The Shadow In The Mirror

Sir M.J. Wasik

ISBN: 978-1-63863-003-6

Cover photo by Aziz Acharki on Unsplash

Back cover photo by Zoltan Tasi on Unsplash

ThePoorKnight.com

'I just want to be treated fairly' It is the cry of the defeated, the motto of the weak. The knight knows that that there is no fairness except that which they can force, a knight does not care if the enemy does not play by the rules, for they know that there are no rules except those the strong create. The knight knows that the only true rules are those which they force on themselves, their character…

Their Honor…

Honor, that internal law in which we live our lives….

It is Honor, not morality, which beats so strongly in the knights, which guides their actions….

It is favoring Honor over morality which frees the knight to act as a knight.

It is their honor which determines whether they raise their sword in defense of the weak, or to prey upon them. It is character which determines whether they will forge the rules to be fair, or only to their own advantage…their honor which makes the knight either a hero of the People, or their enemy….

There is a fine line between salvation and damnation, between being a knight or a tyrant. It is love which draws that line…a tyrant has a great love for the People, where the knight loves the person…

-From the surviving fragments of
What Is Expected of You, By Dunil Gruet

NokoShor Shivna

KanaTukFin

Tuk's Prologue

(Adapted from the House McKray's *Encyclopedia of Colonial History*, and *The First Dragon Empire* by DragonRue Herna Grut)

The Legislative Committee of the Confederate Senate met early in the morning. The air before dawn was chilly and none present liked being rousted from their warm beds. Worsening the grumbling was the fact that President Marius Shadoa had given no reason for the emergency meeting. The hour could be easily dismissed for Marius rarely knew what time it was. He was the type of person who slept only a few hours a night and any crisis meant no more than one. It was still several weeks away from their quarterly meeting.

White Bear sat silently in his chair watching the rest of the Committee members. When he first took the seat in the Senate many treated him as an outsider, an outsider from a weak member nation. It had not taken him long to change their minds about him or the Preserve. It was not easy, made even harder for having to do it quickly. The politics of the Confederacy was threatening to destroy all the Preservatives had worked so hard to create. Officially called the United Forest Preserves, the Preserve was the largest nation in the Confederacy, but its population was sparse. Having given up the lifestyle of chasing after possessions, there communities did not have the money to put up a fight in the political arena.

There were numerous reasons why the Committee had not accepted him easily. The primary one was that he was not one of them. White Bear was no politician. It did not bother him. He had been an outsider for most of his life and became used to it long before the Confederacy was formed. After all, he had fought hard to prevent the plans of the Shadow, for not only the Confederacy, but the Colonies as well. He was the only one who had doubted that Marius had the charisma needed to hold it all together. He did admit that he had grown too comfortable being invisible to those who made policy.

Besides himself, the only other member of the Committee to ever openly oppose the Shadow was Marcus Green. White Bear had never liked the man. It was for personal reasons so he never let it show. Marcus was a warrior who took offense too easily. A deadly combination considering that he was meaner than he should have been so no one would think that he was weak. It was a common problem for people with a warrior's disposition. Dislike was too strong of a word. White Bear never really disliked anyone. It was more of an irritation, and not because of the man's personality but his attitude.

Marcus had the scent of one taught by the Dark Four. Most of Green's mannerism, even his way of thinking, radiated training in Tymalt. It was hard to say for sure. The man guarded his spirit too well, but displayed both the habits and weaknesses of a dark pupil. It was possible that he had been taught by one of the Initiated but it seemed unlikely that one of the Ascended had been Marcus' master. The Dark Four would use racial tensions to their advantage and even foster them, but would not allow a pupil to harbor such feelings. White Bear knew the Tymalt better than anyone and it was written in that tome, 'Any strong emotion hindered control'. Tymalt was about control. Control of others, control of one's surroundings, and above all else, control of one's self.

Marcus had never learned to control himself. To do that one must look inside and strip away all prejudice. Even the simplest ones taken for granted must be cleared away, for they prevent us from seeing what is really there. Green had not even dealt with the apparent ones. He would have been considered a closet supremacist in the Old Earth. He had been furious when the Senate was drawing up the plan for the settlement of the Colonies. Marcus had voiced his opinion frequently as if it could only be that way. He wanted to settle the people according to their ethnic background. This was going against the original plan and the Legislative Committee had not let it go to vote. The only one in the Committee who had agreed with Marcus was Isaac. It was not surprising, except for the two all of the Committee were of mixed heritage as the Old Earth determined race. Marcus as light as day and Isaac as dark as night. In the Old Earth both would have been called racists but the Shadow had made it clear that such behavior would not be tolerated in the Confederacy of the New Earth.

Isaac had eventually put aside the old-world prejudices, to embrace a fully united Confederacy. It was apparent to White Bear, being only an adviser to the Shadow at the time and not part of the Committee, that Isaac had only agreed with Marcus because his followers came from poor and war torn regions of the world and had come to the Confederacy with meager resources. He had feared that those who looked to him for leadership would only receive the scraps of the others. With the ethnic cleansing and religious persecution during the Oil Wars of the last century of the Old Earth rising to a level which would have horrified even the people who had first championed fascist ideals, it was no surprise he would develop such feelings. Isaac gave his approval to the proposal once he had actually gone through the land distribution.

Marcus had yelled and threatened rebellion. He and the Shadow had spent three straight days screaming about it. In the end Marcus had stormed out and went to the group of people he had brought. The Shadow was furious when he learned that Marcus had been urging his people to revolt. They had had a public struggle and it ended with the Shadow changing Marcus' skin to the color of new leaves. Marcus had been furious and had simmered about it over a decade.

It had been just over two centuries now and even though his skin was still green, Marcus had seemed to have forgotten about it. However, White Bear had his doubts. Marcus was not the type to forget much or forgive anything. Even now, as he usually did, Marcus had the look in his eye of someone preparing for battle. Everything was a fight to a warrior and that was their greatest weakness. Only if one learned to wisely choose which battles to fight did one become a foe to worry about. That is why White Bear gave Marcus little thought. He fought everything so never had enough time to know what the effects of their last battle were before he would throw himself into the next one. If he had truly been trained by the Dark Four he did not learn well. He had not even mastered the first lesson, the Law of Proper Action: Examine situation, Analyze data, Act on the conclusion, Store the results.

Today was one of those days which reminded White Bear why he had excepted the appointment as Senator of the Preserve, the largest land mass of the Colonies but the one with the least amount of political power. Marcus thought only of his own power and chose not to see beyond that goal. Like an animal caught in a hunger frenzy, his lust made him more dangerous than he should have been. His attacks would cause damage with none of the benefits which normally comes with success. He was up to something. White Bear did not need his discernment to know that it would be something that was going to rock the very foundation of the Confederacy. Lost in hist thoughts about it, he did not notice that someone had asked him a question. Before he could stutter an apology, the Shadow entered, speaking as he came through the door.

"Forgive me for calling this meeting before our scheduled time but I could not rest until we addressed this issue. It is not a pleasant topic that we are here to discuss today." Marius Shadoa took his seat as he continued. "There is a new force moving across the Confederacy under the cover of dark. It has come to my attention that a cult has sprung up which is a danger to the Confederacy. This is far removed from the occasional cult that is formed from time to time in the more remote parts of our land. They always burn themselves out after a few years but this one has lasted at least a decade as far as my researchers can tell. It could be much longer if they started as a secret. It has spread throughout almost all of the member nations."

White Bear's voice came out as a whisper.

"The Church of Dark Blood."

Marcus just revealed something in his eyes. White Bear was sure that he knew of the Dark Church. Was he behind it or just planning on exploiting it? It was hard to tell. Anyone who spent time listening to the average person would know of it, not that Marcus would listen to people. Although it was forbidden in the constitution of the Confederacy, Marcus had a very extensive spy network throughout the member nations. White Bear needed some time alone in meditation and prayer. His mind was linking the pieces together but the Shadow's words broke the chain.

"You have heard of them, my White Bear?"

"Yes, even though I preside in the Colonies, and the Dark Church has yet to spring up in the Preserve, very little happens in the west without me knowing." White Bear cast a knowing glance at Marcus and received another piece to the puzzle when the man shrunk back in his own mind. "They opened their first church about twelve years ago. So far, their message is one of belonging to the family of the church which pulls in the young adults, mostly males from the richer merchant class. Their teachings however do contain a hint of the Destroyer's hand in it. Their doctrine is a bastardization of Nietzschean philosophy that Lord Green claims to live by. I have not brought them up before because they do not pose a threat to the Confederacy. It will crumble on its own because its leaders are more concerned with their own power to believe in what they are teaching. They lack even rudimentary understanding of the Spiritual War and thus are little more than puppets."

The Shadow blinked twice. The tone of his voice showed he could not believe the words coming out of his friend's mouth.

"I would have figured that you, of all people, would be the first to call for banning this cult. Besides simply conflicting faiths, I have heard that they pray for your demise."

White Bear laughed aloud before answering.

"I too, have heard the same. In fact, their leaders have made it a point that I know. However, those who have put on their armor need not fear the prayers of fools. As for the conflict of faith, just because they have set their eyes on the Destroyer does not make them any worse than any other person. They are still lost, and need to be shown Elohim's love like everyone else.

"Everyone here knows how firm I stand in my faith. All present have seen what, by your own words, can only be miracles performed through me. None of you can deny the Truth. Yet, some of you will not count the cost and follow the Anointed One. How can I then condemn those who have not even heard the Truth when those who are trying to judge them have acknowledged the Way and yet do not walk the path? No, I must flow like the wind, and as for now it blows away from them." His hand came up when Marcus tried to speak. "Do not mistake what I am saying. The lies of this Dark Church will be dealt with but this must be done within the second heaven. The Test of Snakes, if you will. The Truth never has to fear any lie. All I am trying to say is that it is outside the boundaries of the Senate's authority to ban the Dark Church in the member nations when it has nothing to do with international affairs. To do such would remove us from the impartiality which we have spent the last two hundred years building and will show us to be little more than tyrants."

Marcus was steaming with anger from White Bear waving him off with his hand. A gesture that he knew the holy man used often, but he was not a servant to be gestured at to get him to do what he wanted. His voice showed his anger.

"It is true that they have done nothing that is forbidden by law…yet. Are our laws not written in such a way that even though some behavior may be a right, if it is harmful to our society then it is in fact outlawed?"

Marcus pulled out the book of laws. White Bear rolled his eyes. He hated that book. It started as little more than a booklet which anyone who could read would understand but it grew as the years passed not only in size but in complexity. Now it was over a three thousand pages and written in such a way only an expert could find anything. White Bear sighed. The excess of laws creates only strongholds for the tyrants. With only a few turnings of the pages Marcus had the passage he was looking for.

"Here it is. 'Therefore, some behavior would be considered to be harmful to a society when it permeates the society and rots it from within. Such behavior not being directly prevented by law will still be considered outside the law's protection. An example would be such as strong drink. Being not harmful when in small amounts is deadly when too much is taken. Therefore, strong drink shall not be considered illegal by the laws of the Confederacy or the member nations but provinces within said nations may pass laws forbidding or limiting its consumption. Member nations are free to pass laws to punish those who indulge in too much strong drink even if they do not break any other laws.'"

Marcus snapped the book closed and continued speaking

"It is true that neither this Committee nor the Senate can pass a law banning this cult. However, we can and should issue an opinion that the Dark Church, in whatever form it may take, is harmful to society and thus falls under this statute. This is well within our power."

As White Bear shook his head the Shadow was smiling and was almost on the verge of laughing. His two best friends were a mismatched pair. They were opposite as night and day. White Bear, so gentle and meek in nature, could rise on occasion and attack with the ferociousness that scared most people. Marcus was mean spirited and often attacked without provocation but on occasion showed such a depth of kindness that it shocked people who knew him. Maybe they were not opposite, just different. Of course, they both had similar viewpoints as well. Neither one had a high regard for the abilities of the average person. Marcus felt that the average person needed to be guided with a strong hand which was willing to crush those who stepped out of line. White Bear felt that the average person had the ability to be great but too often chose not to be. So the hand simply needed to point the way for those who searched for a better way. It was Marius' turn to speak so he stood.

"Well, it appears, as usual, Marcus and White Bear will be the speakers on this. As it is our custom, as the junior White Bear will speak first.

"I wave the first speaking to the ambassador of New Holland."

Marcus thought for a moment. White Bear was not a great speaker except when it came to his faith but the holy man never did anything without a reason. Marcus had always thought the followers of the man's faith were simpletons, unwilling to except the truth of power. He had underestimated

White Bear because of this and would not do it again. Marcus had his own reasons for wanting to speak last.

"I yield it back to the ambassador of the Preserve."

The Shadow laughed. It often went like such. White Bear stood. He looked around the room. He had trouble finding the words to start. There was so much going on in the Confederacy, so much which needed to be done in the Preserve. Most of it made this issue little more than a trifle. With a sigh he spoke.

"Very well, as custom I will speak first. As Marcus pointed out we do not have the right to ban of the Dark Church but can get around it because we can allow the banning of its practices. However, just because we have the freedom to do a thing does not mean that we should do the thing. If we pass this decree not only will we send the message that we are taking sides, but we will also be insulting all the philosophers no matter what their beliefs. After all, if we allow this decree than are we not saying to them: be careful on what you say for your observations or beliefs can land you in jail?

"Running much deeper than any message we will be sending to the thinkers of our society will be the message we are sending to the average person. We will be saying to them that the Dark Church is valid. Not just valid, but it is something that the Committee does not like, or even worse, we fear. You will not only predispose the wayward youths into this cult, you will push them. They will look at the Dark Church and say we like the message they are giving and the cult will gain in strength. Constant attacks that do not kill your opponent eventually make them strong enough to kill you. In many places they will be forced to go underground and in this they will become stronger. Then we will not be able to follow their acts or counter their tactics when it does turn destructive."

Marcus timed his laugh perfectly. He had expected a much better argument from White Bear. His rival seemed not to be fully into today's debate and this worried him. He pushed the thought away for it made no matter. White Bear was a weak follower of the God of the weak. Marcus threw himself into the debate as was fitting to the Chair of the Senate.

"No offense to White Bear but he is always saying that we send messages. I have never found it so. The so-called thinkers are too busy trying to find their better ways and the masses are willing to believe whatever we tell them. He also speaks as if this cult actually has the power to threaten the Confederacy. It is young and weak so therefore easily dispatched before it can even threaten a member nation."

Marcus ended his turn with that. He gestured for White Bear to take his next turn. Marcus' eyes almost bulged when White Bear smiled and said he had said all he was going to say. Marcus had only made his first point and had much more to say. By stopping the debate when he did, White Bear had prevented him from saying any more. Again, he had forgotten that White Bear was a much better foe than he ever let on.

The vote was taken and ended with a tie. Three to three, thus it fell to the Shadow to make the final choice. It often went this way. The Committee has become polarized between those who were swayed either by Marcus' passion or White Bear's philosophy. He had not been able to figure a way to end it without making things worse. He thought on it for nearly ten minutes. The room was silent except for the sound of White Bear scribbling in a note pad. Finally, the Shadow stood and spoke.

"I agree with both sides. This cult does not pose an imminent threat. However, we must think of future threats of our people. They will be dangerous someday and by banning them now we will be able to stop it before they get that strong. To that end, the resolution to allow the member nations to ban the Dark Church's practices within their area will pass.

"On a happier note, my first child will be born in a few weeks and have decided to name it after Marcus. Really that is all I have to say. Does anyone else have anything that cannot wait until our scheduled meeting?"

After everyone shook their heads Shadow ended the meeting. He started to leave but he was stopped by White Bear coming up to him.

"Can we speak for a moment?"

"I will not change my mind old friend."

White Bear waved his hand in the air, a gesture showing that the vote was of little concern now. None the less, his voice was serious

"Things happen as they must. This is about something entirely different."

The two of them walked to the Shadow's private rooms and the rest went their own way.

Shadow Fire knelt in front of an altar dedicated to Apployan the Destroyer. He had been praying for guidance, with tears in his eyes at times. The Dark Church had been under attack for nearly four decades. They were close to collapse. Even the inner church, the Cult of Blood, was close to rebelling against him. Some of them had started to openly doubt that the Destroyer of the Weak had visited him in a vision. He was about to give up when the altar was engulfed in flames hot enough that Shadow Fire could feel it and his hair singed. The fire was replaced by a figure hidden by a dark field. The figure's voice boomed out.

"The Serpent of Old has heard your laminations and is angered with himself that he has chosen one so weak to spread his message. He has placed me over you and you will listen to me and do our master's bidding. You will refer to me only as the Hidden One and do exactly what I say. Know this, the Great Destroyer has put your life entirely in my hands."

Shadow Fire was quivering with fear. Apployan had promised that there was no after life. That the ever-living soul was propaganda put out to control the weak. His other promise was that if he served him faithfully, he could live until all the stars went dark. A promise also contained the threat that if he failed the pain would last for just as long. He had displeased the master and he would not again. He could hardly get the words out through his fear.

"I am yours to order, Hidden One."

The figure gave the impression that he was smiling before he continued.

"First you will purge the followers of unbelievers. It does not matter who you kill, make it the people you do not like. Just be sure that you make the deaths gruesome and let it known that your knowledge of their betrayal was supernatural in origin.

"Second, the Master chose you because you have the ability to sound like you know what you are talking about. Something you have been lacking of late. Get yourself in order. Do whatever you feel like doing or teaching. You have a free hand in this. Whatever doctrine you put forth you have permission to say Apployan has said thus.

"Third and most importantly, put fourth that the reason the High Committee has banned the church because what you speak is the truth and they fear that. Never do it openly but whisper it in the dark. This will draw people to your near empty meetings."

The Hidden One paused for an awkward moment. His voice took on an angry tone as he continued.

"Know this, I mean to make myself an empire. I have been working hard for the coming rebellion and if you serve well you will be head of the most powerful church in history. If you fail, your head will be on a spear decorating my thrown room."

The man vanished and Shadow Fire sighed in relief. He was no stranger to power but the man radiated so much that it had filled the room. He stood and straightened his clothes. Not the sign he was looking for, but it was better than he had hoped for. His Master had not forsaken him. There were others beside himself who served the Destroyer. Of late, he was even doubting whether or not he had had a real vision. This confirmed that Apployan was not just his imagination. What had the Hidden One called Apployan? Yes, the Serpent of Old. He had heard that before but could not place were. Leaving the altar room whistling a tune, he wasted no time putting his orders in motion.

The Shadow looked over the throng of people who had come to hear him speak. Glancing to the left then to the right the Redicur Guard looked very regal. It was sometimes easy to forget that they were the elite of the military. Twelve soldiers, all strong in the Science and all trained at the Royal Academy. He smiled inwardly when he noticed his White Bear standing in the corner. He was unsure how old his friend was as he did not seem to age at all. It had been over three hundred years since they met and by the way the holy man spoke, he gave the impression that he was much older. Their eyes met and White Bear sent his greeting with nothing more than a movement of an eyebrow. When in public the holy man very rarely showed any reaction to what was going on around him. Many underestimated White Bear for this. They thought that his mind moved as slow as his body usually did. This was something that even the Senate fell into on occasion. In the last two hundred years the Shadow had seen White Bear withdraw further into himself as his mind spun faster and faster.

Very few understood why he had called this man his White Bear. He had started calling his friend that after the first time he had seen him angered. White Bear had actually seemed to grow larger as he moved forward. An illusion brought on by the raw energy radiating from the man and the primal instinct that it inspired in others. Knowing this was not enough to prevent Marius from taking a step back. The three men they had stumbled upon who were mugging an old woman did not stand a chance against the massive man. White Bear moved with a speed unmatched by anything Shadow had ever seen. His actions were a blur. Within seconds the thugs were knocked to the ground and the only one left conscious was being sat on by White Bear until the constables arrived. The Shadow's name for him went much deeper than that incident. Like the great bear this man was slow to action but when he was finally aroused, he became a nearly unstoppable force. Once he had a scent of a problem, he would stalk it without cease until he found the solution.

On the opposite side, almost in contrast, was Marcus showing his every thought on his face. From his impatience that this was taking so long, to his annoyance on having to stand. He often looked like a great hunting cat that could not decide whether to tear you apart or ignore you completely. He often went from one extreme to the other in a heartbeat. He often acted before thinking what the ramifications would be. It was that passion which had drawn the Shadow to him and made them friends. Marcus had opinions on everything and always shared them. He was definitely a warrior, using White Bear's classification of people. Always ready to throw himself into any battle that may come his way even if it had nothing to do with him, yet his plans were complex.

They were there to show support for his decision and the Senate's unity on their choice of his successor. Marcus represented the monocracies of the west and White Bear stood as the representation of the member nations in the east, often called the Colonies. She now stood between the two men. In both physical and mental appearance, she embodied everything they had worked so hard to accomplish in the New Earth. Her hair was near black just starting to go gray. She could be described as neither large nor small. Her eyes shined with both intelligence and passion. The Shadow had almost given up on finding a replacement for himself. Suddenly and without warning he found her. She had written a book. She was not a good writer. Neither showing the skill of White Bear in making the Foggy Path seem attainable, nor the ability to raise one's passion like Marcus. It was more of a collection of notes of her observations over her life. She had only minor skill in the Science so her age would only be a little over a hundred but she was dedicated to the goals of the Confederacy. That was ten years ago and during the time since she had been trained to take over the highest rank in the Confederacy.

Marius had to admit himself that he was almost envious of her. She would be president during the time when the Confederacy started its expansion. Not only had they recently finished repairing the land of north-east Australia allowing it to be colonized but the personal and equipment which would colonize to the north were almost ready to be sent. Marius will still be advisor, but the choice on how to deal with all those unknowns will now be hers to decide. He would miss it but, was also looking forward to other pursuit, the advancement of the Science.

He looked over the area. Several of the levitating ships were hovering nearby. The five represented the peek achievement with the new science. Their only power source was the ambient radiation the nuclear holocaust had unleashed. Even the cameras they held, which would send his speech to the four corners of the Confederacy, were using background radiation. Almost all of the technology of the Confederacy was based on using the elevated radiation found in the land now. There was no longer need to burn fuels to create the energy that allows society to grow. They had achieved the system that so many had worked so hard to create. The Shadow's dream was now reality.

Throughout time every great nation which has risen to that position had an efficient way of systematically exploiting slave labor. The better they are at this system the more powerful the nation. This held true even when machines replaced humans as the slaves. Society had finally found a source of cheap labor that would not threaten revolution from the poor treatment, or without the rot that human slavery brought to the nation. When the electronic revolution reached its full fruits there were no longer a need for humans even to work the machines anymore. Whole factories, cities infrastructures, farm complexes, nearly everything was built and maintained by machines. The amount of energy required for the old way of life was incredible and the energy demand was always more than could be met. Even with the great advancements and expansion of the use of the green energy sources most of the energy was supplied by petroleum.

When White Bear had showed him how the world's conflicts were leading inevitably to a nuclear holocaust, the Shadow had known that he had a chance to create real applications for his discoveries. At first all they had were electrical generators powered by radiation. In fact, that was the extent of his inventions. A scientist in the Preserve, of all places, had found a way to manipulate the strong and weak forces with an item. Already there were dozens of devices that were deemed impossible just twenty years ago. The ships were just one of those items. It had been a score of others who had created the flying ships and the communication systems. The inventions that they had seen in the last hundred years were amazing. They no longer simply recreated the electrical devices of the Old Earth the engineers were finding new ways of using the radiation. It was an exciting time to be alive and he was looking forward to retiring and spending his time in research.

The Shadow was brought out of his thoughts by his wife taking her seat next to him on the balcony. There were still times that he was stunned by her beauty, and this was one of those times. In a real way, this was her day too. And, it had been his wife and her team who had changed their change their genome so they could survive in the radiation. Not just the people, but crops, trees, even the bugs and bacteria now thriving were due to her research. After a hundred years of marriage and three children, everything she had accomplished, the one thing that still amazed him most about her was that she was able to stand him. He knew he was nowhere near the easiest man with which to live. He took her hand as he noted the crowd's noise level steadily increasing. A sign they were starting to get restless. It was time for him to speak so he stood. He let a hush come over the crowd before he spoke.

"Democrats, Nationalists, Republicans and Imperialists,

"In the over three and half centuries since we landed on these shores to forge a new earth, we have come far. We have created a near perfect society of which Socrates would be jealous. We have erased the hatreds of the Old Earth and formed a republic that any outsider would envy. The reason for this address today is…," there was movement behind him, "because I feel," something was wrong, "that it is time for me to resign and appoint a new..." White Bear and Marcus!

The Shadow was surprised by the two jumping in front of him. Both the holy man and Marcus had a thick shield of the Science patterned around the balcony. A flash of light, explosion of thunder and the whole world started to crumble. He heard the screams of his wife and several of his bodyguards. Too late he realized that someone had thrown an attack at him and his two friends had intervened. The contact between whatever Pattern used in the attack and the two men's protective shields had caused an explosion that destroyed the entire wing of the castle. As they fell the protective shield collapsed, even with the combined skill with the Science of both his friends.

His mind raced into combat mode as he used his science to throw the ruble away from himself and land safely. He scanned for future threats. His eyes rested on White Bear. The flesh of the holy man's chest was torn apart, showing bone. Whatever pattern used was a powerful one. White Bear was the only person in the Colonies who had more control over the Science than him, although he rarely used it. He relied on Elohim to protect him from most harm. White Bear was still breathing but might take months to recover. Even Marcus was badly damaged and his skill with the Science would have protected him from the heat of a volcano. If whatever pattern that was used would have hit him, or either one of the two alone, it would have killed for sure. There was no doubt that whoever was behind this had expected to kill him. No matter what words were used, it was an assassination attempt pure and simple.

He yelled for the medics to help his friends. He swirled quickly when a scarf caught his eye. His wife's scarf. Purely from instinct he put his hands out and the huge blocks of stone flew aside like dust caught in the wind. The condition of his wife's body left no doubt she was dead. He scooped her up in his arms as a grief-fueled rage filled his heart. As the tears poured from his eyes he was helpless to stop the Science from reacting to his emotions. The air around him erupted in fire and the ground started to tear itself apart. The destructive force sped quickly out from him. He would kill whoever was responsible for this even if he had to destroy the entire New Earth.

Before the force had reached twenty yards it suddenly dissipated. He turned to vent his rage on whoever dared to undo his patterns. As the flames raced out from him towards the figure, they were dispersed as well. The Shadow slumped as he recognized the person as his youngest child.

"Father, this is not the way."

Of course, the younger Marius was correct. He could not destroy everything. He would have to hunt down those responsible and extract a most horrible revenge.

Twelve men sat around a dark table in an even darker room. The power in the cramped quarters was intense even with none of the men using magic. Magic was a fitting word for it. Everyone present preferred to use the ancient word making the Science sound mysterious. That was not the only reason they called it magic. All of them had gained mastery of the substance not by long hours of study and practice it took to gain control over their mind and body. Without exception, everyone that sat at the table had gained their use of magic through deals with Apployan. They were not practitioners of the Science, they were necromancers. Tainted Truth could not even use magic, he practiced old fashion witchcraft. He called himself a sorcerer and not even Shadow Fire claimed to control the Unclean as Tainted Truth did. There was no denying what he could do through his witchcraft.

Shadow Fire sat in the chair at the head of the table. He impatiently eyed the empty chair. The new member of the Unholy Committee was supposed to join him today. Shadow Fire knew nothing of the newcomer except that the Hidden One had said that he would know the man as soon as he arrived in. That Shadow Fire would know it was the new member because he would not believe that it was him. The Hidden One had said that the newcomer would someday take his place as the Head of the Committee. That was not something that Shadow Fire would allow. After all, was he not the First? Was he not there at the beginning? He was the one who the Destroyer had come to first. He was the first to take the Oath of Destruction. For nearly a hundred years he had been slowly building the Unholy Committee and promoting the Dark Church. No, the Hidden One would be king over the Confederacy but only he, Shadow Fire, would control the Unholy Committee and through it the New Earth.

Everyone in the room felt the use of magic nearby. Powerful magic. A level that was too high except for maybe a handful of people to do alone. Radiation flooded the room. Everyone grabbed their magic wrought weapons and prepared for a fight when a figure appeared. The Unholy Committee pulled magic close to them far beyond their normal levels with the aid of the weapons. The power in the room grew to a pitch that would have fried an apprentice on the spot if they even tried to see the magic. Everyone at the table was ready to fight Marcus Shadoa, first born of the Shadow. It was said that only the Shadow himself was more powerful in the use of magic. This would be a bloody fight in quarters too tight to allow them to use their most destructive spells.

All of them gaped and lost hold of their magic at what Marcus did next. The magic flowed away from him with the ease of one who was born into it. The Committee was shocked. This was not only the son of the man they were looking to depose but a pupil of White Bear, a man who the Committee considered their greatest threat. Marcus should be here to fight but instead he started to speak.

Before the second word was formed one at the table pulled out a hand gun and fired. Marcus only smiled as the smoked cleared. A protective shield had disintegrated the bullet. It was easy enough to fashion a necklace with the Bullet-Proof Ward on it that even those who held low-level offices had them. So common in fact, firearms had become a novelty only used for sport and hunting. Every peace officer and thug in the Confederacy was equipped with the ward. Any fighting had to be accomplished through melee. They had long since entered into a new age of the sword. He shook his head in disdain as he spoke in a manner that showed he had been raised in the best schools.

"You were fools to attack the Shadow the way you did. Foolish indeed to not ask permission of the Hidden One. Luckily for you it has worked out well for my plans. If it had not, I would have come with a handful of my disciples and killed every one of you. Listen to me and listen well, if I had not come to the decision that it would aid me not one of you would have escaped my blade."

The Unholy Committee was still recovering from their shock but Shadow Fire's anger gave him the will to speak. His lips curled up in his trade mark snarl.

"If it is as you say, then why were we not reprimanded by the Hidden One himself, and why now? The attack was nearly a decade ago."

Marcus' eyes filled with a fire and his own mouth curled in a snarl that stripped Shadow Fire's off his face. The first born of the Shadow's tone was enough to make the weaker Committee members look away.

"I will answer you but you will not like it. As you should have already guessed, I am the final member to the Committee. As I know, it is required that a new member must bring both a gift to the Committee and a sacrifice to bind the oath. I bring both now.

"My gift and the answer to your question is that the Hidden One does not know that you are the ones who orchestrated the attack. I only learned of it a month or so ago. If he knew, or if I had known while I still longed to taste revenge for my mother's death, I would be drinking your blood with my dinner. So my gift to you is that I have not, nor will I, reveal your betrayal to the Hidden One."

Marcus smiled when he saw their faces go pale and their spirits radiating fear, all except Shadow Fire. His gift was as much for himself as it was to them. None of them had entered the Cult of Blood in strength. They all had fought for every little bit of power until they reached the Unholy Committee. By then, they had so many secrets to hide from the others that they lived in fear of exposure. He would enter the Committee in full strength and in position to command. Everyone would listen to him and heed. Everyone except Shadow Fire, but he had plans for that man. He continued coldly.

"And as for my sacrifice. No, I am who I am, but that holds no weight here so I will do this formally."

He paused to pull a bundle off his back. Kneeling, he felt the others in the room pull the abundant magic close to them. He smiled. They were all fools. Calling the Science magic forced them to think of it as a thing of mystery rather than a real physical force. Because of that they would never be very strong. It would be fitting to teach the masses such in order to keep them from becoming too strong but those who would lead needed to know the truth. The Science they disciplined into a, what did they call it, a spell. The spell that they cast, an even more primitive term, would bind the oath to him. A simple use of the Science for people as powerful as these.

The Science could not force a person to act against their will but by breaking the oath would cause incredible pain. It was a pattern that would easily be broken by him while leaving a shell which would make it appear that the ward was still active. Even so, he found surrendering to allow the bond to work was hard. After he felt the pattern fall into place, a sloppy forming, he looked up and gave his oath.

"We are in a war. To win this war we must be strong, in our dedication to Perditor and in our dealings with others. I give the oath of my blood to do the will of the Apployan as determined by this Committee. Yet the Master needs a sacrifice more than my blood to show my heart is only for him. As sacrifice I give my name and will be known as Death Bringer, but more importantly I give up all the rights that go with it. I give up the privilege of a pupil of White Bear. Most importantly I give my birthright which is due a child of the Shadow."

He stood and placed the bundle on the table and unfolded it. The Committee member's eyes bulged and even Shadow Fire was shocked. It took them a few moments to recover enough to finish the oath. The Committee went through ritual of binding almost automatically. They were shaken and it showed in their actions.

No one seemed to notice that Death Bringer took his seat. They were too busy looking at the blade. It was the one of the Swords of the Shadow. Made by the Shadow himself, they were more than wrought by magic but were made entirely of magic. Theoretically, it was simply polarizing the magic particles so they formed what was desired. In practice few attempted it, even less succeeded. It was a delicate task with one mistake meaning death, no matter how powerful the wizard. The swords were far stronger than any substance known. It had taken the Shadow nearly a year to make each one.

Once there was three, one for each of the Shadow's children but the first sword had a slight flaw in it and when it finally fell apart the destruction that was unleashed was enough to destroy an entire city. Or it would have, if the Shadow had not directed the flow of the explosion himself and even then, it left a crater over a mile across and rained dust over the eastern lands for months.

The rumors said that their power was far greater than any other item in the Confederacy. The group could not take their eyes off the blade. The patterns were so small and delicate that it was hard to get even and idea of their function. It seemed to be alive, slowing taking in magic and then exhausting, as if it breathed. Even with the power of the blade it represented something far greater. It was a well-known symbol of the Shadoa family. It was commonly known that thanks to Marius Shadoa's foresight his followers were saved from the nuclear attacks. Even though it was not official, the Shadow held the power of an emperor. A power which, even though was not hereditary, would go to his children. This was a great sacrifice for it gave the Committee the power that normally would have gone to Death Bringer. It gave the Dark Church a legitimacy that they had not hoped for. If their plans succeeded, they would be able to claim that their rule was legal. They could point to the sword and to Death Bringer and say that the rightful heir is in agreement.

No one was willing to touch the blade so Death Bringer picked it up. The massive muscles on his dark arm strained. Once the blade analyzed his genetic code it became lighter. He was stronger than most men, thanks to his mother's interest in genetic manipulation, but not even he could have wielded it effectively as a weapon if it was not coded to his family line. He knew only a handful of men who could and only one woman. All of them had augmented their strength through the Science. A detestable practice that overgrows the adrenal gland and shortened the life considerably. Not to mention what it did to one's appearance. He turned towards the wall and it parted for him. He heard gasp from the other members of the Unholy Committee. They had lined the room with lead to prevent the flows of magic from entering. This protected it from being discovered by magic but created a wall too strong for the radiation to get through. This would indirectly show the location of the room to anyone paying attention.

He looked back at the Committee and waved them to follow. He had been showing off and had awed them all except for Shadow Fire. Anger burned in the man's eyes. He was a dangerous man and the only one in the Committee that Death Bringer would have let live. That is if he was not the one behind his mother's death. He would pay for that. Not that Death Bringer cared for revenge. No, he loved his mom but revenge is only a benefit of teaching a lesson to future people who would do him harm. A lesson which White Bear had given; never act without a reason. Death Bringer always enjoyed finding new ways to twist what the holy man taught into his own beliefs. As the Committee joined him in the room, he gave them their first lesson in the Science.

"Magic," the word seemed alien on his tongue, "is not alive. It has no thoughts or desires. It cares nothing if it flows around or through something. It is well and good to place thick walls of lead around something if you are hiding it from your common, ah wizard. Any normal wizard would die if they ever did manage to make it this far from the protective wards you have here.

"No, the threat is from those that hold real power. There are only a couple hundred people in the Confederacy who have such abilities. Most are either my disciples or part of the Redicur Guard. Trust me when I say, we would not last long if the pupils of White Bear were to find us before we are ready. No matter what you may think, the servants of Elohim are not weak. Those of the VoX Temple may not spend long hours in practicing magic but their faith and philosophy give them strength of which to be weary. Some of them could clear this area of wards with a sweep of their hand and could find this hidden room of yours from a hundred miles away if they were looking for it. Believe me as our plan progresses, they will be looking for it. We must prevent detection by using magic instead of blocking it.

"Particles of radi . . . magic always travel in a straight line. Sometimes they hit an obstacle and bounce off, sometimes creating more magic. When controlled you can tell them what to do. Nothing new, but I am sure that the subtle uses have been lost to you. Otherwise, you would not have used walls of lead to hide this room. With the lead you detect something that absorbs the magic which in itself is not a thing to notice. Unless you detect a square or a circle or any other unnatural shape. "

He stripped the walls of its lead with a wave of his hand. The wave was for the Committee. Hand gestures and words were for those who lacked imagination. Those who could not form the proper images in their mind of what had to be done. Another benefit of being taught in his youth by White Bear, he was able to control not only himself but magic with ease. He would give them the false security that he needed to gesture for him to work the Science but not the satisfaction of him also needing to spout some worthless words. Of course, for some of the harder disciplines he still needed to close his eyes to concentrate but that was for patterns which these people would not even begin to understand. He went on.

"Here is the trick." He moved his hands around at random and wiggled his fingers. The Committee would use the gestures from now on. "You set the pattern so it warps the flow of the… magic." Would he ever get used to that word? "The particles that are sent out in a radar fashion will be bent around as if the area is not there. Very much the same way that invisibility works except we are bending the particles of magic instead of light. There are ways of detecting even this but one would have to be close and specifically looking for the slight alterations in the movement."

Tainted Truth spoke in a meek voice.

"What's radar?"

Death Bringer swung on the man, anger thick in his voice.

"Did you people not go to school? Radar? You know, the sending out of rays to determine the shape and distance of things. A simple enough principle that a first-year student could understand it and a third year could use it."

Another one of the Committee spoke.

"But how does the movement of magic show you the shape of things?"

Death Bringer lowered his head. This group was idiots, used to using magic in only in its raw power. He would of course have to kill them all and replace them with competent people, but that would have to wait until after their work was finished. Until then, he had to make do.

Deep into one of the eastern provinces which were collectively called the Colonies by the richer and more influential west, in a village where the town hall, school and inn all shared the same building an older man put down several silver coins on the bar. His voice was as rough as he looked.

"Hello Frank, I'll have my usual."

After Frank had poured the drink and handed it over to the old man he smiled broadly and spoke in a tone which showed many years of familiarity to the other.

"So, Greg, what is the word from the city."

"It is the oddest thing cousin. The Dragoon was there and the whole city was alive with activity. Solders and priests running about like it was the fall festival. Many of them coming and going through traveling gates. I have not seen the likes of it since… well, I have never seen the likes of it."

"Maybe the Dragoon has decided to rebel against his father. I have heard tales from the merchants that the Shadow has become a true tyrant and life is harsh in the western provinces."

"Can you blame him, with his wife being killed the way she was and all. You would not understand never being married, but remember how melancholy I became after my wife's death. We had only twenty wonderful years. Just imagine what it would be like for a man as great as the Shadow who had been partnered for over a hundred.

"I have also heard the rumors, but more than that, I have heard that White Bear had gotten into a fight with the Shadow. They say that the holy man has left the Confederacy. Many are saying that the priests are worried because if White Bear has washed his hands of the Colonies that means that Elohim is no longer protecting us. Of course, the priests I talked to said that was just superstition. That Elohim always protects those that turn to Him."

Frank waved it off with his hand as he spoke.

"Well cousin, I do not know what is going on in the outside but the crops were good this year, we had many births, and even the livestock has done well. There may be trouble in the air but it has not touched us yet."

A large man looked down from the mountain top with a smile on his face. He scratched his beard. White bear's face was one that showed his kindness to anyone who knew how to look. He smiled frequently among friends and seldom around others. The life he had led would be considered a dream by most. For a very long time he had always given up the safety of normality and his own desires to do the will of Elohim. Most could not grasp why he was on this mountain now. When he told people that he needed some time alone to pray they thought he meant a few hours. He had been on the island for nearly five months now.

He had spent that time preparing for the winter. In the old world he would have been considered a survivalist. He did not like that term for it conjured up the image of a fanatic. Some would have considered him a fanatic but those were the people who could not stand to listen to the Truth. He moved down the path to his next snare.

He pulled out a piece of jerky from his pouch as the snow started to fall.

He was looking forward to spending the winter in his shelter. Barring any accidents, he would be very comfortable throughout the winter. White Bear was planning on spending the winter writing about what would come of the Shadow's dream. (His journal of that winter is known to us now as *Concerning the Colonies* and was born from many days and nights of tears.) When he returned to his camp, he checked his supplies once more. He would have liked to have more pemmican but he was far from an expert hunter. He did not fret his shortage of the fat and meat mixture. He had put on several layers of fat in palace life and could afford to lose more than a few pounds.

He was not fond of the meat of the dear-like creatures that inhabited this area but he was not here to appease his taste buds. Very few knew that the Shadow had picked the plants he transplanted to Australia for their useful properties. Most of them from the old America, all of the vegetation had their use, from edible to medicinal to just plan nice to look at. He lit his pipe and fell into a deep thought.

It was Elohim who had told him to have the huge island transformed in secret. It was Elohim who told him to be on the island now. He had heard from the Ferrum so often in his long life that he rarely gave anything a second thought before doing it. This time his spirit and mind warred with each other. He did not want to pay the cost but knew he would anyway. This island, a holy island, was the work of only himself and the Shadow. For decades only the two of them knew of its presence. Tears formed in his eyes. He knew his friend would not be around much longer.

It had been a struggle to come to the island when he knew his friend was in trouble. A friendship which had been born from over three hundred years of struggles, births and deaths is not an easy thing to forsake, even for El Shaddi.

White Bear would not be alone on the island. Even now there were a few score tending the livestock and a few hundred preparing for the arrival of the others. His pupils, their families and a couple of thousand others which were either hand-picked by him or by his elder pupils would be coming to the island soon. The magic needed to transport them would be immense and they had to wait for a distraction. All he could do now was wait for the distraction which filled his heart with grief.

After two years of preparation, they were ready. Shadow Fire had grown to see just how intelligent and cunning Death Bringer was. He grudgingly had to admit a respect for the youth. The first born of the Shadow had pulled everything together in a plan that would stand a good chance of succeeding. It burned Shadow Fire that it had only taken two years to get everything ready. He smiled to himself when he thought of the plans that he had for the youth. He would die at the same time as his father. Shadow Fire would see to that. The youth was too dangerous to have in the Unholy Committee once their common goal was met.

Almost everything was falling in place. White Bear had been gone for months and all indications were that he would be gone all winter. At least that is what Death Bringer had said. Marius Shadoa III, the Shadow's second son was far to the east on duties as the Dragoon. When the senate had opened up the eastern provinces for settlement, it was still wild, but over the last century the population had increased greatly. For the last decade the Dragoon and the Confederate Army had been busy building roads and the infrastructure for one of the colonies. The province was only years away from gaining membership into the Confederacy and what was bothered Shadow Fire most about it was that it looked as if the Dragoon was forming the nation as a democratic republic. Not that it would matter much if the day went as planned.

Shadow Fire was starting to understand more of why Death Bringer had joined the Unholy Committee. He had been a pupil of White Bear but his father favored his second son. At least it seemed that way. After all, Marius was very much like his father in temperament and behavior. He even had the commanding air about him which seemed natural. More importantly the Dragoon was more dedicated the Shadow's dream then anyone else, possibly even more than the senior Shadoa himself. Death Bringer on the other hand cared nothing but for his own power and was frequently angry. Commanding nothing but fear in those who served him. Shadow Fire had learned that Death Bringer was furious and had sulked for a month because the Shadow had given his third born the title of the Dragoon, the leader of the Confederate Army. A force which was more of a work force then an army. Death Bringer had wanted the position but his father said that he needed to get control of his temper before he could be allowed in a position of leadership.

That left only the Shadow's daughter, the First Dragon, and the Shadow Guard to deal with. The First Dragon would not be a problem. She only stayed for a short time in the Shadow City and the ten Dragons who inhabited the city in the training hall would not be able to get to the battle scene in time. Most of them were too new to the form to be able to be much help anyway and would be cut down by the wizards who they had in place. Those wizards would also be prepared to take out the rest of the Redicur Guard that were aroused by the attack. Every city to the west would be attacked at the same moment. It was a coordinated attack that would have been impossible to accomplish without magic. Even in the Old Earth, they would not have been able to coordinate the attacks better.

The first fight would be easy. Once they destroyed the Shadow and taken the cities, the real fight would begin. Alerted by the release of the huge amount of magic, the Dragons would mount a counter attack. With a hundred full-fledged Dragons, along with the military led by the Dragoon, it would be a very hard fight indeed. Shadow Fire for the first time had doubted the Hidden One. The man who was always hidden in darkness had told him that he had a surprise for the Dragons which would end their threat. Shadow Fire could not even imagine what could threaten the massive creatures.

It would take fifty of his high priests to take down even one of the new-formed beasts and even then, he expected to lose forty-nine of each of those groups. Created by the Shadow to combat those wizards who grew powerful and destructive, the Dragons' bodies had been enhanced beyond the point of anything known to the Old Earth. When he had founded the Cult of Blood over a century ago, he had a group of his high priests working on the genetic combination to create these great beasts. The closest they ever had come was to create a single Dragon that was no larger than a man. Unfortunately, those high priests had chosen their human subject poorly, for when he found himself transformed by unbelievable pain into a creature with immense power, he destroyed the stronghold and only one of those priests survived. They should never have used a person they had kidnapped in the night as a subject.

That priest was in the command room now. A very capable man who was almost as cruel as he was. Shadow Fire had broken him for his failure, using magic the man's body had nearly every bone broken and healed several times. Shadow Fire had found that healing made a very effective torture. More painful than the wound which was being healed, it could drive a person mad or even kill them if not used with care. Since then, Death Gate had never failed him and his loyalty was even fiercer. Even so, Shadow Fire held no misconceptions. The mortal wizard only served because he knew that his master was untouchable to him and always would be, but he served well. That is why while the Unholy Committee was fighting the Shadow, Death Gate would be in complete charge of the rebels.

Finally, the signal that all was ready came in. The First Dragon had left the palace and was heading out of the city. The Redicur Guard had been fed the lucky beans. Those wonderful engineered plants which would kill a wizard when they used their magic. It would not prevent them from casting spells but it would grow and cause incredible pain in the guards every time they attacked and defended the Shadow. By the time the battle was over the beans would have sprouted into full grown plants and killed the guards. Every time the guards used their magic it would cause their pain to increase and make using the magic harder. He would have liked to have fed the Shadow a lucky bean or two but it seemed that the man had no need to eat. It would have been helpful. The level that the Shadow used magic the beans would have killed him in seconds.

He left the control room without a word. Death Gate knew the signal and would not fail him. He did not like having to walk but using his magic to enter the palace would have drawn attention to himself.

"Death Bringer?"

Marcus Shadoa turned putting his hand on his blade. Fear rippled across his spirit for a moment and he cursed himself for it. He knew the voice. She was the only person in the entire Confederacy who was better with the blade than him. She had bested him year after year in the international competitions, and he only held the highest rank now because she no longer competed. What irritated him most is that he would now have no means of earning it by defeating her in contest. His mouth curled up in a snarl which could be heard in his voice.

"What do you want, Black Wolf and how do you know my secret name?"

Not moving from her position of leaning up against the wall she smiled. Her tone was as one who had just won a game.

"You should have paid more attention to what my father taught. You have never obtained the balance, otherwise you could have been the greater between us. To answer your questions, I can read you as easily as your plans. Those plans are the reason I am here. I have allowed you to continue in this game you play but use caution Marcus. I have plans of my own and if yours ever crosses mine, you will not enjoy your own much longer."

Death Bringer was hot with anger. He moved forward pulling his blade partially out of its scabbard as he spoke.

"Are you threatening me?"

Black Wolf did not move and her voice remained casual.

"I do not need to threaten you. You of all people know why so many call me the Dark Warrior. Never forget that I do not have my father's reluctance to killing."

Black Wolf turned and left as Death Bringer put his hand to his chest. The reaction angered him even more. His hand had reflexively gone to the scar on his chest. He had received it when they were youths in training together, still friends. They had been sparring and he could not get the upper hand. She seemed to know his actions before he did. His anger had gotten the better of him and he became serious. Pressing in his attack, he no longer cared if he killed her. In an action quicker than he had ever seen she parried his practice sword and struck hard in return. Her practice sword had shattered and sunk a splinter as thick as a thumb into his chest.

He could remember well the cold look on her face as she let go of the hilt and he fell to the ground. There was neither shock nor remorse in her eyes, only coldness. She knew exactly what was going to happen, and had made her choice. Not caring if he lived, she did not even glance at the medical staff when they came rushing up. She simply turned and walked away. The only thing that died that day was their friendship.

Death Bringer returned his blade completely back in its sheath as he came out of the memories. He walked down the corridor in a better mood. That incident had driven a wedge between Black Wolf and her father, White Bear. He was almost at the point of laughter by the time he had met up with the Unholy Committee.

The Shadow was not paying attention to the reports being read to him. His mind was on the behavior of his friend before he left. It was not often that White Bear showed emotion. This time the holy man was choked with tears for almost the whole conversation. His words were even stranger.

"When all seems lost, when there is no choice for you other than defeat, reach far down into the earth, to the very molten core with your Science. With all your force pull it up to you. This must be done"

Then White Bear had left to his Holy Island. The island was another odd behavior of his friend. Over fifty years ago he had come to him and asked for his help. The holy man equally cryptic, just then saying it was a desire of Elohim. All those years the two of them had worked alone in their spare time making the huge island capable of supporting life. It had been struck by several of the nuclear missiles and had since then lost its top soil from erosion. Importing the megatons of dirt and countless plants and animals had been difficult even for the two of them. It had taken them the last ten just to balance the ecosystem, and the Shadow still had his doubts that they had succeeded in that but White Bear had said that Elohim would take care of the rest. Marius did not understand why his friend needed the island or why he was there now. Nonetheless, he trusted White Bear enough to know that it would be for the best, not only for the confederacy but for the New Earth as a whole.

The Shadow was starting to regain much of his former dedication. There would be plenty of time after he had returned order to the Confederacy to ponder why his friend acted so oddly. He looked down from the throne at the scribe. His voice was flat.

"Bring Lord Green to me."

The scribe blinked from the interruption of the report but quickly complied. Only a few moments later the Shadow felt the presence of his eldest son in one of the outer rooms. He was there with several of his friends. Marcus Shadow had been acting strangely since his mother's death. He could not blame his son when he had taken her death hard himself. He was only now recovering. The Shadow did not smile at his friend when Marcus Green entered. His voice was full of heat.

"Marcus, I have been relying on you heavily in running the Confederacy because of my grief because you know my mind better than anyone. But I have spent the last week traveling through the land and found it oppressed. You have betrayed the trust I put in you but worse you have betrayed the people of the Confederacy. I have not . . ." his eldest was entering the thrown room, "decided what…," they were all working patterns with the Science. "Treachery!"

The Shadow jumped from the throne as his son's group threw their attacks. It was fierce and the throne exploded. Quickly, as they had been trained, the Redicur Guard countered attacked. Half threw up barriers for protection from more attacks and the other half attacked. The Shadow stood and brushed himself off. He turned towards his guards when they screamed in pain. Lucky beans! He jumped into action and shouted at Green as he pulled the Science to him.

"They have taken out the guards, put up a screen."

As Marcus started the pattern to put up the protective shield, the Shadow threw his attack. The black lightning bolt was aimed at his son but his son was too quick to be caught by such a raw force. He jumped aside and the upper half of the wizards behind him denigrated.

Death Bringer threw his attack. Confident in Marcus' ability with the Science the Shadow did not flinch when the attack came towards him but started the pattern for his next attack. Only too late did he realize that the protective shield was but an illusion. As his son's magical bolt struck him in the chest and threw him into the wall, he knew all was lost. With all his will he reached out with the Science as he heard them talking above him.

"Stop, Lord Green is the Hidden one."

The science was racing down through the ground.

"Quickly, we must join our powers to get through his protective wards."

He could sense the heat of the rocks but could not focus enough to make the shaft. "First we must block him from working anymore magic."

What a foul word. There, it has reached the liquid rock. With all his might the Shadow anchored the Science into the rock and formed a path for the lava to take. They were starting to block his access to the Science. He could fight back, but his White Bear had told him plainly that if he did his dreams would die with him. He had only one choice if he was going to accomplish what White Bear told him to do. He embraced the pattern that they were working around him. It would guarantee that their patterns would work against him but he had no choice. With the pattern of his enemies linked to his own he traveled the path and pulled all the Science he could from his foes. He could vaguely hear a scream coming from one of them, but he did not care. His own agony was beyond description.

Marcus Green and Death Bringer jumped back. Somehow the Shadow had grabbed the magic with which they were working. They stared at each other with a questioning look for a moment. This was something that neither one of them thought possible. The Shadow and the Unholy Committee were locked in a magic loop. Both feeding each other's spell. One by one they burst into flame. They could not take the large amount of magic moving through them. Marcus jumped into actions. He had to yell to be heard over the screams of his allies.

"Redirect our pattern to that mirror over there, we may not be able to kill him now but we can imprison him."

The two of them worked the details of the patterns together. The ground erupted in lava around them and the tremors started to tear the palace apart. The level of magic in the room was so high that Death Bringer could feel the heat of it.

With all but Shadow Fire of the Unholy Committee dead from the influx of magic the duo accomplished their goal. The Shadow and Shadow Fire were sucked into the huge mirror. They grabbed the mirror quickly as a large wave of lava flooded into the room. Just as the molten rock covered their magically protected bodies, they managed to complete the pattern that carried them to the far reaches of the Confederacy.

I

"People come and people leave, not knowing how they have touched our lives. Those who are most worthy of the title of hero did not earn it through great deeds, but through the sacrifice they made for us. Thus, is the character of the heroes which mark the time we know as the Fire and Blood. They were willing to take on the pain of that time so we could move into the future with a pure heart."

The Dark-Skinned Bard scanned the common room. Appletun was such a small town it did not even appear on the maps of the Minor Bard Circuit. So rare, in fact, were entertainers, that when we first arrived, they had not known what to make of us. A crowd soon formed when it was discovered he was a storyteller. It has been almost four hundred years since the War for Blood and Fire, and the story still captivates the imaginations of the common and noble mind alike, and none could tell as D.S.B. could. When he had taken a drink of the cider which is the town's primary trade, he began his work. Raising his hands, lights grew up from the floor. Within seconds his form was replaced with an aerial view of a city, as a bird might see. As the view came closer to the city, the Dark-Skinned Bard started the first night's telling, the Shadow in the Mirror.

Dracothou would have been an impressive city even if it had not been the capital of KanaTo. Even though it had been centuries since the nation had been an empire it was still often referred to as the Imperial City. The discrepancy was rarely commented about even by the rulers of the other nations, and all who have seen the city agreed that it was a city which belonged to an empire. The architecture of the royal and high sectors dated back at least seven hundred years, to the time when Amic the Great ruled all of the Colonies from the Dragon Throne. They had that subtle beauty which showed its designers and builders were geniuses of the Golden Compass Society, the lost builders' guild which strove to find that perfect balance between function and appearance. Even the mid and low sections of the city, built centuries after the collapse of the Golden Compass Society, showed some understanding in the ancient art of the compass and square.

More than its beauty, Dracothou showed the greatness of the

architecture of Colonies once had. Some of the buildings reached more than a hundred meters into the sky, allowing the Imperial City to house the largest population of any city in the Colonies while only using half the land of the next largest, Jappa, the Capital of Mosk. Yet, it was not the ancient buildings or the size which awed most who visited the Imperial City. It was the magic which was apparent throughout the city. With its magical lanterns which lit the nights of even the worst streets in the low sector and its piping system which brought drinkable water into even the poorest of homes. Even though it was built entirely for humans, Dracothou was a city which was truly built by the Dragons. And after the destruction brought by the Tecmen invasion during the War Forward, it was the last which could claim such a distinction.

Amic Street had been named before Mosk had carved his kingdom from the collapsing Ortis Sol, and even before Ortis had claimed his own from the crumbling United Colonial Empire. A Kaltar walked down this ancient street wearing a style of suit which was common with humans in the north with a look of determination in his eyes. The customary fashion in the south has been the thick wool and dark colors. The thin linen did nothing to hide the cat man's great size and the light color made him stand out. The suit was accented by a red cloak and a few pieces of fine jewelry. With their fur to keep them warm, Kaltars usually limited their clothing to only that needed for modesty. The suit was of a material and quality of cut which was impressive even at court, making Tapps stand out even more. Yes, it was Tapps, Silver was sure of it. There was no mistaking him. Even though black fur was common, Tapps stood as tall and thick as an Ogre, where Kaltars tended to be thin and short by Human standards. Nearly thirty-five years had passed since that fateful night of their parting but the red bandana the Kaltar wore over his eyes was enough. Silver could tell by the way the cat man walked that he was more self-assured and had definitely acquired some wealth. What was most bothering to the Human rogue was that he had heard that Tapps had become a True Magus, master of the magical science. Tapps had not put a streak of silver in his hair as a warning to others. That was an academic custom so Silver did not dismiss the rumors on lack of the streak.

Silver had been furious when he had received the word that his old partner had been declared the Hero of the War Forward. Not only by the northern Kings but the southern ones had leant their names to those who declared the Kaltar's glory. For months he had been in a dark mood. Worsening with each new word about Tapps being honored by this lord and that lord. A little over twenty years had passed since then and Silver had put the Kaltar out of his mind. Silver and Tapps had run the streets together, had called each other brother. Yet just as it is written in Wisdom of the Night: ambition sweeps away all bonds. Tapps had not answered the summons by the Emperor to be knighted and Silver had figured that the Kaltar would never return to the Imperial City.

He was all together a different Kaltar in appearance, but Silver was sure it was Tapps Toya. Tapps had taken their deceased master's name out of respect and that bothered Silver more than anything else. How dare the cat assume that he had the right to take the teacher's name? He was not even part of the Night Culture anymore. It did not bother Silver's logic that he had been the one to betray both Master Toya and Tapps, in his mind the Kaltar was the betrayer for turning his back on the streets.

Tapps walked with a purpose in his steps. Silver was sure that it was a purpose of vengeance and he was the target of the revenge. Tapps stopped and peered towards the rooftops but quickly went on his way. Silver realized he had been holding his breath as soon as he let it out. There was no way for Tapps to see him as he was well hidden by the heat of the chimney's bricks. A small voice in his head told him to be careful all the same.

As Silver climbed off the roof, his mind raced to find a solution to his coming confrontation with Tapps. Silver regretted not killing the Kaltar when he had the chance all those years ago. Now that he had lost the use of the silver fire, he would be helpless against Tapps. Silver knew this better than anybody. He barely was able to stand against the cat man during the last encounter and Silver had realized that the fire he had been granted by the mysterious figure was a powerful magic. How could he stand against Tapps when he had no more power than a rogues' master? Silver was not entirely without resources. He had spread rumors that he had been killed in a rival guild's raid and was having his people look for the best bounty hunters that one could buy or exhort into protecting him. Silver was hoping that would be enough.

The Hero Tapps Toya entered Dracothou reluctantly. This was the place of his growing up, as Humans call it. The city brought back a lot of bad memories and very few good ones. He rubbed the small stone which hung around his neck. When he had left, he had vowed never to return, he had kept the promise for decades. He had business in the city, so he entered in spite of his resolution to the contrary. An old friend of his was from the city and had residence here. Tapps had not seen him since they parted company during the War Forward. He had heard many rumors of his friend whereabouts but none which were reliable. He had need of his friend's skill with money and with any luck Zack would have returned here when he had finished his business with the Shawlls.

Preoccupied in his own mind Tapps nearly failed to notice that a figure on a rooftop was watching him. Stopping, he looked toward his curious watcher, making a point of turning his head. The man was too far away to recognize the face. Tapps would have thought it was Silver but as good as this man on the roof was hidden, he was only hidden from his sight based off heat. Tapps' sight was also based off sound and Silver, knowing this, would never make such an error. Beside Tapps had learned that Silver had been killed in a raid on his guild's headquarters. It was sorrowful news, after all the rogue had done to him, he had forgiven Silver. In a way he was thankful for the betrayal, without it he would never had left the Night Culture. Not only his own, but possible the fate of the Colonies would have been much different.

This rooftop spy was probably plotting the best way to steal Tapps' gold but as this did not bother him, he went on his way. It had been a long time since he was a rogue running these streets at night. There had been many changes through the years but Tapps did not have any problem finding the street he needed. It took him only a short time to find the address he was looking for. From the outside there appeared to be no one home. Tapps walked up to the door and knocked. No reply. With all the skills in the Nightly Arts abandoned, Tapps kicked the door. It swung open with a load bang. He was looking forward to Zack's reaction to finding his door battered in. The man had been across the line for less than a decade and was probably still very much into his wealth. To Tapps' surprise the entryway was empty of furniture.

As Tapps searched all the rooms he thought how it was ironic that this was the very house that so long ago he was caught robbing, an arrest which had changed his life. An event which sent him to prison and at the time he thought had ruined his life. Maybe his life would have been happier. That was a possibility, but it would not have been nearly as interesting.

The only thing he found was a house with its furniture covered. It looked as if the house had been unoccupied for some time. There was no clue to where his friend had gone. He would have to go and ask the Ancient were the old coin biter was. Tapps walked outside thinking of what to do next and bumped right into someone.

Tapps looked around. The leader of the guards nearly fell to the ground from the force of the collision. Some of the guards had their crossbows drawn, loaded and pointed at him. As he looked up at the leader, who was broad of shoulder, Tapps had no need to see the man's gear to know he was a wizard. He could smell the magic woven tightly around the man. The leader of the group took a few steps back and began to speak. Tapps cut him off.

"Could you, sir, tell me what happened to the man that lived in this house? I would very much like to find him and any help that you could give I would appreciate."

The captain looked hard at Tapps and spoke, barely keeping the disgust he felt out of his voice. It could be the early hour or having to deal with a humanike. Tapps could not tell which.

"I do not know who lived here, cat, but it is apparent that you do not realize that in civilized lands it is inappropriate to go around kicking in the doors of a citizen's home. If you . . ."

Tapps knew what lesson the young magus needed to learn and how to teach it. Ignoring the racial slang, Tapps cut the man off again.

"Well, that's all very pleasant, but I am sure you know of my friend. His name is Zackariah Morris, but most often simply went by Zack, a merchant by trade, by the signs he could not have left more than a year ago."

The wizard reddened with anger at the arrogance of a mere humanike.

"I tried to be pleasant and arrest you in a civilized manner but you won't shut up and listen. So we will do this the low-town style. Stand still as my men put shackles on you." He turned towards his men with crossbows. "If he moves shoot him."

Tapps talked gently as the men with the restraints approached.

"I do apologize if I have somehow offended you but I really do not have time to spend in straightening this all out."

The guard's captain just stared at Tapps, as the Kaltar smiled. It was true what he said, he was in a hurry. Regretfully, he had no choice but go with the men. With any luck the area commander would know what happened to Zack. After they shackled him the magus pulled Tapps' papers out of his pocket. The captain's eyes widened in proportion with his mouth as he read. He could barely get his words out.

"Release him."

His men did not move, they just stared at their commander. The captain's voice came out in a roar.

"Take off the shackles!"

The Guards did not know what to think but they knew what to do. Their captain's temper was as legendary as his willingness to vent it on anyone slow at following his orders. After the solders had taken off the restraints the captain handed the papers back to Tapps. His voice was full of a strained humility.

"I must apologize, Lord Toya. My actions have abashed me and if you are willing to come to the office, we can lodge your complaint against me there."

Tapps smiled. Fear was always easy to dispel once you discover the truth. Fear is caused by our imagination of the unknown, what we think might happen. The illusion could be pierced by simply waiting to see what did happen. In Tapps experience, nothing was ever as bad as he thought it was going to be. That is why it was rare for a True Magus to ever feel fear, but by the smell, this one was far from gaining his silver. Tapps voice was gentle.

"There is no need for you to worry yourself with such trifles. I hold no anger towards a man doing his job. However, ponder long on why you broke from protocol and did not ask for my papers before arresting me."

Tapps walked away, wondering to himself why the southerners never changed. As he entered through the city's gate the guard had asked to see his papers. He knew it was because he was a Kaltar. A Kaltar of wealth no less. After the guard had looked at the papers, he was taken to the watch office to check their authenticity. To his surprise they had added some pages to his papers which showed that he had been given the title of Count. It appeared that he also was given some land and all he had to do was go to the royal office and pay some taxes to claim it. The land and title were a bribe, pure and simple. The now deceased king had not wanted his actions in the War Forward to be known by the commoners. This was not the reason he was here, so he had put it out of his mind.

The long list of titles behind Tapps' name was the reason the guard had let him loose. It had been too long since he had spent any real time in the southern kingdoms of the Humans. Many of their laws seemed to be unnatural. He understood now that much of it was because of their tendency to crowd into large cities. Gormec was having similar problems. With the

four distinct cultures forming the nation, laws differed so widely from province to province that it was hard to tell what to do. He had just come from the meeting of the Council. They have been busy trying to draw up a constitution that would be the basic law of the nation. It had not been easy. Humans, Minotaurs, Shawlls and Kaltars had radically different cultures and different ideas of what freedoms and what order must be kept.
At present, it was dependent on the local customs. On his own estate it was custom that an empty house could be used by anyone who had need of it. He had not used his quarters in over a decade so it had been turned into a library which was open to all the workers. The few times he went home he slept in one of the guest rooms.

The only thing that any of the Council could agree on so far was that the law would apply to everyone no matter who they were. Even the Council and himself would be subject to them. Even KanaTo, with an encyclopedia of laws, did not hold such a position. Of the Human nations, called the Southern Lands, only Shouker had the same concept. Eldon was an oddity in the fact that their laws were stricter on their nobility, but they were typically not considered part of the Southern Lands. Tapps considered KanaTo to be the worse of the Human nations. It was true that life was harsher in the slave-nation of Mosk, but race mattered little there. A humanike could not even become a full citizen in KanaTo. Tapps chuckled. He now had a right to form an army in a nation which he could not even carry a weapon.

The gate guards had not seemed shocked in the least about his appointment. No doubt they had heard of him. Besides, Tapps had found that most people in the south, the commoners as they were called, usually did not judge by such vulgar things. Most of them did not understand nor care about the xenophobia which spread through their leadership. For that matter, only the most adept social student would recognize the problem had its roots in the Racial Wars some three hundred years prior. The common people were kept complacent by their search for the illusions they mislabeled needs.

He sped his steps to get to the inn in which he was going to stay. When he neared the place, he walked through an ally to take advantage of the shadows. With a wave of his hand his clothes changed form. He had long since passed the need for gestures to facilitate the forming of a spell but, like so many other new True Magi, it was still habit. As if they were made of liquid his clothes changed their shape to that of a robe. Tapps grabbed the hood and pulled it over his head to hide his face. As his hands left the hood, the whole outfit turned a dark brown. He walked out of the darkness of the alley which was across the street from the inn. The inn, known as the Golden Scale, boasted to be the best in the Colonies. Tapps had stayed there once before and would agree that it was one of the best in human lands, but not in the Colonies. The best in the Colonies was by invitation only and very few knew of its existence. There was also Tear of the Fairy Dragon in Meniopa ran by the Quiz-Thin sisters. They catered mostly to adventurers so entertainment was never lacking. Just as another name jumped to in his head, he arrived at the front desk. Tapps spoke with his normal air of authority.

"I would like a room on the fourth floor."

The clerk looked up at Tapps and appeared as if he was going to say something about status and rank but the youth choked on his words when he spotted a medallion on Tapps' robe. The medallion was the gold circle pierced with a silver lightning bolt. It was the symbol of a Warrior-Magus of the Society of Sword and Spell, a master of combat in both magic and weapons. It was the society's version of the silver hair. Most would not recognize the pendent but members used this inn when they were in town. The clerk could get no words out but "yes sir." In a few minutes Tapps was in his room.

There was a time when a Magus or Warrior-Magus from the Society would be requested to judge disputes. The badge stood for honor, wisdom, and strength. That was a time when the wearing of the pin would gain its bearer respect, instead of the fear it now invoked. Strength was a part of the Society, it had to be strong, but it was power for a purpose. The purpose left the Society long ago, and now even their strength was starting to wane. Even though he was a member, it was not his place to address their problem. Elohim had given him no authority in the matter except in prayer.

Tapps had just knelt in prayer when a knock came to the door of his room. Rising slowly, he wondered who it could be. Very few knew that he was in the city. When he opened the door, he instantly recognized the man bowing deeply on the other side. His name was Keith. A handsome young man, in dark leather armor and wearing the traditional quiver of short spears of the Vagofrons' Insanus Unum. The stripes tattooed on his arm showed that he was not a full member yet. It would be a couple of years before he would officially be allowed to become a Lost One. His hair was the rare color of fiery red just like his mother's, but few brought that up anymore. The youth's voice was strained but still sounded official.

"Tapps Toya, Warrior-Magus, Elder of the Wolf Clan, Protector of the Four Winds, Friend of the Shawlls and the Favorite of the Dragons, may Elohim bless and keep you. I, Keith, son of the Hawk Clan has come with a message from the Vagofron to the Protector."

Tapps smiled as he invited the red-haired man in. This was going to be a difficult meeting for both of them, considering the history between them. It was hard to determine what was going on in Keith's heart. He had learned from his mother to close off his spirit to others but there was too much of his father's teaching in him to do it well. They were called the Lost Ones because they are always outside the circle, by their training they made themselves outsiders to even the Vagofrons. They lived to wield their magic and weapons in defense of the Colonies. Elite warriors and agents of the Clans, many would have liked the honor of being one, but few could pay the price it required.

Tapps offered him a seat but Keith refused and stood with a rigidity which was all too common in official affairs. He spoke with elegance that showed his training in dealing with situations which were distasteful

"I, a son of the Hawk Clan, have been sent by the Speakers to ask for your help in protecting the Clans by teaching the young of the four tribes in the ways of magic and battle. Because such things do not fall in the realm of the Protector, the council has agreed that you will be compensated for the service."

With the message officially given, Keith produced a moderate size bag of coins and placed it on the desk at which Tapps was sitting. Tapps eyed the bag as his mind translated the sound of the metal into amount and type. Five hundred gold coins give or take a few. That would have been nearly half of the Clans' reserve treasury, more than a life time of salary. Tapps thought for a moment. He was not even slightly tempted by the coin. Between the Clan and the Society his needs were more than taken care of. His children would draw from his estate and by any standards could be considered rich. No, if he took the money it would be because he could not find another form of payment which could satisfy the Law of Honor the Clans hold so dear. Tapps slowly pushed the sack of coins back to a surprised Keith as he spoke.

"I do not want gold for such an act. It would better serve the Clans by staying where it belongs." Tapps paused and took a drink of wine. "However, what I will ask is something that the Clans' elder and myself must discuss. I will be at my family graveyard in two weeks' time. If he would like to speak with me then, he is more than welcome to seek me there. If he can wait, I will travel to the Winter Camp after that."

Keith avoided further conversation and left as soon as it was polite. Tapps went back to his prayers, adding the desire that the young man would not succumb to the same stresses which destroyed his mother's love and his father's life.

Far to the west, deep in the uncivilized area which was marked simply as unclaimed on most maps, a large cave gave host to a group which was called the Great Ones, or at least, that was what they called themselves. The group was indeed composed of powerful individuals, and could draw its membership back to the original Great Ones, who ruled the United Colonial Empire until their unexplained disappearance. A disappearance which shattered the unity of the Colonies and threw the Colonies into the Time of Blood. The current Great Ones held no resemblance to those heroes of old from which they took their name. The cared nothing for the welfare of the Colonies or the people which they ruled. Their personal ambition caused them to fight among themselves to increase their personal power, only having to use it to defend themselves from each other. Their meeting hardly could be called discussions, they were always arguments. The tone was no different this time. The voice of the Giant in their ranks was full of enough anger to shake the wall.

"I do not like to be summoned. Then when I get here none of you will admit which one issued the emergency meeting. If I do not get an answer I am leaving."

As if to respond to the Giant's statements, a figure walked out of the darkness. The stranger was one who was permanently etched into all of their memories. When he spoke it dispelled all doubt that it was the Dragoon.

"I am the one who summoned you here."

The Giant sat down. The last time the Dragoon had paid them a visit there was no feeling of power coming from the man. This time it could be felt with the skin. None of the Great Ones spoke. They could only stare. It had been over twenty years since the legendary heir of the Shadow had come to them and decreed a law to them not to get involved in the war-which-would-cleanse-the-way. A decree that they hoped the Dragoon did not know they almost broke. Would have broken if their timing had not been off. It was apparent in his voice that he knew.

"The last time I came to you I gave you an order not to meddle into the affairs of those to whom the fight belongs. You only kept the decree because of your incompetence. A dark time has come upon the Colonies and all of the Elders agree that we have entered the Time of Blood and Fire. Elohim will take care of the Faithful, yet I cannot risk you corrupting who you will. Understand this; there are only two choices for you now. You can either disband giving up your title of KanaUn, or you can force me to strip it from you."

Forgetting the lesson they learned from their last encounter with the Dragoon, the Great Ones instantly attacked. Marius Shadoa sighed. It was obvious that they had planned the attack. The last time they had met he had showed them how petty their magic and power were compared to his own. They must also know, as most in the Colonies do, that he earned the right to dictate what was best for the Colonies. He was the heir of the Shadow's dream, more from sharing the dream and centuries of dedication, than from any right of blood. Maybe it was his own fault for not gaining political power, but he differed from his father in only that way, he had no desire to rule. What he did he did in moments like this, dealing with people such as these.

He never did bother to learn their names but he knew what their specialties were. He could feel the Sanner of the group trying to steal the magic he had already gathered. The Flogg tried to put a shield around him to prevent him from pulling in anymore. The Redinect was pushing the flow of magic into the Giant as the latter pressed in for an attack. They were labels from even before the Time of the Dragon but they fit well here.

The Dragoon did not move as he worked the magic which he had already gathered. With a mental push he shattered the magic-null field around him and focused all of the magic into the stream feeding into the Sanner. The influx of magic was too much for the man. It started with a twitch of an eye and then a contortion of his face. By the time the Sanner knew the influx was too great for him, he was crumbling to the ground. As the Flogg was frantically trying to rework the magic to put up the shield again, a bolt of energy shot from Dragoon and hit the Giant in the chest. The Giant laughed at the lack of effect from the attack. The forces which gave him his size also protected him from magic. Running forward, horror played across his face as he realized that he was shrinking. By the time he stopped a few feet in front of the Dragoon he was the size of a normal human.

Throughout the whole encounter the Dragoon had not moved, gave no outward appearance that he had worked magic. This time his hands shot from his sides, as if he was quickly tossing something in front of him. A visible wave of power emanated from him, throwing everything in the room against the back wall, including the Great ones. They were magically held in place. The voice of the Dragoon was calm and level.

"I see that you band of misfits will never learn to stop your abuse of power. You have mistreated those who look to you for help and in that have betrayed the very names you call yourself. You have left me little choice but to strip you of all your power. Know this, that none of you will work magic again. You will never feel the coolness of it on a hot day nor will you taste its sweetness. Because you have never learned that the proper use of power is in the defense of those without it, you will have no more power than that available to those who you call the little people."

As the Dragoon vanished from sight the Great Ones fell from the wall. As they looked at each other the Giant started to weep. This set off a chain reaction with the rest of them. They could no longer feel the magic around them. To make matters worse, without their power they would not be able to go home. The small empires that they had built around themselves were based on the fact that they could destroy and kill with a wave of their hand. They were now strangers lost in a cruel world. A world that would not understand why they did not have even the most basic skills of society.

That afternoon Tapps went downstairs and asked around about Zack. The only Morris anyone had heard of was the newly formed Family Morris. It did not take Tapps long to learn that the Family Morris had a mansion on the south side of the city.

Tapps headed off. Within an hour he had found the large house. He mused to himself that Zack was doing very well. His current position must have agreed with him. The house in high-town showed great wealth but anyone with money could move in there. His new home was in the imperial sector meaning that he had surpassed being just a rich man but had gained power in politics as well. Zack had finally achieved the coveted Family status. While not as advantageous House Status for international trade, a Family could bid on government contracts and was free from road fees and internal tariffs within KanaTo.

He opened the front door and went in. He grabbed the first servant who he saw by the collar. His voice was threatening.

"Tell the master of the house that one with a sharp blade would like to see the old windbag."

Tapps went to the bar in the study and poured himself a drink. He had just lit a cigar and got comfortable in a chair when a dozen guards rushed in. Tapps blinked twice thinking it was an illusion. It was not like Zack to be threatened easily, but it would be just like him to use his magic for entertainment. After all he was a business man first and it was bad business to form enemies.

These were no mere creatures of minor magic. By the way they held their weapons they were highly trained warriors. He remained seated and sipped his wine when the guards surrounded him. He stood when an elderly woman entered the room. She looked worried and spoke with a grim voice.

"You are the one who broke into my house in high-town?"

Tapps laughed before speaking.

"Yes, of course."

He did not know what Zack was up to but it was sure to be something grand. He would do his part for this was becoming very amusing. The woman did not think the same.

"Why is it that you have come here?"

"I have already told one of the servants. I have come let some wind out of Zack."

The woman thought for a moment before speaking.

"What is your name?"

Tapps was puzzled now. This woman was not playing. She was really concerned about his presence.

"I am called Tapps Toya in the common tongue."

"Lord Toya? I am sorry, my lord, for my bad manners."

Tapps spoke through a wide smile which showed most of his sharp teeth.

"Even though I have been given titles in almost every kingdom, I am no person's lord. I cannot even claim to be my own. I came looking for Zack. We traveled for a time together and I am in need of him again."

The woman eyes took on a look of sorrow but her words came out steady.

"Yes, I know of your travels together. Zack spoke of you often and with a fondness that was not normal for him. He left during the War Forward, and did not return. I assumed he was dead."

Tapps apologized for the misunderstanding and started to leave. The woman stopped him and asked him to stay awhile. Tapps had no real plans so decided to grant her request. They talked of Zack for the rest of the day. Tapps liked her and could understand why Zack had chosen her to be his wife. She was definitely a better business person than Zack was. Zack was a genius when it came to money and trade but his pride prevented him from becoming great. Tapps had seen him ruin several deals just because of a slight insult. Pride could be the deadliest of the vices. Pride could not admit that it was a problem. Those who suffer from pride think themselves too great to suffer from pride, or at the least to let it be a problem. Tapps knew this from personal experience.

This was apparent in the wealth that the Family Morris had acquired in just the two decades of his absence. By the end of their conversation, they had formed a business agreement. An alliance between the Family Morris and the Lord Toya. While still there he wrote a letter to Norkil to send down his eldest child, Sacer, with some administrators to utilize the land and title. As Tapps first born son he would be inheriting the title under KanaTo law. Tapps left the house promising that he would return if he could. He knew where to look for Zack next, but he was not sure when he would have the time.

II

The next morning, back at the main hall of his guild, Silver sat at his desk worried about his own safety for the first time in a very long time. He had no luck in finding anyone who would kill Tapps for him and this just made him worry more. Most of the Silent- Killers who were good enough would not take the job on principal. Those vile enough to be willing to be known as the person who killed the Hero of the War Forward were not willing to risk the wrath of Tapps if they failed. They all had heard the rumors surrounding the Kaltar and would not go near him. Even the House Slar, which boasted to do anything for a price, would not take the contract. To them, and partly to Silver, Tapps was mysterious with unknown power and unknown weaknesses. Silver only had one hope left. He had seen a post of a bounty hunter at a tavern he frequented. He had heard that this mercenary was an honorable person in the naive sort of way. Silver's favorite kind of people. The kind who could easily be fooled and thus, used. He had one of his servants inform this bounty hunter that Silver was looking to hire. Silver was startled out of thought by a knock on the door and one of his assistants entered.

"Sir, the Kaltar that you ordered us to keep eyes on is getting ready to leave the city. Would you like to have him followed?"

Silver needed not to think long, his mind was made for such quick decisions. The type of person who is often right when he answers quickly and often wrong when they think about the question.

"Yes, do it yourself. Always use your magic in invisibility, never stop, never become visible at all. Follow him until sunset and return to me."

As his servant left Silver had the feeling that he had forgotten something. He had been having the feeling a lot lately. The feeling bugged him for hours before he realized what he had forgotten. Tapps used not only the sight of heat but of sound as well. Silver cursed himself. Mike was his top aid and the only person in the guild he trusted. Silver was not sure whether or not Mike's magic of invisibility worked against sound but Silver was feeling better because he had remembered what he forgotten, so the disconcerting feeling had passed.

Mike, confident in his ability, walked on the road about twenty arm spans behind Tapps. On occasion Tapps would stop and look around as if he was looking for someone. Mike thought nothing of it after it happened a few times. Silver always described Tapps as a master rogue just under the skill of himself. It would seem fitting that this hero would be as paranoid as Silver.

Just a few moments before the time Mike would have turned back, they entered Swamp Gate, a town which even now is well known among musicians for the high quality of their reeds. Mike figured that Tapps would go into the one of the small inns but instead he headed straight into the swamp. Mike was uncertain whether or not he should follow. It would be dark in a few moments and he had heard that the swamp was not a place to be after dark. It was called the Swamp of the Dragon. As the legends went, several centuries prior the nation of KanaTo had tried to drain the swamp and use it for farm land. A Dragon as black as night appeared and demanded that they stop. When the King sent a hundred of the best warriors to kill the Dragon, the great creature not only killed the solders but it also destroyed an entire legion of the army it came across. It then declared that the swamp was off limits to any mortal and that if one dared to step foot into the swamp they would die. Of course, as most legends, there was a lack of any real evidence that things actually happened that way and the Dragon had not been seen in at least a hundred years.

When Tapps did not return after a few moments, Mike cautiously entered the marshy land. Silver would be upset if Mike returned with a report of losing the Kaltar. Mike walked into the mud which became ankle deep then leveled out. After only a few minutes of dredging through the mud, Mike made out the glow of a small fire off in the distance. He made his way to it. He came across a camp and peeked into it from the darkness. A small fire had been set upon a pile of rocks. One set of footprints led to the fire and then away again, except for the crackling of the fire there was no sign of life at all in the clearing.

The camp had all the signs of a trap and it did not take Mike long to realize this. He panicked. Turning to run all he saw was a blur of fur. He was hit hard in the face. Lights flashed behind his eyelids as a pain exploded from his nose. All went black.

When he woke, he was bound and lying in the mud. When he looked around, he saw that Tapps' back was turned towards him. Mike figured that this would be his only chance of getting out of the mess he gotten himself into. He struggled a little to loosen his ropes. The Kaltar suddenly stood. Mike went still. Tapps walked slowly over to Mike and placed his face close to Mike's. Tapps roared, spraying Mike's face with spittle.

"Why were you following me?"

Mike just stared blankly back at Tapps. To Mike it seemed that this tactic was enraging the Kaltar. Tapps stood up and paced back and forth a few times. With a sudden leap that frightened the human, Tapps put his face back into Mike's.

"If you do not tell me, I will kill you in a most horrible fashion."

With the words just out of his mouth he racked two fingers of his claws across Mike's forehead just above the eyebrow. Mike just gritted his teeth and grunted but said nothing. Tapps stood and looked at Mike for a moment with a curious eye. Then as quick as lightning Tapps swiped one of his claws across the human's neck. The pain was only slight and it took Mike a few moments to realize that he was bleeding from the wound. He was not bleeding a lot, just small spurts of blood in time with his heart. Not enough to kill him out right but enough to allow Mike to bleed to death over a few moments. This trick was one of Tapps' favorites while he was fighting in the pits for not only did it thrill the crowds, it also assured that Tapps would win the fight.

Mike stared at Tapps who now had a grim look on his face.

"You have only a few more minutes to live if the bleeding is not stopped. I will untie you if you tell me who sent you and why."

Mike closed his eyes and concentrated on how to get through this. The loss of blood was already clouding his mind, or was in fear? Mike could not tell which. He tried to relax and let death have its way. He could not find the peace and panic overtook him.

"I'll tell, untie me."

When Tapps realized he had won, his voice took on a sympathetic tone.

"Tell me who sent you."

"It was my guild master, Silver."

Tapps started to get angry.

"It is a lie you speak. Silver is dead."

"It's Silver, I swear. He spread rumors about his death. Rumors are all they are."

With the words just out of his mouth his bounds disappeared. Then in a flash, Tapps and the camp disappeared. Mike quickly placed his hand over the wound which was on his neck only to realize that it was only an illusion. No magical illusion that he knew of could create the sensation of pain. Mike was not sure what was going on but he was sure that he did not like it. Slipping several times as he ran in the mud, he finally made it back to town. Mike continued to run as fast as he could until he reached the city.

Tapps was watching the man from the branches of a tree. He did not like manipulating the man's mind that way. It always seemed to be like lying to him. But it was the only way he could think of to get the information he needed without actually harming the human. Even so, it was a mean trick to play on the man.

As he jumped from the tree Tapps pondered to himself about Silver still being alive. If it had been a decade ago Tapps would have headed start back to the city to avenge their master's death. He had learned to forgive and felt pity for Silver who must live in fear constantly. Maybe if he could find the time he could go back and put his old enemy's mind to rest. If he could find the time. Life seemed to be getting more complicated of late. There was an evil presence on the wind. He wished Manker was around to help him with this. The old priest had not spent much time with the Frons, not that Tapps could blame him for that. It had to be hard to be reminded of the killing of his wife, and that Tapps had to be the one to do it.

With a sigh, Tapps set off on the journey in front of him.

Angga Del Sella flexed her wings as she looked at a door. She had changed considerably since leaving home. Very few would guess by looking at her the importance she held in her homeland. She bore a scar on her chin, and one on her forehead from a wound which almost cost her sight. She stood with the footing and pose of a warrior who was about to enter battle. She constantly examined her surroundings. Her attitude and wearing the traditional garb of denim and leather, she fit well into that social class of people who collectively are called Travelers. A class that was only starting to gain a kind of the respect which they have now. As a bounty hunter, she lived mostly on the fringe of the Night Culture.

She had joined adventuring groups several times but she had never found one that fit her style. For the past decade she had been making her living tracking down and capturing fugitives. As her reputation grew, she had been approached by the International Order of Detectives with an offer to join. Angga refused, preferring to stay a freelance, the work was not as steady but it allowed her to choose the bounties she went after. It also allowed her time to pursue her interests which were not as economical.

It was one of those interests, her main one which was why she was in Dracothou. When she first came to the land of the wingless ones it had been hard just to survive. It had taken here several years just to get used to the culture. She was comfortable enough now in the human lands, and with herself, that she was able to search for her brother. But she was still not much closer to finding him. While she had already knew that he had left to fight in the War Forward, she had only recently learned that he was part of the mercenary army known as the Panthers. He was remembered by the few who were a part of that group but in Dracothou she found a man who fought by Ankka's side in one of the early battles. The story was exaggerated to warrant the coin he wanted but she had learned that her brother was part of the core group of the mercenary band. It did not shock her to learn that he had taken a lowlander wife. It would explain why he never came home and the wingless ones did have a sort of charm about them. Well, at least some of them did.

The man did not know what happen to her brother after that, giving the excuse that the army had grown too large. She was not sure where to look next, but she figured she could go to Gormec. So far all of her information had come from humans who had only fought under the Panther Banner. She would have to go to the Panthers and see what they knew.

Angga pulled her wings in tight and shifted her Kirtel, the magic of her people, to bind them close to her body. The buildings of the humans were not designed for those with wings. Some of the low town business establishments were built with Ogres and Minotaurs in mind which gave room for her wings. By the look of this door, this one was not one of them. With her wings tucked away, she could almost pass for human. It did not take a hard look to notice the wings but humans often were nervous when she let them spread out. Letting her long black hair fall across her back, she opened the door and walked in.

The room was dark. She expanded a small amount of her Kirtel to heighten her senses. She noted that there was someone in the darkness. The man was stealthy and carried a knife. A test, she thought to herself. She did not like to be tested and she was not in the mood to be playing games. So when the man started to stalk her she let loose with a bolt of crackling black energy from her finger tips. Powerful enough to kill a normal man, it hit the knifeman and threw him against the wall. The man with the knife slumped over. She did not know if the man was dead or not, and frankly she did not care at the moment. It had been a long day and to be summoned by a thief, not asked, but summoned, made her blood boil.

The darkness finally dissipated and Angga could make out a door behind some crates. With a stride which comes with a little too much pride she went to the door. As she reached to unbolt the door, she felt the magical trap on it. withdrawing her hand, she shifted her sight. The faint glow of magic from the door let her read its pattern and adjust adjusted her defense accordingly. She reached out with her Kirtel and unlocked the door. She shifted her magic to open the door but nothing happened. With an audible sigh she mentally checked her defenses and reached out and grabbed the door handle. A surge of power caused her hand to tighten around the handle. She fought the pain and channeled the electricity into the floor. Pulling open the door she examined the corridor beyond it.

There were six doors in all, but only one had light coming from underneath. She let some of her Kirtel slip out of her body and envelope the door to check for traps. Finding none, she walked to it and pulled it open. A human sat behind a desk playing with a long metal item. She stepped in.

"What do you have there?"

Silver slowly looked up at the female, not even seeming to notice the fact that she should not be standing in a middle of a rogue's guild, spoke in a friendly tone.

"It's called a riffle, a piece of technology that was left behind by the Tecmen during the War Forward. I have a buyer willing to pay a handsome sum for one to research on."

She seemed a bit confused and it showed in her voice.

"I thought that such items were illegal and were supposed to be turned into the government."

Silver chuckled.

"This is a rogue's guild after all and we deal in mostly items that are not socially correct. You must be Angga, the mercenary that I sent for."

She was almost able to keep the anger out of her voice.

"I am called Angga, and I am a bounty hunter not a mercenary. There is a difference."

"What you call yourself makes no difference to me. The only thing that

I care about is that you are for hire and that you are good. I assume that you are one of the better ones for you seem to have gotten in here without too much trouble. Well, on to what I sent for you about. Believe it or not, I have of late had an item stolen from me. A bit ironic don't you think. But this item, this necklace, was an heirloom that has been in my family further back than any history can tell. Anyway, it has been stolen by a Kaltar. I offered to buy it from him for more than it's worth but this Kaltar would not part with it. He goes by the name of KanaShor. I would like the Kaltar brought back to me, but if nothing else I would like the necklace back."

Silver went on to describe Tapps and the necklace that Tapps had been given by Master Toya the last time they fought. He knew very well that she would have to kill Tapps to get the necklace from him. In a spark of genius Silver went on to say that Tapps had been down on his luck and Silver had helped him out and that is what hurt the most.

Even with the emotional story Angga normally would have refused the job, but she needed to start collecting funds for her trip to Gormec. Besides, most of her information came from the Night Culture and she could not risk offending such a powerful contact. They agreed on a price and Silver assured her that the Kaltar who she was after was the most dishonorable type and would do anything including lie to prevent giving up the necklace. With that Angga left to search out the Kaltar. As she left, she saw the man who was in the darkness picking himself up. She was glad did not kill the man after all. After getting her belongings from the inn where she was staying, she went into the darkness that surrounded the Imperial City.

Deep in the Southern Mountains, many miles from the nearest village just as the sun made its way to peek over the mountain tops, a man of great stature stood looking over a nearby cliff side. He was named David after his grandfather but because of his large size and the skin of the great bear that he wore, everyone respectively called him Kift.

Those who judge others by their appearance would have known that Kift belonged in the wild. Everything, from his coarse and callous hands to the look in his eyes, showed he would do what he must to survive. Those who have talked to him have always found a man with a keen intellect honed by a formal education. Those brave enough to get to know this great man always found a gentle heart which held no ambition.

Everything about Kift's appearance was in contrast. He was handsome in a rugged way, his face having both the looks of a warrior and a thinker. His eyes had a gently piercing quality and his smile was disarming. He had a lumpy look to him but he moved over the rocky mountaintops with the sureness of goat.

Kift called these mountains his home, almost since he left his schooling nearly a decade prior. Life had been hard in the KanaTo Institute of Higher Learning and he never found peace there. He and his brother had no family and there was never enough money. This made them outcasts among the children of rich nobles who were their fellow students. They both had left the Institute just after his brother's sixteenth birthday. They would not have been able to stay much longer even if they had wished, for their money was almost gone. Trying their hands at the life of adventure, they traveled together for a time. They eventually went their separate ways when the mountains started to call for him and his brother entered the priesthood.

The Southern Mountains are not easy to live in, but Kift could not think of any other place he would want to be. The entire of the Southern Mountains were officially claimed by both Shouker and KanaTo and the little-known Sella Queendom. The boundaries actually were not clear, and few really cared. The Shouker part of the mountain was designated as the Pope's acreage. Unlike such land in other nations, the mountains were not restricted from the citizens. It was open to anyone with the desire to live there. Outsiders rarely came into the mountains and a few of the winged people, who also called this area home, kept a good distance from Kift. Both letting the other do what they must to survive.

Kift shared what he could with the hermits, monks and other Foresters. He had not been there long before words of his past deeds had caused him to be looked to as the area's Silas. And old term from an even older book. He had not realized what that meant at first. He was in essence the informal leader of the hermits and Foresters. He handled the relations between those who lived in the forest and those who lived off the forest. Though with the towns at the edge, Kift had to deal with things more often than he wanted. Each year he made his camp further up the slope. Since last fall only those with real problems were seeking him out.

There was not a part of this area that Kift did not know and know well. At least that is what he thought until a few months ago. He had traded a good number of furs for a field glass. A prize possession for a man such as Kift. Trying it out, he had spotted a small cave near the middle of the cliff. He had never the reason to spend much time examining the cliff before. Erosion from rain and wind had caused the face of the cliff to shear off just before he had come upon it the first time a half decade prior. The loose stones made the cliff difficult to climb and the brown eagles made it dangerous. With a safer route just on the other side of the peak Kift never even thought about climbing the cliff until now.

Kift made his way to the base of the cliff and regarded the height of it. He would have preferred to have climbed down from the top, but it would have taken him at least a half day to get there. With his mind made up, he started to climb. The loose rocks fell to expose jagged ones underneath, cutting into Kift's fingers. The climb was easier than he thought it would be. As he came close to the cliff the brown eagles cried and flew off only to circle and protect the only thing they called their own. Razor sharp talons ripped into Kift's flesh. The bearskin he wore protected his torso but his face and arms were gashed ruthlessly. Blood and pain blurred his vision and made him dizzy. He was no stranger to pain for it is the way that Foresters know they are alive.

Kift pushed upward, for to stop was to fall. It took him a few moments to realize that he had crawled into the cave and the birds' attacks had stopped. He crawled a little farther into the cave before he paused to take care of his wounds. The gashes were deep and hurt with a burning sting, nothing worse than he had felt before. He had no doubt that he would survive this ordeal. Pulling a small lantern out of his rucksack, he lit it with flint and steel. The few lacerations he could not stitch himself he bandaged

He closed and put away his first aid kit and crawled forward. Kift hoped that his pain was not in vain. His fears were quickly relieved when the small cave opened to reveal a cavern full of crystal formations. The light from his small lantern catching them just the right way to throw a hue of colors in all directions. The beauty and wonder of the sight made Kift forget his pain as he stared in awe. He knew the crystals from his training. They were wu crystals or sometimes called void crystals because of their property of perfectly warping radiation around, making them completely undetectable by magical means. Whatever was in the cave would be hidden even by the most magically adapt tracker. If he remembered his training correctly there would be absolutely no way of finding this cave with magic.

It took a while for Kift to regain his composure, completely forgetting his original purpose for being there. He pulled his paper and marker out and started taking notes and drawing sketches. Hours passed before Kift moved from the spot. Even more hours passed as Kift explored every inch of the cave. His bandages were soaked and dripped blood from his elbows. He reached the end of the cavern and spotted a brazier.

As Kift examined the brazier he wondered to himself for a few moments why anyone would put such a thing here. His only conclusion was that someone must have brought it in to form the crystals. It would have taken years to grow all the crystals. He could not come up with an answer to why someone would go through all the trouble. What would be so valuable that such a place would be made to hide?

The brazier was wonderfully carved, four bat-like creatures made up the base, their wings supporting a golden bowl carved with runes. Kift spent some time sketching every detail of the brazier and making sure his drawings and notes were accurate. He sifted through the herbs in the bowl. He noticed for the first time that he was bleeding when he saw his blood dripping into the brazier. He smiled in humor, he had left his mark all over the floor of the cavern. Even his notepad had blood on it. Wondering why he had not noticed it before, a chill came over him. He attributed it to the loss of blood but decided it would be wise to leave anyway.

Kift secured his rope to a stalagmite with a lone-descent hook and started to crawl out of the cave. The rope made the descent faster and much easier. Only one eagle came to maul Kift during his downward trip and it left when Kift reached the bottom. After whipping the rope to release it from the hook he coiled the rope and secured it to his pack. Tightening up his bandages he headed off to have a talk with his brother.

Somewhere off in the distance thunder sounded in a cloudless sky.

Tapps came into a clearing near the center of the Swamp of the Dragon. What he called the clearing was only a large mound of rocks and dry earth with a mark of an old campfire in the middle. Tapps always felt a warm sorrow here for this was the place he buried Master Toya. Back then, he had not known the name of this swamp or the rumors of the Dragon who lived in it. He had talked to the other Dragons about it and had learned that the swamp belonged to KanaFinaPrin.

He had not met the Dragon during the battle against the Tecmen's ships but Tapps did not remember much of that fight. Even the other Dragons would say the name of KanaFinaPrin with awe. From what Tapps understood, KanaFinaPrin was small for a Dragon his age and had an almost humanoid appearance. From the reactions of the other Dragons it was apparent that KanaFinaPrin was a living legend. From what Tapps could learn he had been a great hero during the Dragon/Giant War. Never had Tapps run across the Dragon in the swamp, so he took that as the sign that the Dragon did not mind his presence.

Tapps had set camp and just bedded down for the night when a wolf as large as a small bear with fur as white as snow entered the campsite. He slowly raised and worked the magic around him to shape his body into that of a large panther.

The two circled each other for a better part of a half hour. Then without warning the huge wolf leaped at Tapps' new form. The wolf landed on Tapps knocking him to the ground. Tapps twisted to avoid the large canine's teeth. Tapps brought his own claws to bear on the wolf's side. The wolf yelped from the large gash. Instead of backing off the wolf sunk his fangs deep into Tapps shoulder and tore out a huge chunk of flesh. Tapps retaliated out of pain and brought his own mouth to the wolf's throat. Tapps fangs broke skin but he stopped there. After Tapps released him, the wolf backed up. Wary about another attack from the wolf, Tapps stood his ground while working some magic to stop the bleeding from his wounds.

The wolf started to shift into a human form and Tapps released his spell. His body flowed into its natural shape. After the two men dressed, they hugged. Tapps held the white-haired man at arm's length and was the first to speak.

"Quick, you pup, if your aim was just a bit better you would have won for sure, so what brings you out of the Camp."

"You were always quicker than me and that in itself is enough to make me lose to you every time. The reason that I have traveled so far from the Winter Camp is that I knew that you would not accept the task the Clans set in front of you for a bag of coin and a handshake. So, I have ventured forth to bargain the price in which you ask to teach our young."

Tapps raised an eyebrow.

"Why has the Speaker sent you and not come himself?"

"You have been away from the Camp for too long my old teacher. Silver Bane died four moons ago and I am now the Speaker of the Vagofrons..."

Tapps interrupted.

"Why did not anyone tell me?"

Quick Paw smiled slightly as he spoke.

"It was not an emergency so there was no reason. As tragic as it was it was expected and is, after all, a part of life. As you once told me we are all given a number of days at our birth and we must make each one count. However, there is something that does concern you. The Clan of the Bear says, and the other three Clans agree, there have been many bad omens lately.

"The Elders have spent most of their time trying to find out what it all means. So far, the only thing that has been revealed to them is a great time of war is upon us. A war that will be so great that even we will not be spared. We have to be prepared for the fight and the deaths that will follow."

Tapps took a moment to answer.

"Preparing our defenses will have to wait until the threat is better known. As for the deed you ask of me. It is a heavy task, the compensation must be equally great for this does not fall in the range of the Clans' Protector."

"What is the price you ask of us, my brother?"

Neither Tapps' eyes nor the tone of his voice betrayed any emotion change.

"I want to be taught how to touch the minds of the Insanus Unum."

Quick Paw's voice filled with shock.

"The Insane Ones? That is impossible. Their minds are too well guarded."

"It is true that they close off their spirits to the world around them but some of the healers know how and they can teach me."

Quick Paw stared at Tapps for a moment, and then sighed as he spoke.

"It is a mighty price you ask. I cannot give permission for such a thing. It will have to put in front of the Clan Speakers. They will be the ones to decide. Will you be coming back through the traveling gate with me?"

Tapps thought for a moment before answering.

"No. I have some business to take care of first in Gormec, but I will come to the Winter Camp before the first snow falls."

With that, they talked of happier things until the sun came up.

III

Kift had never felt comfortable in any church. It was not the feeling of confinement of buildings, nor a problem with religion, or any such nonsense. It was the people in the church that bothered Kift. Most of them were merely playing a role. Teachers who had no heat of belief gave the religious studies at the Institute. Those who gave the Sabbath sermons in the school's chapel were not much better. The words were correct but they lacked any real truth in them. They held neither passion nor conviction in what they said. Or worse, holding an image of excitement without any substance.

In his youth he had thought that was all there was to faith. By the time he was fifteen he could tell what point the preacher was going to make a few minutes into the sermon. Like many youths he wanted something more, something deeper, something real. Like many youths, the only answers he got were the same lines he had heard a thousand times before. And like many youths, he got bored and gave up. He never gave up his own faith but had turned his back on trying to find any answers. It was not until his brother entered Shouker's seminary did he become serious about his own faith. It was in the mountains that Elohim found him and showed him the depth possible in faith. Kift had plenty of time for prayer and meditations during the long winters.

It was a country church that had a priest who lived in poverty, not due to the lack of material goods nor because the church did not have enough money. The Shouker government paid his living expense for such a poor community could not be expected to support a priest and staff. The priest chooses to live simply because all the money he could scrap together went to help the poor of the community. The priest of this church believed to be truly humble when dealing with the people he served was to be living under the same conditions they did. This is not a popular idea, especially among the priests of the city, but Kift thought it was a good thing. He would freely admit his bias though. The priest in charge was also his brother.

As Kift entered the church he knelt and prayed for a moment. He understood the need for a temple as a focal point of worship, but why did so many forget the Divine the moment they stepped outside its doors. The sky, a tree, everything screamed out to the glory of Elohim. Even the very people about whom he was pondering reminded him to be faithful. When he had finished whispering his prayer he stood. He reached in his pocket, his freshly stitched wounds stinging a bit when he caught them on his pocket edges. Having no coins for the offering box, he unwrapped the furs from around his lower legs and placed them by the box. He went into one of the back rooms.

As he entered the room the priest stopped his reading of a manuscript at a large oak desk and stood. Their facial features were similar but the priest was a bit taller and only about half the girth of Kift. They had been told since they were young that they were brothers. It was not until they started asking about their life before the Institute that they learned that they were really cousins. With very little discussion they had decided that they would still be brothers. The priest looked at Kift with surprise and said with elegance in his voice which only comes with being raised formally.

"I was not expecting to see you until just before winter when you come to trade your furs. How have you been?"

Kift was always embarrassed that he could not talk with the finesse which came so natural to his cousin. They had gone to the same school, taken the same classes and shared the same experiences until his cousin went into the priesthood and Kift went to the forest. He could not help but have a slight pang of jealousy about his cousin's ability to deal with people so much better than him.

"Well Matt, I ran across something strange during my journeys. I am baffled by the meaning of it." He produced his sketchpad out of his bag and showed Matt his drawings of the brazier. "I was wondering if you could make any sense of it."

Brother Matthew took the drawings and examined them closely. When he finished thoroughly looking through the drawings, he took off his glasses.

"I am not even going to ask why there is blood all over this. Or about the cuts covering your face and hands. Have you heard the legends about the man who we call the Shadow?"

"Of course, I did not always sleep through history class. He was the first wizard of old. His death brought the Time of Pain."

The priest's mood shifted to a solemn one as he spoke.

"He was much more than a wizard. Some say he was an evil man who thought himself a god, others say he was the salvation of the world. Those who know the truth do not talk much about it. He was, without a doubt, a great man who had a dream. His dream he called the New Earth. But I am getting ahead of myself so let us start from the beginning.

"Very little is known of life during the Time of the Shadow except by the most studious of scholars. Before then humans used magic through items of metal and stone, but the people were arrogant. They thought that they had solved all the puzzles of the universe, or at least on the verge of discovering them. People did not know that they were using magic. The Shadow was an educated man for that time. He had graduated from their top schools. Specializing in the field of magic or whatever they called it back then. He was the first to realize the truth behind magic. That some of the energy fields which control its movements could be affected by the mind. He had discovered this nearly twenty years before he realized his dream.

"The Shadow found that if he willed hard enough, he could make strange and wondrous things happen. He devoted his life to the study of what would come to be called the new science. Even though he had created several devices to magnify the effects, he was more and more disappointed for it was not like now when magic surrounds us. Then there were no natural places with an abundance of what we call floating magic.

"I tend to believe he was not an evil man. Some of White Bear's writings of the time survived. They describe the Shadow as a great man, but just a man. He differed greatly from the Shadow in opinion, especially on the subject of technology, but it always had the tone of debate of friends. Hold on, I have a copy of one of the letters from the Shadow that most scholars agree is a reference to the first release of magic which destroyed the Old Earth."

Matthew and Kift moved to the library. After a short search the priest found the book for which he was looking. He flipped through it and stopped when he found the copy.

"Here it is. He writes 'you have asked me why I have chosen this path. Is there no other way than the task I set before myself? Could I not use my position to stop what they are about to bring down on themselves? My answer is no. I worked almost my entire adult life trying to convince people that any technology which is destructive to the planet (even those which are only slightly destructive) must be forsaken. What has this won me except the respect of people who only pretend to care? They claim to agree with me but are unwilling to give up their cars and the toys which clutter their lives. They complain that there are too many people while they themselves consume enough for ten. They become enraged when the price of gasoline increases a few pennies when thousands of children perish from starvation each day. We clear thousands of acres of woodland to build our luxurious homes. We spend nearly a trillion dollars each year eating in restaurants when our neighbors to the south are in the worst famine that they have ever known. In your language I say Huss Ka. No more! No more will I sit by while the ignorant and self-centered destroy the world. We will use my position and the new discoveries made by my group to create a new earth. One that places the wellbeing of the planet and the people above the desire of the rich and arrogant. Technology is a wondrous thing but has only become evil and destructive combined with human nature. I agree with you that machines have allowed us to rid ourselves of using humans as slaves but society only requires slaves when it is lazy. They have taken the salvation that science promised (if you will forgive my terminology) and turned it into a weapon. A weapon of which they are unwilling to realize the danger. We must take away this weapon out of the hands of the children. If this means leaving behind all that is now, all that we know, then - So Be It!"'

Matthew stopped to pour Kift and himself a glass of water.

"Well, the Shadow brought his followers to this land and created the Confederacy of the New Earth. Eventually others learned to use magic but not with the skill which the Shadow had. No one knew the secrets of magic like he did. Even so, the average wizard of that time would be considered powerful by today's standards. The Shadow built an empire around himself and this land prospered into a great nation."

It was not uncommon for Matt to get off subject and Kift was sure that it was the case here. His tone reflected this feeling.

"What does any of this have to do with the brazier I found?"

The voice of Brother Matthew took on a gentle tone.

"Remember back to our Fundamentals of Applied Practical Physics class. The relation between the kinetic and thermal energies. Fire excites the very particles which makes up magic and makes them easier to work. Because the wizard's power comes from them forcing the magic with their will, they will use various items to help them in their works. Typically, there is nothing magical about their brazier. They are simply used to hold the fire that enhances their magic. We do not see much of it today, as the creation of magical items is not well spread, and research is mostly done in the academies. Truthfully, they could use a common fireplace. The average magus' ego being what it is, most of them have fancy braziers made for themselves."

Matthew flipped through Kift's drawing pad and stopped on one of the drawings of the brazier.

"See the supports of the bowl. They are a race of bat-like creatures which were engineered by the Shadow to be messengers. The Shadow took these bat people as the symbol for his family. Like the griffin, they were hunted during the Time of Pain and most believe them extinct now. I am not an expert, but I believe this brazier once belonged to the Shadow or at least one of his descendants. There are two of which I know. One in the museum of the Institute and the other is in the hands of a private collector. It is quite a prize you have found here cousin. It will be worth a king's ransom to a collector."

After several more hours of personal conversations, Kift stood. With a hug and a thank you, he left the church. He walked into the forest to think.

When Angga was sure she was far enough away from the city where the guards could not see her, she let go of the magic which kept her wings wrapped close to her body. The bat-like wings unfolded to rise well over her head. Her wings were the cause of much of Angga's difficulties with the land-bound. Maybe it would have been different if they were the feathered kind of most of her people, but the dark leather often caused a reaction. There was not much she should do about it, but there were times this affect had helped her impress the serious nature of the situation. As small as Angga was, she could be terrifying to some. Especially she spread her wings fully and she let the black flame of her Kirtel engulf her and her Salk, the traditional weapon of her people.

After taking to the air, it took her less than an hour to reach Swamp Gate. Once on the ground it took her only a short time to find the tracks that the cat man had left during the encounter with Mike. Angga could not make sense of what had happened. The Kaltar had spent some time in a tree as the human ran around in the mud. It looked as if the human was in a fight with himself. After the human ran off the Kaltar jumped from the tree and headed deeper into the swamp.

She followed the tracks until around midnight, and then found a dry spot to spend the night. Far removed from the pampered life she knew in her youth, but Angga had lived such a life for so long that she was just pleased that it was dry. She rose with the sun and started off again. She had reached the camp where Quick Paw and Tapps had stayed the night and after a close examination realized that she was only about half a day behind him. With any luck she would have him and be back in a week. There had been a fight between two large creatures. There were too many tracks to tell exactly what happened to them. Later a human had entered the camp. She knew that the human and the Kaltar parted company and went separate ways. She was happy that she did not have to fight them both and hoped the Kaltar would be alone when she found him. She picked up her pace and went to head KanaShor off.

Blood and bits of flesh covered the walls, floors and even the ceilings of the corridor and adjacent rooms. Mutilated bodies littered the area like discarded dolls. The scene was the same all over the underground complex which sprawled under the heart of the City of Jappa, the Capital of Mosk. The attack had been swift and deadly, and as vicious as only vampires can be.

Elson walked through the hallway followed by a dozen of his guards. The carnage filled him with both ecstasy and anger. He was the Degeath, the leader of the Vampires of Mosk and these were his personal quarters. He had held the headship of the cult for almost two decades, but had unofficially been its leader for much longer. His father cared little about actual power, as long as he had the title. When Emperor Mosk the Betrayer disappeared, he was sure that he would have to fight his brother for the cult. Mosk the Dark cared nothing for the vampires and Elson had no desire to have the kingdom. It was a convenient partnership. Together they were able to kill their other siblings without a civil war and the wholesale destruction that goes with it. Their father's legacy would survive, not that either one cared for anything as abstract as legacies.

The cult had weakened since he took it over. The Society of Sword and Spell had doubled their attacks and that cursed Kaltar gave them no rest. He knew that an attack would be attempted. The Vampires of Mosk had a long tradition of progression through death. One took an office by killing the holder. One kept office by being strong enough to survive such attacks. Guards were employed to counter the advantage of hidden attacks, and more guards to protect against those guards. It had been a delicate balance of assassination and counter-assassination. But Darrik had gone too far. Even with the anything goes philosophy of the vampires, he crossed a line which could not be forgiven.

The attack had come in force. It had never been done before, although even that could have been forgiven, if not commended. But Darrik had brought outsiders into the very heart of the Dark Complex. No vampire who did not belong to the Cult had been in the Complex since it was built. The raid by the mercenary vampires had killed at least a quarter of the Vampires of Mosk before they were defeated. Elson knew that it would have been much worse, bad enough that Darrik might have succeeded, if a stranger had not warned him. Elson spoke softly without turning towards his lieutenant.

"Find Darrik and bring him to me. In any condition you want, but alive. Kill any vampire or mortal found with him. Whether they belong to us or not."

His lieutenant left quickly. Elson was in a mood which many knew meant that death could come quickly for those who even showed a hint of disobedience. As the slaves started to clean up, Elson entered his office. The stranger was there. He could smell the man's rituals. The man was an annis. A vampire sacrificed others for power, an annis sacrifices themselves. They were usually weak and cowards. This one was neither. His name was DeathGate, which showed that he followed the old ways. Traditionally an annis would choose a name they considered terrifying. Modern ones usually rejected this custom. He also reeked of sorcery and of the Forbidden Blood Rituals. This stranger worked hard to give the appearance of being just an Annis but he was much more. Elson's voice was cold.

"I still do not trust your motives but your advice was correct. For that I owe you a blood debt."

The stranger looked through his cloak as if for a lost item. His smile showed teeth sharper than any vampire's. His voice was full of humor, and carried a hint of dark power.

"A blood debt? Interesting, it tells much that you practice it. Very well, there is something you can do for payment. Do you have a current map?"

Elson sent a slave to get one. As they waited for it DeathGate told the head Vampire of Mosk what he needed to do to repay the debt.

Tapps walked through the forest admiring the serenity that only beings with a righteous heart or great power could do. Tapps had both. During his travels he had learned many secrets and mastered many skills which were useful in life, but he had also done many things that he regretted. Because he had mastered the skill of magic it flowed through him and surrounded him constantly. He did not know when he started his studies at the Keep of Secrets that it would have the benefit of increasing his lifespan as well.

He had found peace with himself after the War Forward. More importantly he had placed his faith in VivusDeus. He never considered himself a religious man, but he prayed frequently and felt LingueArdeo move him. He now enjoyed spending time alone. It gave him the opportunity to pray whenever the mood took him. He was in deep prayer or he would have noticed Angga coming up on him before she spoke.

"KanaShor?"

Tapps, startled out of his thoughts, took a moment to find his voice.

"Yes, that is me, but I rarely go by that name in the Southern Nations. I am called…"

Angga cut Tapps off.

"Defend yourself for I mean to bring you to justice."

"What?"

Tapps was taken back as much by her appearance as from her words and few things shocked him anymore. With her large bat-like wings and her snow-white skin she looked like one of the Unholy Council from the Giant Kingdoms, the daemons of the Cult of Blood. He did not react quickly enough. Angga's crackling bolt of black energy hit him squarely in the chest and threw him back several yards into a tree. Tapps was momentarily stunned but recovered quickly. He had barely regained his footing before he leapt.

With a sweep of her wings, Angga flew straight up in the air. She let loose with a bolt that clipped Tapps' right arm. Tapps did not even seem to notice the energy ripping his flesh. He landed in the spot where Angga had been. He quickly turned and with an outstretched hand shot a black bolt of his own. It hit Angga in the abdomen.

Angga smiled to herself, she did not even feel it. When she readied another shot the pain started. Magical fire grew out of the spot where she was hit and engulfed her. What ever it was, it was feeding off her own magic. All but the pain left her mind. She started to fall to earth, plowing through the treetops. Just seconds before hitting the ground she managed to push the fire off and spread her wings. She hit the ground hard. Lifting herself up a few moments later she checked herself to make sure nothing was broken.

Except for the smoke still coming from her charred clothing she was unharmed.

Not in the mood to play any more games, she pulled her Salk. She had come to realize how precious the gift from NetThin was. It was Ogre Steel and carved with red runes. It was sharp, incredibly so, but its most amazing feature it would magnify her Kirtel. She could ingulf it with the same deep dark blue flame which she could shoot from her hands and even use it to create a protective field around her body. She scanned the area for Tapps but could find no sign of him. She started to back track him from the last place she had seen him.

To her surprise, when she arrived where she had run across Tapps, he was there. Hunched over the spilled contents of his bag, he was carefully putting them back in his rucksack. Angga decided it would be more prudent to hit him with an overcharged bolt rather than the one of her normal ones.

"KanaShor, you will not escape me that easily"

Tapps looked up at Angga and disappointment washed over his face. He brought his hand to his head and rubbed his temples to ward off his growing headache.

"I do not know what injustice I have caused you but let me assure you I am truly sorry. If there is anything, I can do so you can forgive me and get on with your life, let me know."

"I cannot be bought off and it is not me you have offended."

With that she fired the bolt of energy she had been building up. Tapps was expecting it, so he easily dodged to one side and leap towards her. He had not figured on Angga being able to recover her magic so quickly and was caught off guard by her throwing another. He was hit in the chest with the bolt just as he dug his claw into her side. Angga screamed in pain and slumped to the ground.

Tapps looked at her with remorse and almost said he was sorry. He had not meant to kill the lady. He dropped to her side to save her life. He noticed too late that she was smiling. He was too slow when her hand came up and black crackling fire surrounded his head and rippled through his body. Tapps slumped to the ground in a smoldering heap of fur.

An acolyte entered White Bear's office and spoke without waiting to be acknowledged.

"Sir, there is a communication."

White Bear acknowledged the message with a nod and a hand gesture. He was in the middle of a thought and did not want to ruin it. Admiral Turner would be expecting a response soon. Realizing the acolyte had not left, White Bear turned his head and examined the youth. From his accent and appearance, he would be a convert from the Asionic Empire. White Bear did not have to try hard to recall what he needed to know about the man. His name was Chang Tzu. The name alone told much of his history. He was the product of over two centuries of the Asionic Empire's selective breeding program. When eighteen he had been assigned to the Emperor's Guard unit responsible for purging any teaching that did not hold the Emperor as God. He started his carrier as an agent to infiltrate the Order of Truth. He did his job too well.

Tzu learned everything that the Order had to teach and, in the end, decided to serve Elohim. Many still thought he was a spy but White Bear knew different. The man was honest about his faith and that was why White Bear ordered him to come to the island. Chang's final test would not come for some time, a time when he would have to choose how to best to serve his Emperor. The price on Chang's head was now a hundred thousand tughriks, a price the holy man knew had been placed there so Chang could infiltrate deeper into that Order. White Bear spoke softly as he stood.

"There is more, mister Tzu?"

Chang spoke with all the respect that is due a master.

"Yes sir, they said it was important that you come. I overheard something about Shawlls using video communication."

The news set White Bear in motion. He threw on his cloak and ran to the communication room. Excited workers parted for him as he entered the room. One of them spoke, her voice full of energy.

"Sir, the being is Shawll of an old form, but the transmission is not coming from the Colonies but from a ship in orbit."

White Bear acknowledged the information, but already knew this. Shawlls were the reptilian like beings, found on earth only in the Colonies. With that land's ban on technology, they would not be using such transmissions. The person on the screen was not a Shawll. Coming to the computer console he recognized the face on the screen. He pushed the button to transmit and spoke.

"Mas'l Curshel, what is wrong?"

The reptilian face showed no discernable expression, at least none in which any in the room could discern, but even with its thick accent the worry was apparent in her voice.

"You are right to say something is wrong. The Kallete have destroyed Rirs. They launched attack. We are a police force and will not last long against them. Time is short. The Kallete have followed us here. Let me give you message."

The face of the reptilian person was replaced by a figure that appeared human. White Bear had always marked that if it was not for the Rirsts averaging eight feet in height they could easily pass for human. This particular Rirst White Bear knew personally. He was Kul and had been the leader of the Trinity Alliance for over sixteen centuries. The man had taught White Bear many things. Even with the calm look on Kul's face, White Bear could see the stress in the Rirst's eyes. The man in the recording spoke with the calmness which was a common trait of his race.

"My old friend, the time that we have discussed has come. The remnants of the Trinity Alliance have shattered and the Grietun Accord has been broken. I have wept for the coming of this time but even I did not foresee the destruction which the Kallete would bring. Only a handful of the Rirsts have survived and we are being hunted with the purpose of extinction. Do not cry for us, you have your own work to do. Remember in service of the Source, death is a prize.

"My wishes on those we sent to you have not changed. They must be left to find their own paths. Do not interfere even if the path they choose leads to destruction. Do not go to them but wait until they come to you. They must come to the Source willingly or not at all. This is the way of our people.

"The cost to send this message was too high for me not to include that it has been my great honor to call you my pupil all these years and to see you to come as far as you have. Know that I have always held the highest…"

The screen went to static. The technicians frantically tried to fix the problem. White Bear knew that they would not be able to. It was beyond their skills. He stood up and walked outside with Chang following behind him. The aid spoke eagerly.

"How is it that the person on the video was speaking Asionic?"

White Bear smiled at Tzu but took some time to answer.

"He was not. He spoke his own language but when Kul speaks, we all hear him in our native language. Most of the Rirsts who choose to follow Elohim are gifted such." White Bear pointed to the sky. There were streaks of lights and balls of fire streaming through the air. He pointed out one of the fire balls. "That was the ship that carried the message. The galaxy is aflame in conflict but it is nothing compared to what this planet will someday unleash upon it."

Tzu examined the sky. The patterns of the lights were those which would be present if a great number of ships were fighting each other.

"Aliens?"

White Bear shook his head.

"Some, but the others shared our faith and that made them our brothers. It all depends on how you define your family. If one must be of the same culture and ethnicity of you to be your sibling, then you will never know the unity our faith allows. Ponder this in your meditations today, but now go and summon the elders for a first light meeting. We have much to do. We have only a couple of decades to prepare humanity to reach out into the stars."

As Chang left White Bear returned his attention to the sky. All those deaths just to reinforce the order not to interfere. Kul knew how much he wanted to go and collect the children he had placed in the Colonies all those years ago. It tempted White Bear every time he thought of it.

IV

Near Tymalt Morgan adjusted his ponytail as he entered the city of McGovern. He did not want to return to the city. It held nothing but painful memories for him. High Tymalt Boreta told him that he needed to face his past, without mastering the pain he would never reach the level of Tymalt. Of course, Boreta was correct. It was a weakness in him which was often an area of attack. A look, a certain tone-word combination would cause him to react. As it was written in the Tymalt – when an opponent can cause you to act without thinking, you have already been defeated.

Like everyone in the Order of Tymalt, he was naturally gifted in True Sight. It was more than truth-saying or empathy. The higher talent was a way of seeing the world how it really was. The Order defined it as not being fooled by the illusion by which the common people live their lives. The Tymalt taught that everyone was born with the lower and higher talents. Almost at birth the talents warred with the culture-reality, the structure of society. The great insight that children have is eventually replaced by what society says they should feel and see. A few never develop the blindness that prevents them from seeing what is real. This was always a byproduct of terrible pain, or maybe the cause of the pain. That was something which was much debated within the Order. There were few in the Tymalt who had not been forged into greatness by some abuse or tragedy. It was the pain, or more truthfully, trying to overcome that pain is what drives them, what makes them Tymalt.

There was a time when the Tymalt raised children from birth. Through strict training and controlled pain, the Order had created generation after generation of High Tymalts. It even continued for nearly five hundred years after the defeat of Apolloes and the rest of the Unholy Council. The downfall had come from internal strife and bureaucratic waste. Too many of the leaders were more concerned with maintaining their control over the Order than advancing knowledge. Most of their records would have been destroyed, but High Tymalt Boreta had read the signs correctly when the Tecmen first appeared. He had ordered all archives be sent to the Temple of the High Tymalt. It was found in Nuguluseam, and overlooked the graveyards which made the city famous. By the time the Asionic Empire attacked in full, and destroyed most of the order's northern training halls, their records had been safe.

Morgan had just reached the level of Near Tymalt when Boreta had ordered him to clean up the Order's library. He was not pleased with the assignment. With the great number of journals, notes and reports which were flooding in from the satellite house it was going to test his control. He almost refused it and rebelled when he walked into the archives and saw the terrible shape of the library. The contents of the other libraries had just started arriving, but the main library was in disarray. There had not been a librarian in over three hundred years and it had been even longer since anyone cared about what was found in the catacombs.

Before he could even start, he had to clean out the massive labyrinth of their subterranean library. Many of the books had turned to dust, or were decayed to the point of uselessness. Luckily most of the dehumidifiers were still working, but he still spent the first month hauling out the rotting paper. At the end of the month, he made a discovery that excited him. One of the books had fallen out of the barrel he was using and shattered on the ground. When Morgan picked it up, he noticed, if he looked close enough, he could make out some of what the author wrote. It was in the ancient language of Templen but he still could make out most of it. He spent the rest of that day translating the tome. It held wisdom far beyond what the Order now knew.

He shared his finding with Boreta and the old man just smiled. Morgan requested an assistant and received three. They were Failed Tymalts, for one reason or another they found it too hard to progress beyond where they were. They could not let go of the pain which had forged them. Usually, such people were expelled from the Order but High Tymalt Boreta had refused to send them away. It was just one of the controversies that constantly surrounded the leader of the Order. In his two decades in the position Boreta had proved that he was truly a High Tymalt and not one which was simply granted the title for knowing what to say. He used even his opponents to advance his own plans. As it was written in the Tymalt – only those without control destroy their enemies, use them instead to destroy your own weaknesses. High Tymalt Boreta understood their philosophy better than anyone else in the Order.

It had taken Morgan and his three assistants almost five years to finish gently extracting the fragile tomes and transposing them to the new books which would eventually be magically preserved. When they had finished the preserving of the ancient records Boreta made the three assistants the Order's official librarians. In the fifteen or so years since then the High Tymalt had Morgan doing research for him while the librarians catalogued and organized the works. By the time Boreta had sent Morgan to this city the library had lived up to its name and there were two dozen Failed Tymalts taking care of it.

Morgan had always had a deep respect for his master but the more he researched the more he became awed with Boreta's genius. The High Tymalt's plans became clearer with each passing day. One of the first things that Morgan looked up was the traditional uses of the Failed. Besides just being the librarians in the ancient days they also did the tasks that the apprentices now did. More than just being servants many of them were great scholars and craftsmen. By the time that the Unholy Council had been banished the more skilled Failed had taken over the administration so that the Tymalts could concentrate on teaching and their own control. After researching several other topics for the High Tymalt, Morgan knew that Boreta saw what none of the other High Tymalts did. That the Failed were the backbone of the power the Order used to have. The fall of the Order had been caused by the pride of the Tymalts and High Tymalts. They could not see what use the Tymalts could have of those which never learned to control themselves.

It was the writings of Jomas, the founder of their Order, which had given Boreta the ability to set the new culture at the last meeting of the High Tymalts. Most of Jomas' writings had succumbed to the passing of time but what words were left had reached across time to cut into not only the High Tymalts but Morgan as well. So effected was he by them that he committed them to memory. He spoke them softly to himself, a practice used to reinforce memorization.

"Never mistake control for enlightenment. Do not make the mistake of relating power with forging the heart. The difference between a Tymalt and a common is not control but seeing the world how it truly is. In the moment that you think, because you control those that do not see Tym, you are better than them, is the moment you prove you are not Tymalt but a commoner. A lesson you must learn is that even those of us who see all of the Invisible Pattern controls very little of it. It is the great masses of the common who forge Tym, we can only flavor it. If you give into the pride of enlightenment you become trapped in that pride. Pride is the deadliest poison to the Tymalt. The moment you believe that you are better than someone you will stop seeing them for who they are. A person who has something to teach you, and a person who has energy in Tym."

The last line was a paraphrase of the Tymalt. Morgan was only now starting to realize how deeply he had been affected by Jomas' writing. It was as if he had seen what would happen to the Order and had written those words for this time. It was this pride, this feeling that the Failed had no use. The belief that the Tymalt was more than just a leader of humanity and had no need of anyone but themselves. This pride had caused the fall of the Order even though many tried to blame it on their rivals.

He wished they could blind himself to the truth in this area. It saddened him to think that the Tymalts, who take an oath to lift humanity out of the mud it lived in could wallow in it themselves. Most still said that it was the VoX Templers that had broken them. Many accepted this without question, as the Templers were the only group in the Colonies who matched them in the manipulation of Tym, the threads of fate. It was apparent from the records that they had a shared history, and there was an indication that they were once the same group. This could very well be true because only real difference between the two orders was their faith. The VoX Templers were Xristzen where the Tymalt were Anaelist. Again, something both of them believed without question. Morgan stopped as part of verse twelve of the Tymalt rushed through his mind and spirit.

Anything that we accept without question is not faith but foolishness.
Questions strengthen truth into faith.
Questions destroy the weakness of falsehood.
Some Questions are foolish to ask,
Made even more foolish by not being asked.

Morgan realized that no one ever questioned the part of their belief when it came to the Divine. They question constantly the way the Tym works, but not once was he encouraged to question the Order's teaching that Elohim and Apployan was just two sides of the Divine. That they were opposed but equal, an equality so complete that it insured that neither would succeed in completing their goal. Did the VoX Templers question their faith in the Divine? He had believed that they did not, but had never asked one if it was true. The High Tymalts always talked of them in a condescending way, all except Boreta. Morgan would have to ask his master about this when he returned to the temple.

Morgan was broken out of his thoughts by someone watching him. No, he could feel three of them. Instantly he realized that it was not him that they were watching but the youth who was picking his pocket. With a quickness that comes decades of honing one's reflexes Morgan reached out and grabbed the youth's hand. The young man tried to run but Morgan's grip was complete. The youth tried to break free as Near Tymalt Morgan spoke in a soothing tone.

"Calm yourself and look at me."

Morgan let go of the youth's wrist when their eyes met. At first Morgan thought that he was only reflecting himself in the youth but the eyes did not lie. The young man, no more than twelve or thirteen, saw Tym clearly. Most likely better than Morgan could himself. He had already relaxed even though Morgan had given no indication that he was not going to harm him. The youth had known it even before Morgan had made the decision himself. There were High Tymalts who could not read him that well. Morgan spoke in order to probe the youth.

"My name is Morgan. How is it that you know that I am not going to turn you over the guards?"

The youth shrunk back in himself. Morgan reassured him with a smile. The young man also had the pain that goes with seeing what others did not. The youth spoke in an almost a happy tone.

"My name is James. I was watching you for a while. You hate this place and especially the guards. That is why I chose you as a slip."

All accept his name was a lie. James was a good liar, his abilities would normally have focused the person on what he wanted them to see, and probably could talk himself out of just about anything, but a Tymalt, even a Near Tymalt, was not so easily fooled. Morgan gave some thought on what to do next. It was clear that it was Tym that brought them together. Tym was more than just fate or accidents. Everything moved along the Invisible Path and every action affected how that path took shape. As it was written in the Tymalt – the choices we make, gives us the choices we have.

James looked on with surprise when Morgan unbuckled his money purse and poured out three gold coins. He was even more shocked when Morgan handed the purse to him. Morgan pulled it back just as James' hand reached for it. Morgan had something to say first.

"I am not giving this to you. Everything has its price. You will have to do something to earn it."

James examined Morgan. The Near Tymalt could feel the youth probing him. Morgan almost laughed when he realized what had James worried. The youth was worried that Morgan could be a pervert. Morgan opened up and let James' probe have its way. He knew that the youth would not find anything that would bother him. Like all the Tymalt he was practically chaste. One cannot seek to fulfill desires and still keep control. It was one of their highest teachings. Morgan smiled when James spoke.

"What do you want to teach me?"

The question took Morgan by surprise. Whiltha, the ability to determine the motives of others was common, most people often used it without thought, and just as often did not pay attention to what it was telling them. Highly tuned at such a young age showed a forging by an incredible amount of danger. What had James gone through to give him such a high ability to be so accurate? Morgan spoke honestly.

"I belong to the Order of Tymalt, and we teach people how to control their own fate."

James frowned. He spoke as he pointed down the street.

"You are like the priests there?"

Morgan looked to where James was pointing. It was a church with three priests standing in front of it. The three who had brought Morgan out of his thoughts in the first place. The church was most likely a satellite Temple of the VoX Templers. Neither the building nor the priest's clothing gave any indication, but it was apparent by the calmness radiating from the priests. Morgan raised his right palm and placed his left on his abdomen as he bowed his head. The priest who stood in the center returned it with an ease that came from frequent use of the greeting which both Orders shared. Morgan spoke when he turned back to James. The youth had been watching him intently.

"Our teachings are very similar. The difference is in who we serve. The priests use their abilities to serve Elohim, we serve Humanity. The Order of Tymalt is dedicated to lifting all of humankind to a place where they can have control of their own lives. You must make a choice now. You can choose them, choose to become a Tymalt or you can simply walk away and I will pester you no more."

James looked over at the priests. They had been kind to him, but Morgan was offering him the ability not to be pushed around anymore. He knew that walking away was not an option. He could learn on his own but he knew he would be trapped. That was what these two were offering. To see the whole world and not just the little one he found himself in. He closed his eyes and let his mind and spirit tell him what he should do. He could see the effects of either choice. Choose the priest's and go on glorious adventures with his best friend and to be killed in a land he did not know by creatures he did not recognize. Or to choose Morgan's way and break with his best friend but come to rule an empire where they will name him a god. There was a third way, but he could not see where it led. His sight was blocked by thick fog. All he could see through it was a shining light on the other side. He knew the third choice was the one he should take but it was still far in the future. It was a path that he would have to decide, no matter what he chose today. What Morgan was offering excited him far more than what the priests had. James opened his eyes and spoke to the smiling Near Tymalt.

"I will let you teach me."

Morgan laughed when he handed the bag of coins to James. It was apparent that the youth had forgotten about them. Morgan then pulled out a small and well-worn copy of the Tymalt and handed it to James. He spoke in a friendly tone of ordering.

"I cannot take you with me now, the coin is for you to live on until I return. It will be several years before you may come with me to start your formal teachings. This will test your commitment and your patience. You have two assignments to prepare you for entry into the Order of the Tymalt. First you must meditate on the meaning of each of the sixty four verses of the Tymalt. Do not worry if you do not understand them at first, just read them and think about them. If you come to one you understand then strive to understand how it relates to your life."

Morgan paused and glanced over at the VoX Templers. The man was smiling. Was it that he was actually approving of James becoming a Tymalt? There was much he needed to learn about the Order of the Vassals of Xrist. James' voice made him realize he had been distracted. Do not control your wandering thoughts, only control when you let your thoughts wander. Morgan pieced together what James had said from memory.

"What is the second thing?"

Morgan returned the smile to his face before answering.

"Stay alive. As long as you study your Tymalt, no matter what you do or where you go I will find you and bring you into the Tymalt. Until then I cannot teach you anything so we will part company now."

James turned and left without a second thought. Morgan watched him go. As soon as he became a full Tymalt he would return for the youth. James was not going to be an easy pupil, but the kind the Order needed. He turned to go talk to the priests but the men had already left. Morgan resumed his walk and stayed in the city of McGovern for three more days before returning to the Temple of the High Tymalt in Nuguluseam.

James walked straight to his alley. He called it his alley because no one else wanted it. One of the sewage lines were open in it and gave the whole area a stench. He could easily put up with the smell to have a place to call his own. The smell was enough to even keep people from using it as a shortcut. At the orphanage they had no personal possessions. Even their clothing was handed down from the older kids and would be mended and handed down when he outgrew them. So when he found that no one of the Night Culture had claimed the alley he decided it was the place for him. Now he not only had an alley, but a bag full of gold coin and a book. The book was worn but it was his. The orphanage and the church which his best friend spent most of his time were both in low town. The most he ever hoped from his cutting of purses were copper coins. He did manage to get a quarter or half coin from time to time, and had even gotten a silver once but had never even seen a gold before. He knew that they were very valuable. James also knew that people would think that he had stolen them. He would have to find a place to hide them. First, he wanted to know how many there was.

Twelve gold, thirty-two silver and five copper. He pocketed the copper and one of the half silvers and decided where to hide the rest. Climbing up the side of the building he placed the sack into an old bird's nest. It was his safest hiding place because of the numerous hornet's nests on the eve. The hornets that infested the area were nasty creature which attacked anything that came near their nest. They would even latch onto and mercilessly sting rocks thrown by them. A pass time which he had long since grew board with. For some reason they never attacked either him or Kaymid.

After dropping to the ground, he made sure that the bag could not be seen from the alley. Feeling that his treasure was secure he sat on a discarded bucket and started reading the Tymalt. He did not know how long he sat there until a voice brought him out of his reading.

"What do you have there?"

James looked up. It was Kaymid. The only one at the orphanage who saw the invisible threads as he did. Kaymid spent all his free time at the church. James did not like the priests. They were nice but in James' experience when someone was nice to you, they wanted something. As nice as the priests were and how much they gave away, whatever they wanted had to be big. It angered James at times that he could not figure out what it was. His best friend enjoyed spending his time there.

Kaymid looked around the alley. He cringed his nose and then ignored the smell. He did not know why James would spend his time in this alley when he could be sitting in a plush chair in the church's library. James and Kaymid did not get along very well most of the time. James was far too reckless, too willing to risk getting in trouble for Kaymid to enjoy their escapades. He was sure that his friend most likely found him boring. Still, Kaymid had to admit that there was a bond between them which neither one of them could understand. When they were younger, they used to think that they must be brothers. Even though they could not understand each other's behavior they often knew what the other was thinking. They would defend each other the best they could. Each would sneak food to the other if one of them did something wrong and had to miss a meal as punishment. Kaymid was the one usually sharing his meal.

It was not that Kaymid did not break the rules. Since they were young together, he would always be the one weighing the risk. If he thought the chance of getting caught was too high, or the punishment too much, then he would not do it. James would go ahead without fear and this often landed him into trouble. Kaymid had to admit that there were times when he envied his friend's freedom in this. It was apparent to Kaymid that James was trying to ignore him so he rephrased his question.

"Is that the Tymalt?"

James snapped his head up. His surprise quickly left him. Morgan did say that they taught the same thing. The priests made Kaymid read all the time so it would make sense that he would have read this book as well. He wanted to be alone but was still happy when Kaymid sat on the ground next to him. That was why they were friends. They acted out of each other's needs. Even when one of them did not know what they needed the other one would provide it. James was happy alone and was sometimes irritated with Kaymid for sticking around, but he always was disappointed when he left. Kaymid spoke with some interest.

"The priest told me that verse twelve is the one that I need to learn the most."

James turned to the verse Kaymid mentioned. He read it but it did not make much sense. Acting from his friend's lack of understanding, Kaymid spoke again.

"It means that sometimes doing the right thing means you have to do it in the wrong way. That sometimes you have to break the rules. Don't look at me that way. I do not understand it any better than you. They have a simplified version in the library. If you want to understand that book you will need the priests and their library. Come, we can go now. The library will still be open for several hours."

James looked back at the book in his hand. He had to admit that he did need help. The verses of the book were full of phrases that did not make sense. It said things which were contradictory. In order to fulfill one's desire for control one must first rid themselves of the desire for control. What was that supposed to mean. How could you have something by giving it up? James stood up and followed Kaymid into the library. As the months went by their friendship returned to what it had been like when they were very young. They spent all their time together studying the Tymalt and talking about what it meant.

V

Tapps woke to the smell of a campfire. He tried to stand but failed. The thick leather straps that bound him were carefully placed so his claws could not reach them. His body ached all over and his head throbbed in beat with his heart. He almost let out a moan when he turned his head to the side to look at the winged woman.

"How much are you getting paid, bounty hunter?"

Not stirring from her spot in front of the fire Angga's voice was cold.

"More than its worth, cat."

Patience showed through Tapps' voice when he spoke.

"That was not an answer to my question and I am surprised to hear a racial slur from someone of your education."

Angga faltered. Her voice remained without emotion but there was a touch of fire at its edges.

"Well, KanaShor, if you must know. You are worth one hundred coins. Do not think that you can buy me off, I do not betray a trust put in me for any price. I will not betray anyone for a cat that steals from their master. What do you mean one with my education?"

Tapps ignored her question.

"A hundred silver, is that all? I figured that he would put real gold on my head." Tapps paused in shock as if a fist had hit him in his face. "Steal from their master? What lies have Elson filled your head with? I have not been a rogue for almost three decades."

Angga still did not stir from the spot where she was sitting in front of the fire.

"It was not Elson that sent me. I do not know such a person. I was hired by a man named Silver. He told me of your dishonorable deed."

"Silver? You believed a man that acts more like a thief than a rogue? I assure you that I stole nothing from Silver and am planning to take nothing from him. As for dishonorable, I know nothing of such things, it is not the way of a Vagofron."

Angga struggled hard not leap up at the words. She turned her head slowly and stared at Tapps for a while. She had heard of the clansmen. It was part of her education. Vagofrons, in the old tongue as in the language of her people, translated into the Wandering Protectors. She knew little of them except the legends and half-truths she gleaned from her story books. Their purpose seemed to be to protect the world against beings who become too powerful and threatened the balance of life. They were broken into four clans, holding honor and family above all else. She had never met one of the Clans before, or at least never met anyone knowing they were part of the Vagofrons. All she knew about them came from her reading. There was no conviction in her voice.

"I do not believe you."

Tapps shrugged.

"My papers are in my rucksack, and my badge of a Warrior Magus is in the inside pocket."

Angga rummaged through his pack and found the papers and badge was he said they were. She dropped the bag when she saw the medallion. The gold circle with a silver lightning bolt.

The papers were most likely forgeries. She could not believe that he had honors in every one of the Southern Nation and even the title of Count in Kanato. That nation was too xenophobic. Nonhumans could not even hold the lower offices let alone one of nobility. She had to get an endorsement from the International Order of Detectives just to carry a weapon within the nation's borders. Luckily her refusal to join them had not soured her standing with the organization.

Buy the look of his clothes, the Kaltar had some wealth but he did not look like a dandy. There was confidence in his eyes but not the arrogance which came with noble birth. The clothing, like the papers, had to be part of some game the Kaltar is playing. This man was a con-artist and there could be little doubt that the papers were forgeries.

The medallion was a different matter. What she knew about it was limited but it was enough. It was the sign of a Warrior-Magus of the Society of Sword and Spell. No one would ever dare to use the medallion without being a member. She weaved her Kirtel to examine it. Sure enough, there were over a dozen spells on it, several of which were active. All of them were beyond her ability to tell their purpose. The small circle with a lightning bolt through it was the most magical item she had ever seen. She hoped she kept the awe out of her voice.

"They could be fakes."

"I was heading in another direction but can easily divert my path to the winter home of the clans. If you need further proof then I could take you there and allow you to speak to the elders."

She examined Tapps for a long moment. He was much larger than the other Kaltars she had met. She had never traveled farther north than Eldon. There was always enough work in the human lands. It was possible that he was part ogre. She had heard that such things were happening. She could not tell his age. His fur hid the ways she knew of telling age but from the tint of gray and the way he carried himself she put his age in the fourth decade.

The legends said that none but one of the clans could find the winter homes. If Tapps could, it would prove that he was who he said he was. She had been fooled before. It was common for the poor not to get a fair trial and she had been convinced too often that the criminal she hunted was innocent. She was not sure if she could risk his escape if he was lying. She knew she could not risk the alternative if he was not. Finally she nodded.

"I will travel with you to find out if what you speak is true."

They moved out with Tapps securely tied around the arms and wrists. Travel was slow.

Kift stood at the gates of the Imperial City of Kanato. He wondered, for at least the twentieth time, why he had talked himself into coming here. He had gone to many small towns to try to sell the information about the brazier but all had told him to seek out Zilly's Antiques in the Imperial City. He had gone to one of the larger towns first in hopes of not having to come to the city. The innkeeper in that town had also turned him towards the city.

"If you looken to sell something, then Zilly's your gal. If she can't find a buyer fo't, it ain't goin to get selled."

The innkeeper had no other useful information. Kift's dislike of cities bordered on the feeling of hatred. To him there was nothing worse than a city, with its foul smells and corrupted people. He only felt comfortable in the forest with its clean air and wild animals. But he had something to do in the city so he reluctantly entered hoping that he would soon be heading home.

He knew this city well. After all, he had been raised in it. Even so, it held no feelings of home for him. Most of his time at the Institute in this city was horrid to him. He had found a sort of peace. The only time he left the dorm was to go to his classes or to the Institute's gardens. Back when what is then the Royal Sector had been all there was to the city the gardens had been the King's Woods. They were large, nearly three hundred acres and one could spend a whole day there without seeing anyone else. Kift laughed. There was another time he left the dorm. Whenever Matt had that look in his eyes that he was going to get in trouble and needed someone to stabilize him on a night out.

It seemed like a much larger than the city Kift remembered and it took him nearly the rest of the daylight hours to find the place. He entered the quaint little shop and went straight to the counter. A middle-aged woman was in a back room behind the counter. She had dark skin with long black hair and the deepest and darkest eyes that Kift had ever seen. She had never lost her attractive looks from her younger years and had a schoolgirl bounce when she walked to the counter. She examined Kift so quickly that it would have been missed by one not trained in such things, which meant Kift did not notice it. She smiled sweetly when she spoke.

"My name is Zilly. What do you have to sell?"

Kift spirits rouse a bit at the greeting and without saying a word pulled out his drawing book and notes on the brazier. Zilly put on a small pair of spectacles. Spending nearly an hour going over Kift's drawings and notes and checking with several tomes, she finally looked up and spoke.

"You're good at taking notes even though your drawing leaves a lot to be desired." She paused for a moment and examined Kift. Her smile returned as she continued speaking. "I am convinced of the authenticity of your find. I will give you six hundred gold up front for the notes and another four hundred if you point out the location to one of my boys."

Kift could only blink for a few moments. He had not expected to get nearly as much. Kift was only figuring a hundred gold would be the most, and would have been very pleased with fifty, and would have settled for ten. He knew this is the part where he was supposed to haggle. Kift examined Zilly. She would have read him well and thus her offer was on the low end. He did not care about the money so did not try to get more. By the next morning he was heading home with two large sacks of coin and a teenage boy in tow.

On the other side of the Unclaimed Lands, high in the Barrier Mountains which separates the Colonies from the Land of Blood, the nations of the Giants, a woman sat in a dark room which was at the heart of the Enforcer's headquarters. She had been there three days without food or water and was planning on spending another four in prayer and meditation. It had been Black Wolf's custom since accepting her father's faith to spend both the Holy Weeks doing such. A voice that was not the Divine broke through her thoughts.

"*Master?*"

Black Wolf opened her eyes. As first she thought it was an unclean, for her pupils knew not to interrupt her prayers. She let her senses expand and realized it was Hohn Petre, her second in command. That would mean that it was something that he could not handle, which in turn meant that it was serious. Her father's teachings prevented her from worrying. Find out the facts before you apply your imagination on what could be.

"*Yes, what is it?*"

There was some slight hesitation from Hohn. There was only one person that could make him nervous.

"*The Dragoon is here to see you.*"

She smiled.

"*Show Marius in.*"

She bent over and lit a candle. The light would put Marius at ease. With all his power he was still very much oriented on the physical. She understood. He took after his father. She nodded when he entered.

"*You still fond of pastries?*" Waiting for only a moment she continued verbally. "I often forget that you never learned to listen with your spirit. What brings you to see me? Have you decided that you will try to court me again?"

The Dragoon laughed before he spoke.

"It is an understatement to say that it has been a very long time since I was that small boy who followed you around my father's estate. No, I just wanted to let you know that I disbanded the Great Ones."

She raised an eyebrow before speaking.

"If they had been in my care, I would have taken a group of the Enforcers a century ago and taught them a few truths about leadership. But then, you always did have a kinder heart than me. I am a bit disappointed with you. You have never been the type to play games. Why do you stall in telling the real reason you came?"

Marius Shadow actually looked a bit nervous.

"Yes. Well, I was wondering if you have any idea of what is going on."

Black Wolf laughed coldly. This is the reason he had been so nervous. He never understood her relationship with the holy man.

"Why Marius, have you not gone to see White Bear? Were you not my father's pupil?"

"He would not tell me anything but to be patient. He forgets that such a thing is not easy for me."

Black Wolf wore a smile but her tone was philosophical.

"Yes, he has told me many times, and I have long since found it to be true, that one of the hardest things to remember is that not everyone thinks like our self." She paused for a moment and her voice had a serious tone to it. "However, he has not forgotten this. No, he never seems to forget to apply his own teachings to himself, which is what I have always found the most irritating thing about him. If my father said to be patient it is well within your abilities. I have come to respect, yes even admire, his calling, and more importantly, his ability to maintain his purity under the pressure."

Black Wolf stopped and poured a glass of water for the Dragoon. She continued speaking in a casual tone once he had sipped from the cup.

"As for what is going on in the Colonies, all I can say is there is much activity with the Unclean. My Enforcers have been busy. The number of Annis have doubled and not just the hags and twisted, but the ones with real power. The vampire cults are multiplying and becoming more aggressive. All in all, a time of Fire is coming quickly. More than this I do not know."

The Dragoon's nervousness was gone.

"Not exactly what I meant. Will the Gates be opened?"

Black Wolf's face showed a bit of compassion which she was not commonly known from her.

"No, it will be some time before you have to face your brother. The axe is still secure and the two have not made their choices yet. Besides father said that he will not be alive to see it. He is still far from death." her voice became gentle. "Do not worry about the future. You know that all of us are behind you. It was he who betrayed your father."

"I know, I know. That does not make it any easier."

"Doing the Will of Elohim rarely is. Often what is best wars against what we desire. There are things that even we cannot change. We must accept them and let them happen as they must."

The woman which was once infamously called the Dark Warrior blew out the candle. She went back to her prayers after summoning an Enforcer to show Marius out. Not another word was spoken.

Miguel looked up at his three cousins. They were the Four Horsemen of TelTet, or at least that was what they were calling themselves. They were on an important quest, or that was how they thought of it. The truth was that they were four young men, like so many others who were simply seeking fame and fortune. It had been Dyrrel's idea and if his constant boastings could be taken as proof, he was in charge of the adventuring group. They had decided, which meant Dyrrel had decided, to find the Swords of Lux Orbis. According to the legend they were four swords, which when welded by a group such as theirs were unmatched in power. They were supposed to have been forged during the war against the giants, and were especially designed to be used against those using Dark Powers.

That was what they were doing disguised as manual laborers. They had found employment in the remodeling of the Draco Castle. They had been there a month and learned a lot. Miguel wiped the sweat of his forehead. The castle was an impressive sight. It was at the very heart of the city Nuguluseam, a city spoken of often in his history classes. It was sometimes called Graveyard City due to almost a quarter of it held the family graveyards of nobles and the rich. It had been such since the Time of the Dragons, when Amic Grutt laid his wife to rest at the southern base of the Holy Mountain.

Nuguluseam had been attacked hundreds of times over the centuries but had never been taken. No force had ever been able to stand against the Draco Army backed by a militia which fought hard to protect their city. It was the last of the independent cities, even though Mosk claimed to represent it in the Council of Southern Kings. Dyrrel said the history of the place did not matter for an evil man who went by the name of Death's Fang now ruled it. That was what had been bothering Miguel. The rumors and the real information did not add up. Many said that Death's Fang was a vampire but the locals just laughed at this. The evilest thing that could be said about the man was that he let the people of the city choose a council which in turn decided policies of the city. Miguel knew that inherent flaws in such a system would lead to wide spread apathy but had to admit that Nuguluseam did not show such behavior. The only reason for the city's success was the leadership of Death's Fang. Miguel voiced his doubts to the group.

"If Death's Fang is such an evil person why is he having this section of his castle converted into a hospital? And paying for it himself?"

Dyrrel snorted. They had been over this a dozen times. For being the smart one of the group Miguel was sure slow to learn. His irritation showed in his voice.

"Look, we know that he disappears frequently, leaving the people of this city without a Lord. Even when he is here, he pays little attention to what they do."

Rick spoke out

"I don't know Dar. They seem to like it that way.

"Shut up Rick. People say he is a vampire but more than that, people say he has Day Break. He has one of the swords Rick, preventing it from doing the good it was designed for. We have already been over this and it is settled. We will be ready soon."

The foreman yelled for them to get back to work. The fourth of their group, Paul, had not paid much to the conversation. He did not care enough to listen. He enjoyed the manual labor, and had already earned himself a raise. He was not sure what all the fuss was about. Life could not be better.

A few hours before sunset nearly a week after being captured by Angga, Tapps caught the scent of nearby humans. Tapps was still bound like a convict, but his legs were free. He crouched, his tensing muscles sending ripples through his fur. Scanning the shadowy forest around him, he could hear breathing. Angga noticed the change in the Kaltar and decided she had better find out what was going on. Tapps could smell the slight fear that came from every good warrior before a fight. Angga landed next to Tapps. She opened her mouth to say something but before the words could form, a bolt of Palm Lightning crackled through the air and crashed into her. Everything went dark for her and she crumpled to the ground.

His movements a blur to the normal eye, Tapps broke his bonds and leapt at the wizard hidden in the bushes. Before the wizard had time to realize that Tapps had moved he laid dead on the forest floor with his chest ripped open. It was rare for Tapps to kill anymore. The wizard would have lived but Tapps had overestimated the protective wards on the man.

Tapps stood to full height and examined the heat signatures of the bandits in the bushes. He had entered the Shortan, the blood lust. Since the days of the War Forward, he had learned to master it rather than it mastering him. Once it had forced him to kill his opponent, now the only power it had over him was to make his eyes glow red. It still heightened his senses and movement, still numbed any pain, but it no longer drove away his thoughts. It truly became oneness with the combat which the legends called it. Those who knew it, knew how dangerous it was, to the foe of the person, and to themselves. No wound, no matter how great would be felt until after it was over. Only death could stop one in the Shortan before the fight was over. Tapps spoke with calmness.

"I am Tapps Toya, your wizard is dead, and it would be wise for you to give up the fight."

If the bandits knew his name, they gave no indication. If they had any wisdom, they did not use it. They attacked. There were only eight of them so Tapps decided that he would not need his claws. All of them rushed at once and Tapps used that to his advantage. Moving again in a blur, which only a few could manage, Tapps grabbed the arm of the first man who lunged at him. Before the pain of the broken bone could register in the man's mind he was thrown into another. Another attacked, a swing, a block, a broken nose. The conflict did not last long before the would- be ambushers fled. He almost took chase but the sight of Angga tore him back from the void. With a struggle Tapps brought himself out of the Shortan.

He dropped to the ground from the pain. One of the bandits had managed to stab him through the ribs. Working some magic, he repaired his lung and muscles and sedated the pain from the rest of his wounds. He quickly went to check on his fallen captor.

Death's Fang looked over the table. He had been so busy lately that this was the first time he would have time to enjoy a meal. There were many in the Colonies which considered Death's Fang the most powerful person alive in the Colonies. He would often respond to such people that they did not understand power, that those who spend their lives searching for power have never learned that it is found in the simplest things in life. Such as the roasted chicken and carrots on his plate. He smiled and looked at the officers of the Draco Army. They all knew power as well, and its price. Each member of the Draco Army had killed a Dragon, membership into the army had been their reward, their punishment. Their duties kept them busy and they too were looking forward to the pleasure of a quite meal.

After offering a prayer to VivusDeus he started his eating. Just as he focused on the flavors of the first bite, the door to the dining hall was violently thrown open. Four men came rushing into the room with their swords drawn. The smallest of the bunch did not bother looking around the room before he spoke.

"We are the Four Horsemen of TelTet and mean to destroy your evil vileness."

Death's Fang looked down at his food. Was he being tested? He shook his head when the four men spread out in an assault formation. The officers started laughing. Death's Fang was not amused. With a sigh he decided it would be better to talk with the youths before deciding what to do.

"Evil vileness? Forgetting the silliness of that phrase, I fear that you have mistaken me for someone else. There are very few alive who can honestly claim injustice by my hand and I am sure you are not among them."

Dyrrel, considering himself the leader, was the one who spoke.

"We know that you are a vampire who holds the sword of Daybreak, preventing it from doing the good it was meant to. We demand that you had it over to us."

It had to be a test. Death's Fang joined in the laughter of his officers. Those who know him could tell that it was to control his anger. He stood for affect and his voice took on the tone of a parent correcting a wayward child.

"A sword? Do you know me? Have we shared a meal me? A bottle of wine during a late night of conversations? Are we family or clan that you can demand anything from me? You have barged into my house uninvited and threatened me. Normally I would have spent time explaining your misdeeds. However, you have found me in an uncharitable mood. With everything which is happening in the Colonies, at this moment you are not all that important. This sword, a piece of metal with just a bit of magic in it, is just as unimportant. I will set a place for you to think about what I said and what is important in life."

Death's Fang sat down and the four horsemen suddenly found themselves in a prison cell. He put the four youths out of his mind and went back to his meal. There would be time to deal with them after they had time to ponder what they did.

Angga awoke to see Tapps sitting against a tree, fast asleep. His ears twitched with the slight sounds that the forest makes in the early morning. She noted that he had a bit of blood at the corners of his mouth. She wondered if he changed his clothes. She had not noticed any in his bag, but what he now wore had no tears or stains of blood. He had also returned the necklace to around his neck. She tried to sit up but the pain kept her from it. Her almost inaudible sigh as she sunk back down into her bedroll woke Tapps. He fixed his senses on her.

"I'm glad to see you awake and well. We will rest here until you are feeling fit to travel. If that is adequate with you?"

"What happened?"

"We were ambushed by some bandits and you were hit by a *Palm Lightning* spell."

"No, no, I mean, how did you get out of your bonds and why did the bandits let us go?"

A small smile lifted the corners of Tapps' mouth.

"Well, first of all, the leather straps you had tied me with were never really able to hold me, even with their enchantments. As for the bandits, they did not let us go. I let them go. After the wizard was taken out the rest were easily dispatched and ran in the end. I could not take after them and look after you at the same time." Tapps sighed as he continued. "It was not a fair fight. They were ordinary men. Hopefully they will learn a lesson from the fight and find some honest work."

Tapps stood and stretched. Angga watched as his massive muscles rippled under his fur and wondered if it happened as he said.

"If you could break the bonds so easily, why did you wait? Why not break them before? Why did you not flee in the night?"

Tapps quickly turned and faced Angga. She could not tell if Tapps' face showed anger, surprise or both. He spoke in almost a whisper.

"Honor is an illusion." He took a deep breath and raised his voice to talk to Angga. "I said that I would take you before the elders of the Clans and that has not changed. I did not break my bonds before last night because I wanted to make you feel comfortable. If you thought I was securely tied and unable to run you were less likely to fear."

Angga looked hard at the Kaltar then glanced around. This was not where they were the night before.

"Where are we, and how did we get here?"

"There was a Kurrut nearby and used it in case the bandits decided to return and tempt fate." He paused his train of thought to answer the questioning look on Angga's face. "The Kurrut are a handful of traveling stones left over from the Time of the Dragon. The Frons keep them in working order and their locations a guarded secret. I have been told that once nearly everyone could travel quickly all over the Colonies, but now only those with both the magic and understanding can use them. As to where we are, the base of the Central Mountains, deep within the forest of Lift-Kin.

Angga's shock was apparent in her wide eyes and in her voice.

"Is it safe? I have heard that the Forest People do not tolerate outsiders."

Tapps laughed before answering.

"Only believe half of legends and none of rumors. It is safe to travel through the land of the Culrete. That is, it is safe as long as you follow the laws of their nation. For us that means simply to take no more from the forest than we need. If that rule is followed then they will not harass you. At least, they have never bothered me. Oh, they come and watch me for a while but have never approached me. In truth, I do not think that they know that I can tell when they are around. I am not so arrogant to think that there are not times that I cannot"

As soon as Angga was able, they started their travels again. By the time they reached the winter camp she did not feel that she needed to ask anyone about Tapps' honor.

Erkgare's muscles strained as he lifted a small boulder. He slipped the boulder into its place in the dam. As his fellow Goblins went to work with the smaller rocks and sand he rested. He was getting too old for this kind of work.

The Goblins were created as a labor force by the Cult of Blood during the Rule of the Giants. It was not enough for the Cult to give the Goblins a shorten stance, only a little more than a meter. That would not have separated them from the rest of humanity. The cult went further and gave them a horde of warts, moles and other lumps on their deeply folded and sickly-green skin. As if that was not enough, the facial features were twisted and misshapen. Greatly uneven ears, a diagonal mouth and eyes, and a nose which was nothing more than two holes. Even their hair, which was only in patches, seemed to be designed to make the Goblin a hideous being, at least by human standards.

Erkgare like most Goblins found beauty in their form. Over the centuries, even Humans had grown used to their appearance. At least in his experience few Humans showed any reaction to his presence, in one way or another. And he had a lot of experience with Humans. Erkgare was an

Erlking, a leader Goblin. The engineering that the Cult had done to Goblins to create his kind was similar to what they did to the Ogres. He was many times stronger than a common Goblin, as strong as the strongest of Humans. He would have given up all of his strength for a normal life span. The oldest Erlking of whom he had heard lived only a little over five decades. He was reaching his fourth.

As he stood to get the next boulder, he spotted a dog running towards them. The way the animal moved he knew it was a Gytrash. No doubt with a message. Erkgare was the goblin elder in this area of Mosk. He smiled. All through the Colonies his people were slaves. Yet, in many ways they were freer than the peasants. It was because of the Gytrash that they still could continue their work.

Erkgare walked into the woods. The dog followed and sat on the ground for a few moments. Erkgare nodded and the Gytrash shifted into a goblin. The new form looked similar to Erkgare. They were not able to shape perfectly into the form of another goblin but close enough to trick a Human. Few Humans ever paid enough attention to Goblins to tell them apart. Erkgare voice showed his curiosity.

"I am Erkgare, I was not expecting a message. What specialty is needed?"

The Gytrash smiled as he spoke.

'Erkgare, I not here from another province. I come from the Center. The Highest Goblin called a meeting. I am to take your place. The meeting is of utmost important and you are to use the gem."

Erkgare blinked. Each Goblin elder had a gem which could be used for teleporting. He had never used it before. There was never the need for such quick travel that would warrant the risk of a magus detecting them. Long ago, it was decided that it was better if no one knew where or who the Goblins' leadership were.

Putting out his hand, he waited for the Gytrash to put his palm in his. Erkgare shared a quick bond with the shape shifter. Not the real bond which he shared with the goblins in his care but enough to let them talk with each other over the distance. It was a precaution in case a question came up that only he could answer. Erkgare headed towards his hut knowing that the Gytrash would keep his people safe until his return.

VI

Luxas entered the throne room of the Draco Castle. He was a tall thin man who by his walk, his clothing and manor it was easy to tell that he was of noble birth. His smile showed that this never entered his mind. Death's Fang looked down from the Draco Throne. His tone was one of familiarity.

"Luxas what brings you to see me. It is rare for you to leave your mansion in the wilderness."

"I regret uncle that it is not social in nature but clan business which brings me from my retreat. It has come to my attention that some of my family has insulted you and I am here to ask, by privilege of bond of kin, that you hold them no ill will."

Death's Fang blinked. His voice showed he was caught off guard, which was not something which happened often.

"Insult? There has been no... Oh, the four men with the poor manners."

"Yes sir, they are of my family and I do have a duty towards them. They have been listening to the stories of my first daughter. They have gotten it in their head that they too will be great heroes like Tillent."

Death's Fang smiled at his nephew. Their bond was more than one just of family or friendship. It had been born from the shared defeats and victories of war. After thirteen hundred years, the bond had only grown stronger but Luxas has never completely rid himself of seeing Death's Fang as the Commander. The image of his uncle leading the original Great Ones as they cut a path through the armies of the Cult of Blood was forever in his sight when he looked at his uncle. The Dragon/Giant War was one that neither one of them talked of much. Death's Fang voice held the tone of concern.

"I understand, yet they want Daybreak. I think they are planning on collecting your family swords."

Luxas laughed.

"I did not say that they were the brightest in my family." Luxas thought for a moment. "What is it going to cost me so you will give them the sword?"

Death's Fang shook his head as he spoke.

"While their determination can be commended, they are trying to reach beyond their place."

Luxas was already expecting the response so was prepared with his answer.

"That may be sir, but do have you not always say that one does not know what they can do until they try? That each of us has to discover our greatness for ourselves?"

Death's Fang shook his head.

"Yes, but there is a difference between seeking greatness and seeking a fantasy. One gets in serious trouble when they define their own greatness, by others instead of what it is in them to be."

Obviously, Luxas was just prepared for that argument.

"There can be no doubt of that, uncle, and I do not argue that their greatness will be found in the family. It is just that if they do not try, if they were to go back to the family now, they would always be in the grip of the fantasy of what could have been. They are young and must learn themselves, they must come to that awareness on their own. They are stubborn, as much of that part of my family is, and I see no way of them understanding that a life of adventure is not for them without first living such a life."

Death's Fang laughed. There could be no arguing with that. the traits were obvious from the short time he had dealt with them, and Luxus kept track of all his decadents so would know the youths well. That was a trait Death's Fang did not fully understand about his nephew. These youths had to be at least ten generations removed but Luxas would see them like grandchildren. He still was not convinced but ultimately it was Luxas responsibility.

"Very well, Lux. As for the cost, the most it is worth is the hassle in finding where I put it. No offense Lux, but it is of poor make, they do not hold the power they once did. So, we shall call it a Ravia."

Luxas smiled and nodded consent.

"No offense taken old man, I was still very young when I made them and did not understand the effects time could have on something" as an afterthought he added, "or someone."

Luxas thought that getting the sword would cost him, and cost him much. The four youths were fifteen generations from Queen Tillant, so Death's Fang would feel the family concerns would overweigh the other considerations. It was understandable to Luxas. Death's Fang's grandchildren had had children by the time the Shadow was over thrown. Nuguluseam had originally been a country retreat for his family, and in all the centuries since, most of the city had become related to Death's Fang. So the concept of family for Death's Fang did not hold the same meaning as it did to most. That is why the declaration of Ravia shocked Luxas as it did.

Ravia, in the Ancient language, was that which is given to family, something which is given with no thought of be repaid. Using the Ancient word Death's Fang was letting Luxas know that he would not have to do anything in return. He was not one to keep track of how many such favors he had done for a person. The two talked on friendly matters for nearly two days before Luxas left. It was not until then did Death's Fang called up the Four Horsemen of TelTet. He did not speak until they were very uncomfortable under his gaze.

"You have come in here not only insulting me but everyone who serves me. If it were not for a friend of mine who petitioned on your behalf, I would have left you in the cell to starve. Your benefactor secured your release, by honor that you do not yet understand. You have fixed in your minds on being great adventurers. Yet, your first duty is to your family and to your clan. It is to them you should go and be hero. You will not find your glory with a sword but behind a plow. My advice is to go home now. You're free to go."

One of the servants presented the sword Daybreak to Daryl and the Four Horsemen of TelTet left the city of Nuguluseam very happy about being out of the prison. They gave no thought on who their benefactor might be or to the words of Death's Fang.

Kift's mood was joyous. He put a hundred of the gold in the Shouker National Fund for himself. The hundred gold was enough for a modest person to retire on. Far more then Kift would ever need. There were many who would not make that much in their entire life. He lived a life of simplicity. Seeing the decadence of his fellow students at the Institute, Kift came to understand at a young age that luxuries had a tendency to ruin the pleasure of simple things. How the seeking after constant pleasure eventually stripped all pleasure from life. He had dedicated himself to the path of simplicity and detachment in order to more fully enjoy life. So Kift put the funds in the National Fund incase ill health or an accident were to prevent him from living off the land. The rest of the money he put into the Fund in the name of the town. Though Kift would never learn of it, that gift would allow the town recover from the tragedy which would soon strike it, and ten years later plant the orchards which would produce Shouker's Gold cider.

It was not the money which had him in high spirits. It was from finally being finished with the distraction and being able to go back to cave. He was looking forward to the hard work it was going to take to finish stocking his home with winter supplies. From the animal signs he was already seeing, winter was going to be bad. It suited Kift just fine. He had borrowed a couple of books from his bother and was planning on spending the winter catching up on his studies. He spent the harshest months of winter doing just that, and in the best of moods.

The mountain region which surrounded the winter camp reminded Angga much of the rocky cliffs of the Sella Queendom. For the first time since she first left, Angga had a feeling of returning home. It was a gentle tugging on her heart, the kind which we find so easy to ignore. The mountains of her growing years were further south so they were much colder. The snow would already be thick for weeks and her people would be living on their winter stores. Their feathery wings were adapted well for living in such cold weather. Angga shuddered. Not much was ever said about why she was born with Mankarian wings. Well, her uncle did have wings like hers, but he would only say that it was the place of her father to talk to her about it. The only answer she could get from her father was something about things happening as they must. She was broken out of her thoughts by what suddenly appeared before her

The valley was filled with thousands of multicolored tents and hundreds of covered wagons that displayed even more colors. Tapps had said that the colors tell the stories of the people that lived there. Tapps did not see the colors so he was unable to tell her much about it except to point out the complexity. Each color had a meaning, and by combining certain colors it would change the meaning. She mused on how the wagons could have been hauled into this forestry valley when mountains surrounded it at least fifty miles thick on all sides. It took them almost an hour to get to the heart of the encampment. The magic was intense. So much so, that she did not have to weave her own to sense it.

It was called the Winter Camp, but a city would have been better description. There had to be at least twenty-five thousand here, and from what she heard most of them lived here year around. There was a Summer Camp, somewhere in the south, but apparently it was used mostly only a meeting place, and temporary housing.

As they walked through the area, she noticed that what she thought were wagons were in fact small buildings. Little more than wagons without wheels. The few of which she could see inside showed that they were storage areas and homes. There was no extra space in them. The Vagofrons spent most of their time outside, even in the coldest of weather. Trees and bushes were throughout the camp. Just enough to give ample shade during the summer but not enough to hinder movement. Even if it was the size of a city, it was spread out giving the feel of a camp that had been pitched randomly in a forest.

No one seemed to pay them much attention except for some of the young adults. She smiled. The young men probably found her attractive. She knew that she was not beautiful by Human standards, she knew that many found her attractive because of the exotic nature of her bat-like wings. The presence of all the races. Having Humans, Kaltars, Ogres and even Shawlls in their ranks must make them comfortable with anything. She wondered what the young Human ladies were looking at.

It was Tapps. She turned her head up to get a good look at him. Kaltars had a kind of beauty to them, the elegant feline grace. It was true that he was handsome, but from the overt nature of the lust in the young ladies' eyes it had to be more than that. She had found that many, both male and female, would be attracted to someone for no other reason than position, wealth or some other abstract of power. Her uncle, NetThin had told her once that it was not a shallow response that many make it out to be. It was in fact an expression of the most primal mating instinct. In his view attraction was based on the perception of a fulfillment of a need or want by the person or object. He would go on for hours to say that love was when this need and want fulfillment flowed both ways. She wandered what need Tapps' fulfilled

She looked out at the camp again seeing so many different races' children playing together. Her mouth opened wide. There was a baby wingless Dragon playing with the rest of the children. She turned and asked Tapps about it forgetting her former embarrassment. Tapps glanced over at the dragon before answering.

"That is Kilic. He is actually a Shawll but of an old form. Though, don't tell him that. Right now, he believes himself to be an Ogre. A year ago, it he said he was a Minotaur." He continued when he noticed the puzzled look on Angga's face. "The old form has not been seen in centuries. Shawlls are excellent adaptors, their genetics allow them to change their physical shape in only a few generations to better survive their environment. That is why there are so many different types from the single old form. As for Kilic, he appeared a little to the north of here about five years or so ago and has been traveling around playing with the children ever since. He is a great mystery, which not only the Clans and Dragons are looking into, but the forest people and The House Coxcomb as well."

She had a hundred more questions but was unable to ask them before Tapps stopped and turned towards a man sitting in a chair in front of a large tent. The only man she saw so far wearing weapon and armor. They exchanged a few words in Clan Speak and then Tapps spoke in the Tradespeak seemly for the benefit of Angga "And his captor is here to see them."

The man in the chair seemed almost dazed, which must have been from the sudden change in language. After a moment he stood, bowed deeply at the waist and walked inside. After a very short time he came out and gestured for them to follow. She was about to say something but Tapps was already in the opening. She quickly followed. They walked through several rooms and stopped in front of a hanging tapestry. The art was expertly woven, showing some wolf-like creatures bringing down a deer. The guard pulled the tapestry aside and Tapps walked through.

The inner chamber held four short tables scattered with papers. Pillows of a hundred different colors and shapes lined the floor behind the tables. Four Humans and one Kaltar along with a score of aids made up the occupants of the room. All of tables were turned slightly to the side. Allowing the people behind to look both at Tapps and QuickPaw who sat on a throne of pillows in at the head of the tables. An older man stood next to and slightly behind the youth. QuickPaw raised his hand in welcome when Tapps entered.

"I, QuickPaw, Warrior, Tactician, Speaker for the Clans." The old graying man who stood next to QuickPaw bent and whispered something in his ear. Tapps smiled, showing most of his teeth, as QuickPaw continued. "Oh, yes. Speaker of the RonThinVagofron, bid welcome to Tapps Toya, Warrior-Magus, Friend of the Shawlls, Protector of the Four Clans, Favorite of the Dragons and if I may say, an old friend of mine." The old man seemed to be getting irritated as he leaned down and again whispered something into QuickPaw's ear. "Sorry again, I may not say an old friend of mine but we bid you welcome anyway." QuickPaw looked at Angga. "I see you brought a visitor to us. What is the occasion, please tell?"

The old man started to bend down, apparently to correct QuickPaw again but must have thought better of it, for he straightened out without speaking. It was hard for Tapps not to laugh. It was apparent that QuickPaw was toying with his etiquette advisor. He took a step forward and bowed slightly. Such a meager bow would have been an insult to the Speaker of the Clans coming from anyone but the Protector.

"Thank you, Speaker, for asking. This most honorable lady that stands before you is my captor. She captured me through superior skills and talents. She allowed me a favor and traveled here with me to seek knowledge. I now humbly ask that you freely answer any questions she puts to you."

QuickPaw nodded his approval. Tapps always hated these formal meetings. He thought they were degrading to the clans to have such a high respect for ritual when the leaders dealt with each other. Tapps felt that one could get more accomplished over the dinner table than a bargaining table. He gestured at Angga to step forward as he took a step back. She spoke with a confidence in her voice that showed she was use to dealing with important people.

"I was hired by a man who assured me that KanaShor was a person without honor. The time I have spent with him has led me to believe that I was misled from the start but I am not blind to how cunning he can be. I came to the clans because your honor, even though differing from the rest of the Colonies, is highly respected. I have but a single question. Is KanaShor a man to be trusted?"

It started as a slight chuckle here and there but soon soared into a symphony of laughter. The whole room was laughing except for Angga, a clerk and the old man who stood next to QuickPaw. The advisor's face was getting red with anger. The clerk chuckled a bit but glanced around trying to figure out at what everyone was laughing. Angga looked at Tapps, who only shrugged his shoulders and smiled. QuickPaw was laughing so hard that he fell off the large pillow on which he was sitting. Noticing a stern look from his advisor, he quickly sat back up and regained his posture. He motioned for everyone to calm down before he spoke.

"His honor is in question then?" Humor was still thick in his voice. "Let me tell you about this Kaltar who some call KanaShor. He has been my mentor and a close friend since before I was allowed a voice and was the Clans' Protector even before that. He has never failed to come when the clan or myself has needed him. Mind you, I am not saying that Tapps is without faults. There is not a being alive who does not have some secret that they have hidden. Tapps has not always been successful in preventing the darkness which we have in our hearts from affecting his actions. Yet, in the ways of the Clans which is little known outside of us, we know all of which is Tapps. There is none who is more respected among us. We trust him, with our lives, more importantly with our love, and with the Clans there is no honor greater than that."

Angga looked as if she was expecting the answer, but shot a quick glance at Tapps when that name was mentioned. She barely had recovered enough to thank QuickPaw and step back. QuickPaw looked around and adopted a solemn tone.

"Now to the business at hand. Tapps has agreed to teach the young in the ways of sword and magic, but he asks a price . . ."

Silk, The Speaker of the Rat Clan interrupted QuickPaw.

"He has no right. He is the Clan's Protector. It is his duty."

Silk was a thin, wiry man who had a look to him which showed that he was one always trying to find out your secrets. It was a fitting appearance for the Speaker of the clan that was in charge of information gathering. Angga thought about asking to be excused. Before she had the chance, Tapps stepped forward. He opened his mouth but before could speak QuickPaw stood and the room went silent.

"Enough! The floor will open for debate in a moment." Tapps had never seen QuickPaw exert so much authority before. Tapps smiled, QuickPaw will make an excellent speaker. QuickPaw sat back down as he continued. "It is true that it is unusual for the clan's protector to ask a price but this is a strange time we love in and everything must be weighed. Normally I would just agree and give him what he wants but he asks a large price. He wants to learn the secret of the Forgotten One. He wants the elder healers to teach him to touch the minds of the Insanus Unum. The floor is now open,"

Silk was the first to speak.

"Like I was saying. He is the Protector of the Clans. It is his responsibility to that position. This gives him no right to ask any price."

Tapps looked at Silk in such a way that it made the leader of the Rat Clan sink down in his seat. Tapps understood Silk's behavior. The Insanus Unum were independent of the Clan Speakers but worked for Silk more than any other of the clan speaker. Each of the four clans had their own speaker, an administration leader, just as the Clan had its own speaker but it was the elders who made most of the decisions, and Tapps knew that it would be them to make the final choice. Tapps' voice was calm.

"It is true that I have no right to ask anything to protect the clans but what you ask of me is to teach the young to be warriors. Teaching pups and kittens is not in the realm of the Protector. You knew it was outside of my sphere of influence and authority. That is why you sent the gold in order to entice me. I am also sure that you knew that I would reject it out of hand."

The Speaker of the Cat Clan, a beautiful Kaltar named Jenifer stood, brushing long black hair out of her eyes as she spoke.

"I am sorry Father, but I must act in the best interest of my clan, no matter how it may affect the family. So, I put to you, why such a heavy price? Why such a guarded secret to teach young ones how to fight?"

Tapps smiled inwardly. Jenifer was still young, but was turning out to be a good clan speaker. She was a reluctant warrior. A fighting leader from the clan that was responsible for the Clans' security.

"The answer comes in two parts. First, I must divulge many of my personal secrets of power if I am to teach the young and to teach them well. That is a secondary concern obviously. The second and most important reason is that if I am to be Protector of the Clans then I must be able to deal with any threat to the clans even if it comes from within. I ask this not for personal gain but for the betterment of the Frons. Who here doubts that?"

QuickPaw was the one to ask the next question.

"Why? There has never been one that went against the way of the clans."

Tapps sorrowfully smiled as he spoke in the Clan Speak so Angga could not understand.

"We are too fond of saying that line. They cannot betray us. Their training insures their loyalty. Just because we say something often does not make it true. It happened when you were still young. Silk and some of the older aids will know the truth of my words. An Insanus Unum did the unforgivable. He attacked others of the Clans. He did not stop there. Some said that he had found his mind and could not take the stress. Others say that he dealt in the magic not even a beast should. For whatever the cause, he went on a killing spree. The rogue Protector had destroyed out two towns totally. I mean, he killed everything living in them.

"I came across the second town during the attack. Just one of the red hairs was able to hold off a dozen of his comrades. The rogue was defeated finally but at the cost of many of our people's lives. Let us not forget QuickPaw, when a similar thing happened to your sister. She was the leader of the Insanus Unman, second only to me in the leadership of the Warriors. We are still unsure why she did what she did. It is true that there has never been a Lost Ones who has ever betrayed the Clans directly, but there have been those who have broken under the pressure of that life.

"This is why I ask for what I ask for. The secrets of the Insanus Unum protect them from having their spirits attacked but it also curses them to be truly alone for their entire lives. That is a terrible strain on anybody." Tapps switched back to the common tongue. "Even so, I will also ask that you to submit it to the elders and have them think about this long and hard. I have some family business to take care of in Gormec, but I will be back before the hard snows. I will expect your answer then."

Tapps was about to leave when he was stopped by Keith stepping out from behind the tapestry where the Insanus Unum kept watch. There was a small room behind each speaker. It was a custom dating back to from when the Clans still fought each other. The Lost Ones were the first to act independently, to act in the best interest of all of the Clans and not just the one they belonged. That was where their name, the Lost ones, originated, they were considered lost by their original clan.

"If you will, wait a moment Protector?" The red hair youth turned towards the Speakers as he continued. "Speakers, even though I have not finished my training I have been given the authority to speak on the behalf of the Unams. Will you hear me?"

QuickPaw smiled at his nephew.

"Of course, the Insanus Unum have always had a voice."

Keith bowed to each speaker in turn before speaking.

"Even though I have forgiven Tapps," Keith faltered but quickly regained himself, "for what he had to do. Even though I have rid myself of the hatred, it is still difficult at times to look at him in fear that the hatred will return. You well know my pain, struggles and anger. So, you know that I speak true when I say that we are in agreement with Tapps. Even I can say no ill against him. He has never failed in his duties or abused his position.

"Every one of the Guardians of the Clans shutters at the thought of the breaking. We work hard to close ourselves to others, but to fragment from ourselves is terrifying. An Insanus Unum in such a state cannot be subdued. In every case, going back to the beginning of the records, we have had to be killed. We have long known that it starts slowly. Very few seek help and those that do there has been no hope. If Tapps could learn to defeat a Broken One without death then he can teach others and the elders could learn how to treat it. As the voice of the Insanus Unum, we say that we have nothing to fear from granting the Protector's request and much to gain."

Keith again bowed to each of the speakers and went back into his hiding place. Tapps turned and left the tent without waiting to be dismissed. He was too tired of dealing with ceremonies when there was evil in the air. He had felt it before although he did not want to believe it. He could not ignore it any longer. It was getting worse. As soon as they had got outside Angga spoke.

"Tapps?"

"Yes?" Tapps turned towards here then laughed as he continued. "With all ritual and pomp of official meetings beside the point, the Clans do no put much important on formality. You may call me by my familiar name if you like."

Angga smiled, she never thought that KanaShor may have been a family name. her voice showed a bit of hesitation.

"I was wondering if I could go with you to Gormec. I have never been in cat country before," Angga paused briefly, "no insult intended."

"None taken. I was raised among humans in the Imperial City of Kana To and have seen most of the Colonies since then. I have outgrown being offended by racial slang for they are only used by the weak of mind." Tapps looked at Angga with a look of a teacher in his eye. "No insult intended."

Tapps then burse out in laugher suddenly and load enough to startle Angga. He spoke with a smile that showed most of his teeth.

"How could I say no? You are my captor after all. I will be leaving in the morn."

Angga had a thousand questions. Everything was new and she wanted to understand it all. She spoke quickly in an unconscious fear that she might lose too much time.

"The girl with the human hands called you father. You do not look old enough to have a child of that age."

Tapps spoke with anger in his voice and instantly regretted it.

"She is not a child! She is a warrior to match any in the camp." He consciously calmed himself and his voice went back to its normal tone "I am surprised that you noticed her hands. They, and her hair are the only thing that shows that she had a human mother. Yes, she is my daughter. A True Magus ages slowly and my fur hides most of my age."

"You are married?"

Tapps sighed. It took him a long time to answer. Apparently, it was painful for him to talk about.

"It was a long time ago. I am a widower but my children carry on with the traits of their mothers. Only my eldest is like me in temperament and we have had our differences."

Tapps lowered his head. It was the first time that Angga had seen any sign of remorse in the large Kaltar. An awkward moment grew between them. Tapps did not speak again until he made arrangements for her sleeping quarters.

Goblins pressed in on each other as they waited for the Highest Goblin to arrive. The meeting hall was huge but they filled it. Many had to stand outside the doorways. Erkgare looked around. This was a throne room and by the style, it was human. He examined the art and furniture. It was similar to what was popular in Mosk but did not feel as dark. It was more than the abundance of windows. The art itself was lighter. Just as much carnage and warfare but one came to the impression of a victory after a long struggle rather than the theme of pleasure in the violence. No, this castle was not in Mosk. Only a border lord could get away with such a deviance from the national theme. By far, this castle had too much wealth to be a mere guardhouse.

Erkgare was still pondering where they could be when the Highest Goblin came in. Erkgare's heart sank. She did not look well. He shuttered on what it meant for the future of his people. He knew he was witnessing the beginning of the prophecy. The Goblins of the Peace would lose their direction. The Goblin King would come, but not until after a great length of time. In the meanwhile, it would be hard. They would fragment and many would choose their own king. His people would struggle with each other the way that the humans did. It would be soon. Many had expected it. After all, she had led the Goblins for the entire of their history. For the first time, Erkgare was thankful for his short lifetime. He would be spared from the pain of seeing his people fall apart.

The room went quiet as the Highest Goblin took her place to speak. Her voice showed the strain which standing was putting on her.

"Listen to me Goblins of the Peace, for I am Elohim's voice to you. Our people have been through a lot since our escape from bondage. We did our part to build the United Colonial Empire and to help usher in its golden age. Even though that empire fell apart and we once again felt the pain of sword, whip and chains we never failed in our duty. It has been a privilege to have lived within Elohim's will and to know our path. We have been blessed because of that. Even while being slaves to the Humans we are free. What has it mattered to us that we have not been respected as long as we fed the Colonies."

Cheers erupted through the room. That was the Goblin legacy. It was the identity which the Goblins held on to. They had been genetically engineered as slaves, to be docile, complacent and obedient. They had been designed to bare injustice and suffering without complaint. It would not be the years under the Rule of the Giants which would define them. It had been when the Highest Goblin had found freedom while still being a slave. It would be here teaching which would unite them and define them. To be a Goblin is to suffer, freedom was found I having a purpose for that suffering. To suffer for each other, and for the benefit of all of the Colonies was the legacy of the Goblins of Peace. She spoke again once the crowd had quieted.

"We worked tirelessly feeding ourselves and the humans, even when they gave us no help and fought each other for the land we were plowing. It is important, more than ever, that we never forget our duty or our legacy. Each one of you must make it a priority that a system of teaching is established. It must be accomplished with most haste, for I will no longer be able to be a focus for our people. I will not live out this moon cycle."

The room erupted in moans of grief. Erkgare just stared. He had the feeling that there was more. That there was something else that would make matters worse. The room quickly became quiet again when the Highest Goblin regained the strength to continue.

"Do not mourn for me. I have long since tired of this mortal coil. I am ready for my prize. Do not weep for what is to come. There is too much to do to allow your hearts to be overwhelmed by grief. We cannot escape the collapse of our culture, but if you work hard, we will come out of it stronger.

"My energy is quickly fading but there is one more matter that I must address. The Wild Goblins are becoming restless. They will most likely invade as soon as they learn of my death. There has already been raids in the outlying villages here. Luckily, the Dragoon knows the truth about us and holds no ill will. Those of you in the other human lands will not be so lucky. Keep diligent in your relations with the humans and give them aid in tracking down the Anear.

"Remember that whether in life or death I will always give my prayers for you. It has been an honor to serve you.'

It was apparent that she wanted to say more but did not have the strength. As the Highest Goblin was helped out the Erlkings started talking with each other. Erkgare did not feel like conversing so he activated the stone and went home. Having figured out that they were in Nuguluseam gave him no joy. There was a lot to do. Mosk would be the worst when the wild goblins started their night raiding. The authorities would not investigate much and would most likely grab the first goblins they found. Luckily, he was in the north so they will have to go through Gormec before they came to his area.

After debriefing the Gytrash he told the news to the goblins in his care. The weeks that followed they worked on the dam and discussed the ways to save as much of their culture as possible. They had just finished both when the message they did not want to receive arrived. For the first time that any of them knew the Highest Goblin had been wrong. She had outlived the moon cycle, but only by a day.

VII

Within a month, Angga and Tapps reached the large town of Tosha. Altering the flow of her kilter to bind her wings, Angga looked around gleefully. She was amazed at the similarities between this mostly Kaltar town and the human towns she had visited. Herds of cattle and sheep on the outskirts of town and the buildings were just like their human counter parts except for some cosmetic differences. She stopped in front of the blacksmith to watch him pound on some metal. He looked just like a human doing the same job would but instead had red fur covering his large rippling muscles instead of just skin. She realized just how foolish she had been. All the stories about the Kaltars from the humans she met painted them as savages, more animal than human.

Angga had slowed her pace in her amazement so she had to run to catch up with Tapps as he entered the inn. Making it inside, she kept close to Tapps' side. He went straight to the counter and said something to the red tiger-striped clerk behind the counter. Angga recognized the language but had never learned the purrs and hisses of the Kaltar language. She never found it advantageous to learn any more than some of the local dialects of the Imperial Language which was often called Trade Speak by the humans. Tapps seemed to argue for a few moments with the clerk and abruptly walked into the bar.

The common room looked very much like its human counterpart to Angga. The only real differences were that there were no chairs, only low sitting tables with large pillows and the decorations were more of furs and trophy heads of fierce animals. Some of which she had only seen in drawings. She had never really been an adventurer. Never even been to the Unclaimed Lands.

Tapps found the table he wanted and walked up to it. His manner of speech and the way he held himself showed he was used to being in the lead. He said something to the brown furred Kaltar at the table. The cat man rose from his table and stared Tapps in the face, difficult as it was only coming up to Tapps' chin. They exchanged angry words with one another with their lips curled. Angga could make out none of what they were saying but the few times that Tapps' name was mentioned. She thought for sure that the two men were going to try to kill one another but the brown furred Kaltar suddenly grabbed his drink and stormed over to the bar. Tapps sat at the table. Angga just stared open eyed. Tapps looked up at the still confused Angga.

"Are you going to have a seat or are you going to eat standing up?"

Angga sat down abruptly on a pillow and looked around. None of the Kaltars had paid any attention to the exchange. She leaned over to Tapps and kept her voice in a whisper.

"I have always been told that life in Gormec was much more savage but what was that all about?"

Tapps put his hand over his mouth as he started to smile. There was definite humor in his voice.

"Savage? That would depend on what you mean by the word. Most of those who call Gormec home would consider the southern Human lifestyles barbaric. Consider how much of their lives they give up just for luxuries." He warded off her protest with a wave of his hand. "I was raised by humans, so I to spend too much time seeking after luxuries. As to what just happened, I would have settled for any table but that invites too many challenges. Because of my size many would assume that I did not take this table because I am a coward. I have long since grown tired of fighting. I had my fill of it during the War Forward. By taking the table of strength beforehand would prevent them from testing me."

Excitement was apparent in Angga's voice.

"Did you fight with the Panthers?"

Tapps looked away for a moment. When he returned his gaze to Angga his face held a sorrowful smile.

"Yes, we fought and killed side by side. At the time we were so happy with our victory. It had to be done but I cannot forget the Tecmen, mere youths, that died by my claws. Even after all these years it is still difficult to talk about. It is even harder to think of those that lost their lives following me."

Angga wanted to ask about her brother, but she could not find the words. The huge Kaltar looked so fragile, the opposite of his usual demeanor, that she could not bring herself to cause him more pain. They both were just silent.

As she struggled to find the words, a serving girl came to the table who

Angga thought must have found Tapps attractive. Tapps did not seem to notice. He said a few things after they ordered and handed her a bundle of letters. A few moments later she returned with the drinks and gave Tapps some letters.

"Tapps, if you can see, why do you wear the blindfold?"

Tapps brought his hand up to his mouth and smiled wide enough to pin his ears back. He responded after bringing his hand back down.

"My sight is based on heat. Because of my eyes being without pupils many believed I was blind and I wore the blindfold since before I even have memories. In the fighting pits they kept me wearing it to give the crowds more of a thrill. The cloth does not block my sight only dampens it. I have been told that it is very much like smoked spectacles that a Dragon I know wears and are beginning to become popular with the humans she runs with. The world seems just a bit too bright without it. I really do not need it but I am used to wearing it."

A plate of vegetables arrived for Angga and she looked at Tapps.

"You're not going to have anything to eat?"

Tapps looked at Angga and the smile came back to his face. His voice was full of warmth.

"You're just full of questions. I spent many years living with the Shawlls and . . ."

"The lizards?"

Tapps cringed slightly. As nice of a person the Angga was, she had the cultural insensitivity of those of the South.

"Yes, the reptilian beings that live mostly to the west of here. While I was there, I learned many of their secrets and picked up much of their culture. There are many advantages of being a True Magi trained in part by the Shawlls."

"I know you eat your meet raw. I was taught many things in my youth. Among them were the practices of other cultures. I have a hard time eating low land meats but understand that is entirely based on taste. I would not be offended."

Tapps laughed before answering.

"No, it is not that at all. It is just that I am in the middle of HolTem, a time when . . ."

Tapps was cut short by a gray furred Kaltar sitting down at their table. The stranger looked hard at Tapps for a moment then with lightning speed lashed out at with his hand. Tapps caught the stranger's claw in his own. A startled Angga stood, almost knocking over the table. Her Salk was half out of its sheaf before Tapps' laugh made her reconsider. Tapps spoke in Tradespeak with a wide smile, looking awkward hiding his teeth behind his hand

"You are getting slow, old man. Maybe you should retire and open up an inn somewhere."

The stranger smiled not showing his teeth.

"Too many years of running this place has made me slow Smiles, who is this mountain dweller you bring to my establishment?"

He turned his attention to Angga who had finally regained herself enough to sit down. Tapps gave another hardy laugh.

"This is Angga, a bounty hunter from far to the south of here. She has captured me, so I sit before you a prisoner." Tapps looked over at Angga.

"This is Nilkees, the manager and part owner of this fine establishment."

"Captured your heart most likely." Nilkees turned his attention to Angga and bowed slightly. "Anybody who could bring this old alley cat down is worthy of my respect." He turned back towards Tapps. "I was expecting you weeks ago. This arrived for you."

As Tapps spoke Nilkees handed him an envelope that held Tapps' personal seal.

"I had an unexpected detour. I was planning on going to my estate but from the last letter, Secar and Norkil are handling things well enough. If you two will excuse me I am need of your office."

Nilkees nodded his consent and almost immediately turned his attention to Angga.

"How do you like traveling with Tapps so far? A bit on the wild side, is he not?"

Angga laughed

"I worked for a long time to have control over my own life and since meeting Tapps it is as if the world is entirely different than I thought. Immensely larger and a lot harder to control."

"He has that effect on people. I saw that in him when we first met. In fact, it was why I took him on as an apprentice. That was a long time ago, probably back about the time you were being born. He grew faster than I had thought he would, and had been on his own for a good while before the War

Forward."

Angga's curiosity was peaked

"Did you fight in the war?"

Nilkees smiled slyly.

"No, I was tracking down a lead in the Unclaimed Lands. Well, more truthfully, I was on my way back from tracking down a lead when I was captured by some Wild Goblins. I spent most of the war trying to win my freedom. I am regretful that I missed it. I would have given my nose to see the battles first hand between the Tecmen and Tapps' Panthers."

Angga's eyes grew wide, and there was no mistaking the shock in her voice.

"What do you mean by Tapps' Panthers? You mean that Tapps is the Tapps?"

"You did not know? Why would you? Tapps rarely talks of the war and when he does it is usually focusing on some kind of nonsense about how the Tecmen were people and should be mourned. Tapps is the commander of the Panthers. Well, officially Tapps retired and disbanded the Panthers after the war. Unofficially they are still around, there is a half dozen of them that live in town. Even though he has not taken direct control since the war they still consider him their commander." Nilkees paused and rubbed his chin while he stared at Angga. He leaned in a bit as he spoke more quietly. "Why do you travel with him? I mean what is your intention?"

Angga faltered. She was beginning to ask that same question. She knew that she was developing an infatuation with the Kaltar. Before she could answer Tapps returned to the table without comment and handed a few letters to Nilkees. Angga blushed slightly. She took a drink of her wine to hide her checks. Her embarrassment was instantly gone when something the gray Kaltar had said struck her odd.

"Nilkees, how did you know I am from the mountains? Have you been to my homeland?"

"No, I have never gotten a chance to travel that far into the so-called civilized nations but in my adventuring days one of my comrades was a Mankarian. Well, you see, your wings are not a clear signal that you are from the Sella Kingdom. . ."

Angga corrected with a bit too much fire in her voice.

"Queendom."

Nilkees attitude changed at her tone. He took on a much more serious manner.

"Yes, the Sella Queendom. I have never heard one of the Mankarian wings have anything good to say about the Sella family. Considering the way you are treated there."

Angga was getting angry.

"What do you mean the way we are treated?"

Nilkees sly smile returned to his face.

"It is true that I have only known a few Mankarians who are from the mountains but I have it on good authority of the biases the Queendom holds. How your law does not protect you simply because your wings are not feathered."

Angga was about to explode.

"Good authority! What do you consider good authority?"

Nilkees thought for a moment before answering.

"It is true, he may not have been a good example for he did end up in prison. However, NetThin seemed to be very bright, as he showed me more than once, and he did spend a good portion of his time researching the history of your Queendom. He was preparing a revolution so he may have been biased against the royal family."

Angga's anger left instantly. NetThin a rebel? That did not make sense. I could not be the same one. She spoke hoping to keep her fluttering stomach from sounding in her voice.

"Are you sure his name was NetThin. Are you sure it was not NetThen, Mankarian wings are very common in the Then family?"

Nilkees laughed before answering.

"I am very sure young lady. He was the one that gave me the scar which runs down most of my back, and taught me to read the southern alphabet before the fur had lengthened to cover it. I spent a total of two years apprenticing under him, and what little magic I know I learned under the blunt end of his Salk. And we escaped together when his brother was getting married. Yes, I knew him and his weapon well."

Angga had a thousand questions but wanted to get the conversation off the topic of her uncle. She did not know if Nilkees saying that he recognized her weapon, but if he did not, she did not want to risk him finding out who she really was. She jerked her hand away from her Salk when she realized she had placed it there when Nilkees had mentioned it. She hoped her voice was steady.

"Again, how did you know that I was from the mountains?"

Nilkees smile turned into a knowing grin before answering.

"Oh yeah, even without your wings show that you are Mankarian you could be from one of the few settlements in Shouker. There is a good size population of Mankarians there. You, however, still smell like one of the mountain people. Not many would be able to even smell you or know the difference but I have traveled a lot. Nothing gets past this nose of mine. Like the trouble that is walking in the door."

All three looked towards the door and a few seconds later a white-furred Kaltar followed by two large Shawlls entered. The white Kaltar motioned and the two Shawlls walked to a table. The lizard men picked up the Kaltars who were sitting at the table and threw them aside. The white Kaltar slowly walked to the table and sat down.

Tapps started to rise but stopped when Nilkees put his hand on Tapps' shoulder.

"It is all right, big guy. His name is Snow. He took over the local rogue guild and is a lot worse than its last master. He shakes down the local business owners and nobody can touch him because of his men. Every one of them nothing more than thugs. The old ways are dying. I fear we are becoming more like the Humans every day. The elders won't do anything. I think they are afraid of him. I wish for the old times when all we had to worry about was the occasional cut purse. How much crime can a town support?"

Tapps got a look on his face of someone who just found a gold coin in their pocket which they did not know they had. Nilkees and Angga got worried looks on their faces. Nilkees was the first to speak.

"What are you up to Tapps?"

"Nothing that does not need to be done, my old friend. Get all the people that Snow is strong-arming and have them meet me here tonight."

Tapps grabbed his bags and headed up to his room. Angga stayed downstairs and talked to Nilkees about Tapps and eventually about her uncle.

The thick forest southwest of the Gormec territory was as quiet as jungles get. A small party was making their way through the dense undergrowth. They had left their homes in the hopes of finding fame and adventure. Two Humans and an Ogre were the group in whole. All three just at the age that they could call themselves adults. Only a few hours into the jungle in the central part of what the Colonies call the Unclaimed Lands and they were already getting on each other's' nerves.

"Stop bumping into me, Albert!"

The young Ogre looked hurt by the words.

"I'm sorry Wil, I have hard time walking in forest."

"Will you two shut up, we don't know what lies in this jungle and whatever it may be will know we're here if you guys keep at it."

Wil spun around his face red with anger.

"Elwyn, whatever is out in this jungle is going to know we're out here because of Albert is stomping around like a bull on dried leaves, not because we are arguing."

Elwyn looked as if he was going to say something but he was interrupted by the Ogre's shouts.

"Snake, big snake, don't let him eat me."

Both humans looked around towards the direction they were headed to see a large jungle snake lifting itself off a rock where it had been sunning itself. Elwyn pulled his sword.

"Die you evil beast, kill him guys."

Elwyn started to charge until he realized that both his friends had taken off in a run in the direction from which they had come. Elwyn ran after his friends. All three of them ran until they got home and never thought of adventuring again.

The jungle snake looked towards the commotion the three made and opened its mouth as if in a bored yawn. Then it slithered into the jungle.

Not an hour had passed before a Plain Shawll like no other came to the same clearing. She stretched her snake-like body which was nearly twice as long as a human is tall. Near her head she had a pair of powerful arms and shoulders that from the back, gave her the appearance of a giant cobra. Her tongue flickered out of her mouth. She tasted the scent of large mammals that had been in the area recently. She was not hungry so she did not hunt after them. She looked around the clearing with eyes as orange as the fruit that bares the same name. Spotting the rock that the jungle snake was sunning itself on, she thought to herself that it would be a nice place to take a nap. Curling her body around the rock, she used the end of it as a pillow. Yawning, she exposed two large fangs the size of a man's forefinger and fell asleep in the afternoon sun.

Her name was UnamKrint, our just simply Krint to her brood. Even though she shared much of the appearance of the Shawlls she was in fact a

Dragon. A very young Dragon. Normally she would have never been allowed to travel on her own, but she had a mission. A mission for which she had been trained for the two short decades of her life. She was to find the mammal who she had been bonded to when she was still in the egg. It was time for them to complete the bond and make things right. Most of the time she could feel in what direction he was but there were other times that she could not sense him at all. At present he was not far away. As long as he did not start moving again it would be no more than another week and she would find him.

That night Tapps entered the common room where all the merchants had gathered with the confidence that was as much his trademark as the red bandana he wore over his eyes. His suit was of the formal style of the south and he wore the medallion of the Society's Warrior-Magi on his lapel. Around his neck he wore the torc of the Protector of the Four Clans of the Vegofrons. He scanned the room and was surprised to find an Ogre there who wore the traditional priest vest. He took a deep breath before he started.

"For those of you who do not know me, my name is Tapps Toya, Warrior-Magus, Protector of the Vagofron and Friend of the Shawlls. To let you know that I have reason for what I do, I will tell you a secret of mine. Long before the War Forward I ran across Nilkees and we traveled together for a time. After the war he told me he wanted to open up a bar. He did not have enough money, but I had more than enough. When the new Gormec was founded he came to me with a deal. I would put up three fourths of the cost of this inn and he would put up the rest and run it for us. We are business partners and I take fifty percent of the profit." He turned his attention to the bishop. "Abbot, you honor me with your presence but why are you here? Has Snow stolen from the church?"

The priest stood. His voice was surprisingly low and soft for an Ogre.

"It is I who am honored to be in your presence, Lord Toya. The Grace in you is well known to the Temple of the VoX. In my training there, I have heard much of the Hero of the War Forward. Snow steals from the Church only indirectly. We do not have many in need in this town but we do have some. Every silver which Snow takes from my friends is a copper they cannot give for the needy. As it says in the Upior; People go hungry only because of those who desire more food that they need. I am here to give a Blessing to any decision that the town comes to."

Few things surprised Tapps anymore, but an Ogre as a VoX Templer was one of them. There must be a story there and Tapps would have to hear it later.

"I am glad of that, but please do not call me lord. I am nobody's master. Especially one such as you."

"So why did you call us here? What plans do you have?"

A plump female Kaltar who owned the bakery got to the point. It was so apparent on her face that she was getting impatient that a human could have recognized it. It was odd to see such a large Kaltar. Tapps put it off as the influence of the more human foods present in the culture and from the lack of the daily hunt. Tapps turned to the female and smiled with only a hint of teeth as he spoke.

"The reason I called for you is that I am planning of getting rid of Snow. He does not follow Noktorace so is only a thief. Anyone that does not follow the Law of the Night does not fall under its protection."

A large red furred Kaltar stood. His large body rippled showing the many years he had spent as a blacksmith. Even with his size he still looked small compared to Tapps.

"I suppose that you will be setting yourself up as the new guild master?"

Tapps was waiting for the question so he was prepared for it.

"My friends, your town is growing fast and soon you will be a city large enough to support many guilds, but it has been many decades since I have been a rogue. I have no wish to run a guild or to reenter such a life. Someone will fill the void. But rest assured that it will not be me."

The crowd seemed satisfied, most likely more from his reputation then from his words.

"So how do you suppose to get rid of Snow. He has over a dozen thugs and even a wizard?"

"Leave that up to me. All I need is for you to tell me every detail about Snow and his thugs even if you think it is unimportant."

The room was buzzing when the Kaltars talked it over among themselves. They finally agreed to let Tapps do what he wanted and started to tell him about Snow and his men. They had just finished when the door of the inn violently flew open.

Snow walked into the bar with a young Kaltar beside him and his two Shawlls following close behind. He looked around the bar and then at Tapps. He whispered something in the boy's ear and the boy took off out the door.

Snow looked at Tapps with contempt in his eyes.

"Well, well, what do we have here? A party and nobody invited me?"

Tapps faced Snow and took a step forward. Snow's Shawlls went to confront him but Snow gestured with his hand and the two lizard men stopped. Tapps snarled a bit when he spoke.

"This is a private party. Some of my friends welcoming me to town. I do not count you as one of my friends so you were not invited. If you would be so kind to leave, it would be appreciated."

"Apparently, you do not know who I am. I am Snow and I run this..."

Tapps cut Snow off. He no longer kept the anger from his voice, or his teeth hidden.

"I know who you are, but let me tell you who I am. I am Tapps Toya." His voice took on the hiss of the Shawll's language. "Hisk sweee tuus kanashorfin."

At his words, the two who were with Snow stumbled back a few steps as if Tapps had reached out and hit them with his fist. He brought his speech back to the Kaltar language and his attention back to Snow.

"I have nothing but contempt for you. You insult all those who practice Noktoran. For the dishonor you bring to rogues I should cut your heart out, but I am afraid that it would be quite messy and your blood would stain the carpet. So, I will give you a chance to leave town and save your unworthy life."

Snow just stood there making sure that Tapps was finished. He looked around the bar again and smiled. A Human with a streak of silver running through his long black hair walked into the room. Snow lifted one hand before he spoke.

"Well, it looks as if I have a mutiny on my hands. I have never heard of you blind one but my pets seem as if they do. It really makes no difference to me. You should not worry so much about my blood staining the carpet, but yours, for I do believe that the odds are in my favor." Snow turned towards the wizard. his tone was casual. "Kill him."

Snow turned to leave. He had not taken another step before he heard a scream and the thud of his wizard hitting the ground. He turned around to see Tapps smiling at him while lighting a cigar and his wizard curled up on the floor holding his head. Snow had a puzzled look on his face, but only for a second.

"So Master Toya, you are a mind scrambler as well. It still makes no difference for you are but one. Things being as they are, I still have the advantage. It will be interesting to see what will come to pass in the next few days."

Snow turned and left after slapping one of his Shawlls and telling him to bring the wizard along. Tapps apologized to the shopkeepers and bowed slightly when the bishop passed. When the last of them were gone he sighed and slumped onto a large pillow. Nilkees grabbed a bottle of wine and joined Tapps at the table. Nilkees took a large gulp of wine and then handed it to Tapps. He waited until Tapps took the bottle before he spoke.

"I think you handled that well."

"Snow recognized my name but not my face. He is nearly as old as you so should have been there during our fight against the Tecmen. He fears me probably because of all the rumors about me. This is what we want but the timing is all off. The people I sent for are not here yet. There is no telling what Snow will do tomorrow."

"Or tonight, my blind friend."

Tapps took a swallow from the bottle before responding.

"No, he will not act tonight. Snow is not like us. He is a thinker, there is no doubting that. He will weigh each option carefully before deciding what to do. He will not risk anything on a hasty move and will wait until at least tomorrow. I am just puzzled on why the two mountain Shawlls are working for him."

"From what I hear he paid for them when they were still very young and had them raised to be his body guards"

Tapps shook his head, Gormec was becoming too much like the human nations. Too willing to exploit their neighbor for personal gain. Tapps could not help but wonder if that was what the future was really going to be like. The two friends finished the bottle of wine in silence and went to their beds.

Angga woke to the morning light. It was later than she wanted, but even after all these years it was still hard to wake early. After getting dressed she entered the common room which separated Tapps' and her bedrooms. Tapps was sitting on one of the plush chairs which faced the fireplace. She thought the scene was a bit odd with him not moving. Frantic thoughts ran through her head. Tapps would always awake and greet her at the slightest noise, but he still did not move even when she ran to him.

She was relived to find him still breathing. His chest rose and fell slowly.

His ear would twitch from time to time but not nearly as much as they usually did. Angga was tempted to rouse him but decided against it. She sat on a couch and waited.

Eventually Tapps sat up. He removed the bandana from his eyes and looked at the widow. His face turned back towards Angga before he spoke.

"What time of the day is it?"

"Nearly midday. What was that all about? You just sat there."

Tapps smiled and for the first time Angga realized that showing the teeth was a human expression. Kaltars showed aggression by barring them. She was about to mention it but Tapps cut her off.

"Good, the first of my people should be here any moment." He paused and seemed to realize that Angga had asked a question. "I was praying. If you have not noticed, I am easily distracted, but in my communion with VivusDeus I sometimes become completely unaware of the physical world. Because of the danger I do not allow myself the deep prayer except when I am in a safe place. I usually do it in my own chambers but I was sitting here when the mood struck me. It was . . ."

Tapps was interrupted by a knock on the door. Angga looked at Tapps, who was smiling again. Angga went and answered the door.

"You little brat!" Angga's voice broke with anger. "You have a lot of explaining to do!"

A boy who looked to be no more twelve or thirteen was standing outside the door clutching a skunk in one arm and a small stick in the other. His smile turned to a horrified look and he took a step to run. Angga was ready for him and took off after him. As soon as Angga got a step out the door the boy twisted in mid step and ran into the room. He slammed and locked the door with an agility that seemed unnatural for his age. Angga started pounding on the door and screaming almost immediately.

"You little vagabond. Just wait until I get my hands on you. I'm going to take that twig of yours and snap it over your backside."

The boy calmly walked over to the chair that Angga had been sitting in and plopped himself into it. There was laughter in Tapps' voice when he spoke.

"Herman, will you ever change? Go open up the door for the lady."

The boy looked surprised as if someone just asked him to jump into a well. His joy was betrayed by his northern dialect.

"Go open the door? Ya crazy? Do ya hear what she's planning ta do?

Do ya?"

Tapps just looked at the Herman. The boy placed his skunk in the chair, patted her on the head twice and handed his stick to Tapps for safe keeping. He walked to the door with all the sorrow of someone who was heading for the gallows. He slowly unlocked the door being careful to do it silently. He turned his head to show Tapps his great big smile. Quickly throwing open the door, Herman ran to stand behind Tapps.

Angga walked in the room trying to remain calm but her face was red with emotion. She looked at Tapps and the boy which were both smiling enough to show most their teeth. She turned even redder and her voice cracked with the anger.

"Tapps, you know this child?" She continued, not waiting for Tapps to answer. "You know he is a con. I found him one winter. He was so pathetic. Huddling in an alley corner, shivering like a wet cat. Well, I took him into my home. I fed him, clothed him, even tolerated that mischievous skunk of his. How does he treat me? He took advantage of my kindness, that is how. Waited until the whole town knew that he was in my care. Waited for the whole town to know that he could charge things on my accounts. Then out of the sky, he charged up over a hundred coin in small things. Things easy to carry and sell in the next town I suppose. Left town that same day and there I was worrying that some bandits made him do it. I see now that I was taken for a fool."

Herman got a hurt look on his face. Tapps was surprised when he heard the boy tell the truth.

"What ya mad about. I did the same ta Tapps here. Ya don't see him running around threatening me. Do ya? No, and I took much more from him and in gold coin ta boot."

"Five hundred twenty-four gold and two silver to be precise. If I am not mistaken, and I am not, I tracked you. If memory serves me right and it does, you learned your lesson from the episode."

"Yar memory is getting faulty in yar old age. I turned myself in to ya and ya didn't have a chance of catching me."

Tapps smile widened. "Did to."

"Did not"

"Did to"

"Did not"

"Did to"

"Did not"

"Did to"

Angga wanted some answers so she broke up their games. Her voice still stressed with the anger.

"So Bobby, what brings you to this town?"

Herman composed himself and his natural accent turned into the more formal southern dialect.

"Tapps begged me to come help him with whatever recent trouble he got himself into. Did not."

Tapps smile widened.

"His real name is Herman, and I asked him to come help me. Did to."

Tapps did not think that Angga could get any redder, but it showed on Herman's face that he knew it could and he was planning to take it there. Angga ruined his plans by speaking first.

"What can he do? He is only a child."

It was Herman's turn to become red and it was apparent that he was about to yell and scream at Angga. Tapps decided it was time to put an end to it and made his voice just loud enough to stop Herman from speaking.

"This child, as you put it, is the best Rougbat I have ever met and without a doubt the best actor that the Goblin Players have ever produced. If there is anything he cannot do through magic and slight of hand, he can talk you into thinking that you just saw him do it."

Herman blushed and looked down towards his feet. His voice was almost a whisper in his natural northern accent when he spoke.

"Thank ya," and said a bit louder so Angga could hear, "did not."

Tapps almost laughed as he spoke.

"Besides he is not really a child. He is not much younger than you. It is just that his natural ability in magic has retarded his growth. Did to."

"Did not."

"Did to."

"Did not."

"Did to."

"Did not."

Angga could not take it any longer. She left and went downstairs to the common room to hear the minstrel play. After she left, Tapps and Herman laughed for a while. Both of them got a glass of wine and a cigar then started to go over the plans for the town.

VIII

Herman left town under the protection of invisibility, the same way he had entered the town in the first place. When he felt that he was far enough away that no one would be watching he shifted his magic. As he felt the pattern that kept him invisible dissolve, he thought for a moment and let the magic that kept people from seeing the silver in his hair fade as well. His hair was almost completely white with only a few strands of black. He thought that the silver was a good contrast with his dark skin but the sight of it often made people nervous so he kept it hidden most of the time. The wizards of the south painted a strip of silver in their hair so many people believed it meant something. There was a time long ago, when the Dragons still ruled, when a wizard reached a certain level of ability, they would mark their hair with silver as a warning to others. There was no system then to tell a person when to dye their hair. It was left up to each wizard to decide when they were powerful enough that others would need to know. The custom had even been held under the rule of the Great Ones but now it had become political. Not how enlightened one was, but that they knew enough. The color of his hair was natural. As far as he could tell it was unrelated to him being a Trualja, a Natural Wizard, one born with the ability to manipulate magic.

He had not known what the big deal was. The teachers who Tapps had arranged for him were impressed that one so young could manipulate magic so well. It took him awhile to understand that he was different from even other Trualja. The wizards who tried to teach him, or study him in Herman's opinion, had dealt with Naturals before, just not one like him. He was not simply Trualja, but one which was born with such ability that it rivaled a True Magus in power. They could not even come up with a good theory to why one so young could work magic as well as one who spent their life studying it.

Not that he was really that young. Although his body may have appeared to be just past its first decade, he, in fact, had just had his twenty sixth birthday. A byproduct of being born what was called an Upior in an ancient tongue. He looked away from the town and fought away tears. Many have sold their souls in an attempt to have the kind of power which was at

Herman's finger tips. He would give up anything just to be normal.

Herman pulled two small crystal marbles from his pocket. He threw them into the air and they disappeared. He could do what needed to be accomplished without the marbles but it was easier to have a prepared item do parts for him. He had dozens of items, to do things that he could do with a thought. His least useful item was the stick he always carried. It was not much more than a twig, but it held three patterns for magical attacks. He made it after am encounter with some thugs in Jappa. His warm smile and natural charm were considered a sign of weakness in the capital city of Mosk. The three youths knew he had a considerable amount of gold on him. He had been accepted into the Mosk's University of Medicine and Magic and had been carrying the first two years' tuition on him. The three thugs wanted the entire fifty gold. To make matters worse, they were not satisfied with simply taking his money, they had also beat him viciously. He did not like to admit it but he had been afraid. His fear had prevented him from working any magic to protect himself. He had made the stick while in University in case he was in a similar situation again. Luckily, he had never needed to use it in the five years he spent in the University.

The thugs were caught and, against Herman's wishes, were publicly tortured and executed. In Mosk the execution of justice for a crime, even as severe as beating a young child would be left up to the family. However, in order to draw students from outside of Mosk, Emperor Mosk the Dark had placed all of its students and staff under his care. By beating him the thugs had attacked a member of the Imperial Family, or at least that was how the nation's law worked. Herman felt sorry for the three youths. The torture they received was especially severe because of Herman.

The University had the idea that Herman was only eight so they thought they had a prodigy on their hands. In a way they were right. He had been only eighteen and already knew enough to pass their entrance exam. Like most Trualja, Herman was a genius but sometimes he had difficulties with details. The only reason he had known enough to pass their test was that he had plenty of time to study when on the road with the Goblin Players. He was one of the few humans who were allowed to join the Goblin's acting guild. It was more than just the time, he was driven to learn by his desire to help his sister. That is why he entered Mosk's University of Medicine and Magic.

The University was harder than he thought it would be. Along with the education the experience taught him humility, at least a little. It would have taken him an extra year if he had not been so versed in magic already. He graduated with honors only in magic. He was preparing to leave when he was recruited for a special program at the University. They were very vague with the details and this had peeked Herman's curiosity. He entered the program and had spent the last three years learning to be an assassin. He did not find out the purpose until the second year and had almost left. That was when they started teaching about plant and animals and the various poison uses.

It was not simply curiosity, but curiosity of the secret knowledge they would be teaching. What they knew about the use of poisons went far beyond what was believed to be known. It did not surprise him, after all Mosk was considered the Land of the Royal Assassin. A place where Silent Killers were respected, and there was no law against murder. That may not have been enough to have kept him there, but they were also starting to teach him how to fight.

His sister had already taught him the basics use of a blade but Herman was no warrior. Their style of fighting was more fitting to him, how to take out a target silently. Right before the letter from Tapps came he had just officially became a Royal Assassin of Mosk. He received his first orders the same day that he had been asked to help Tapps. He was supposed to be in south Mosk killing some noble. There would be a price put on his head when he did not meet the contact. It did not bother him. He now knew how to protect himself and others from an assassin and because of his magic, no conventional force could take him.

It was also at that time Herman had just finished the black orb which constantly floated around him. he had spent countless hours working it so it would be invisible to normal sight and to all but the most detailed examination by magic. Originally it was meant only to deflect arrows or darts which were direct at him. After learning what he did in school, he added patterns to it that would also filter out dust from the air and even streams of liquid. It would have been much easier just to create some Wards to do the same thing, but the orb was much stronger than a ward could be, and would not be subject to the same measures of disrupting them.

Pulling his cloak's hood over his head, Herman headed back towards town. By the time he had reached the town his marbles had found the targets. They were three large Kaltars who walked into a shop. A few minutes passed and they walk out stuffing a sack of coins in their purse. Walking towards the thugs, Herman spotted a beggar on the side of the street. He ordered his marbles to return and walked over to the beggar, dropping a silver coin. He kept his voice level and in a tone which showed he had done this before. He had not completed mastered Vrenic, the Art of Voice, but was skilled with it enough, not only to sound older, but to sound as one who was used to issuing orders.

"Tell the guild that the Puppet Master is in town and he will pay the usual cut for an outsider."

The beggar eyed Herman for a long moment and finally spoke weakly.

"Thanks for the coin sir, but I don't know what guild you are referring to."

"Do not play games with me, I have traveled all day and am not in the mood. Will you tell the guild or not?"

There was so much authority in Herman's voice that all the beggar could do was nod. Herman hated using the inflexion of his voice to cause fear but he had not lied. He was not in the mood. He reached out his hand and his two globes dropped in his palm. Pocketing them, he looked for the thugs and saw that they had moved farther down the street. If all went well, he would be part of Snow's guild within a couple of hours. If things went wrong, he would be dead. He swallowed hard and cursed Tapps for the trouble he put him in. He walked fast to catch up with the hoodlums as they walked into another shop.

It was a leather shop. As he entered, he spotted a small leather poach on a table by the door. As much out of habit as from the plan, Herman reached out and grabbed it. When he had realized what he had done, he cursed himself for being a fool. He could have ruined everything. If he was caught the plan would go afoul. Slim chance, Herman thought to himself. He had not been caught since before he started his training as a Royal Assassin. His hands were too quick for that anymore. He followed the three Kaltars into the next shop. It was a silversmith. Herman was surprised that the town would have such a shop. But considering that it was the major trade town with Mosk, and thus all of the Southern Nations, it was most likely rapidly growing in wealth. Herman smiled, confident that his hood hid it. He started filling the folds of his robe with silver. He was careful not to take too much from one area. He was so gleeful that he almost missed the three bandits leaving. Having the stuff, he needed it was time to make his move.

He stealthily stepped up to the thugs and cut all three of their purses. He tucked two of them in his robe and half turned. He dropped the third pouch on the ground and let out a faint curse. The three strong arms turned to see Herman picking up the sack. After a quick hand down to his side the largest one grabbed Herman by the collar. The gray-furred lifted Herman off the ground a growl. His words heavy with a Kaltar accent.

"Why you little kitten, I'm going to have your heart for supper."

Herman twisted as if to get away but he made sure that all the silver and the bags he had stolen fell out. He even dropped his own money sack. As all the contraband hit the ground the three cat men's eyes widened. The Kaltar who had Herman by the collar gave him a small shake to see if anything else would fall out. When nothing else did, the gray-furred Kaltar looked at Herman, humor thick in his voice.

"You steal all that kitten?"

Herman made his voice quiver with false fear.

"No, sir."

"Well, I'm not sure if I believe you."

The Kaltar with the black tiger strips chimed in, apparently the smartest of the group.

"Rrik, maybe we should take him to Snow."

The calico picked up Herman's stolen goods while the gray one spoke.

"That's a good Idea. Glad I came up with it." he turned his attention to Herman. "You're going to go see the boss."

Snow did not sleep at all the night of the encounter with Tapps. He had been kept up by his fear. He had heard many rumors about the exploits of this Tapps, the supposed Hero of the War Forward. Snow, for the first time, regretted not joining in that war. He had been in the south, learning the art of business. He was working for the Great House Slar, the best of the Great Houses in Snow's opinion. They did not limit their practices by any ideals of ethics or honor. Profit by any means was their motto, at least internally. He had done well in the House, and the only reason he left was because the land expansion of Mosk, and the founding of Tosha had opened up a direct trading route. He knew that the beginning of a Gormec as a nation was the best place to start his own house. He had picked Tosha because it was at the center of trade to the southern nations. He had already started expanding into more legitimate business. He had just bought a caravan to start shipping cargo and trading with Mosk. Construction of a warehouse was scheduled to start after the winter. All of it under his real name. His rogue guild would be at the center of it, giving him a pool of thugs to intimidate any potential rivals.

At the time of the War Forward Snow was sure that it was not worth risking his life for, but at least he would have known if this was the real Tapps or just some pretender. Even the legends of the real Hero of the War Forward were too grand. Who really could believe them? After talking to his Shawlls about what they had heard of Tapps' travel in the Shawlls' land, he was beginning to believe and they had confirmed, that he was the real Tapps. It was true that Tapps was only one Kaltar, but if half the tales were true then he would need a lot more than the twelve men to take on Tapps. Just before sunrise he decided to have his men to make another round of collections, in case he needed to run for it. He was not a man who really believed in the Shadow World, but he had spent a lot of time praying during the night to whatever gods might listen that Tapps would not make his move before he got the coins.

His day was filled with nothing but anxiety. As it got closer to sunset his fears decreased, Snow always felt safer in the dark. Only a few moments before the sun would take the its last look over the world, a knock came on his door. Fear choked his words as he told the knocker to come in. He barely managed to get the words out. Some of the fear loosed its grip on him when he saw his head thug walk in with a human child in tow.

"Rrik, what is this?" he barked

"Lord Snow, I caught this urchin cutting my purse I would have killed him right on the spot but I found this on him."

With that, the large gray-furred Kaltar dropped the silver and gold on the desk in front of Snow.

"Child, why did you steal my men's purses when you already had so much gold?"

Herman quickly noted Snow's human style desk and human way of talking. It would reflect his human style greed. In just a few seconds he decided the best role for him to take. He was an orphaned youth from the north who blamed Tapps for the death of his father. He was following the first rule of a cover story. Keep it as close to your real life as possible. He smiled before he spoke in the northern dialect.

"Ya can never have enough, besides I was not plannen ta get caught."

"Plans don't always go the way they are laid. If you would have shown up yesterday, I would have taken you in with open arms, but things being as they are, they call for a different approach." He looked up at the Rrik. "Kill him quickly and silently. Dump his body where it will not be found for a couple of days."

Things were going bad for Herman. Not that he had to panic about the threat but he did not like having his plans disrupted. He had to think fast. His first thought was that he was trying too hard. Forcing himself to relax, he took a step forward, dodging the large cat man's paw. He opened his mouth and just let the words come out.

"Ya can't kill me. I have somethen ta do before I die."

"What may that be, kitten?"

Snow's curiosity got the better of him. Herman relaxed a bit for he knew that he had snagged Snow on his hook and all he had to do was wait for the fish to get tired of fighting. He still had a bit of nervousness in his voice. Not all of it from his act. If Snow had anyway of detecting lies, he would be lost. Herman used the first skill he learned with the Goblin Players, his eyes became watery on the verge of tears.

"I have ta avenge my father's death. I don't know his name. All I know is that it was a huge blind Kaltar who always wears a red bandana over his eyes. He was the cat, uh, Kaltar that I saw kill my father."

"Tapps." Snow quickly got the joy he felt under control and continued the questions. "And how is a child supposed to reek revenge on a highly trained warrior?"

Herman almost smiled. He held it in check. A prideful smile would be deadly. He knew that the fish had tired and all he needed to do is to pull Snow in. He returned to the role he was playing and spoke with a tone of naive determination.

"Well ya see Lord Snow, it was Lord Snow, wasn't it?" Snow nodded. "My father named me Kerfun. In the old language it means birth magic. Since before I coud walk I controlled magic. I yem what mar people call a natural. Well, not to sound big headed or anythen, but I have become quite good."

To add flair to his performance, Herman let his hood fall to expose his silver hair. One of the thugs actually whistled. Snow's mind raced with a thousand ways to use the child but he quickly discarded all but two. Either he could use the boy to slow Tapps down while he escaped or he could use the might of the kid's magic to confront Tapps when the blind man did not expect it. Snow needed time to himself to think so he told Rrik to take Herman to his wizard. He looked at the boy and spoke with excitement in his voice the gold and silver back to Herman.

"I am sure that we can find a way to work together in a way in which we will both get what we want."

Snow slumped back in his chair after the two had left. It took Snow a good hour before he finally made up his mind how he was going to use Kerfun. Snow truly relaxed for the first time since his confrontation with Tapps. He even allowed himself a small glass of wine. He had a plan and, if the kid was as half as powerful as he appeared to be, it would happen without any problems.

The wizard walked into Snow's office. He still had a headache from the run in with Tapps. He was covered with sweat and his robes and hair was singed and still smoked a bit as he moved. He walked up to Snow's desk and stood there impatiently. After enough time had passed that Snow knew the wizard would be irritated, he looked up from his desk. Snow was taken back by his wizard's appearance but he quickly regained his posture.

"Kern, what happen to you?"

"I tested the human child and like he says, he is a natural. The kid's power, as young as he is, exceeds my own."

Snow took a thoughtful moment to reflect on what the wizard had said. He mumbled a few words so soft that Kern could not hear. Then Snow lifted his head and raised his voice.

"That still hasn't explained your appearance."

"Well sir, I started out probing him with the basic detection spells. He has wards in place that prevent such detection spells from working. The kid seemed surprised when I told him about them. Most Naturals have a few wards on themselves for a hundred different things and not even know the wards are there.

"I have even heard of natural wizard never knowing that they controlled the forces of magic. They just thought that they had good luck or that strange things always happen around them. I even once met a fishmonger in Winbeat that before the war..."

"Wizard, the boy!"

Snow's patience was thin and did not feel like listening to the hours of background which the wizard always thought necessary for the laymen to understand what any magus talked about.

"The boy? Oh yes, the boy. Well, like I said, I didn't learn anything from the probe spells so I started on to the next test. I set up a wall that was made from purely magical essence and told him to unweave it. Well unlike us wizards that have to think about the steps of a spell, a natural merely thinks about something happening and it does." Kern went back to the boy's story when he saw Snow getting irritated again. "Well, how far someone can get through the wall in fifty ticks shows you somewhat how powerful the person is. I let the fifty seconds pass and looked at the wall. It was no longer there. A wall that took me a good ten minutes to put up he took down in mere seconds. He didn't stop there. I didn't know it at the time but he had destroyed the patterns of most of my protective wards I have placed on myself.

"Because the wall test did not show the extent of the kid's powers, I decided to do the Mixing Bowl. I informed the child what to do. The process is quite simple. He imagines putting all his magic in a magical sphere that I made with my magic. When he finished that, I weaved in a little of my own magic to probe his. The child had put so much power in that when the little amount that I put in overloaded my sphere. Something I have only heard of happening with the most powerful of adepts. Well, my sphere exploded. If it were not for the fact that the child absorbed most of the blast I probably would be dead now." Snow's eyes got wide with worry. "He's alright sir. The kid has so many protective wards on him that his clothes didn't even get singed. I can only guess that the child could have taken about twice that explosion and still be standing."

Snow looked up at the magus with a smile on his face.

"That is all for now. On your way back to your room tell my astrologer that I request his presence."

Herman sat on the edge of a bed in the room they gave him. He smiled to himself while he ate. He enjoyed out smarting people but the way he fooled the wizard who had tested him was something right out one of those storybooks that filled Tapps' library. The wizard had no imagination in testing his power and used textbook tests on him. Like any good slick who comes across a textbook scene, he used textbook tricks. Dispel the wall, such a childish game. Herman thought that the wizard must have been playing with him. When he finally realized that the magus was not joking, he got busy. He turned the magical wall invisible to the wizard's spells and started turning off the wizard's protected wards. As complex as the magus thought they were, they were in fact very simple to turn off. The man did not even have the skill to be a village wizard. The man knew a lot about magic, but had very little understanding of its nature.

When he had erased all of the wizard's protective spells, he had just enough time to pocket a small medallion that had caught his eye when he first walked into the wizard's laboratory. Time ran out and the wizard looked for the wall. He did not see it so he thought Herman had dispelled it all. Herman laughed again. Fill the sphere. It was the stupidest thing Herman had ever heard. It was a test for a novice to see how much potential they had.

He decided to have some fun with the test. He put the magic in place that created the most volatile pattern he could think of. While the wizard prepared his own magic Herman positioned himself where the orb would be on the other side of the magical wall. When the wizard had put his magic in the orb it agitated Herman's pattern. The orb exploded. The wizard was more use to Herman alive, so he put his arms up and made a face like he was trying to use powerful magic. All he really did was direct the blast towards himself. He let just enough of it hit the wizard so that his tester would know that he had no protective wards. By the time the blast worked its way through the magical wall it was so weak that Herman's protective spells absorbed it all.

Herman laughed out load as he finished the last of his food. The wizard had left in a hurry allowing a servant to show Herman where he could stay. He prided himself on his ability to read people well and knew exactly where the wizard had gone. Without a doubt he was telling Snow that he was the most powerful natural that the wizard had ever seen. It was not a lie, he probably was the most powerful natural the wizard had ever seen, after all the old man could barely call himself a wizard. He realized that he was still hungry so he grabbed the empty plate that once held his dinner and went to find the kitchen. He was always looking for a free supper and trying to find the kitchen would let him get a good idea where things were in the building.

A knock came to Snow's door. The door opened slowly after Snow gave his reply to come in. A venerable Kaltar with the graying fur of old age walked in slowly. The Kaltar was older than most thought was possible and it showed in his walk. Snow stood out of respect. The old Kaltar was the only person whom Snow would temper his attitude around. Not because of any fear or fondness for the stargazer but because Snow was very superstitious, even though he would not admit it to himself, and would not even choose what to have to eat without his fortune teller.

When the old cat man had taken a seat in one of the hardly used chairs at Snow's desk, Snow also sat. Snow was about to say something but the old Kaltar stopped him by speaking first. His voice showed his age even more than his walk and sounded if it was an effort to breath like a man lifting more than he could carry.

"You want to know what will happen if you confront our blind brother. I cannot say for sure, but I do know that he is destined to fight a great foe in the future. A foe more powerful than I have ever ran across in my life. I have seen a vision in my dreams. In the dream I was standing in a large room. Its walls were made of some black rock that absorbed all the light in the room but I could still see. In the room were you, the blind one and a dark god wearing an even darker cloak which seemed to be made of a lightless fire. You were lying dead on the ground with the large blind one standing over you. His claws were stained with your blood. He turned toward a dark cloaked figure and said, 'another of your servants have fallen'. The fire-cloaked god turned towards me and handed me a large gem. He smiled as I looked up from the stone. I could see all the pleasures of the world in his eyes and a hint of a secret. He said to me in a voice that was thunder in my ears that I was to tell you of some of the secret that was in his eyes. At this point I awoke.

"Since then, a mere hour ago, I have read the stars, read the tea, even the cards which I have not done since my youth and they all tell me the same thing. If you confront this Kaltar, either now or in the future, you will die." A gentle look came over the ancient Kaltar's face. "Dear Snow, you have been so kind to me in the past years. I realize how hard that is for you. That is why I cherish it so much. I do not want to see harm come upon you, but I am not blind to the vengeance that you will want to seek on our brother that chases you from your home."

The old Kaltar stood slowly. The strain of it showed on his face. He paused a moment to caught his breath before speaking.

"I have marked a place out on your map. There will be an expedition to the south in the Human territories of Shouker that will uncover an ancient tomb. Go and join them. Late at night while the others are sleeping take this gem." he produced a large dark red stone. "Place it where you are instructed. Reap the power of the havoc that you let loose on the world. I have no family so I do not care of what you will make of the world."

Snow reached out and took the gem from the fortune teller. As the ruby left the hand of the astrologer he fell to the ground. Snow quickly went over to him. The old Kaltar was dead. He died the moment that Snow had taken the gem as if the gem itself had kept the old cat man alive.

Fear once again tightened its grip on Snow. So many unanswered questions. What did the stargazer mean when he said that he would be instructed? Was his running going to prevent the vision of his death or just postpone it? Snow's thoughts were in a whirlwind of confusion. He quickly started packing. He stopped several times to look in the large ruby that he held tightly in his claw. He thought he could almost see a face in the crystal but he attributed it to his paranoia. By morning, he was several miles north of the town. He had left word with his magus and Shawlls to meet him in the town to the west. A meeting he had no intention of keeping.

Somewhere off in the distance, thunder sounded in a cloudless sky.

IX

Three men stood on a shore looking out across the Sea of Storms. The beach was calm, with only a slight breeze in sharp contrast to the storm which raged only a few miles off shore. None of them knew about the signs which warned of coming troubles in the east, nor would they have been concerned if they knew. They could have easily been mistaken as Travelers, a group of adventurers, as that was how they appeared. They did not enter the Unclaimed Lands to in the search of adventure, but in search of themselves.

All three of them were from the Colonies, but from ages past. Their stories were different but shared one thing in common. They had awoken in a sea cave, with their last memories being of running across a mysterious man with a lantern of blue-colored flame. Leaving the cave, and the silver coffins in which they had been sleeping, they had found a world much different than the one they knew. In the two years since that day, the hardest part that Thorin had to deal with was that history had recorded his death.

Thorin stepped forward to the water's edge, as if to get a better look. Standing nearly six and a half feet, he was by far the largest of the group. He was also their leader, even though they had never discussed it. It was his personality, and training, to take control. In his own age he had been an officer of the Combined Army of the Nations of the New Earth Confederacy, now called the Shadow Empire. He had reported directly to the Dragoon, and had just received word that a rebellion had started when the man with the lantern appeared. It still frustrated Thorin that the rebellion had toppled the Confederacy and he had not been there to do anything about it. Thorin glanced at Cesdakar when the man stepped next to him.

Cesdakar was a strange man who never shared where he was from and was the only one of them that did not show any curiosity about how they came to be where, or when, they were. His skin was a light red and lacked any hair, like that of new born mice. Cesdakar always had the hood of his cloak up and his sunglasses on hiding his huge irises in bright-red eyes. Even in the most overcast days he seemed to be irritated by the light. Only at night did he seem comfortable and would take off his sunglasses. It was his behavior, not his appearance, which seem oddest to Thorin.

Cesdakar did not seem to have the slightest understanding of even the basic social workings which most took for granted. He was polite, maybe overly so, but had a temper which was deadly. Temper was not the right word for it, and that was what seemed oddest to Thorin, Cesdakar simply never got angry. When the group had been surrounded by wild goblins as they first entered the Unclaimed Lands, he had walked directly up to them without even his sword drawn. Even knowing that wild goblins would not listen he tried to reason with them anyway. This in itself would not have been worth noting for it had become apparent that Cesdakar was a holy man of sorts. But when the goblins attacked anyway, Cesdakar drew his sword and fought with a skill which impressed even Thorin. It was always that way, Cesdakar did not shout, did not warn, he just drew his sword and attacked.

Luckily Cesdakar rarely took offense, even for those things which would have had Thorin fighting. Except for theft. Cesdakar had never said where he was from, but where ever it was, theft was punished fiercely. While they had been in Mosk, He had cut off a man's arm at the elbow for trying to cut his purse, a purse that was empty because he had earlier given the little money he had away. When Thorin had asked him about the incident Ceskakar had spoken as if he was quoting something. Those who ask shall receive, those who take shall be punished.

Thorin spoke not really expecting a reply.

"It is going to be a hard crossing."

Before Cesdakar could answer, KuAra yelled from the tree line.

"The storm is magical!"

Cesdakar only nodded but Thorin snorted to bite back a sarcastic comment. KuAra was a wizard of some ability and spoke with a manner which only comes from a formal education and a lifetime of dealing with business. Thorin could barely tolerate the man. Thorin was often irritated by KuAra's constantly hopeless attitude, and he had a hard time not yelling at the man for his way of always stating the obvious as if it was a world altering revelation. Even the meaning of the man's name was irritating, or the way that he always reminded them that it meant Energy of Peace, in the old Imperial language. KuAra had come from the time of the United Colonial Empire, just shortly before the disappearance of the Great Ones.

That was the reason they were standing on the shore watching the storm. KuAra had lived in the city, which was supposed to be an island beyond the storm. The city of Nora had been the capital city of United

Colonial Empire. When they read of the history of the city KuAra had the idea that it may still be intact. Thorin could not deny that his reasoning was sound, so they headed out into the Unclaimed Lands to see for themselves. According to history when the United Colonial Empire had collapsed a renegade army had gathered on shore preparing to ransack the city. On the shore where they now stood. The storm had appeared during their crossing, destroying much of the army, and preventing anyone from reaching the city.

KuAra spoke in a knowing tone which Thorin found most irritating.

"This is a good sign. If the storm is still active that means that no one has reached the city."

Thorin snorted again, but he spoke anyway.

"Or that someone has reached the city and taken control of the storm. We will not know until we get there. So, how are we going to get through the storm?"

Cesdakar chuckled as he spoke.

"With prayers and strong arms to row with."

This made Thorin laugh. Cesdakar thought prayers were the answer to everything, which normally would have bothered Thorin, except every mention of prayer was also accompanied with a practical solution. Thorin was still laughing when he heaved the axe on his shoulders and headed towards trees to start with the boat.

The rest of Tapps' people started coming right after Herman started his task. They filtered in for the rest of the day and into the night. Mostly Kaltars but a few Ogres and Minotaurs marked their numbers. They were ready by the time morning came and Tapps started his plan in motion.

Tapps examined Angga, disguised with a smile, over the breakfast table. She was not beautiful enough to make heads turn but was attractive enough to make him wonder why she had not married. She talked little of her upbringing but it was apparent she was used to servants. She had a tendency to see people only as their function. Yet, there was more to it than that. Tapps looked with the Eyes of Righteousness, letting Elohim show him what he should see. There were wounds on her heart which kept her distant from others. It was the obvious motivation which had led her to the life she now led. Another way she could separate herself from the people around her. Her pain was old and not nearly as bad as many with which he had dealt. He would be able to help her. Whatever reason she picked up the blade for a living was not there anymore. She continued on as a bounty hunter only because she has been doing it so long, she had forgotten that there is more to life.

Tapps had been giving her much thought lately, not only in terms of helping her, but because she looked like someone he once knew. His memory was crystal clear for years. He could tell you what he did, second by second for the past five years. So, whoever she looked like, he must have known a long time ago. Angga noticed Tapps smiling at her and blushed. She excused herself for she had business to attend. Who she reminded Tapps of was at the very edge of his mind but his thoughts were changed by Herman walking in the door. When Herman got close to the table Tapps grabbed the youth by the ear.

"What are you doing here? If anyone places you with me our plans will be ruined."

Herman chuckled. His voice full of sarcasm.

"Don't you worry, father dear. Snow left town in the night and his wizard and lizards followed him west this morning. So far his head knockers have not got a clue of why their boss has left."

The two left the bar together. As they walked down the street, they were confronted by almost all of Snow's thugs. Most carried lead filled clubs but a few had short blades pulled. Only the older Kaltars carried a Hepur anymore. The culture of the hunt was dying. Even though he had never been a part of it, the thought made Tapps sad. There had to be a way to hold on to what the hunt teaches, maybe a festival of some sort. Tapps decided he needed to write Gormec's council about it before he left. Tapps stepped forward with a grim look on his face. His voice was even but in a strong tone.

"Who is in charge here?"

Rrik, the gray-furred Kaltar who had grabbed Herman the night before, had proclaimed himself the leader in Snow's absence. Tapps examined the Kaltar and knew that the man would not listen to reason. It was written on his face. Tapps' fist came up with lightning speed hitting Rrik hard under the chin. Even as large as the gray Kaltar was, the strength of the blow caused him to fly back several feet before landing in a heap of broken flesh. It was a very old trick but it worked. An annoyed look came over Tapps' face. His voice came out in a roar.

"So, who is in charge now?"

No one replied for quite some time. Finally, a fearful brown-furred

Kaltar stepped forward. Fear broke the Kaltar's voice

"I am, now."

Tapps took a good look at the man, his voice filled with the sound of authority.

"I do not wish for a conflict between us. It is pointless for us to fight at this time. Snow left town, leaving you behind to slow me. You are all free to find your own destinies, but if you decide to fight your destiny will end here in your death."

The matter-of-fact way that Tapps said it made all who heard know it was no idle threat. The brown-furred Kaltar thought for a minute, then walked back to the group of villains. They talked it over among themselves. On occasion their voice would raise and then someone would look over at Tapps and they would go back to whispering. Suddenly the brown-furred Kaltar turned his head towards Tapps.

"Were did Snow go?"

Tapps was surprised by the words and slightly stumbled on his words as he spoke.

"He fled to the west."

The group went back to talking. In a little while they started arguing. Tapps was starting to get impatient when they broke into two groups. The brown-furred Kaltar walked up to Tapps with a black-furred one. The black fur was almost as broad of shoulder as Tapps but not nearly as tall. The brown-furred Kaltar spoke with a little less fear in his voice.

"We are simple rogues that do whatever the boss tells us. But self-preservation is more important than any loss of face. The ones that follow me will head west to seek out Snow and..."

The brown-furred Kaltar stopped talking and got a look which showed that he was trying to come up with the right words. Tapps growing impatient again broke off the brown fur's thoughts.

"That will be acceptable you may go your own way. What about you?"

Tapps turned towards the black-furred Kaltar. The black fur spoke in a tone that can only be spoken by those who think they are morally right. Herman thought to himself that he could mimic that tone.

"Snow left us behind to slow you down or to stop you all together. Then that is what Snow will get."

With the words barely out of his mouth, he struck Tapps across the face with his club. The strength of the blow forced Tapps' face to the side. The blow had hurt and it angered Tapps. Like a striking snake, his hand came out and grabbed the black fur by the throat. Tapps' fingers almost touched in the back. Tapps lifted the Kaltar off the ground, anger making spittle come out with his words.

"I have fought the giant wolverines of the Unclaimed Lands. I have wrestled with the great brown kift of the south. I have eaten the hearts of beasts a thousand times fiercer than you. You will neither cause me fear nor be much of a delay to my trip. The time it would take me to kill the lot of you would not allow Snow to get a dozen steps."

Tapps threw the black fur into his group. Herman stepped forward. He had known Tapps long enough to know when he was starting to go into one of those Shortan things. Herman understood them, even though his were much different. He placed his hand on Tapps' arm, he could feel his muscles tense as Tapps popped his claws. Herman hoped his words would be enough to soothe his friend. Herman knew well that to use magic on Tapps would trigger a much different but more violent instinct in him.

"Remember who you are and who you serve. Remember how far you have come from the pits."

The youth's voice brought Tapps back from the fringe of his blood lust. He looked down at Herman. His expression showed gratitude and his voice was gentle.

"Take care of them as you see fit."

Rrik awoke just in time to see Herman raising his hands over his head. The young man's hands started to glow as a dark red energy encompassed his body. Herman rose a few feet in the air. A wind started whipping around him, and within seconds it was pulling up dust around the youth. The particles of dust reacted with his magic and started to explode in showers of sparks. His cloths shifted into a suit that was red like fresh blood. Suddenly the area was filled with a blinding light and loud screams from the Kaltars who confronted them. Seconds later the whole group fell to the ground. Gray strands of smoke raised from their fur. Their breaths were shallow and it would take a close examination to tell whether the lived or not. Herman gently landed on the ground and his cloths changed back to the rags that he wore before. He smiled and gave Tapps a wink. He did not have to make a show of it but like any good slick, he liked to be posh.

Everyone gathered was impressed but for different reasons. The crowd was awed due to the sheer power of the magic. Tapps knew how powerful

Herman was. The boy had on several occasions shown that he could manipulate power far greater than anyone thought possible. But power was one thing, control was always much harder. The spell he had used was called Overload. It created a field around a person which caused the senses to be hyper-acute and at the same time magnifying the stimuli. The target's mind would literally shut down to protect itself. Tapps had enough skill to do the single person version of the spell. Herman had taken out over a score. Tapps had not realized that Herman had learned so much control over his magic while he was in school.

It seemed to Tapps that it was only yesterday that he tracked down Herman. He was the son of Mark and Tapps had his promise to fulfill. Before Tapps had found him, Herman had turned his sister into the skunk with which he traveled. Tapps had asked many of the wizards who he ran across about the spell to change her back but none knew one. Even the wizards at the Keep of Secrets did not know of a spell. There were plenty of spells that could change the shape of people but none of them last very long. Permanent Transforms were only legends from the Time of the Shadow. She was not trapped in the form of a skunk but had actually become a skunk. Tapps had went about teaching Herman control of his magic as the Society of Sword and Spell went about researching a spell to help his sister. Tapps knew only the basics then, only enough to be called a wizard. Herman learned all that Tapps knew within months and had taught himself the rest.

Tapps had arranged teachers but Herman had called them all fools and ended up alienating every one of them. Herman was a Trualja but there was something about Herman that went beyond the label. Like all naturals the ambient magic reacted to his will, but for Herman it was much more like him and the magic were united. The more Herman came to understand himself the more he understood magic. Herman was often at odds with the Society because of that. When he would hear one of the members talk of magic, he would either go into laughter or lecture them. Still, he was always welcomed. He was one of the only a handful of nonmembers who knew the location and had access to the Keep of Secrets. Tapps most likely would have forced Herman to stay at the keep but the truth was that the reason the Society was eager to have Herman there was they wanted to study him. Tapps would not make such a choice for the youth.

As Tapps and Herman walked back towards the inn, Rrik made his way out of town as the rest of townsfolk were locking up the badly hurt Kaltars.

He liked the way things had been going for him with Snow and swore revenge on the large blind Kaltar for his wounded chin and pride.

Just before dark the town started its celebrating in the tavern. When Angga walked in, she quickly scanned the bar and headed towards the table that held Tapps, Herman and Nilkees. She sat at the only empty spot at the table. Tapps smiled at her and spoke causally.

"I see that the princess has returned from whatever would take her away from my side during combat."

Angga looked at Nilkees questionably. He had admitted figuring out who she was but had promised not to say anything about it. He simply shrugged to say that he had kept his word. Angga eyed Tapps for a moment. Tapps realized that she was judging something. He was not sure whether it was something he said or something that may have happened. He just kept smiling. Deciding that he was only playing with her, she answered his question.

"Yes, all went well." She lifted up a blade and sheaf of exceptional beauty and make. "One of the runes had broken out of my blade. I was never able to find a smith who could replace it. The smith here is very skilled and was able to do it in only a few hours" Tapps examined the hilt and scabbard carefully. He nodded at Angga and she tied it back on her side as she continued. "I heard that there was some excitement. What happened?"

Nilkees laughed. His smile was so wide it almost showed teeth. His voice was full of humor.

"Secrets everywhere."

Tapps shook his head. The words meant that his old friend had figured something out but was not going to say what it was. Nilkees was by far the best person who Tapps knew at figuring out and keeping secrets. From the look on Angga's face and the way she held the blade, they both were involved in the secret. Herman broke the mood by starting to tell of the day's events. The youth seemed to enjoy the task immensely. To Tapps' surprise Herman was able to capture the excitement without losing the truth. After the story had finished, they drank, sang and danced until the morning sun could be seen, then Tapps, Angga and Herman headed to the winter camps.

About the time the trio had entered the Fron's winter home Krint had almost caught up with them. She was a couple of dozen miles north of the clansmen's winter home when the magic she had been given no longer pointed towards Tapps. The white water had fallen from the sky yesterday and it took her longer to warm herself on a rock with each passing day. She made her way through the forest careful not to come in contact with any of the two-legged mammals. She had some close calls with them early in the year after she had come out of the thick forest. It had happened when she had entered their above ground pits. The ones who were not running towards her making terrible low-pitched noises and trying to poke her with sharp metal sticks were running away making even worse high-pitched noises.

She rubbed her shoulder where one of those sharp metal sticks had struck her. It was only a scratch but it was a lot more than she was used to getting with her scaly hide. She learned to avoid the mammals. She did not blame them and had been taught to expect such a reaction. They were used to Shawlls but she shared only their shape. Some might mistake her for a plain Shawll because of her snake-like body, but her appearance was much different to those who were familiar with those creatures. Her skin was dark, nearly black and her scales were spiked in the manner of the mountain Shawlls. Her size was twice that of a normal Shawll. She knew that she must look very fierce to the soft-skinned mammals.

She did not know how she was going to find the mammal she was looking for without entering their pits. She was uncomfortable with the Imperial Language the humans used, but she was sure that the mammals must have been able to understand her. None of them seemed willing to talk. All of them either ran away or tried to hurt her. Her pit parent always warned that the two-legged mammals could be dangerous but they had never said how excitable they are.

She shivered from the cold. The temperature was well above a dangerous level, but she was used to her pit parent's cave. She had been in the mammals hunting grounds for nearly two seasons now and she had found no clue on as to where her mammal was or how he could move about so fast. Her pit parent had said that her search for him was the final part of her training. When she was hatched, she was told that they were linked in ShorUn, in spirit and blood. She did not understand it.

What she did understand was it was getting late in the day and the weather was getting colder. If it became much colder, she would have to find a pit in which to hold up for the white-water season. She shivered more from the thought of spending the cold days alone than from the chilly wind that had started up. She had never spent any time alone before this trip. She had never spent a white-water time without the heat of her pit siblings.

Occupied by the thought of spending the winter alone she failed to notice the small black bear until she almost ran into it. The mammals called them bears but she knew it as CorSenShor. She had never seen one before but the pit parent had told her that the CorSenShor were impossible to take as food. It happened during the period the mammals call the Time of Pain. Something in the way in which their bodies use the magic which flows through them prevents them from being harmed. There was only one way to take out a CorSenShor but her pit parents did not tell her the way.

With not enough time to flee, she curled herself, preparing both physically and mentally for the combat and her death that would follow. She allowed herself a few seconds to morn. A tear ran down her chin, not because she would die but because none of her pit would be here to feast on her fallen body. She almost fled when the beast did not attack, but spoke.

"Well, well, I've seen a lot of strange things, living as close to Humans as I do. I sure have, and my mama always said that I would see a lot more but you're the strangest snake I have ever laid my eyes on."

She got light headed, and swayed a little. Regaining enough of herself to speak, the strangeness of it all made her Tradespeak even more broken.

"Youss talss?"

She had not regained enough of her composure to say anything else.

"Of course, I talk. I'm a black kift, or a jour bear, or whatever other silly name the Humans have put on my kind. You're talking, so that makes you a Shawll. I must admit you're the strangest Shawll I have ever seen, not that I have seen that many. The ones I've seen have got two legs but like I said I have not seen very many. My names Grizzly, on account I had a temper when I was young. My mama used to say that I must have grizzly blood running through me. I'm too small to be a grizzly besides my mama always said that if the large kifts were intelligent they would be dangerous. What did..."

"I am seeking my ShorUn." She had not realized that she had spoken until the bear stopped talking and looked at her. Then he started speaking again in the same tone, as if he had never stopped speaking.

"So, you are Shor Un? Why were you walking, well, slithering through my forest?"

It took Krint who the Kift seemed to have named ShorUn, a little while to realize the bear had asked a question. She looked around nervously to see if there was a way she could flee. She wondered if the CorSenShor was angered. She laughed at herself. She was acting like the mammals who chased her out of their pits. Most of the nervousness left her. A little remained and it showed in her voice.

"No, I am UnamKrint. I look for mammal. Have words for my ShorUn, Friend of Shawlls. I need pit to sleep in before white water gets high."

"UnamKrint? Odd name, that it is. ShorUn, hmm? Have words for him? Friend of the Shawlls? Well, can't tell you that I have seen too many humans hanging loose with the reptiles, that's for sure. Like I was saying I don't see to many Shawlls and the ones I see, I don't talk to very often. My mama always said, you do your thing and let the lizards do theirs. White water? You must mean snow." He lifted his snout in the air and inhaled deeply. "There is a storm heading this way. The snow will be over my head. If you promise not to eat me, I will let you stay in my den. Like my mama always said a warm den is better than a honey comb. The den is not as sweet, but it don't come with little bees trying to sting you either."

Grizzly laughed to himself as if he said something funny and started walking off on all fours. He abruptly turned his head towards Krint.

"Well, you coming?" He turned his head and started walking before she had a chance to move. "It's like my mama always said, you can lead a squirrel to the acorns but you can't make him harvest."

Grizzly talked all the way back to the den. Sometimes to himself and other times to Krint. He seemed to enjoy her company and having someone to talk to. He even listened from time to time as long as the Shawll kept it short. She spent the winter months there having fun talking to the bear but she missed the pit and wondered if she would ever find her ShorUn.

X

"We got to go back. We are going to die!"

Thorin could barely hear KuAra's complaining over the roar of the storm. The small boat they had crafted was being violently thrown about, and it was all he could do keep his oar in the water. Between the waves and the wind, they had made little progress since hitting the main of the storm. KuAra's magic was keeping most of the water out of the boat, but the shield was constantly failing due to the strength of magic of the storm, or its wind.

Thorin was irritated, no he was angry. He had not survived countless battles, just to die from drowning. Thorin would not accept that he would die in some meaningless manner. To fuel his anger even more Cesdakar had stopped rowing and, by his posture, had started to pray. Thorin was trying to yell at him over the storm when Cesdakar's voice could be clearly heard.

"Source of All, if it is your will for me to die now then I welcome my entry into the Hope that has been promised. I ask you not to save my life. I ask not even that you save the lives of my companions. I ask only that before we die you will show them your glory so they may come into the blessings of the Unity."

Thorin started to move towards Cesdakar in order to make him stop his silliness and get back to rowing when he lost his balance. He had been thrown to his hands and knees because the boat had suddenly stopped it rocking. Even though the storm still raged in the distance they were centered in an area of calm. Thorin stared at Cesdakar and then at KuAra. KuAra only shrugged. Cesdakar straightened his sunglasses spoke with an expression rare for him, a smile.

"It appears that it is the Will of the Source that we live today. But even when the Source moves so openly, those of the Unity must still do their part."

Thorin did not say anything, but followed Cesdakar's example and returned to his oar. KuAra was still asking questions as he manned the rudder. Cesdakar ignored him in order to give his strength to rowing, and eventually KuAra gave up. It took them hours but they made it to the shore of the island. They had barely finished securing the boat when the storm rushed into the calm path they had gone through. KuAra did not waste time returning to his questioning.

"Will you now please explain what just happened? I noticed no change in the magic."

Cesdakar examined the sky as the two continued watching him. he then turned his attention to the storm still raging around the island. He then examined the area around them and then each of his companions. When he finally spoke, it was in almost a whisper as if he was afraid of waking someone.

"It is the will of the Source we make it to this island, or at least one of us. As we lacked the ability to accomplish that, the Source moved to our benefit.

Thorin weighed Cesdakar's words but KuAra judged more quickly and instantly rejected them.

"A miracle!? You are saying that you performed a miracle? That is just impossible, miracles are impossible!"

Cesdakar nodded his head and responded with patience in is voice, a common trait which both his companions found irritating at times.

"As I understand the meaning, a miracle is when the impossible happens. As nothing is impossible for the Source of All, I can only I agree with you. Miracles are impossible."

Thorin almost laughed at the look on KuAra's face. The wizard actually sounded angry over the Cesdakar's words, and his voice reflected it.

"Do not play word games with me. Are you really trying to say that you performed a miracle, something beyond what is possible with magic?"

Thorin did laugh when Cesdakar's expression became as one expects when a parent is trying to explain something to a child. Cesdakar's voice, however, did not sound condescending as he thought it would.

"No, that is not what I am saying. I am not claiming that I worked a miracle, or even that one was performed through me. The Source acts according to the will of the Source, I am only here to make sure you know it was the Source."

KuAra let up on his questioning of Cesdakar, sure the strange man was some form of wizard. He would spend the next several hours trying to find a magical explanation for what he had seen. Thorin spent only a minute or so examining Cesdakar to make sure the man was serious. Then he shrugged his shoulders and turned his attention to examining what was on the island. He was an old soldier, and had learned to accept what he saw. Thorin did not doubt that it was a miracle. The Dragoon had believed White Bear had performed miracles, most likely saying something similar to what Cesdakar had said.

The Thorin and Cesdakar had headed towards the city that was supposed to be on the island. KuAra eventually followed when he tired of his examination of the storm.

The elders of the Vagofrons agreed to allow Tapps to learn the secrets of the Insanus Unum, and he started his teaching of the youths as soon as he returned to the winter camp. Angga had agreed to help and was eager to teach the young to fight with a blade. Tapps was thankful for the help for he had never even picked up a sword. He had never even learned the use of the Hepur well, the traditional weapon of the Kaltar. It had taken him a long time to learn that aggression was not typically the best option in conflict resolution. When he had to fight, he still preferred his claws. They were longer, harder and sharper than the ones of a typical Kaltar, a product of the genetic experiment he was. Angga wielded her Salk like a master from Eldon and had a natural skill in teaching the young. Of course, it did not hurt that nearly every young male was enamored with her.

Herman did not spend much time with Tapps and Angga. From time to time, he would help Tapps with classes on magic. He spent most of his time with Kilic. Herman and the strange Shawll were inseparable. Tapps was glad that over the winter the two of them became actual friends. Herman desperately needed a friend because of what he was putting himself through. Herman was tired of looking so young and had decided to speed up his aging. Tapps wished that the youth would have spoken with him first. Then, Herman always kept his own council and only looked to others for information. The time of life which he was entering put pressures on a person even when it was spread over years. Tapps could not fathom what was happening to Herman when he was condensing it into a winter. For someone of Herman's natural abilities, the emotional confusion that happens at this age often has adverse effects on those around him. It was more than once Tapps had to lecture Herman on not daydreaming about women in the nude. For a typical boy it would be a normal lesson of growing up, but with the magic at Herman's finger tips when he wondered what a female looked like under her clothes, her clothes usually disappeared. No ward or spell could protect from the level of power which was at Herman's command. The short days of winter passed too quickly and Tapps did not have the time to waste dealing with Herman's incidents.

Just after the first permanent snow Herman had caused a problem once again. This time was much worse for it involved an Insanus Unum. The member of the elite warriors of the clans did not take kindly the walls of her tent disappearing while she was bathing herself. Of course, keeping with the tradition of the Insanus Unum, it was not modesty but just the intrusion that angered her. The story had reached Tapps when one of pupils had informed him at the beginning of class that she had chased Herman for nearly half an hour fully naked throughout the camp. Tapps had had enough. He was about to send for Herman to inform him that he would be going to the Society when his plans were foiled by Herman himself. Herman entered and spoke with a thoughtful expression which looked unnatural on his young face.

"Tapps, I'm going to leave."

Tapps was taken back by Herman's words.

"What? Why?"

"I just have to. . . I . . ." Herman paused. The look on his face appeared as if he was searching for the right words. A problem he never had except when there were no words to express what he meant. He continued, still with an unsure expression and tone. "My magic is becoming very volatile. I should have let you have those stogy old people teach me how to control it before now. It is very much like my thoughts are not my own. I am going to find a secluded place to spend some time."

Tapps recovered from the shock and knew that Herman would do what was best. His voice was warm.

"You could go to the Keep. They know how to train you to get control again."

Herman laughed and then went silent abruptly. He sometimes felt so alone because no one could understand what power was really like. Most True Magi were like apprentices to him, but he had to hide it. When people found out that one so young could wield so much power they would treat him much differently. Tapps had been not been like them. The Kaltar never treated him as anything other than a person needing his help from time to time. Herman knew that Tapps could not help but to be the way he was. Even Tapps forgot Herman's true age from time and time and had to be reminded.

"No, I thought of that. My temper is starting to be too short. They will push me, and no matter what the Society thinks they would not be able to last long if I lose my patience. It will be better for everyone that I go find a cave to spend some time in until I am in control again."

Tapps smiled widely. Herman was remarkable and it would be very interesting to see how he ends up affecting the Colonies. Tapps nodded as he spoke.

"Well, if that is what you want to do, I will not try to stop you. If it is something that you must do, I would encourage it."

Tapps gave Herman a party to make his departure happy and a gold pocket watch with Tapps' and Angga's faces engraved on the inside. It had a little magic to make it run and a little more to make it glow in the dark. Tapps was worried about Herman's decision to leave suddenly but soon forgot about it. Herman was only nine when Tapps had tracked him down after the War Forward. Through the boy's wit and magic he was surviving then. Surviving, was not the right word, he was prospering. In fact, Herman's wealth was beyond counting.

At that time, Tapps would have not given the young man much thought except he had promised Mark to find and look after the boy. He did his best but at times he felt that Herman was taking care of him. He stopped worrying shortly after Herman was out of sight and a student came up and asked him a question, but he could not help but think that he still should be worrying about the young man. There were dark times ahead for the youth, a challenge he would have to face, and face alone. No, not alone, just without Tapps. When not to protect those in our care is often the hardest thing to know.

Tapps spent the next morning a few miles out of camp working his thoughts out by pounding his fist against a tree over and over again. The fight between the tree and Tapps did not stop until the tree fell from the deep gouges which Tapps' fists left in it. His muscles strained when he hefted the tree onto his shoulders. He paused on his slow walk back to the camp to rest and to study the invisible wall of magic which protected the Clans' winter home's location. Tapps felt the power of the wall and wondered how many Herman's it took to raise it. A quick wave of envy flowed through him then it was gone. He was considered a Warrior-Magus by the Society of Sword and Spell, a master of combat in both melee and magic. He barely commanded enough magic to wear the pin. Compared to Herman he was little more than an apprentice. Tapps thought about it until his next class with the young men and women.

Herman looked back at the winter camp. Even hidden by the Dragons' magic he could still see it. Even as powerful as Dragons are, they had nothing compared to what he held back. He leaned against a tree and closed his eyes. He had lied to Tapps. He had not been having trouble with his magic. It was true that he had made some mistakes in the patterns of his spells. He dealt with magic which had no spells. The most famous incident with the Insanus Unum was a flux in the magic of the area. He had been working on selective invisibility with the help of Kilic. He had been attempting to make the camp invisible only to the Shawll. More than a mere illusion, he was trying to make it as if the camp did not exist at all. Where the target would see a tree, they would also feel one. It was difficult to fool two senses let alone all six.

He had accomplished it with singular items but was thinking on a grand scale. Working patterns all morning Herman had managed to finish half the camp. When he sensed the flux-wave coming in the magic he quickly altered his patterns to compensate. He accomplished this at a speed that the best scholars said was impossible. Over a thousand patterns in less than a minute. He had done it without thought, and what he remembered of the working surprised even him. It was as if the magic worked itself. He had discovered something about his own use of magic. There had been a mistake in the part he had consciously worked. A slight alteration he had forgotten to include. The magic fused with the fabrics of the walls and broke down the material when the brunt of the flux-wave hit.

He never liked to admit when he made a mistake in any area, but especially with magic. He was so far beyond anyone else, it often felt that it belongs to him, that it was his. Tapps had taught him the basics of spell patterns, and Herman had expanded it from there. By the time Tapps had arranged teachers, Herman had already gone beyond what could be taught. Even the Dragoon could not teach him for more than a few months. The Dragoon, now there was a man who knew how to wield power. Not with raw force but with subtle nudges. Even though it was clear that Herman would outpace the Dragoon in power, if he had not already, Herman considered the man as his better. The only one in the Colonies. It was not his power which caused the fondness, but that the ancient man truly cared. Those who knew the Dragoon by his various names he went by would think that he was a selfish man. He kept track of nearly everything in the Colonies and was behind some of the most famous incidents. He tore apart the McGovern family in order to get a sword. A sword he then turned over to a peasant. There was not a noble he could not play like a pipe.

Many thought the Dragoon played games with people's lives for mere amusement. Such motivations were alien to the man. He found his joy in his duty and his hobbies. Herman had been amazed that such a busy and powerful man would spend time in such a mundane task as gardening. No magic, no servants, he kept sixteen acres of land by his own hand. The Dragoon spent most of his time weaving plans for the betterment of the Colonies. The time working on his garden was spent on formulating those plans. He preferred the slow growing trees and plants because he said that it reminded him to be patient. His every thought and action were to keep his father's dream alive.

Herman lowered his head. Maybe he should visit the old man. He had no plans of his own and the Dragoon always would find something for him to do. All he knew was that he had to leave, to get away from her. He had a crush on Angga when he had stayed with her. Now it was different. Before it was a child's simple attraction, now it was growing into an obsession. The intensity of it took him by surprise. His world started revolving around her. He lived to be in her presence, to hear her voice, to see her smile. He had hope in the beginning, but he soon realized that she would not come to want him. He felt like a fool for expecting that she, that anyone, could see him as anything but a beast.

Fighting back tears, he would gladly give all his power if it would take away the chaos and the loneliness. There was always pain. Everyone he met had wounds which jumped into his own heart. He had grown accustomed to feeling the pain of others. It was just a matter of realizing that the pain was not his. But it wore him down and when he grew tired the chaos would win. When he succumbed to his own pain, he could not deal with that of others. He did not have the energy and easily became irritated. He would start to hate them for having pain. He would often regret such feelings.

There was no safe place from the pain except in solitude. Tapps used to be a refuge from the world. Before his wives died, his smile could be felt for a mile. Now there was such pain underneath. Even though the Kaltar had long since stopped feeling the pain himself, he had never dealt fully with the loss. He had just learned to ignore it. Herman knew his obsession with Angga was caused by his own loneliness. He was just coming to realize that he had always allowed himself to be driven by his pain of being different. He had used fantasies to sedate the pain but they only made it worse in the end.

Herman's obsession had stripped him of his defenses. He took her wounds as his own and it robbed his strength. When he realized his obsession and the depth in which he was submerged in the chaos, he knew that it was not safe to stay. It was always there, threatening to overtake his well-organized mind and bring the pain with it. A pain which always tempting him to use his magic for…he pushed the thought away. Better to die then to let that happen. Most of the time he floated in pain, was comfortable with it, but there were times that he felt like he was drowning. These were time when he felt like an alien to the world and sometimes even to his own body.

When he was younger, he never understood it. He could not realize what was happening until it broke him and he would lash out. Now he had come to recognize it early and get away from people. He still did not understand what it was or why others did not feel it. He knew it was linked to his power. It was his greatness and his weakness. It was what let him look into the hearts of others, and that was what made him a beast. Anyone that knew him, knew that he could kill them with a thought. Few ever feared him for that. But let them know that he could feel their heart, that he knew the secret pain that hide even from themselves, and they would run in fear.

That was his lot in life, to be feared, hated or awed by anyone who truly knew him. It was the same with those who wanted to teach him. They were just using him in a different way. Teachers who feed on some sort of emotional desire at the expense of their pupils were those who sought him out the most. There are many forms of addiction and Herman found the emotional ones were the hardest to recognize, hardest to rid oneself of, and by far the most devastating.

He knew he was no different. He would not allow anyone in. It was easier to feed his addictions with fantasies. But fantasies being safer than love was only an illusion, for in the end they were far more painful, far more destructive. Herman had read somewhere that the desire for something is what prevents us from acquiring that thing. Was the same true for love? This was at the core of Herman's present distress and he knew it. He knew well what people desired. There were few people that he could not manipulate with ease. There was nothing physical he could not get. But the key to his success was he never cared. Money was only bits of metal. What were all the kingdoms of the Colonies compared to a single friend who cared more for you than themselves? That was why Tapps was so dear to him. The man was very much like a child, simple and trusting. He missed the old Tapps so much. Tears attempted another assault as Herman slumped on the ground.

As if in response to his loneliness, Marlyn wiggled out of his backpack and licked his ear. Scratching her neck, Herman could not hold back the tears anymore. Marlyn had been his greatest crime, making him worthy of any punishment that the world would deal him. She had taken care of him, looked after him. She had worked from before dawn to after dark to make sure that he was safe. She put up with the comments and suggestions regarding her beauty with a smile, just to keep him fed. He was her little brother and, with their parents' dead, it was her duty to look after him. Herman shuddered as the tears increased from the memories. When he was eight a group of rogues moved into the building, they lived in. It did not take him long to become acquainted with them and to find that he could make a lot of money aiding their endeavors. His magic allowed him to acquire enough wealth in only a few months to buy back the sword Marlyn had pawned to feed them during a bad winter. She had instantly known something was wrong and confronted him when she gave it to her. They argued and he lost his temper.

The pain prevented even tears as he relived the moment. His anger had stripped him of reason and before he realized what he was doing he had changed Marlyn into a skunk. He knew instantly what he had done and it had turned his anger into grief. He had spent years trying to change her back. That was the fuel for his desire to learn more, to understand more. If he only knew enough, he could make thing right. The chaos had grown worse, harsher as time passed and he slowly came to realize the truth. He had not changed her shape into a skunk but actually changed her into one. In essence using her life to create the skunk. He had killed the only one in his life who had ever loved him.

He did not attempt to hold back the tears anymore. He let himself sob uncontrollability and the chaos to consume him. An hour, maybe two, passed and it was night before he could regain control of himself. He finally stood and cleaned himself. Anyone seeing him now would say that he was in a good mood. He had learned long ago to always smile. To smile when he was sad, to smile when he was angry, to never stop smiling no matter what he was feeling in his heart. It was what people wanted. It was the first lesson one learns in an acting guild. While a Goblin Player he had seen too many of his fellow actors forgetting who they were. He left when he noticed it starting with him. Herman laughed bitterly. That was the question. Who was he? He had succumbed to the same madness to which the other actors had fallen prey. They called it the role sickness. Life was just a show. He played a part and nothing more, and the part he played was a carefree and joyful youth. Only those who paid attention to his eyes would know that he was not truly smiling. He was not feeling better, only numb. Above all else he was an actor and no one would see anything other than the jocular youth he wanted them to see. He should visit Marius.

Putting on a smile, Herman teleported to the antechamber. It was the only area in the tower that was not protected. Even Herman lacked the power to break the wards preventing traveling. He waited a few minutes. Maybe Marius was gone on business. Herman looked out the window to the garden below. It was nothing compared to the over five hundred acres of the Imperial Garden of KanaTo. Still the beauty of it put all others to shame. It was not the product of a thousand gardeners working to please their master, but the work of a single man to please himself.

Kift treaded carefully through the forest side as the dead grass crunched under his feet. The shadows were thick and death was in the air. He examined a nearby tree. It was dead, as was all the other vegetation of the forest. It was worse than death, it was the complete lack of life. Even the dirt was dead. Darkness engulfed the forest and Kift looked up. The sun was dark and a shadow covered the land. The shadow reached down from the sky, grabbing people and animals alike. Eating some, twisting others so they would serve some evil deed. It grew larger and darker with each death and seemed unstoppable. If it was not conquered, it would not stop until the whole world was consumed. He tried to get a look at the great shadow, but his eyes could not take it all in. All he could make out was a darker part in the middle of the darkness.

Suddenly Kift found himself in a peaceful meadow at the edge of a crater. It was late spring and the song birds were in full voice. A young deer started to run as the ground erupted around it. A huge wolf made of shadows pulled itself out of the crater. Broken chains still clung to the shackles around the wolf's legs. The wolf tore the meadow apart, killing everything in its path but eating none of it. The world turned dark and Kift knew that the beast would destroy the entire earth with no regard to what it devoured. He frantically ran, searching for who released the wolf. They would know how to put it back. Wherever he ran there was nothing but destruction. He stopped as he spotted the wolf again. The wolf turned towards him and smiled.

Kift looked down at his hands. In them was a large key. The key he had used to unleash the beast on the earth. He would not believe it. Throwing himself on the ground he hid his face in denial.

He opened his eyes slowly, knowing it was only a dream. The dream was the same as it was yesterday and the day before. The dream was always the same. He spent the whole winter haunted by the nightmare.

After leaving the guild, Snow traveled to the north throughout the night and most of the next day before he entered the next town. Ignoring the innkeeper's questions, he got a room for the night. He had slept only a few hours before he awoke in a sweat. Bad dreams of Tapps handing his heart to a shadowy figure kept him from sleeping again. It was a little after midnight when he packed his things and headed east under the cover of darkness of a night without a moon. It was an omen, but the meaning of it escaped him. He headed west until he reached the center of the Confederacy and headed south.

Snow had taken plenty of money and his papers showing he was a merchant so travel through Mosk was unhindered. KanaTo was a different story. The border guards were too well trained not to notice a merchant traveling alone and without goods for sale. His papers showed that he worked for the House Slar, but they were outdated. Luckily Snow carried no weapons so they had no real reason to detain him beyond the few hours of questioning. All of the other towns were the same except for Telpep. The Telpep guards actually expected him to stay until his papers were verified. In his stay he learned the reason for their mistrust. The House Slar had been banned from doing business in Telpep. It was not hard for Snow to find out the reason. The House had sold a shipment of hand forged swords to the army which turned out to be mold poured. The swords had never made it to the front as the first officer to see one could tell the difference. The quartermaster lost his position and the House Slar while admitting the salesperson was an agent of theirs but denied liability for the misrepresentation. The Duke suspended the House's franchise license in the province until the matter was settled. Even though Snow cursed the inconvenience he felt lucky that the Slar chapterhouse was closed.

Snow waited in the city just long enough that the guards would not be paying as much attention to him. By the time the letter came saying that he was no longer with the House, he had already been gone two days. He traveled to the Shouker sleeping in the coach. In case they were searching for him he did not want to waste the time staying the night at inns.

The trip through Shouker was miserable. There was no coach service, even the wealthy was expected to travel by foot. He was a bit surprised to find that the peasants freely offered rides in their carts. If he was walking and a cart passed him by without offering a ride, it was because there was no room in the cart. Snow was unsure what to make of it. Still, he cursed the nation for not having a coach system. Even with the rides he did not reach his target destination until spring was in full bloom.

"Two more of our teams have been killed. All indication is that it is the Black Glove."

Silver's eyes widened at the news. His voice showed the stress he had been under.

"The Glove? They are silent killers. Why would they be attacking us?"

Mike gently rubbed his temples before answering. They had discussed the subject at least a dozen times.

"We have had reports that they are expanding into other areas besides assassination. They merged with the Golden Clan guild and have been squeezing everyone else for the past two years. They already control the Imperial Sector and are now starting to move into High Town."

Silver threw his hands up. His eyes hurt and it was becoming harder to think. This was Tapps doing somehow. His guild members had been unruly. He would not be surprised if half of them were Greenwoods working for the Black Glove. Mike was the only one he trusted. Silver looked up. Mike had said something else. He was about to ask about it when a thug busted in.

"We are being raided.

As Silver stood hastily, throwing back his chair. Mike spoke calmly.

"Where and by who?"

The strong-arm voice was hard and hurried.

"Here, but they wear no colors."

Silver's eyes were wide in disbelief. Mike jumped up and went into action. Turning to the strong-arm his voice was clear.

"Get the rest of the guard and block off the catacombs. Make sure you hold it for at least five minutes. After that do what you can to get away." He turned to Silver as the thug left. "You will be their primary target. We must get you to safety.

Silver shrugged.

"What's the use? All is lost. Tapps has won."

Mike grabbed Silver by the arm pulling him along like a child. In just a few minutes they were out of the building and within an hour Mike had Silver in a safe house. Mike finally relaxed. He had personally bought half a dozen safe houses and had not shared their location even with Silver.

The guild master had been on a slow decline since the Kaltar had come to town, slipping further into an extreme paranoia. Mike had never known Silver to fear anyone, but this Tapps was different. Having met the cat man Mike knew there was reason to fear. Yet, this was not a rival. In fact, Tapps gave no indication that he even cared what was going on with Silver. There was a history between them that the master rogue would not talk about. What dealings Silver could have with the Hero of the War Forward were beyond Mike's understanding.

Mike spent the next day gathering information. All six of their hubs, including the safe houses and fronts, had been raided at the same time. Some by the city guards but most of them by rogues not wearing any colors of a guild. The Silver Guild was no more. Only a handful of rogues who were still faithful survived. Mike sent them a letter to make their own way. Luckily Mike had never let his face be known. He had always worked hard so those who knew his face did not know his power and those who knew his title had never met him. Only five, besides Silver, knew both his face and rank. All of the others were dead. He had been born and raised in the guild. Only a little over twenty, he was a better rogue than most twice his age. He had no problem getting a job as an orphan, many times working for the Black Glove. The cut as a freelance was not as good, but it would let him and Silver survive until the guild master got on his feet.

Ukkert pushed herself into a large crack in the wall of the cavern. Letting the coolness of the rock drain the heat out of her body, she waited. The Cold Sleep was like dying, as if life itself was draining from her. She had long since mastered the anxiety that often accompanied it. Only the young had problems entering the Cold Sleep. Closing her eyes, she did not notice the hours and then days go by. She was a Shorlin, the Blood Guards, Protectors of the Deep Ground. In the hibernation-trance her thoughts mixed with the rest of her people. She was one with all the other guard parties in the Cold Sleep. Their spirits united together to worship the Source and protect her people from nonphysical attacks

The physical attacks all came at once. Anger and pain came from the linked spirits when the Goblons attacked in the west, Rorwi in the north and Ares in the south. She did not have time to register all of the attacks when her eyes suddenly opened. The sounds of the advancing Gremits reached her ears. The bond shifted to only her guard party. As scores of Gremits charged through the cavern, she dropped from her hiding place. It would take minutes before her body warmed enough for the Gremits to see her. It would be the same for the few dozen of her kin. It did not matter. The Gremits would press the attack to the last of their number. She attacked with the ferocity for which her people were known in the Deep Ground. The small furred bodies of the Gremits did not stand a chance against her sharp claws.

Yet, the rat-like creatures had claws of their own and sharp teeth which could penetrate the rocky hide of the Shawlins. No more than a foot tall, the Gremits were able to tear large chunks out of her flesh. Ukkert avoided as many as she could but she could not avoid them all. Hour after hour the Gremits came. Hour after hour her and her party fought on. Eventually the wounds started to take their toll. One of the party dropped. Then another. Two more. After ten hours of combat the last of the Gremits and sixteen of the forward eastern guard were dead. The price was heavy but only a few hundred of the Gremits made it through and they were easily taken care of by the middle eastern guard.

Ukkert dropped to her knees. There was not a part of her body that was not gouged, ripped or sliced. She was tempted to let herself dissolve and join the Unity. Her mate was dead. Her brood was dead. The pain of her people overwhelmed her. She felt herself slipping away. The Blessed Hope of the Unity was calling her.

No! She broke her connection with the link. She still had her duty. She did not wait for someone to come and help her up before she stood. The other races of the Deep Ground fought too much among themselves to join forces like this. All of them attacking at once could not be accidental. The Dark One was preparing something on the surface. That was something with which the light dwellers had to deal. She gave it no more thought as she found the fungi that would help her wounds. After applying the quickly made salve on her wounds, she examined the battle scene. Ukkert ignored the scavengers that always came to feast after a battle. She would not harass them, all Shawllin knew that without out them there could be no life in the Deep Ground. She did grab a few for a meal before crawling up to her hiding place. Slipping into the hibernation-trance, she knew only that as long as one life was still in the link, the evils of the Deep Ground would not plague the nights of those on the surface.

XI

The winter passed slowly for Krint. Even with the company of Grizzly she missed her own pit and the brood with which she was raised. She had never been told why the ancient had chosen to raise her, she had never asked. When the snow was its thickest, an Ogre showed up. Slowed by the cold, UnamKrint was barely able to keep her head from being split apart by the large mace that the surprised Ogre carried. It turned out that the Ogre's name was Ampkel, and he was a friend of grizzly. He was a priest of sorts. The belief of his people was that most the evil which affected the earth was a physical force which could be fought with sword and shield. Of course, the best way to serve Elohim was to rout out this evil and crush its skull. His sect was located just north of Eldon in the Confederacy of Dukedoms. He had known Grizzly for most of his life and they were close friends.

Ampkel had never seen a Shawll before and had to admit in his apology to Krint that he had freaked when he saw her. They became good friends on his many trips to Grizzly's cave and by the end of winter he had agreed to come with her and help her on her quest. Grizzly had to put his voice in to tell everyone that he had decided to come along too.

"My mama always said that it is better to be able to tell your part of something exciting than having to listen to an Ogre tell you a boring tale. At least that's what my mama always said."

He threw in the last when he noticed Ampkel raise an eyebrow to the Ogre part. Ampkel was a High Ogre. The High Ogres were a family of Ogres and Minotaurs who kept the traditions of their culture. The family was the best educated in Gormec and were well trained in the science of magic. His family was returning to Gormec and Ampkel decided to go adventuring. Krint had never seen the magic of the mammals before and was amazed at what he could do. Krint decided that Ampkel was a noble man, even if he claimed that he had no other choice. The families of the High Ogres were very strict on keeping with the honors of the people, the Peace of Gor as they called it. The large mace he carried was a family artifact that was said to have been made just before the fall of the United Colonial Empire. Ampkel wore the mace since his youth and it seemed natural for him. Whether it was on his hip or in his hand, it was as if the mace was a part of his body.

All three of them left the cave a week after last thaw. They headed east to the sea coast to charter a ship to KanaTo were Ampkel had a friend who may be able to help. On their way they came across a tree stump that had been created by some unnatural means. Grizzly walked up to the stump and examined it. He took only a short time before he spoke.

"It has been done by someone of great strength, see how deep the gouges are? Interesting. It was downed with small blades and clubs." Grizzly sniffed the ground and then the air. It smells like a Kaltar, even though it is odd to find one this far south. Even odder to see one destroy something that could not fight back. The way I see it is that this thing is mad, out of its mind, that is. We have nothing to worry about though, this happened some time ago. Let's carry on our way to the coast. It's like my mama always said if you go looking for trouble your bound to end up in a hunter pit you can't get out of."

They continued on their trip with Ampkel wondering more and more why he let Grizzly come on the trip. Krint was wondering more and more if she would ever figure out mammals.

As the first thaw of spring started its work of filling Broken Wing Lake, Kift decided to visit his brother. He was not sure if Matthew could help with the nightmares, but it was a good place to start. Grabbing his pack, he headed towards the town. He had the nightmare once more on the three-day trip, but he mostly the nights were without dreams.

Kift arrived the morning of the Sabbath. He waited outside for the sermon to finish. He had always put his trust in Elohim but felt out of place in church. At times he was sure that the people, in their best cloths, stared at him in his furs and leathers. He knew that it was not so, but that did not stop the self-consciousness.

People started pouring out of the church to signal the end of the sermon. A Kaltar caught Kift's eye. It was strange enough to see a Kaltar this far south, let alone one with a fur color as rare as white. With his preoccupation with the white-furred Kaltar it took him awhile to realize that there were more people than usual. It took longer for them all to leave, but they finally did and he entered.

He prayed at the alter for a short time then dropped a few coins in the offering box. He had made sure he had brought money this time. The winter had been hard on his legs without his best gaiters. He found his cousin's study. The priest would always go to study after Mass to work on the next week's sermon. Mathew's inspiration came when he spoke. He would be taking notes on the items he did not have time to go into today. Kift paused at the door, and then knocked. He waited for a reply before entering. Kift saw that his brother was still wearing the ceremonial robes. Matthew started to speak before he looked up.

"What can I do for...Kift! How are you? I was not expecting to see you for a couple of more weeks. What brings you out of the mountains so soon? You find another artifact?"

"No, nothing like that. My sleep this winter was plagued with nightmares and it has me baffled as to the meaning of them all."

Matthew thought for a moment before speaking.

"I am not very good with dreams. The Sanhedrin does not like us dealing with dream-readers and I do not have many books on the subject." Mathew paused and smiled warmly at his brother before continuing. "Those who are recognized researchers of dreams agree that most of them come from a troubled mind. But Kift, you have always been sensitive to spiritual things. You have become even more so since you moved to the forest. There is a point to these dreams. I am sure of it. Tell me about them and I may be able to help."

Kift sat down and told his brother of his dream. He finished with a change to his last dream.

"The scenery changes and I am standing on the walls of a city on top of a huge mountain. The wolf brings death to the humans even more ferocious than to the animals. I can see the sea many miles away. Nothing lives in the land. It is worse than the Great Desert for it holds no life. The wolf destroyed it all.

"I turn to see the inland and it is the same. The wolf is behind me, smiling. Instead of the shackles he wears a collar with large chains coming from it. It looked as if the beast was chained to some large wall to prevent him from doing what he did. The end of the long chain still held the lock which had bound him. I drop to my knees as I know that I was the one who had turned the key to open the lock. The key was in my hand. I ran to throw myself off the mountain but I always wake before I can get to the cliff's edge."

The priest gave a thoughtful look before speaking.

"How well did you pay attention in ancient history class?"

Kift laughed. That was a loaded question to which his cousin already knew the answer. Kift had never gotten less than an honor for a grade but rarely remembered much of the material that did not interest him.

"Not much, enough to pass the class, of course."

The priest smiled. He had forgotten for a moment what his cousin was like in school.

"During the last decades of the Shadow Empire, the Cult of Blood was just beginning. They had a much different beliefs than what developed from the Rule of the Giants. Among these beliefs was what was called the Shadow World. This was their name for the Second Heaven, or what some writings call the spiritual realm. It was said that the Cult was able to summon creatures from this realm. In truth they practiced a dark art which tried to physically manifest unclean spirits. Most who perform BablayoCiferian rituals do nothing but waist time. The few who actually managed to accomplish something usually only manage to have their person taken over by the creatures they try to summon. It was said that through an evil pact, the leader of the Cult of Blood was immune from such possession, and it is believed that modern Summoners try to form the same pact. Unfortunately for them, the pact which kept the leader of the Cult of Blood from losing his sanity, or even if he was able to stay sane is unknown to them."

"What does all this have to do with my dreams?"

Kift was getting impatient. The priest only smiled as he continued.

"Be patient brother, I am getting to that. Not a lot is known about the founder of the Dark Church and the Cult of Blood, but it is a common belief is it was the Shadow. What happened before the Time of Pain is up to debate among us mere scholars as there are not clear records which survived. The early writings paint a picture of the Shadow as a hero but by the time he was overthrown he is made out to be a tyrant. Either way, at the time of his imprisonment we see information starting to indicate that the Shadow was behind the cult. It is common belief in Shouker's schools that this was done to create acceptance of the Dark Church. Most reject the idea, but those who hold to it frequently point out that the Shadow and the leader of the Cult of Blood disappeared at the same time. It is possible that the prison that is keeping the Shadow is weakening and the unclean forces are preparing themselves."

Kift felt like this was getting nowhere so he made his question more to the point.

"Why me? Why my dreams."

Brother Mathew smiled warmly as he spoke.

"You have often voiced your envy on how I deal with people. But truthfully David, I have always envied you for how sensitive you are to the world around us. The way you feel an area in your heart is a Gift which is rare and precious. It is why you have such a hard time in cities.

"If something is about to happen in the Colonies you would know of it long before me. I have long told you that you needed to find yourself a master. Now, you have no choice. I have been waiting for the right time to give you something. It will help you immensely." Matthew took out an old book and a bundle of loose papers and handed them to his cousin. "This is a copy of the journal of Amic Redwolf and my notes on the subject. He writes of one who keeps records from the beginning of time. He writes as if she is the greatest mind in the world. His opinion cannot be fully trusted for it is apparent that he loved her, but if only a tenth of what he says is true then she would be the one to guide you."

Kift laughed as he spoke.

"Amic Redwolf? How does this help? That was over two hundred years ago. Even a True Magus would not have survived."

Matthew face became grim. He closed his eyes for a few moments before answering. Kift knew that his brother was praying.

"She is not a magus, but a Dragon. I know it will be a risk to intrude on one such as her, but she is the one who you need. I tell you not only as your brother but as your priest. This is the path that Elohim has set for you. You must prepare your part in the future and there is no other who can help you."

They both left the church together. They would have spent more time talking with each other but Mathew needed to make a call on one of the eastern villages in his care. With a hug the two said their goodbyes and Kift headed to his hogan and then where he had found the brazier. After a day and a half, he found that there was a camp at the bottom of the cliff. The eagles that had once dotted the cliff with their nests had all been killed or run off.

A tear ran down Kift's cheek, he never meant for it to come to this. He watched men going up and down ladders that they had put up to get to the cave. He watched for hours and rage filled his heart. He did not notice the slight sprinkle or the cold breeze that blew through the valley. For a long time, he knew nothing but the hatred he felt for what he had done. It was not until sundown that he came out of his thoughts. Even with the setting sun the men who worked the cliff side did not stop. Kift had enough of the watching. He turned and walked away. The tears which filled his eyes had made it impossible for him to notice the white-furred Kaltar walking out of a tent. There was enough of a moon that he was able to all night to get rid of his feelings.

Snow had followed the advice of his truth-seer. He had volunteered to take the night shift in the beginning and was about to give up on the whole thing. Every night he spent time in the cave alone. Night after night nothing happened. It was all becoming very frustrating. He did not think it was fitting for him to be doing manual labor. Snow thought such work was beneath him.

After he forced himself to eat some of the cooked meats, he started his shift. The night's talk was that they had uncovered a mirror in the cave. It had been completely encased in the void crystals. The find was greater than that of the brazier, for by all indications it was the Mirror of Knowledge. A magical device which was supposed to have been created and used by the Shadow in the ruling of his empire. The writing on the mirror was the same as the brazier. In the dim torch light, he made his way to the large chamber that held the brazier. He examined the mirror. Spots of the mirror were tarnished nearly to dust. The areas that were not tarnished did more than just reflect light, it seemed to magnify it. It was framed in steel, which even with its apparent magic was layered in rust when it was found. Some of the night crew had spent the first half of the shift restoring it. The carvings were the ancient language in the ancient alphabet. He ran on of his talons over the writings wondering how they etched them so to deep. He read the inscriptions.

'W.T.H. – for blood and wealth with the. . .'

Snow stopped. He was not proficient the ancient tongue, he did not even know what the letters were. It made sense to him all the same. It must have been that he had only been able to overhear some of what the writings meant. It must have been the magic. After recovering from his shock, he started reading again.

'W.T.H. – for blood and wealth. With the wealth carved by the forces of the dark fire and life of one who desires only the will of Elohim, the one imprisoned is free.' There was a part worn away. 'By blood and gems for life and power the other is saved.'

He did not understand what it meant but he was sure that he had to place the gem in the brazier. Going about his work as usual, he waited until all of his coworkers had broke for the late-night meal.

After making sure that all had left the chamber, he took the huge gem the astrologer had given him and placed it in the brazier. Nothing happened for what seemed like hours but could only be a few minutes. It would not be much longer before the meal break was over. He was about to give up when a booming voice came out of nowhere and drowned out all other sounds.

"Quickly now, set the pattern and set the herbs ablaze."

Snow turned on his heals, nearly falling over. The voice came from the mirror. A glowing face appeared in the mirror. The face moved radically over the surface of the mirror as it spoke.

"Quickly, set the herbs aflame and set the patterns."

Snow's head spun. He could make no sense out of what was going on.

"What pattern?"

The white glow of the face turned a dark red and its voice raised.

"Just set the fire. I'll do the rest. Do it now!"

The force of the face's words was so strong that before Snow realized he was moving, he had grabbed a torch from the wall. He paused before placing the torch in the brazier. He turned his head to ask the face what he will get in return, but the fire in the face's eyes made him think differently. As he touched the flame to the herbs, he closed his eyes to rid himself of the image of the face.

A lightless Fire blazed up in a column engulfing the ceiling of the cave. Snow covered his face with his arms to protect it from the heat and dropped to his knees. He heard the mirror shatter behind him. The ground began to shake violently. The noise, heat and tremors seemed to last forever. After it stopped, it took a few moments for Snow to realize that it all had ended. His ears still rung while he looked up.

Standing in front of Snow was a tall and slender man. The man's skin was as white as Snow's fur. His long flowing red hair seemed to disappear in his cloak made of a dark fire. The man looked down on Snow and his voice was full of sweetness.

"You have done well. You have sacrificed your life to release me and for this you will gain the power of," the man looked around as if searching for something. He continued with a sinister smile, "the Shadow. The blood you sacrificed will forever bond you to that power and the wealth makes our fate as one. Rise for it is not fitting for the future ruler of the New Earth to be on his knees. Soon we will both rise to be rulers of the land. You as its king and me as its high priest. It will take a short time for you to get to full strength, but I will weave some protective wards around us. The Faithful will be here soon and we must prepare for them. If you but trust in me, I will help you realize the greatness inside yourself."

Snow was lost in it all. It seemed like a dream to him. The haze did not lift when they floated down from the cave to the camp below. It did not lift when the man offered an ultimatum. Join the forces of the returned Shadow or die. The battle that followed was short and Snow broke out of his trance to find the mangled body of a human in his arms. He only vaguely remembered the power flowing through his body. The disgust that Snow felt was overwhelmed by the pleasure of the life ebbing out of his victims. It was like a powerful drug and he wanted more. Before his mind had caught up with his body he had reached out and grabbed another human. With a mere twist of his wrist the man's neck broke. When he had dropped that body he looked towards the man he had freed. The man was standing to the side watching. He looked at Snow and smiled. Someone or something whispered in Snow's ears.

"Sanguis vigor."

The words excited Snow's mind. He knew neither the language nor who had said the words, but the meaning of it was clear. Blood is the life. Snow realized that he should be afraid, but the pleasure which flowed through him was too great. All he could do was throw his head back and laugh. He knew that his soul was damned but the greatness of his desire for power pushed the care for such things out of his head. He knew that the man he had released was the essence of chaos, a son of disobedience, possibly even the Abomination of Desolation. Snow did not know what that meant, or even if the thoughts were his own, but the greatness he felt coursing through his body made him only want more.

As Snow walked over to the man, he realized the sun was coming up. The man raised his hand in front of his face to block the sunlight. The tone of his voice was philosophical.

"How long has it been since these eyes of mine have seen the sun? When you have learned to live the Darkness even a little light is painful." He turned towards Snow. "Remember what I have just said. It is the secret to keeping our power. You may call me Divinus. Come my lord, we have power to gather."

They headed towards a small town that was not too far from camp. The strange man spoke mostly on the nature of power along the way.

A few minutes later a man crawled out of the cave with shaky hands. When he reached the bottom of the ladder he looked around with a blank stare. He seemed not to notice, or at least did not care about, the carnage around him. The man crossed himself. He did not know why it just seemed to be a reflex. Slowly a look of mild surprise came to his face. He could not remember anything before the embers in the big bowl. Not his name, not even where he was from. He shivered as a late season snow started to fall. Not knowing where he went, or why, he started walking. Not down the path but to the west into the woods.

Somewhere off in the distance, lighting crackled through a cloudless sky.

XII

It had been a hard day of training. Tapps was about to call it a night and head off to sleep when he was surprised by Angga asking a question.

"Tapps, how did your mate die?"

Tapps turned away long enough for Angga to regret asking the question. He finally turned and spoke with a smile on his face that did not touch his eyes.

"About a decade after the War Forward, nearly eight years ago, the fight between the Magi For Magi and Clans was at an intense stage. My duties to the Society had brought me into conflict with the Vampires of Mosk. Between the two, I was spending most of my time away from home. At the time I was tracking down a renegade. A Vagofron who was planning on helping the Magi for Magi destroy the Clans. The Frons have foiled several of their plans in the past and the Magi for Magi's would love to see the end of us. The renegade did not know that I was after her, or so I thought. I followed her trail for days and soon I realized that she was heading back towards the winter home. She was very close to my family. If the truth be known, she was the mate of one of my dearest friends. I do not blame her. The Insanus Unum close off their spirit so it cannot be manipulated. This prevents them from connecting with people, so on occasion they just snap. To make matters worse, we had had our differences when I first came to the Clans.

"She was one step ahead of me. I went through her possessions and figured out where she would be striking. I went with all my speed to my estate in Gormec, but I was too late. Both of my wives were already dead..."

"Both?"

Tapps sighed before speaking.

"Yes, both. I was a different Kaltar back then. I knew only take and nothing more. Do not mistake my words. I loved them both but I have come to understand why most cultures have taboos against multiple mates. The lack of cultural rules help the Vagofrons accomplish what they need to get done, but there are always problems that arise when social conventions are slacked.

"On the way back, I was ambushed. The renegade thought she could take me. Whoever was pulling the strings was greater than any of us. At the sight of her, and the vampires with her I just snapped. I lost all my reason with the death of my wives and I struck with everything I had. They did not stand a chance against my fury. I still do not know who was really behind the attacks, but whoever they are they won the battle."

"I was so devastated by my wives' death that I was practically useless for over a year. They were not warriors or wizards. They were ordinary women who had no power except for that they held my heart. I loved them with all my soul. They had loved me and taught me how to love. They taught me there was more to life than the thrill of the kill and I learned to be careful when I must. Most of all, they taught me that it was alright to be human."

Angga had already heard the rumors but wanted to know the truth.

"You sound as if your wives were human."

Tapps smiled sweetly. How long had it been since he had talked of them?

"They were. I was raised by humans and many of my tastes run parallel to theirs. In my younger years I longed to get back to my animal side, to get back what humans had taken from me. I went into the Deo Vicis."

Angga interrupted Tapps with a look of surprise on her face.

"The Dying Land? I thought it was only a legend."

Tapps chuckled.

"Most of my life has been a legend, but the testing ground is real. I went there to find myself but I stayed too long. When I finally walked out of that cursed jungle I was more animal than Kaltar. If it was not for the Shawlls, I probably still would be not much more than an animal. They taught me the true meaning of nobility. My wives taught me to love, but if it was not for a feathery winged man named Ankka I probably never would have learned to truly care about others."

Angga stumbled back as if Tapps had reached out and slashed her with one of his claws. Her voice quivered when she spoke.

"What happened to Ankka Del Sella!?"

It hit Tapps like a Finger Lightning spell. He finally figured who Angga looked like. He dropped to one knee and took Angga's hands in his. He gave a sorrowful smile when he looked up at her face.

"You are his younger sister. I do not know why I did not think of it earlier. He talked so much of you. Do not try to deny it. You're Sella, are you not?"

Angga looked around to make sure that no one was close enough to hear Tapps' words. Her face red with either anger or embarrassment, Tapps could not figure out which. The corner of her mouth twitched when she spoke.

"Yes I am, now tell me what happened to my brother."

Tapps hesitated. Angga looked so fragile to him right then. He did not want to hurt her, but he knew it would be worse to lie.

"He is dead. It was at the end of the War Forward. We had just fought the battle that drove the Tecmen back into the sea. Apparently I was marked for death. For one of their shadow hawks came for me. The large black bird that was more metal than hawk came from the sky. I did not see it until it was nearly on me and it was too late for me to do anything. Ankka saw it and acted fast. He flew from the sky behind the bird and grabbed it just as it was getting ready to strike me.

"The shadow hawk dug its poisoned claws into him. Ankka hung onto the bird with all his strength until they had flown over the ocean. It was a beautiful sight in a morbid kind of way. The white wings of Ankka fighting the near translucent black wings of the shadow hawk. It looked as the sky held the fight of heaven and hell. An Unclean and a Messenger locked in mortal combat. They both plunged into the sea. I have no great love of getting wet, but I ran after them and jumped into the water. I had pulled Ankka out. His wounds were not bad but the poison had already worked its way into his blood. His arms were already turning the black that shows the victim of a shadow hawk. I could do nothing for him seek vengeance by destroying his attackers."

Angga had kept herself from crying until she looked at Tapps' face. She knew he was locked in the memory of that moment. Long streams of tears ran down his check. Angga Sella put her arm around him. It was easier to comfort Tapps than let herself feel the grief.

Keith walked up and abruptly stopped at the sight. He turned to leave, but Tapps' voice made him pause.

"Keith, you need to speak with me?"

Keith spoke without turning.

"It is not important. It can wait."

Tapps said something else but Keith did not listen. His thoughts were only on getting away. He managed to hold back the tears until he had gotten to his tent. He felt like such a fool. He was just the son of a poor priest and a warrior who had lost her name. What hope did he have that one as wonderful as Angga could want him? He had never known a woman like her. The way they talked the world seemed to melt away around him. There were moments when he looked into her eyes that time itself seemed to stop and her beauty was all there was. As he started the mental exercise his mother taught him to harden the heart, a last wave of self-pity rippled through him. Every free male of mating age in camp wanted her. He had been a fool to think that a man like him could win her heart. She was a hero, and it was only fitting her love would belong to another hero, and he knew he was no hero.

The wind whipped the banner around with a fury. Duke Duran laughed. He was almost to the city which marked the center of Duke Marks's territory. His retinue was large, consisting of a full contingency of warriors. They were not needed, as the two dukes had been friends since they were Lieutenants together during the War Forward. Even so, people wanted a show when the lords traveled, so Duran obliged.

They entered the castle with his team. It was nearly twice the size of his but he held no grudge to his old friend for prospering. That was the reason for the meeting. With the death of Prince Markus the Confederacy was starting to fall apart. Prince Markus left no heirs and some of the dukes were starting to withhold their taxes to the Confederacy. Both Mark and Duran felt that a Council of Dukes would be the only path to prevent a civil war. He had no doubt that the council would work. The dukedom of Mark was by far the richest and largest in the Confederacy of the Northern Nations and his own held most of the military might. With a partnership between the two, the other dukes would have little choice but to keep the peace.

Duke Duran slid off his horse when Duke Mark appeared in the courtyard. His left leg slipped slightly on the rock ground. He had lost his real leg during that last fight of the War Forward. In the twenty years since then he had become accustom to the prosthetic limb. Tapps had given him a magical leg which allowed him a greater movement than the wood one he had used for years, but still not nearly as much as the one of flesh and bone. Almost everyone knew of his injury but no one ever brought it up. No one except Duke Mark. Then again, Mark had the left side of his face crushed in the war. Mark truly did not care about his appearance, and would be the first to admit that it was true except when it came to romance. Duran grudgingly have to admit that he was still a bit self-conscious about his missing leg although he had always thought himself as not being the type that would have been bothered by such a thing. Grabbing his cane, he walked over to his old friend and they hugged. Mark was the first to talk.

"It is good to see you again. I hope that Elohim has blessed your family with good health."

Duran laughed before answering.

"More than we deserve, that is for sure. My eldest has joined the military and she is doing very well. Even though she is growing into a great leader she still shows no interest in my dukedom as a whole. My second is quickly growing to be a great administrator. He will most likely be my heir. What about you? Still, living the bachelor life or has some pretty thing caught your eye? Knowing you, she would have to be a warrior to match your own skills."

Mark bellowed in laughter but unconsciously touched his face.

"No, no I have been too busy of late to think of anyone other than what use they can be put to. Maybe once we return peace to the land, I will have time to look. But, come, you must be hungry and tired. I have prepared a light meal and your beds. After then we can have our ideas put on paper."

"I will gladly take the meal but I am eager to get on with this. We must act as quickly as possible."

Mark bowed slightly as he spoke.

"I am yours to command."

The two talked as they walked. Mark had been a lieutenant under Duran in the War Forward. They were both cousins of nobles. They had been eager officers back then, fed on the romance and glory of war. They had earned their own nobility with their victory. Mark was as natural a leader as Duran but was younger. Duran and Mark were two of three close friends when they fought under the Panther Banner. When they joined the Panthers, Duran broke the force in two and had each of them take command of a half. William had not survived.

The two entered Mark's office and he gave the order to have the meal sent up. By the time it arrived they were deep in conversation on what would be the best way to save the Confederacy.

A man, who no longer looked like he belonged in the world of humans, laughed as he pulled on his cloak. He was Death Gate, a high priest of the Cult of Blood or at least he was when there was a Dark Church. For the first few centuries after the banishment of his masters he had started several cults. Every time some cursed people would show up and ruin his plans. Something in the back of his mind urged that there was a link between all the adventurers over the years but it did not matter to him.

The room was lit by magical lanterns scattered about the room. Skulls from every race and the stench of burnt sulfur and rotting flesh filled the room. Even the naivest child upon entering the place would recognize that it was a sanctuary of evil. Not that anyone could enter his inner sanctum without his permission. He was sure of that. It had taken him almost a year to create the room, the one above which acted as his laboratory and the one below which was his bedroom from a tower at the very center of the castle of Duke Mark. The War Forward had been a blessing for him. With the destruction of the old northern kingdoms, it left the land open enough so that not too many people traveled this far north. With the formation of the Northern Confederacy after the war it was a nation that had a large supply of eager people, but not much wealth. He had appeared to Duke Mark as a True Magus. The Duke was taken back at first at his hunched over appearance, but quickly recovered. Death Gate, calling himself Kerko, had said he would work for free if he gave him the tower as his own. The Duke agreed and soon became the dominate lord in the land.

He further bonded the Duke to him when he most recently arranged several contracts with the House Slar. The House was one of the most powerful trading houses in the Colonies and it had great influence in Mosk. Of course, his contacts were not in the house but in the Vampires of Mosk. He had never revealed to them who he was, but they had similar goals. From the practices of their high priest, Death Gate could only surmise that the cult had been given much of their secrets of the Rituals by Backbitter. They had his signature on them. Which mean that the cult had been operation since his last appearance. He had just happened to be there when one of the lower priests had started a rebellion. With Death Gate's help, the high priest was able to easily put down the usurper. The high priest knew that he owed a debt of blood for that, and was quick to repay it with a well-placed letter that changed the official policy of Mosk. Mark's Dukedom was now the primary trade province in the Confederacy.

That had only been a short time ago and already the city had become true to the name, and one fitting for a duke. He did all that for the duke but not because he liked the man. Far from it. The duke was one of those people who would do the right thing even if it cost him his life. One of those warriors who dedicated their sword and their life to Elohim. It rose the bile in Death Gate's throat. No, he did it because he needed the duke to be rich so he could get the resources for his own work.

He had been working on finding the location of all of the gates that would release his old masters. He had been granted a long life by the Destroyer. Of course, such powers were not without their price. He shuddered at what price that would be. If the god Apployan did not overthrow Elohim, then the punishment would be eternal.

He had located six of the Gates but the other five had eluded him for nearly a century. That is why he had picked this tower. One of the gates was actually in the room upstairs. His knee cracked loudly when he walked over to his work desk. His flesh was starting to become corrupt again. He had just performed a blood ritual but he could not waste the power on keeping his body in peak condition. It will be a long time before it would be safe to make another sacrifice to the Destroyer. He did not know what the effect would be.

He went over his map again. The tome he had found the month before had given him the clue. Using the new information and the gate in the tower he was able to find all of the gates but one. The first one. He lacked the power to open them out of order. It was possible that the Giants beyond the Barrier Mountains controlled it. If that was true then he could not understand why the Giants had not opened it. With the first one open he would easily open the others. He pulled a book from a shelf and had just opened it when the temperature in the room rose considerably.

The newcomer radiated the evil power which his masters had. Death Gate threw himself prostrate as the man spoke with a voice full fire.

"You have done well to keep the faith Death Gate. I remember you when you were an acolyte and it was I who blessed you with your first promotion."

Death Gate almost looked up at his recognition of this man as Shadow Fire. His head jerked back down before he reached the man's knees. Looking at a master's face would mean death. He did not even dare ask the question about the master's death.

"Your behavior now does baffle me though. Why is it that you cower in front of me like a child? Have I not always told you that I expect only strength from those who follow me?"

Death Gate was shocked. Then suddenly he understood what the master meant. Shadow Fire had never treated him like a grub. It had been that way with the others only after Shadow Fire had been killed. He stood, it was hard to fight the habit of giving the impression of fear on his face. He jumped slightly when Shadow Fire started laughing.

"I see that those who took over the Unholy Council wanted servants who cowered before them and shook with fear every time they spoke. This would be a great attribute for a cup bearer but not from those who use your name in your absence. Remember your punishment Death Gate?"

"Yes sir"

How could he forget? It was the reason he was so misshapen.

"And you remember what it was for?"

"Yes sir. I failed you, but my crime was not reporting something which you should have known because I feared your punishment."

"And what did it teach you?"

Death gate was starting to get his confidence back. This was without a doubt Shadow Fire come back to life. In an instant, all of his self-conditioning on how to behave in front of the Unholy Council was wiped away and he was a new man. He was Death Gate, High Priest of the Dark Church. Second only to Shadow Fire, Great Prophet of Perditor, Destroyer of the weak.

"That I could say anything to you and not fear retribution as long as I say it with respect."

Shadow Fire smiled. He was pleased when he had felt Death Gate working a ritual with his signature. He had been shocked when Death Gate had prostrated himself. What pain Death Gate must have gone through to be conditioned like such. He had picked the man because he was strong willed. He would never have great power but was powerful enough to gain control of his body. He looked down at his servant. Strength was reentering the man. Shadow Fire was pleased and it showed in his voice.

"I am now back and require you to serve me again. You have much to do and only a few years to do it in. All things must be prepared for when I give the signal. Go into the Trance so you will remember everything."

Death Gate eyes glazed over as he set the patterns in his mind which would allow him to have complete recall of everything said. He nodded to Shadow Fire when he was set, and his master spoke the plans in a condensed language which was called Short Speak during the Time of the Shadow.

Not caring about appearances, Herman materialized at the front door of a modest home. He went to enter but it was locked. That was odd, Willie never locked his door. He opened a small gate to his private storage and reached inside. Giving it a second thought, he returned the key to its place and closed the gate. He knocked on the door.

After a few minutes an Azerian answered. Herman could tell instantly that he was very talented in magic. By the way that his whiskers twitched nervously, the rat man was talented enough to tell how powerful Herman was. Herman smiled. He always liked the sewer crawlers. Before the Azerian could mutter a question, Herman spoke.

"I am looking for the Azerian named Willie."

The Azerian really became nervous and looked as if he was about to flee. His voice was shaky.

"I am Willy."

Herman's smile became genuine.

"Sorry, I am looking for Sir William Eldie."

Willy opened his mouth, but before he could speak a cheery voice came from inside.

"It's all right, let him in. Herman, I'm in the den."

Herman waited until the Azerian stepped back before he entered. Walking straight to the den he avoided eye contact with Willie as he poured himself a drink and pulled a cigar from the humidor. Gathering his strength, he turned to face his friend. To his surprise, Willie had crossed the room. The odd looking Azerian reached out with his paws and caressed Herman's face. He smiled as he stepped back. Willie's voice was happy.

"I did not believe it was you when you first came in. It has been some time, even so, I was not expecting you to have grown so much. You are on the verge of manhood." Willie returned to his seat. "Not that I am complaining, but what brings you to see me? Have you figured out how old I am?" Noticing Herman glancing at Willy he continued. "It is alright to talk in front of him. He is, in a way, my nephew and has become my pupil. In fact, he has information that you may want, but that can wait."

Herman laughed.

"That was not my motivation but now that you mention it, I think I have figured it out. How many questions do I have left?"

Willie pulled out a notepad before answering.

"Thirteen. Use them wisely."

Herman smiled as he pulled out a book from his backpack. He scanned his notes before speaking.

"Let's see. You are not built like a normal Azerian, more bipedal and not comfortable on all fours. You knew Death's Fang before he went by that name. You do not have the melodramatics which is common with Azerians." Herman looked up and smiled. "You served the Great Ones as Liberian?"

Willie laughed.

"Yes, you have been studying. Twelve left."

"Were seven years lost in the raid of Cornelias?"

"No."

"Eight?"

"Yes. You have ten left."

"Have you had your birthday this year?"

"Yes."

Herman's smile widened.

"You are Sir Eldon Ward-Wilson, known to the populace only as the Keeper of the Library during the rule of the Great Ones, which your father was one of that group. You were born in the spring of the twenty second year after the Dragons' Abdication which makes you six hundred forty-eight years old."

Willy watched with wide eyes as Willie clapped his paws in excitement. He knew that the Old One was the oldest living Azerian but he had no idea that he had such a history. He paid close attention when Willie spoke.

"Very good, I see that you have finally started doing real research. However, as I have always told you, there is no rest for the gifted. So, let us move on to the next puzzle. Why did the Great Ones disappear?"

Herman's eyes widen. He started to protest.

"That is not a fair ques. . ."

Willie interrupted Herman by raising his paw.

"If life was fair, all would be condemned to hell. The question which has plagued scholars for hundreds of years may take the rest of your life to answer. It is true that it is not a fair question. The ones which teach us the most never are. Just as the pain which brings you here is not fair, but it gives you so much." the ancient Azerian turned towards his nephew. "Please tell Herman what you told me about the man you called Mark."

Willy relayed the story of his time spent with Herman's father. How the Tecmen had captured him and turned him into a monster by filling his body with cybernetic. How he died fighting valiantly against the Tecmen in the last land battle and where he was buried. It was apparent to Herman that the Azerian had cared for his father and believed him when he said he spent three days crying over the slain body. Even now it brought tears to Willy's eyes. Herman did not feel anything, not sure if that was good or bad. Someday he would have to visit his father's grave to find out if he had no feelings or if he was merely suppressing them.

Eventually the conversation turned to lighter subjects and by the time Herman left he was in a genuinely pleasant mood.

Thorin sat on the Dragon Throne, the very seat from which Amic the Great had ruled the United Colonial Empire. He enjoyed sitting on the throne and would spend hours there with his own thoughts. It made him feel back in command, but more than that, it reminded him to what he had dedicated his life. It reminded him of his oath. As an officer it had been his Honor to protect life, peace and property. It had been his dedication to that duty which had propelled him up in rank and contributed to him being accepted by the DRAGON project. He had only finished the first part of it when the man with the lantern had shown up.

Even though it made KuAra uncomfortable, they had set up their camp in the Imperial Castle. Thorin had insisted, not only because he felt more at home in the military setting but also because was the only part of the city that was not in need of serious repair. The city was much smaller than Thorin had thought it would have been. It would be not have been much more than a town during his time. Thorin was also surprised by the fact that there were no monuments. While there was artwork everywhere it was almost universally in the form of Dragons. The only statue of a human he could find was one next to the throne, and it gave the impression that it was watching over his shoulder while he was sitting there. The way that KuAra spoke of Amic the Great, Thorin had expected there to be a hundred-foot monument to the man on every street corner.

They had been in the city now for months, and Thorin was ready to leave. Food was not much of a problem as there was an abundance of wild fruit, and some livestock that had been roaming the island. The problem was that it was boring. Cesdakar kept himself busy either by praying or spending long hours sitting and watching the storm which surrounded the island. KuAra had the task of figuring out how to turn the storm off so they could leave. Thorin had nothing to do but to try to keep in shape.

The wizard was in the throne room working on the device which he said maintained the storm at that very moment. He stuck his head out just as Cesdakar entered the room. KuAra's voice reflected his frustration.

"This is impossible". KuAra paused as he noticed where Thorin was sitting. "You know I hate when you sit there.'

Thorin only shrugged.

"You have said both, many times. What is it now?'

When they first arrived KuAra would fume for hours about Thorin sitting on the Dragon Throne, but now he mentioned it more out of habit then true concern. He gestured at the storm device as he spoke.

"According to the log, there was not teltar. None at all, not even a telprot."

Thorin snorted humorously. KuAra had been trained for some sort of technical work with magic and had the habit putting everything in the language of his profession. Thorin responded hoping he kept his apathy out of his voice.

"Simplify it for this old solider.

KuAra glanced at Cesdakar for some kind of support but the holy man only shrugged. He turned back to Thorin and spoke with a bit more frustration in his voice.

"They used the storm control system and tied it into the long-range communication in order to teleport the population and a large amount of supplies. It was an ambitious plan, but there is no target location. There is nothing in the system of where they went."

Thorin waved his hand dismissively.

"That is not such a big deal, Kua. Most likely they just had it where their destination was erased when they arrived where ever it is they went.

It showed the state of KuAra's agitation that he did not notice the abbreviation of his name. His words were almost a shout.

"No, you do not understand, they did not go anywhere. They did not teleport themselves. It had to be some sort of grievous error. They disincarnated themselves along with a considerable number of supplies."

In spite of himself, Thorin became curious. A mass suicide? Why then did they not destroy the city as well? Why only some of the supplies and not all of it? There was a mystery here. Thorin leaned forward as he spoke.

"Explain to me exactly what happens when someone teleports. And put it in simple terms."

KuAra motioned for them to join him by the device he was working on. He started when the two of them came near.

"Teleporting is not like gating. Gates set up a connection, a doorway between the two. Teleportation breaks down the person into energy and some small particles, then reassembles them where their target location is. If that location is not worked out in the teleportation spell then it would simply tear them apart. There is simply no target location at all, it is written as if they were planning on going nowhere.

Cesdakar spoke with that tone common with those who see the world as others cannot.

"The Source is merciful to answer the prayers of those who are caught with only the wind as their bodies."

Both KuAra and Thorin turned towards him and spoke in unison.

"What?"

Cesdakar looked around for a while, as if looking to see if anyone was there to eavesdrop on them. He often did that even though it was clear that the three of them were the only ones on the island. When he eventually spoke, his voice was barely above a whisper.

"The storm is just water and dust like any other, but its heart is sad. There is a life to it which is crying out for help. I have not been able to help for there is no body to heal."

Thorin understood instantly. His voice was a shout compared to what Cesdakar's had been.

"The storm is the people of the city."

KuAra looked at both of them as if they each had sprouted a Dragon's head out of their back.

"That cannot be…unless…if."

The wizard turned back to the device and pulled off several of its panels. After some time, he finished his examination. When he spoke both his tone and expression were grim.

"Cesdakar is correct. I do not know why they did it, or how, but they set up the teleportation to put them back in their original spot when the storm system shut off. Whoever did this must have miscalculated because the control crystal cracked under the stress. Now that I understand what happened, it will be easy enough to route power so the storm will dispense. All I have to do…"

Cesdakar interrupted the wizard with a shout, and for the first time the two heard his voice have a tone of command.

"No!"

KuAra took a step back but still spoke with some authority.

"There is no other choice. They are degrading too fast. These who are lost in the chaos of the storm increase every day. Within a month there will be no one left to save. There simply is not the time."

Cesdakar place his hand on the hilt of the sword.

"The we have a month to find a way. Failing to save them I can accept, actively ending any chance of their salvation I cannot allow. The Source will show us the way."

There was no fear in the response of KuAra. His voice was a mix of sorrow and anger.

"Ces, these are my people! If there was a way to bring them back, do you not think I would try it. Even if I could find the equipment, I needed to make a wu crystal it would take me at least a month to grow it, and that assumes I get it right on the first try. It is already too late for them, so unless you have another miracle you can pull out of your…"

There are those moments which a person knows what they have to do. Different cultures throughout history have called it many things, and given many causes for it. Regardless of how it is viewed, such times are unmistakable. It was in one of those moments which Thorin reached out and grabbed the two conductors before KuAra or Cesdakar realized what he was doing. His only rational was something that KuAra had said weeks before. Only the human mind and body is better than wu crystals in the shunting of magic.

As the energy flowed through him, the sensation reminded him of the alterations he had received when he entered the DRAGON project. Radiation flowing through him, changing his flesh to absorb, store and release it. That was where the similarities ended, this was much stronger, and he could feel his body heating up.

In the back of his mind, he heard that voice telling him to let go. That he would not survive. He ignored it, focusing only on controlling the flow of the energy through the device. It was not hard to dispel the fear. After all, he would fulfill his duty, his purpose. He would die a hero, give his life in the defense of life, and that was enough for him. Just before he lost himself in the haze of pain, a touch of humor filtered through his thoughts. He always thought dying would feel much different.

XIII

Tymalt Morgan adjusted the strap holding his ponytail in place. It was hard to admit, but he had been taken by surprise by High Tymalt Boreta assigning him to this position. It had only been two weeks since he had been tested and he had just been allowed to call himself Tymalt. Boreta had given him just one piece of advice. Boreta had gotten where he was by following what he considered the highest meaning of Tymalt: Seek the truth in everything.

Stopping at the door he made sure his uniform was perfect and adjusted his iron starburst. The Tymalt's uniform was a suit of the southern style. Its coloring and cut were tailored for each Tymalt, in order to portray a sense of control. The iron starburst, with the symbol of the Tym at its center, was the symbol of the Tymalts. It was identical to those worn by the VoX Templers, except theirs were gold. Testimony of the shared history of the two orders. Once he made sure that his appearance was correct, he entered the room.

With a quick scan Morgan went to an empty seat. Without saying a word, he took his place among the members of the room. He allowed himself a small smile. He knew that the ones present would take it as a sign of him being proud of being asked to join. Giving it some thought, he realized it was pride. Not for being part of them, but because he was stronger than them. He quickly purged himself of the pride. As it was written in the Tymalt – pride prevents us from seeing what is real.

Everyone in the room had given up everything which would make them truly powerful for the petty gifts they had. A Vampire, a Praus and an Annis. All three had made a deal with the Destroyer to gain their power. The Order of Tymalt had only a single rule about dealing with spirits, never.

He watched them as they talked with each other. They gave away too much information that could be used against them. The one named Death Gate was driven by his fear of death, which would be why he became an Annis. Like all his kind, the Vampire was consumed with his lust for carnal pleasures. Indulging their appetites more and more until there was nothing left but pain, and rare moments of normalcy. Searching only for a release from the pain, the classic addiction cycle.

The Praus was a different story. The only one in the group Morgan he could not shred apart in seconds. The ultimate stoic philosophers, selling their very bodies to perfect their minds. No more pain, no more pleasure. At least not that of the body. Without the body the pleasures and pain of the mind are magnified. They are not apathetic, they are hate embodied. And filled with a pain Morgan knew, all too well, from his own youth.

As a youth all he knew was that pain. That was before the Order, before a Tymalt found him and taught him control and power. As it was written in the Tymalt - one must be detached enough to neither wish harm on another nor to refuse to do them harm.

Sensing the soon arrival of the caller of the meeting, he straightened his posture and placed his hands on the table palms down. The other three present looked at him. They would not understand that it was the sitting attack position.

Shadow Fire entered the room followed by what appeared to be a guard. As a faint smell of burnt hair reached Morgan's nostrils, he was sure that this man was one he could respect. Not a stranger to power, and real power at that. Morgan started to understand why he was here. The High Tymalts would not allow this man to rule without knowing what he was up to. It was Morgan's ability in Derica, seeing a person's heart, which was needed here. Shadow Fire looked around and smiled at him, apparently feeling the probe.

"I am sure you already know who I am, so let me get to the point. I have called this meeting for one purpose and that is to officially reform the Unholy Council. I have chosen the four of you carefully to be the Chaos Lords. You represent the most powerful factions of what is left of a once magnificent church. The Dark Church will once again rise and bring the human race to the purity it needs."

The Praus spoke out.

"With you as the leader?"

Shadow Fire smiled as he answered.

"Of course, what of it? Horich, you discarded your body in order to advance you knowledge. How much farther would you have been able to go if you had a free hand on this side of the Barrier Mountains? To run your personal and social experiments with a free hand? Would you not follow me in order to pillage the Library of Shouker? With the tomes found there you might even be able to find the Pyramid of Data. You, Elson, what price would you pay to finally be rid of the Order of Sword and Spell. And to the Order of Tymalt, I can only offer the ability to freely exercise your philosophy."

Morgan thought for a moment. His voice was as void from emotion as his mind.

"We already freely exercise our philosophy. There is no law which can bind us except those which we bind ourselves with. Still your goal is a lofty one, and I can admire that. I am weary, though, of any words from a worshiper of the Unclean. I am sure that we lack the strength to accomplish such a task. As it is written in the Tymalt: one must count the cost before one attacks."

The Praus chimed in.

"Our enemies are too strong. I had to sacrifice a half dozen Giants for a distraction just to travel here. The Enforcers will come as soon as they learn of our presence."

Shadow Fire shook his head hiding his ignorance of the Enforcers by agitation in his voice.

"It is true that our enemies are strong, but not by themselves. We must divide them. I am personally turning my attention into bringing one of them to our side. Of course, I mean the …"

Horich interrupted Shadow Fire again.

"The Protectors will not be fooled by your sweet words. I have tried to corrupt the Dragons for centuries. What makes you think that you can find a weakness in them?"

Shadow Fire stared hard at the Praus until the undead wizard had to look away. He was beginning to think he made a mistake with this bunch. In the silence Morgan spoke.

"It is written in the Tymalt: having no weakness is the greatest weakness. Besides I have never met any without a weak spot. In fact, most have such a large one that they are easy to control, even you, Horich." The Praus stood. The anger in his movements caused his skin to crack and fall away. Morgan smiled as he spoke. "Thanks for proving my point."

Horich sat down. Knowing that his anger was about which the human spoke. Was it possible that Shadow Fire had learned the weakness of the Dragons in his long imprisonment?

Shadow Fire was laughing. He liked the Tymalt. The man was a warrior to the core, not just of flesh and blood. The man did not even flinch when one of the most powerful wizards in the Colonies was about to attack. Could it be true that his Order knew how to attack a person's spirit as a physical thing? He had only learned about them through Death Gate. The Order of

Tymalt held onto the Philosophy of White Bear but rejected his faith. Shadow Fire would have to learn what they knew. That could wait. Now, he had to deal with the Council.

"This Council is forming whether you're a part of it or not. A yes or no is all that is required." He continued when all of them said they were in. "Very well, I will be dealing with the Protectors myself. Death Gate, you already have your orders. Elson, start unifying the minor cults of Vampires and Annis. Do it as silently as possible as not to arouse suspicion until you are strong enough. Horich, wage a war against the Dragons in the Barrier Mountains with your Giants. This will distract them until I have put the wedge in them. There are many VoX Templers who will most likely get involved. We will need the Tymalts to aid Death Gate in dealing with them."

Shadow Fire paused when Morgan shook his head. The Tymalt spoke with a tone which showed there was no debate with what he was saying.

"There will be little challenge from the Templers except to your unclean. They do not break their vow of nonviolence lightly and will not confront you in that manner. We will deal with the Templers, but in our way."

Shadow Fire smiled to hide his ignorance. There was a history here that he did not know, but it would work in his advantage.

"Very well. Along with the Dragons, I will be dealing with the individuals who pose a threat if they were to join forces. We can worry about making our bylaws and the splitting of power when we have a firm grip on the Colonies.

After getting more details on the various plans, the members of the new Unholy Council went their own ways.

Silver had plenty of time to think since he lost his guild. It was the kind of thoughts that have the chance to change one's life. He probably would have had come to some life decisions if he was not preoccupied with the dreams which had been haunting his nights. At times they were the best dreams that he could remember. Others times they were the essence of fear and he understood what nightmares really were. One night he would dream that his silver magical energy had returned and the whole world was at his feet and even Tapps was kneeling before him. In others, he had gained his silver magic back but he was unable to use it without it consuming him. Tapps was there and was coming closer. Tapps always won in those dreams.

He had traded his soul for the energy, not that he believed in the soul.

A man calling himself Death Gate had come asking for his soul, but eventually got around to him wanting something else. Silver had known it would, it always came down to business. In exchange for the power, all Silver had to do was to kill Tapps. At the time, he had thought that prison had finished his partner and thus was getting a one-sided deal. By the time Tapps had returned, he had forgotten about the deal. The power had left him shortly after that, but not before he had a chance to consolidate his power in the guild. Now he felt the energy bubbling up from the darkest recesses of his heart. Pulling him somewhere, pulling him to confront his oldest enemy.

Silver walked the streets with the hood of his cloak pulled over his face. He had read once that one human constant was that the only people treated crueler than those outside the group are those inside the group who do not follow the social rules. It was the same with the people of the Night Culture, probably even more so. Silver had not been one to play by the rules. It had never mattered when he was on top. He had made the rules. To him honor among thieves was only a fantasy from novels.

He made way to his apartment in Low Town. It was small and had a leak in the roof. Silver was almost grateful for this because it would drown the roaches which were always running in and out of the cracks in the wall. Mike had done well in acquiring it. No one cared who came and went, and it was cheap. With no way to bring money in and the need to keep a low profile the place was just fine. He blamed all of his bad fortune on his bad dreams and blamed them on Tapps Toya. He longed to have his vengeance on Tapps and get his life of a master back. He was very tired of groveling day in and day out and relying on Mike just to feed himself. He knew that the dreams that he had been having were a clue about the way to seek his revenge. He had paid some attention to what his old master had taught them. He cursed the dead man for all the times which the memories of Master Toya came to him. He cursed the dead man for ever teaching him about dreams.

That knowledge was making him find a destiny that he did not want. He would either succeed or be dead, either way he felt that his life would be better. He did not have the courage to find Tapps and face him, so he decided that he would seek out the shadowy figure who was always in his dreams and thoughts. At times he was certain that he heard the figure's voice in the day as well. He could not be sure. It was usually too hard to tell when the fighting in the apartment next to his was loud enough to overpower his own thoughts. He always hated spring with all its rain and the mud that would collect on the city's streets. He entered his small apartment and cursed aloud. A new leak had sprung. The water had soaked the straw mattress which he called his bed. He made up his mind right then and there that he would seek out this shadowy figure and put an end to his miserable life.

He grabbed his small rucksack and filled it with an assortment of clothes. He went over to the dresser that looked as if it was going to collapse under its own weight. He pulled the bottom drawer and removed its false bottom. An obvious hiding place that would not have worked if it was not for his living quarters being what they were. He pulled out a large sack of coin. He smiled to himself. His speech was thick with the slang of the streets but he knew that money can be a great translator. He finished packing and changed his clothes to his well-made, but worn, outfit. The denim pants with the thin leather overcoat would hold up to the life of travel well. He had to make only one stop on the way, to pick up some supplies to replenish his disguise kit. Master Toya had discovered that he had a talent for it, so he had hired an expert actor to teach him. It was only a hobby while he was guild master, but it had come in handy since his fall.

With all his supplies in order, he penned a note that told he was going to drown himself in the swamp and was coded with a place for Mike to meet him. He left town with a smile on his face. For the first time in a very long time, he laughed out loud. In such a great mood he did not even care that he did not know why he laughed.

Fire. Hot and painful fire. His world was made of fire, and when Thorin realized this, he knew he was not dead. He floated in that place between dreams and awake, where imagination intensifies the pain and gives meaning to it which the conscious mind would not accept. Thorin could hear the mumbled voice of Cesdakar in prayer, and he faded back into the cool relief of unconsciousness.

The fire was gone, but there was still pain. Thorin could hear a voice he did not recognize.

"It should have killed him. A recovery is too much to hope for."

"You do not know the Source, or Thorin."

That voice was Cesdakar, Thorin was sure of it. He tried to open his eyes, to wake fully, but his eyelids were too heavy. He fell back into sleep to awaken again hearing the subdued voice of Cesdakar's prayers. Someone else was speaking as well.

"I have not explanation for it but there can be no doubt. He is healing."

Healing? Yes. He was healing and Thorin could feel it. This time he did manage to open his eyes. His first sight was Cesdakar. The sunglasses which protected the holy man's eyes from the light of the room's lanterns did nothing to hide the happiness on Cesdakar's face. There were two other people in the room. One was KuAra, even though Thorin did not recognize him at the first glance due to the strange outfit the wizard was wearing. Thorin had never seen the other man before. Turning his attention back to Cesdakar, he asked the only question which seemed important.

"Did it work?"

Cesdakar simply said yes, but the stranger stepped next to the bed. His voice was filled with a respectful awe.

"You saved over eight thousand of us. You are a hero to every one of us."

Thorin took a moment to process the information, and glanced at KuAra when he spoke.

"KuAra said this city held at least thirty thousand."

The stranger faltered and it was Cesdakar who answered.

"Yes, many were lost in the storm."

Thorin nodded in understanding, even though the nod was only in his thoughts. He turned his head towards the stranger.

"Can I assume that you are the leader of the city then?"

The mad started then spoke in an apologetic tone.

"Yes sorry. I am DragoRue Henra Grutea, yes, a grandson."

Thorin smiled his voice full of humor.

"Grandson?"

"Sorry again. I am still having trouble dealing with the idea of so much time passed. It is a kind of habit because of my name to automatically answer the question of relations, as that is always a question."

Thorin laughed and instantly regretted it because of the pain.

"Related to who?"

KuAra spoke up quickly.

"To the Amic Grutea, of course."

Henra shot the wizard an irritating glance, as Thorin voiced his question.

"So, you are the emperor's grandson. Then that would make you the heir to the Dragon Throne."

KuAra nodded his agreement but Henra shook his head with a laugh. His voice was a combination of humor and buried regret.

"The Empire was never strictly hereditary. My position of DragoRue, or leader of this city as you put it, is as much as I want. It is the level in which I am most qualified. To make myself DragoKeen would to go beyond my competence to limit the bureaucracy."

Thorin tried to respond. He tried to ask the questions he wanted answers to but a wave of fatigue prevented him. He closed his eyes and before falling back to sleep, he heard Cesdakar herding the other two out of the room.

Kift did not understand the vision he was having. He dreamed of dark castles and horrible deeds. A mountain forest torn apart to make a center of power. The animals twisted into horrible slaves to an evil master. The people who lived deep in the mountains forged by fire and pain into beasts which seemed more made of shadows than flesh.

Nightmares had been with him since he left his brother's church and in the months of travel, he had gotten used to it. It was not until he had the visions while he was awake did he really start to worry. He needed to find the help for which he was looking.

In the book which his cousin had given him there was written only the general area that the Dragon would be. If she still called home the mountains in which he now walked, he would find her. By the time he had reached Draco Mountains, it was almost summer, and was no day of midsummer. If he had been one not used to such a life he would have feared the coming winter. Instead, his thoughts were often in the mountains he called home.

With winter needing to be prepared for and no sign for what he searched, he was ready to give up and find a place to hole up. He would have to start gathering supplies he would need. It was only by chance that the same night he decided he would have to look elsewhere for his answers, he noticed a light on a distant mountain top while he was relieving his bladder.

When the sun rose, he headed towards the area where he had seen the light. It took him a full week to reach the area and he could find no sign of what had caused the light. He set camp as the sun set. As darkness of true night covered the mountains, a light shined from behind him. He turned and the sight caught his breath in his throat.

The side of the mountain was transparent with the strong yellow light coming from behind. He stood and touched the translucent wall. His hand felt nothing. He had seen magic before in his youth. The basics of magic is a required course at Kanato's Institute of Learning and for a time he had thought that he had wanted to be a wizard. That was until Elohim called him to the forest. Making the puffs of multicolored smoke that he learned to do was nothing compared to this. He walked through the mountainside after grabbing his gear.

The natural cave was large. Its walls were lined with natural crystal which caught the light and changed it into a multitude of colors. As he wandered deep into the cave towards the light, he wondered to himself for the first time why he was really here. The visions were hard on him but to seek out such an obscure teacher was crazy.

Kift stopped dead in his tracks. Lying in the main chamber was a huge reptilian beast who Kift had only seen in a drawing. He knew that she would be one but he had never seen a Dragon before and was taken aback by her. Her skin seemed to radiate a light of its own. Black, orange and yellow running in patterns that made the hide of the Dragon seem as if it was made from molten rock.

The Dragon did not seem to pay any attention to Kift. She was staring into a gigantic brazier. The size of the brazier, and the flame within, was as large as a house. It looked like a small cook fire next to the Dragon. Kift dropped to his knees when the beast swung her huge head towards him. Her bellowing words hurt Kift's ears.

"I have been expecting you, Kift of the mountains. The animals speak kindly of you, and more importantly, LingueArdeo tells me of your need. I am honored you have chosen me to guide you on this path."

Kift tried to stand but could not. He could barely get his words out.

"I have been plagued with nightmares. They now haunt me even when I am awake."

Kift tried to say more but he was taken back by what happen next. The great Dragon shrunk. Her form took on the appearance of a stunningly beautiful woman. Her skin was as dark as night, and contrasted with hair that was fiery red and moved as if it had a life of its own. Kift closed his eyes as she moved closer with outstretched arms. Her hands caressed Kift's head and face. Her skin was hot to the touch and slightly burned, but somehow was soft beyond belief. The touch was sweet but surprisingly short.

Kift open his eyes to see the Dragon-woman looking down at him. Her words were as sweet as her touch, but with a hint of fire.

"It has been a long time since I had anyone in my cave. The last was a thief. He stole some of my treasure. I learned this transformation spell to track him down. The man turned out to be a better thief than I thought. I retrieved my treasure but, in the end,, he had stolen my heart. Since his death I have never let another RoFin into my home.

"I would not have let you find me, but your need is great. The world's need is great. I do not know whether or not your future role is important in that fight. But it is important that you are there."

Kift did not understand and it showed on his face as she continued.

"As for your dreams, you have been linked with the man who is known by some as Shadow Fire. This in itself is not the cause, but he has set an Unclean to harass you. It will not bother you while you are with me, yet you must gain your defense against it before you leave. You will have a lot to learn so that you can cast the Unclean from you. In the coming years expect to feel like a child in school once again."

Snow was awoken by loud laughter. It was the voices from nowhere again. They had been plaguing him for some time. They had grown in numbers since they came to this valley high in the Southern Mountains. They hinted of knowledge just out of sight. No, it was more like they tempted him with all the power of the world, just beyond his fingertips. Divinus had returned from wherever he had been and was just starring off into the darkness. Snow would not let the chance go by to ask Divinus a question. He knew that this man, or whatever he was, would make himself powerful and bring Snow with him, but once they got there, Snow was planning to do what it took to have all the power for himself.

"They are telling me something, but I cannot make it out. How do I hear them clearly?"

Divinus was silent long enough that Snow was not sure he had heard. The man answered just as Snow was going to ask again.

"Listen if you like, but do not do anything they suggest. They are willow wisps, tricksters, nothing more. They are minor spirits which are useful only for information, but if you live in their allure, they will own you. And, by no means, ever allow them to enter you, not even for a moment. If you give them entrance, they will drive you mad. It is better to ignore them, but let them stay near and you will gain their power. We have other things to occupy us now. People are already on their way to meet us. We must finish making a home suitable for the Chaos Lords. My friend Snow, there is so much out there that you will never see, but if you listen to me, you will rule it all. All will call you master. You are the Shadow returned. No longer will you have to pay homage to anyone, for you will be master of all you see. Not just the Colonies but all of creation will be yours to command. But enough talk, we have much work to do before the first lord arrives."

With the words spoken Divinus raised his arms and a searing black energy flew out of him. Snow felt the energy within himself. He was helpless to stop the magic from flowing from his body. He did not know how he controlled the magic or why. Out of him the darkness rushed and went into the mountains with a roar. After several hours, the mountains around the valley grew as if a giant hand was pushing them up.

He should have been awed by the sight, but he cared for nothing but the power flowing through him. It was the same every time, but never as pleasurable as the time before. Snow's spirit soared when the birds and the goats and all that lived in the mountains twisted to his vision. He seemed to spend a lifetime changing the mountains, and it seemed to last only a heartbeat. As quickly as he fully realized the power was flowing it stopped, and all he was left with was an aftertaste. He longed for it back. He was changed on the inside and he knew it. He perceived the world in a whole new way. Not only could he see the magic around him now, but the very forces which controlled it. It was like the willow wisps that hovered around him. He saw them swirling around him like small dim lights, or more accurately small lights made as shadows. He saw how the pattern changed when he touched a tree, a rock, moving as if it had a mind of its own. He saw a small release of it when he reached down and crushed a frog in his hand. The balls of energy crowded around him and brightened as power exploded from the creature. The magic became excited where the frog's blood fell to the ground. A willow wisp whispered in his ear.

"Blood is the life."

The words echoed through his mind. The meaning of a small phrase hit Snow sharply. He controlled magic like a True Magus, but only through the willow wisps. Their numbers grew and now there was at least a half dozen around him at any time. Always whispering secrets in his ear which even the wisest of people should not know. Now they were showing him the power which was found in life. Power that was kept in the blood. He stood the rest of the night watching the flows of magic returning to normal, or at least as normal as it could with the darkness controlling it.

He saw so much power in the living things around him. He knew no way to pull it out of them without killing them. Snow kept trying to find the secrets of the blood. He knew such a path would damn his soul, but he did not care. After all, he had always denied there was a second life. The power was a wondrous drug that held Snow in a lock of dependence. It was sweet and he felt forever young with it. He could raise buildings or tear them down with only his will. When the power was gone and Snow could find nothing around him to kill, he was left with a hollow feeling inside. A feeling like he was weeks dead and the worms had already started to eat him from the inside.

It took them a few months to shape the valley to its final form and another month to change the path of a high mountain river to run through the center of the valley. By the time they were ready to start with the buildings there was already a large group of people who had come to serve the Shadow. Some came to serve hi. Others came determined on his destruction. All that came were twisted and warped by the time Divinus and Snow were finished with them. By the time they completed turning the area into a truly magical city, Snow had learned many secrets from the willow wisps. They assured him that he was the most powerful person in the Colonies. He no longer found any pleasure in the blood rituals, but like any addict he now did them simply so he could function. Still, like all necromancers, he was driven. There were always more secrets to learn, more power to gain. He would not stop at simply being a god, he would be the Most High God.

Divinus had been spending a lot of time with the Chaos Lords. They were people who were chosen to be people of power in the New Shadow's Empire. Snow smiled at the thought that he was the Shadow. Still, he did not like that Divinus was the one who chose them, or the fact that he did not even get to meet them. The willow wisps told him to be patient, that there would come a day that he could rid himself of the man from the mirror.

Divinus was now talking with one of the newcomers. For some reason this made Snow jealous. Not jealous that Divinus was spending the time with the lady, but that the female was not his. It was not that he wanted her, not in any way, it was more that he just did not want anyone else to have her. It had taken him several days to realize that the woman had the same effect on all the men of the area. She was not a Chaos Lord but had somehow created for herself a position of nobility. Snow was thrown off guard by the sight of what happened when Divinus and the lady approached. One of his willow wisps circled him violently and then collided with one that surrounded the human. The two bounced around as if in some sort of dance. Both the lady and Divinus bowed deeply to Snow. Divinus spoke crisp and sharp as if speaking to a superior. The complete opposite of his pattern of speech when they were alone.

"My Lord Shadow, this is Lady Eveitio Validus, the woman who you granted the position of countess. Remember, my lord, we spoke of her the night before last?"

Because of the show, he had not been paying attention. One the balls of energy whispered in his ear, telling him what he should say.

"Yes, of course." Snow did not remember any conversation, but then Divinus often did things without consulting him. No matter how it irritated him, Snow was smart enough to play along. "How do you do Lady Validus?"

She smiled. It was apparent she was impressed by the Shadow, but she was used to dealing with powerful people.

"I am doing better than I have ever in my life, Lord Shadow. I have served you faithfully most of my life and enjoyed your blessings. I am overjoyed with your release from your prison. Most of all, I could not be more excited to be serving you as one of your lords."

"We will talk about this later. When I am not so busy. Chancellor, we need to speak again about the palace help. If you would please excuse us, Lady Eve."

With that, Eveitio bowed deeply again and started to walk away. Divinus took the look of deep thought, but showed happiness in his voice. "Lady Eve, I like that. It contains the familiar name yet still maintains the proper formality. Yes, I think that you will do well to set up such a culture between the nobility."

Snow was taken a little aback by Divinus' attitude. He quickly decided that it did not matter what Divinus did as long as he knew why. He made his question quick and to the point.

"I do not trust your motivations. Why are you setting me up as emperor?"

Divinus laughed.

"I have told you before not to pay attention to what they tell you." He motioned off handedly to the willow wisps before continuing. "First of, you are the Shadow. You must have felt it before now. A sense that you were greater than what the world was letting you be. I am not setting you up as an emperor, I am simply letting you be the emperor you already are. Besides what I need to do so we can rule the world I cannot do from the Emperor's seat. I care nothing for empires or ruling. My only desire is for my faith. I set you on a throne not of a king but an emperor. I do this in order that the Dark Church can take its rightful place as the spiritual leader of the world.

"It will all come to pass that we will have the whole world at our feet and then I will enjoy turning the role of servant to someone else so I can turn my attention solely to my faith. Until then I know of no one else you can trust. Almost all of the Chaos Lords are here but we have much to do before we announce to the world the Shadow has returned."

Snow thought about it for a little while and then nodded his head in approval. They walked together for some time talking about women and power, and mostly about their plans to conquer the Colonies.

XIV

The moonlight shone down, lighting the meadow in a thick forest. It was an overly obvious place to hold a meeting of evil intent, but the four heavily cloaked men which was having the meeting cared nothing of image, or anything which could remotely be considered a human concern. They were focused on a single goal, and anything and everything was judged by how effective it was at advancing that goal. Creatures would be a better description of them, Horis thought to himself as he watched them form the nearby trees. Even though their bodies were those of men, Horis knew from experience that these four could not be considered human. They were Presicree, true undead. Human bodies with the living spirits gone, replaced by an Unclean. Horis, as one of the Five Horsemen, knew of their kind. He had been there over four thousand years ago when the very first Presicree was made.

It was a simple enough process if one had the courage and strength to do it. The hardest part of it was controlling the Unclean well enough to force them into the body. While the evil spirits gained much by being anchored into the flesh, apparently, they faced some sort of punishment, or pain if the body was destroyed. Horis knew about it, but very little of the details needed in order to do it. His specialty was intrigue and strategic manipulations. He had little dealings, nor desire concerning unclean. He understood enough to know that these four had to be very old. By the way they filled out the cloak, or rather did not fill the cloak, their flesh was completely desiccated and all which would remain of it was tidbits clinging to a skeleton. They could easily be destroyed which meant they could easily be threatened.

Horis had crossed the sea from the land of the Tecmen to the Colonies in search for Amon Umenpire, the one who had gathered and trained the Horsemen, his old Master, and the only one that he trusted to answer a question which had been burning his mind. A question in which the answer, no matter what it was would change his life. Horis did not understand why finding Umenpire started with these four but it was the path in which the Pattern clearly showed, but Horis was old and experienced enough to know how much the Unclean, and their prince, Apployan the Destroyer could influence the Pattern. He simply waited and listened.

One of the four, one which still had its speech, for the other two would have lost that ability long ago, spoke with toneless, emotionless and almost mechanical voice.

"We have lost Death Gate. He follows Shadow Fire with no regard for the will of the Master.'

After a short pause one for them spoke, sounding so similar to the first that Horis could not be for sure if it was not the same one. There was no movement, nothing to indicated which one of them was speaking.

"He is only groundling, and does not have the drive to dethrone the Redeemer. The Master agrees, we can never count one of them as totally one of us. Look how we lost Open Palm."

The four grew silent once more and if it was possible, they had become even more still at the name. Horis almost leapt out when he heard the translations of Umenpire. It was a name in a language so old, it was forgotten by the time Horis was born. A language he had heard spoken only by Amon. Horis's mind started searching the pattern to place the clues together. Who were these four Presicree if they knew of Umenpire?

Horis was deep enough in thought that he started when one of the skeletons spoke in a voice like the others.

"The Master agrees. Death Gate cannot be lost to us. He is needed to open the gate which the One will not be able to. Even though Shadow Fire works the most of the Master's plan, Death Gate is more important. The Master does not know what will happen when Open Palm confronts Shadow Fire. He may be lost to us as well, but it is not important. The Master's plan will continue and we must be ready for our parts."

The other three spoke in unison.

"The Master Agrees."

Horis had enough of waiting. He stepped out into the moon light. All four turned towards him, and he could see the dark red light of their eyes. According to legend, and Horis believed was true, the light was a reflection of the Unclean's hatred of all life. One of the skeleton figures raised its bony hand and pointed at him. The hand shot out a flame of the same red of their eyes. Horis simply ignored the Presicree fire as it hit him and seemed to be absorbed into his chest.

"Come now Presicree, I know well enough you have no power over me which I do not allow. If you mean to kill me you will have to do it with those bodies you have stolen. But that will not be easy for I am Horis the Hidden.

Now, tell me where to find this Shadow Fire."

In unison the four Presicree repeated his name with an angry hiss. After a long moment of silence one of them, the oldest for even the bones were starting to decay, spoke with a hatred beyond human understanding in its voice.

"The Master does not agree with you being here. Go back to your place in the plan. You belong across the sea."

Horis had dealt with Unclean enough over his long life to know how to get the information he needed from them.

"If you want to keep those pieces of matter, then tell me where to find Shadow Fire. Tell me or I will destroy you all."

When all four let out a haunting laugh, Horis was genuinely shocked, which he could count the years since that happened in centuries. Threats always worked with the Presicree, at least threats one was able to follow through with. He was further shocked that the next one who spoke was one of the skeleton figures. One who should have lost their ability to speak.

"Horis of the Five, do not think we are mere Presicree or even Presis of a star. We are the horses on which the riders will come. Of the rebellion only the Master is greater than us. Give up your pursuit of trying to find Open Palm, and the Master will grant that you will ride a white horse."

Horis looked at the four for a long moment, looked as if he was going to say something but abruptly turned and ran. He ran as hard and as long as he could. It had been a long time since he had been afraid. Like so many other emoutions, he could count the time since he lost felt it in centuries but those four was beyond anything he had dealt with.

One of the Presicree turned towards the other three.

"Horis is almost lost to us. We should not let him live."

Another one of them spoke

"The Master disagrees. We may lose Horis, but the Master's Plan will be advanced by it. The three which are left will be ours forever because of it."

The other three spoke in unison.

"The Master agrees."

Then they turned and walked back into the woods in different directions.

XV

Herman Alexander-Coxcomb walked down the main street of New Shadow City. He now appeared in his in his mid-twenties, closer to his actual age. Tall and fit, almost bordering on thin, his gait was of as usual. As one who was unaware or unimpressed with his surroundings. It was always the latter. He was unaware however how his attitude and appearance drew the attention of the ladies while he walked down the street.

It had not taken long for the chaos to return after leaving Willie, so he had spent the last few years in a self-imposed exile. Two years of it being deep in the Unclaimed Lands. He had practiced over and over again every known exercise of True Magic, pushing himself at times to the point of exhaustion. It was dangerous, and he now bore the scars of a True Magus on his body. Not that anyone except another True Magus would recognize them as such, or believe one so young could have survived the transformation of his nervous system.

Herman took no pride in his new status though. He rarely thought of it, and when he did, he had a sense that it was a waste of time. he had only risked his life because he thought it would help with the chaos. But the feeling that the world was spinning out of control had only increased. Having learned everything, he could from the texts he had he decided to return to civilization.

With his new senses he had instantly noticed the new city that grew in the Southern Mountains while he was gone. Only two years and a full-size city had sprouted up. Herman figured that checking it out would be a good diversion. It definitely had the look of being wrought by magic but it lacked the normal residue. In fact, there was no more magic or wizards in the area than found in any city. Yet, there was a sense of power.

He had planned to teleport himself inside the city but there was a shield preventing it. He could have broken through but not without collapsing it. He knew that those who had it raised would not have been happy to have such an expensive ward ruined. It was better to teleport near and walk the rest of the way then drawing too much attention to himself. There was something very interesting going on here and he was going to find out what it was.

Herman stopped and closed his eyes. The power had the same feeling of that which came from the old priest Manker. No, not the same, just similar. Manker radiated authority and trust. This was power, real power. It was as if the city focused the power of the citizens. He sent out strands of magic to start gathering information, but before he could gain any insight he was interrupted by a tap on his shoulder. The voice indicated one used to giving orders.

"There is no loitering, boy."

Herman opened his eyes and put on a smile before turning around. The man was the largest human that he had ever seen. Most likely the man had used magic or chemicals to induce his size. By his uniform he was some sort of police. The man had some sort of power but it did not come from any skill in magic. The symbols on his cloths showed an ancient form of ranking.

Herman scanned his memory for the relevant information. When he found what he was looking for, he spoke.

"I have traveled a great distance, Sergeant, and was gathering my bearings before finding appropriate lodgings."

The sergeant smirked as he spoke. Herman could tell that they must get many vagabonds coming to the city.

"There is a flop house five blocks that way."

Herman was surprised. He looked down at himself. His smile widened. He always wore the best of cloths but instantly realized that he was still wearing the cloths he had worn in the wild. The denim and leather were common among adventures, and was popular with rebellious youths as well. His outfit was of the highest quality but were well worn. Not to mention that he was carrying a skunk under his arm. Still, he did not like being responded to such. His tone showed that he did not approve of the treatment.

"I said appropriate lodgings."

He simply turned and started walking. The guard followed him. Herman decided that he would have to stay in the city for a while to find out what was going on so he altered his cloths. Without the flash or sparkles that most wizards add to such spells, his cloths changed into the finest possible. He was not a tailor so it did not fit as well as it should. He preferred the tailored look and always had his cloths custom made. He turned his head and gave the guard a smile. Herman knew that the man would not follow him anymore.

Looking around, he was not sure how long he would stay. At first, he thought of using one of his standard cons and then laughed at himself. He was looking older now and would not be able to pull off the helpless child act anymore. Well, it was about time that he updated his image anyway. Checking his purse, he headed off towards uptown.

It did not take him long to find the hotel in which he was going to stay. It took even a shorter amount of time for the two gold coins he put down on the counter to convince the clerk that he was a proper resident. After inspecting the apartment, he told the attendant that he was expecting his luggage within the week and tipped him a silver. The suite was finely furnished which included a large fireplace. It gave him an idea of what his new image would be. He went to open a teleporting gate and remembered the shield. He gave it some thought and found his solution. It took him a few seconds, but the gate open.

Herman walked into the gate into his private storage. It was located far into the Unclaimed Lands, over a hundred meters below the ground. He had only slightly enhanced it to warp magic around it so it would not be hard to locate for any wizard of even moderate power. In the civilized lands it would never have been safe, but this far into the wilderness, one would have to know its location to find it.

It had started off as only a small room but had grown to a full-size warehouse. It contained not only the riches which he had acquired over the years, but the items he had created as well. Putting permanent patterns into an item was a hobby he enjoyed. It required an intense amount of knowledge, but very little power. It helped more than anything else with control. All of them were crafted not because he wanted it, but because he wondered if it could be done. He had created many in his late teens. He had had little control over his power then so had found it easier to rely on items for the more delicate spells.

Herman placed Marlyn on the ground. She always enjoyed running around in the place. He headed towards his clothing section. Looking at his massive wardrobe he realized that most of it did not fit him anymore. He could deal with that once he decided what look he was going for. His first inclination was to dress as a dandy, as he was interested in exploring the Games. But discarded the idea, because like with everything he did he needed to stand out. Marlyn ran up, jumped on him then ran off again. He normally would have played tag with her, but it had given him an idea.

He headed to the back of the room. Opening a passage in a rock he entered his secret room. It was small and highly protected. It would take a wizard stronger than him just to figure out it was there. He never cared for wealth, so he cared little about any of the contents here except for what was in this room. From the shelves he pulled a sword, a sweater and a small medallion. All three had come from the family of his mother. All the items in the room, and even himself, were all that remained of the Alexander family. He had spent some time tracking down his heritage. His grandfather had been the youngest of the family Coxcomb. He had been reluctantly sanctioned by the house when he joined the military. Herman's grandfather had risked much to follow his dream, but his father had been cast out of the House Coxcomb when he married Herman's mother. She was of minor birth, but still a member of the Alexander family. The two families were bitter rivals just as the two Houses they controlled were fierce competitors. Hurnik or Mark as he was called at the end of his life, had gone a step further than his own father. In marring one of Alexander family, he was sanctioned to the point that all he was allowed to keep was his name. Herman had no official claim on the House Coxcomb or the family, but as the last surviving member of the Alexander Family he was the sole heir to their fortune.

Not that it mattered, most of the House Alexander's holdings were destroyed when the Tecmen first invaded. His wealth was not great compared to that of a Great Houses, or even a Minor House. Still, we was but a single person, and the investments that had survived meant that Herman was never in the want for money. Herman cared little for money, for it could not replace the family that the Tecmen invasion had taken from him.

So many people were just like him in that regard, lost so much during the War Forward. The Tecmen brought a destruction with them that the Colonies was only now starting to recover. Herman wished that he could hate the Tecmen, but he could not. They were just like everyone else, just simply another culture. Just another group that struck out at others from the misguided belief that it would make their lives better.

Herman placed the watch he had received from Tapps in the room. He did not want to risk reminiscing anymore, or the tears it most often brought, so he quickly left. He walked back to his dressing area. His new self would be one that always kept up on fashion so he dressed accordingly with the exception of the sweater. Its magic adjusted its size to fit him. It was spider weave made during the height of the magic of the United Colonial Empire. Even though it felt like fine wool, it was really weaved from very small threads of a magical alloy named Fortis. Besides protecting like a suit of plate, it also had many magical properties. The most important to Herman at the moment was the sweater's ability to regulate the metabolism of the body. It would keep him cool enough not to sweat and warm enough not to shiver. He could drink all he wanted without ill effects and would not have to worry about being poisoned.

After putting on a loose pair of paints and a cape, Herman turned his attention to jewelry. It was very popular to flaunt wealth using such tidbits, but Herman decided that he would not follow suit. He picked out a simple gold bracelet and watch. For the medallion he chose a silver necklace. No one serious about fashion would wear silver and that is why he did. It would be noticed and he wanted to draw attention to the medallion. It was small and simple but the pattern was the symbol of power. Very few would dare to wear it. It was the royal seal of Amic Gruet, the ruler of the United Colonial Empire. Many take it as a noble sign of arrogance, a way of saying that one is better than everyone else, but a few scholars knew the truth. It was the symbol of true power, love.

He belted on his sword, which was also out of fashion. It was a rapier, and the thin blades have not been used for generations except by a few families. In fact, the younger courtiers stopped wearing blades all together. It was a nice sword but was neither magical nor fancy. It was fully functional and had been well used by his grandfather. It was a warrior's blade, not one for appearance. It was exactly what he wanted.

Once fully dressed, he paced the rows of shelves working through the role he was going to play. Slowly working out every detail of the character's personality and history. Hours passed as he made a new person come to life. Stripping his habits and replacing them with new ones. He eventually walked over the mirror.

He was now Alexander Hermes. The only son of a poor country noble raised in the courts of his city-living uncle. A stoic who was indifferent to the pains and pleasures which the game has to offer. Above them, willing to play only as a favor to the lady pursuing him. He was stylish but was not a slave to the whims of the popular. He was known for being generous and polite to everyone including servants, but was bored by nearly everyone. He would not tolerate being dishonored even in the slightest, but forgave easily. A man of wealth, but not enough to threaten those who care about such things. A bit of an eccentric, which can easily be forgiven for he was genuine and honest.

Not so smart as to be a threat to those who only pretended to be intelligent yet enough so his opinions were welcomed. Yet something was missing. He knew instantly what it was. He replaced his cape with a cloak. The cape lacked function, only a dandy would wear one. Alexander was not one to care what other people thought of him. After grabbing Marlyn, he returned to the hotel to start his new life.

Brother Matthew felt out of place in his new church. It was in the city of Saint Peter and was the second largest city in Shouker. It was, of course, a promotion of sorts for him. He was still an Abbot but now had several friars under him. The larger church meant a better chance of promotion, though that was something he cared nothing about. He felt closer to the occupants of the farming communities, those who spent their lives in hard labors. Many might have considered it odd because he was raised in the posh lifestyle of academics. It had been what he had seen, and what he had done living that lifestyle which had left with a distaste for it.

It had been almost three years since the destruction of the town which was under his care. An anniversary he was not looking forward to. The actions of the Holy Council still baffled him.

He had presented himself to the Sanhedrin shortly after his town was attacked. He still did not know what had happened. He was at one of the outlying villages on a routine visit. When he returned to his town it had been burnt to the ground. Whatever attacked the town had left no one alive. The destruction was complete, not even the stone around the well was left intact. He reported all to the Council and they had told him that they would look into it. A few weeks later he was assigned to this church as assistant to the Southern Abbot of Saint Peter. He never learned what the Council had discovered, but last month he had received his orders to take over command as the Southern Abbot. His boss was retiring and the promotion came as no shock to him.

Once his turnover was complete the first thing, he had done was raid the priests' offices. All the gold and silver that belonged to the church which was being used for decoration, everything that was not used in the rituals, he had sold to fill the poor box. That had not set well with the Friars and Called under his command. They were further upset when he had confiscated the jewelry which belonged to the church for the same reason. All that was left when he was finished were those items that had been sanctified.

Abbot Rosincran was not against the rich priests, or the ones from the rich families. Jewelry and silk were simply their custom, but the church could not itself be exhibiting riches when people were hungry. Mathew knew the arguments and agreed with most of it. The exhibition of wealth by the Church showed the grandeur of Elohim, gave people an understanding of Golden Eternity. Yet, that was only if their eyes were focused on the life beyond death. Mathew knew that most, especially those who had to struggle just to survive, did not have the time nor inclination to fix their hearts on such an abstract reality. To them, the wealth of the Church only pushed the thorn of poverty deeper into their flesh.

Mathew wished he could apply his decree to uptown as well but it was even more important in the Southern District. It was often called the labor district because the River of Hope ran through the southern part of the city. The constant movement of cargo located the day work in this area. Even Shouker's day laborers were only one step ahead of destitution. In fact, his abbot had the largest budget in Shouker. The city, being the trade hub of the nation, had a large number of unskilled laborers. Nearly all of the city's poor fund was allocated to his district. Could not these priests see, if not the pain it caused, at least the bad taste it was to flaunt their wealth.

This was the reason he liked dealing with the simple people in the small villages. The harsh winters of Shouker made it necessary for them to pull together. As Saint Shouker had once written 'The greedy thrive during the booms but it is the generous who survive the bust'. Matthew knew that this was true. In his own town everyone was always quick to split their meals with anyone who came along. His only friar then had come from the very town in which his church had been and one would not have guessed that he was a friar to look at him. So much unlike these city priests with their silk and fine wool garments.

He wished that the entire Priesthood would adopt the practice of the Order of Saint Stephen. His latest memo was what had gotten him in trouble. He was very clear that the only clothing which the District of Southern Saint Peter would buy for its priests was the simple ones that the Order wore. That was the problem he was dealing with now. His entire priest staff was outside his office. He knew that he was in for a fight. He knew that most of his troubles were because of his age. He had just reached his third decade and most of the friars were at least half that again. They resented having things changed by one so young. It made matters worse that he looked at least five years younger than he was. His face took on a truly boyish appearance when he smiled. Not that he would be doing it much around them for a while.

He could not put off the confrontation any longer. Gesturing for his assistant to open the door, he braced for the fight.

The priests entered quietly. He had picked this room for his office for a simple reason. It was small, only having enough room for three extra chairs. The two abbots under him and the most aggressive friar took the chairs, the rest had to stand. As soon as Matt looked up from the paper he was reading, everyone started talking at once. Everyone except for Abbot James. Everyone knew that he had hoped to become the Southern District's Abbot. He was a man who always had the look of a predator in his eyes. If he was not as strong in his faith, he could have been the worst enemy that Matthew had. They had fought when Matthew first took over the district, but now he seemed to have taken to an advisory role. Matthew would have liked to talk to him alone. Matthew raised his voice, which had such a commanding quality that the room went silent.

"I will not change my mind on this. We have no. . . "

He was cut off by everyone talking again. Matthew stood, but this had little effect. Brother Matthew took a sip of his coffee. His eyes rested on the movement of the dark brown liquid. He felt like such a hypocrite. Even though he paid for the expensive indulgence out of his own meager allowance, could not the money be spent on something better? The same battle he was fighting with them he had been fighting with himself. He was spoiled and knew it. How many people could have been fed with the silver he has spent on the luxury of the stimulant? At that moment he despised the cup in his hands. It was as if it was a poisonous snake and he threw it across the room. The priests went quiet when they were sprayed with warm coffee and cup shards. Matthew knew that most of his anger towards them was from his own shortcoming. He knew full well that what we find most irritating in others, we are guilty of, and usually to a greater extent. Realizing this, it was easy to calm himself while he pulled a piece of paper from his desk. He read it with a stern but gentle tone which made the others forget how young he looked.

"Three hundred twenty-four people in our province died last year from the elements. In our province another two hundred sixteen died from hunger. Just because your calling is not for the poor does not mean that you can ignore them. We are the representatives of the Xrist to these people. If we do not show them Elohim's Love then how are they to see it? If we do not love them then how can they believe that the Most High does?"

There were tears in Abbot Rosincran's eyes, and he wanted to say more but lacked the strength. He dropped to his chair and rubbed his forehead. The priests present were abashed. They had been swayed not by the young abbot's words but by his own apparent repentance. The silence was broken by the door opening. Matthew could feel the Spirit flooding the room. Whoever had just come in was strong in the Anointing. He got a good look when the rest of the room went silent and the priests parted to let the man through. Brother Manker walked up to the desk and looked around.

"Everyone out. I have something to discuss with your Abbot." He looked down. "If you would, I would like to you to stay as well Brother James."

His voice was soft and non-obtrusive but everyone did not hesitate. Manker was only a friar, but everyone knew he had the authority of a bishop. Not in the running of the government, but the authority of office. Many had already started calling him Saint, even though both him and the Sanhedrin did not allow such talk, and Manker openly discouraged such descriptions of himself.

Once everyone left and the door was shut, Manker took a seat. He was an old man and looked even older. Many had said that he aged ten years when his wife died and Abbot Rosincran could feel the wound. Even so, he radiated all the authority for which he was famous. His voice was strained as if he was carrying a heavy weight.

"I have heard of what you have been doing here Brother Matthew. I must say that I approve. What I am about to say should not go beyond the door. I have been talking with the Sanhedrin and soon the entire church will be going to the vows of the Order of the Sabaoth. The Sanhedrin wanted to initiate the vows of the Order of Saint Stephen, but they listened to me about this. Not every priest is called to complete poverty. We cannot expect everyone to give up their own wealth. But that is not what has brought me here.

"First to you brother James, I know that you hold no resentment for being passed up for the district Abbot. Know that it will be yours soon, you just have to be patient for Elohim has other plans for Brother Matthew."

Manker turned towards Matthew and smiled warmly before continuing.

"As for you, all I can tell now is to keep yourself in shape. Both physically and spiritually. A battle is coming soon and you must be ready for it. The Council has only a glimpse of what is to come. On that I am not yet allowed to tell but it is enough to allow us to be ready. My only advice would be to keep up with what you have been doing."

Manker stood and after bowing slightly left the room. Matthew and James spoke for a while and then went about their business. With the help of James the rest of the priests in the Southern District of Saint Peter were soon giving up their luxuries voluntarily.

Divinus entered the war room and addressed Snow. After the generals were dismissed, he spoke freely.

"The currents have been telling me very much lately. To start, it tells me of a man of your race named Tapps. We must get to this man. If he can be convinced, he would make a great addition to the hall of power."

Snow eyes widened. He did not want Tapps to be on the council. He only wanted him dead. And his voice showed it.

"I have come to call this man enemy. He has done great harm to me in the past and I was planning on having him killed as soon as I got a chance." Divinus thought hard and seemed to be listening to someone.

"I understand your hatred, but you must put it behind you. This Tapps was chosen by the First Dragon. He is at the phase in which he can still be turned to our cause. He must make his choice soon of either becoming a Saint or a Deamon. His power is too great for us to fight at a distance and we cannot risk bringing him close unless he embraces the Destroyer. With any luck he will be the first modern to sit on the Unholy Council.

Snow did not like that implication and his tone said so.

"And if he does not?"

Divinus smiled in a way which sent chills up Snow's spine.

"Then you may do what you will with him. I have some errands to run and will be gone for some time. I will be back in about two moon spans. I am confident that you can manage that long without me. Do not be eager for battle. Instead sharpen your military skills on the winged people who share these mountains. They have little contact with the outside world and are not great combatants. I will look forward to seeing what you have accomplished when I return."

Before Snow could respond Divinus turned and left the room. Snow was beginning to get annoyed; it may be time to get rid of his so-called advisor. A willow wisp whispered in his ear. For now, he would have to put up with the man's insolence, just because he needed him. He did not yet have enough control of his powers to be rid of Divinus. The time was coming quickly when he could rid himself of the man, just a bit of patience was needed. He mused to himself that it did not matter. He knew where the Tapps' weakness was and he did not have to confront him directly. He waited for Divinus to leave and called for the human called Silver to be brought to him.

There is an old saying that is as true now as it was when it was first written in the Tymalt. Only those who are willing to fall the farthest reach the highest peaks. Silver had fallen far. He had plenty of time to think of his old master's sayings locked in a cell deep in the Castle of Shadows. He had been a fool and he knew it.

Feeling called, Silver had entered the New Shadow City, the City of Chaos as it was commonly called. He had heard that the Shadow could bless men with great power or send a creeping black energy into them that would kill him slowly and painfully. Silver mostly heard about the latter. He shuddered to think of his body swelling and swelling until it finally exploded. The whole process could take days and from what Silver heard one would be insane from the pain by the time death took them. Silver was sure that he was meant to be here so had to risk it. He had to find a way to revenge himself against Tapps. The only other choice was death. He had to talk to this Lord of Shadows. He had to talk to the Kaltar who people called the Shadow, or was it something else he needed to do? Silver was not sure what it was but he was compelled to do something.

He did not understand himself when he walked straight to the central palace and demanded entrance. He had always been more of a thinker than that. In the weeks that followed he was sure that he had been under a spell. How else could you explain him ranting and raving like a mad man?

He jumped when the cell door started to open. Two large and grotesque men entered and grabbed him without saying a word. He was sure that this would be his death. He did not know why they had just not let him starve to death in his cell.

XVI

Snow threw his head back and laughed heartily. It was the first time he understood what he laughed about since Tapps had thrown him out of his guild of rogues. He had just heard Silver's tale. Snow was on his throne and Silver kneeled in front of him. Silver looked like a beggar and not a very good one at that. It had taken Silver a little over a year to get to the heart of the new Empire of the Shadow to seek an audience with the Dark Shadow. Snow had overheard that phrase, and liked it much more then calling himself the the Shadow reborn. Dark was how he felt. It implied hidden power, and the wiliness to do what needed to be done.

The pathetic human in front of him looked more like a drowned rat than anyone of importance. Snow had not understood why his last Blood Ritual had led to this man. It all came clear when he heard the master rogue's story. Except for the physical difference, the two of them were the same. They both were raised up and took over their guilds from a weak master. Both had been ruined by that cursed person named Tapps. The hero spending his early life in fighting pits, and then a guild, explained much about him.

This man named Silver he could use. Even if he was a human, he seemed to know Tapps well. Snow knew that the man did not share his desire for revenge. No, Silver was obsessed. Like an ill raised youth, Silver had let his passion take away his reason. But still, this obsession had its advantage. Just in listening to the human tell his story he had learned twice about Tapps than he had known before. It was interesting to know that his enemy was raised in a gladiator pit. He had guessed that his blind brother had a strong sense of honor, but it was more than that. The time that this human and Tapps had been trained together would give him much insight into his foe.

He would have to keep this human close for a while. As an afterthought, he made Silver a general in his army. The man was used to ordering people around. He would make a fine general again once he cleaned himself up.

It took Alexander Hermes only three months to become a full member of the Courtly Culture. He was considered an up-and-coming youth. To the generals and nobles, he had just enough ambition not to be a lay-about, but not enough to be a threat to the plans of others. He had acquired the reputation as a master player. He would never even admit that he entertained women privately. He was also known for never smiling, which he used to his advantage when he did entertain by smiling frequently.

He knew he was considered a full player when an invitation for an Eveitio Ball came to him. He knew it was because of Shelly, General Albert's wife, that he received his invitation. He had presented himself as available to partake in the courtly game, but most of the ladies would give up when it became apparent that he would not be conquered. Lady Albert was determined. For two weeks she had hinted and stole away to spend time with him. He would always receive her in the friendliest manner, but would not allow it to go farther. His indifference only proved to make her more passionate in her pursuit.

When the invitation arrived, he knew it was her doing. It was Lady Albert's way of saying that she could do great things for him, if he but agreed to be lovers. He would go to the party, and thus let her know that he is willing. He knew that she would take it as a victory and would stop her play. He had no attention in going through with it, he would not be conquered, but it was a way to stop her pursuit. Both would walk away feeling as if the victory was theirs. No matter why one played, the best victory in the Courtly Game was one where the adversaries thought they had won.

He had clothing especially made for the occasion. He would not give up his usual style but as he was being introduced to the highest circle of the court, he needed to present a strong image. Appearance, after all, is the obsession of such a life. Appearance without substance was what the Courtly Game requires. The hardest decision had been the choice to leave Marlyn behind. He did not mind the rumors about his sanity caused by him so dutifully caring for a skunk, but a party was no place for her. In all the preparations the night of the ball arrived quickly.

It was a pleasant evening so he decided to arrive by foot at the huge complex used for these parties. More importantly he was going to be slightly late. He knew that the Countess would take it as an insult and thus notice him. He had learned all he could about Lady Eve. She was loved by all the lords and hated by most of the ladies. She had a great number of courtiers including, if the rumors were true, the Dark Shadow himself. All indications were that she indulged none of them. It could be true or it could simply mean that she was a master of the game. Either way she would be his entry into the royal court.

After showing his invitation to the guards he entered the ball room as if he owned it. Handing his card to the valet, he scanned the room. He kept his countenance calm to show that he was not worried about being late. He did not rank an introduction, but knew that Lady Eve would ask about him. She was looking at him now. He nodded a greeting and continued his scanning. It did not take him long to find Lady Albert. He slowly made his way to her. He spoke politely with General Albert and his wife. He allowed her to introduce him to various people. He was always courteous, but they held very little interest for him. He kept an eye on Lady Eve. It was nearly an hour, but she did go over to the valet. He looked away when she started to talk. When he knew it would be safe, he looked back. The door attendant was going through the cards. Alexander knew he pulled out his because he had his made with rose colored paper. He had accomplished his real objective tonight, so he threw himself into the introductions. The contacts would be useful once he was in the royal court.

He scanned the room for General Silver. For such a small city, there were a lot of generals. Silver had a strong street accent from KanaTo. Herman would have determined which city Silver was from, but Alexander had not spent much time in that nation so could not tell Silver's accent came from the south west section. The general lacked even the slightest ability in matters of court. His few real exploits were well enough known that only the ladies of the third court would even converse with him openly. It was also well known that he had a taste for slaves, and if rumors were true, he had a large harem of them. This would work to his advantage, for Hermes knew as soon as he was introduced to the man that Silver wanted to be a player. The only reason he was tolerated at such parties was because he was an advisor to the Shadow. His position, and his position alone, made General Silver worth befriending.

He found the general making a fool of himself by the buffet. Alexander was too far away to hear the conversation, but it was apparent that Silver was telling a story that none around him believed. He turned to excuse himself when his eyes met with those of Lady Eve. He nodded a greeting and raised his glass. To his surprise she gestured for him to come over. He gave his assent and without worrying about appearances leaned over and whispered in Lady Albert's ear.

"If you come tomorrow night, I will smile with my eyes."

He walked away, knowing full well that she would know it was in reference to their conversation that only love would make him smile with his eyes. He moved unhurriedly and the Lady Eve seemed anxious to receive his company. Maybe she was not a master player after all. When he approached she put out her hand. He took it gently and pressed it to his lips as he bowed. It tasted like honey and the touch sent an energy he was not accustomed to through his body. He almost lost his composure and slowed his raising.

When he looked into her eyes the world melted away. He quickly let go of her hand when he realized he still held it. He let Lady Eve introduce him to her companions. If any of them noticed his initial discomfort they did not give indication. He took a seat and joined the conversation. It was light and became mostly about him. He answered their questions openly and politely, but his mind was occupied with the Lady Eve. He wanted to look at her. He feared that if he did, he would be discovered.

Both her eyes and hair were dark, in sharp contrast to her light collored skin. Her figure was of proportions which left no doubt that she was a woman. Hermes was drawn to what was beyond her beauty. She had a way about her that instantly put him at ease, yet, left him completely confused. More than once, when their eyes met, the entire world would disappear and it seemed they were alone.

The group spent most of the time talking on trivial matters that did not compare to her. Only once did he feel compelled to speak. The conversation had moved to the topic of power and someone mentioned that Sir Alexander must have something to say because of his medallion. He spoke unguarded and with a smile which did not touch his eyes.

"Power? Yes, I know a few things about power. I have searched for it most of my life. I wear this ancient piece of jewelry to remind me that I have yet to find the greatest of powers. All other forms of power are but shadows of a dream compared to love. A love that radiates through time and space is worth more than all the gold and swords in the Colonies. Indeed, one may count themselves the most fortunate person alive to know this kind of love for even one day. That is why Amic the Great took the symbol of love as his own and declared it also to be the symbol of power."

Hermes was immensely pleased with his words but only because they had pleased Lady Eve. The enjoyment of just sitting next to her made the rest of the night go by quickly. When it ended, he did not want to go but could find no excuse to stay. He reluctantly left but found himself smiling, even with his eyes, on the way home as he thought about the next time he would see her.

A man warmed himself by the breakfast fire. The woman in the other room had a slight cold so he decided to let her sleep until she woke on her own. He owed her that much for all she had done for him. A few of years ago he had come out of the nearby mountains nearly frozen from the early spring cold. She had found him collapsed at the edge of her farm and taken care of him. Since that time, he had helped her with the farm work. Her husband had died years earlier and she had no children to help, so there was plenty for him to do.

He moved outside to start his work. It still frustrated him that he could not remember who he was. He only came to remember his name a few months ago. She was reading from one of the few books she had when they came across the name of Marius. It seemed to fit him. He was not sure why but it just seemed like his name.

There were other things that were odd as well. The language she spoke, even though he understood it perfectly he had a hard time speaking it. His accent was thick and he stumbled on words frequently. He seemed to be much more conformable with what she had called the ancient tongue. Most of the books had short quotes in the old tongue and he understood them perfectly.

A week ago, things had become very confusing. The world suddenly took on an odd appearance. A fog, which was not a fog, appeared. It moved through and around everything and if he concentrated hard enough, he could get it to move how he wanted. Marius did not know what it was and he feared that his illness had taken away his sanity.

Elizabeth came out of the cabin with an irritated look on her face. He knew why. She was upset that he had let her sleep in. She was not one to let a minor illness prevent her from doing her work. He decided that it would be wiser to avoid her until lunch.

Angga Sella walked through the winter camp enjoying the time between classes. She had to admit that that the culture was impressive. For a people with such a strong pride of who they are, they welcomed outsiders with open arms. In the years she had been there, many had come and joined. Even the renegade Gargoyle who came from the Unclaimed Lands were welcomed. A nation of misfits. She could understand why Tapps would take it as his own.

Tapps was called to perform a duty of his office as Protector. She was shocked to find that he had to deal with a Dragon. She did not get the details of exactly what he would be doing. She knew that both the clans and Tapps were in good standing with the Dragons, but that was far from interfering with them. To make matters even worse he had gone alone, saying something about respect and Rolfins. Whatever that meant.

With Tapps being absent it was the first time she really noticed Keith. He was a handsome youth some ten years her junior. He was one of the warriors of the clan and the Spirit-child of Tapps. Since her arrival he had been around. He had been assigned to help her become accustomed to life in the clans. Until Tapps left she had only asked him about the various customs of the Vagofrons. They spent most of their time talking about Tapps. The youth had both a strong admiration and a strong anger towards the Kaltar. When she asked him about it all he would say was Tapps did what he had to do.

It had taken her some time to piece together that the woman who had killed Tapps' wives had been Keith's mother. What a burden for the youth to carry? Still, Keith was one of the most generous and forgiving persons who she had ever met. He spent most of his time with her, but when he was not, he spent his time helping others. Everything from digging a new post hole to repairing tents. He did this even though the Insanus Unam were excused from those duties.

She had asked him about it and he said he was only following his father's example. Apparently, his father was a holy man of some sort and had left the Frons when Keith's sister had come to age. Keith had once said that his greatest shame was that he had not yet been able to forgive Tapps the way his father had.

Keith was serious most of the time and the way he spoke reminded her of her father. The way he analyzed everything before speaking. He even had his moods like her father. He was in one of those moods when Tapps returned. Although she did not notice because of her preoccupation with Tapps.

Alexander sat in a plush chair in the Iron Tooth tavern holding a note in his hand. The exclusive club allowed only the top generals and nobles as members. He was only half paying attention to the conversation, something about a hypothetical campaign, as he was preoccupied with Lady Eve. It had been almost a month since the ball. He knew he had become drunk on her smile. His passion would be his downfall if he could not control it. He had had several chances to see her again but politely declined the invitations to the various parties if she would be there. He had to gain control of himself first.

He had to do it quickly for he only had two weeks. The note in his hand was an invitation to a private party given by Lady Eve at her own residence. He could not refuse. Not only because it would ruin his plans, but because it was handwritten by her and informally signed. A party invitation could be declined no matter who it came from, but refusing a personal request was a major courtly offence. One that would earn the animosity of the sender. He was called back to the conversation by General Spith asking him a question. He did not like the man. The general was the type of man who would not control his appetite for the sensual. Alexander was polite, but did not hide his strong disagreement with the general.

"The key to winning KanaTo is not in countering their advance military on the open field. They are a rich nation and even their foot soldiers are equipped with weapon and armor. The Dragon Riders and the Imperial Elite are impressive, but all of KanaTo's might rests in two cities. Their power is centralized. Take and hold Telpep and the capital and your victory is assured. No matter how many battles on open field you lose.

General McGovern chimed in from the next table.

"You have forgotten McGovern City. My father holds most of the power in the east. His force would be able to crush any army which came against it. Thus one would have to defeat the McGoverns before they could secure KanaTo."

General Geran rolled his eyes. Alexander gave him a knowing look. The young McGovern was little more than a spoiled child. A shame really, because like all the McGoverns, there was great potential in the youth. Master Hermes decided to ignore the rudeness of joining a conversation uninvited and favored the young general with a response.

"That is true. The McGoverns have always held great power, even when their holdings have waned. However, I have met your father once and instantly knew that he was a wise man. One smart enough to know that any force which could take the Dragon Throne and Telpep would be very strong indeed. Even if he could muster enough to defeat such an enemy, it would leave him too weak to hold even his own land.

"No. Confronted by such a force your father would use the elegance for which your family is famous. Duke McGovern is a master player without equal. His passion is not for the ladies but for power, and if rumors are correct his ambition includes the desire to sit on the Dragon Throne. More likely, if he faced such an enemy he would parley a peace in secret and gain for himself a kingdom from eastern KanaTo.

"As we are only making believe, I would venture to say that any McGovern would recognize such a force capable of threatening KanaTo long before it became known to the rest of us. They would use their prowess in the game to increase their own power no matter which side won. There would be many ways of doing this, but as a McGovern I am sure I would not have to tell you of them.

"All I am really saying is that even though the holdings and forces of the McGoverns are the strongest in the nation, a smart enemy would not have to face them directly in order to gain the rest."

Everyone hearing understood the thinly veiled insult. Most prepared to get out of the way, a few prepared to back Alexander in the conflict. Everyone knew that the young McGovern was there for the very reason that was just spoken. To make matters worse for the youth, the name McGovern was often used by the nobles to mean one that could not be trusted. However, the challenge never came. General McGovern was too pleased by the flatteries to realize that they were really insults directed at the honor of him and his family. Knowing that the child of a noble would not understand, Alexander turned back to the generals at his table. He spoke with a tone fitting to the victory he had just won.

"That proves my real point. Forward attacks should only be used if your foe is so weak that your victory is assured, or if they are a distraction from your real goal. This is true in all aspects of life, whether it is business, power or the ladies. It is all the same. But I am sure that I do not have to tell you gentlemen this."

They all laughed except for Alexander. He had already retreated into his mind. The generals would take it that he was giving serious thought to what they were saying. After all he was but a youth and they had much more experience. What he had said had affected him more than the others. He had to decide what his real goal was. His goal has always been the power, but now he was not sure. All he could think about was her. Did he really want her or was he a victim of the game? Was this one of those short-lived desires on which it was based? Was she the distraction or the goal? He needed time to think. He was about to excuse himself when General Albert burst into the room.

The general had his blade drawn and was yelling for Alexander. The butler tried to restrain him but General Albert gave him a blow with his basket hilt. The servant went down, the wound looking severe. The general was a large man used to combat. In a hurried pace he moved towards Master Hermes throwing several chairs out of his way. Alexander stood calmly when Sir Albert approached the table. The general's words were contorted by his anger.

"you. . . you. . ."

Not being able to find the words to express himself, the general lunged his sword at Alexander across the table. Master Hermes dodged it easily. In the same motion he pulled hard on the general's arm and yanked a call cord from the wall. By the time Sir Albert realized what was happening, he was belly down on the table, and Alexander had his arms tied to a leg of the table.

The general thrashed and screamed about honor and duels.

Eventually General Albert calmed enough to get loose. He stood and looked around. The other generals were looking at him disapprovingly. The youth, who was the object of his rage, was calmly cleaning out his pipe. The general had made a fool of himself. He straightened out his uniform and apologized to those present. He turned to leave, but Alexander's words stopped him.

"Sir, a private word with you?"

The general stood motionless for a moment before turning. When Alexander saw the man's face, he felt real compassion. The general was not a player but a true gentleman. The crime committed was not against his honor but his heart. The general's words came out cold.

"There is nothing you can . . "

Master Hermes gently cut him off.

"Sir, on my honor, and all that I hold dear, if you will just hear me out you will have satisfaction."

The general reluctantly consented and they retired to a private room. Alexander gave an order for coffee with sugar to be brought. Both too expensive for the general normally afford. After the drinks arrived, he lit a cigar and handed one to the general. He spoke openly.

"I have dishonored you, but not in the way you think. I have entertained your wife privately." He put up his hand when Sir Albert went to rise. "But I never touched her. I would not have. Neither would she have allowed me. I have affronted your honor by believing you to be like the ones out there. I see now that you really love your wife. I will give you a piece of advice which you would be well to take to heart. Go on a picnic with her this very afternoon. Make it a secluded place where you will not be disturbed. Talk with her. Show her how much you adore her. Most of all show her the tenderness she knew from you in the beginning. To her you are a husband not a general. She is your wife and is there to shore up your weakness."

The general eyed Alexander suspiciously before saying anything.

"I must be wary of any advice that comes from you. After all she told me of your proposition. About the night that..."

The general looked away. Master Hermes spoke softly.

"She did not come to me that night. I would not have offered if I thought she would. But think on this and I will leave you to make your choice. She told you. Her motivation is clearly that she still wants you. More than that, she still wants you to want her."

Alexander stood and walked into the common room. A doctor was working on the butler. As he headed towards the wounded man, General

McGovern spoke with a sneer.

"So Alex, what did you tell him?"

Master Hermes did not bother to look towards the man as he spoke in an irritated tone.

"General McGovern, I have given you no leave to call me familiar and my business is none of your concern. Even if it was, you would not have understood."

There was no cloak to this challenge. McGovern stood and was apparently ready to answer. Alexander was not paying attention so the McGovern grew awkward and sat back down. Master Hermes approached the doctor. The physician looked grim as he stood.

"It is hopeless. He needs a Medical-Magus. There is not enough time to get one."

As the doctor moved to the basin to wash his hands Alexander turned to one of the servants.

"Go fetch the magus, and tell him that I will double his fee."

Master Hermes bent over and placed his hand on the butler's forehead and sent out strands of magic. The pain started for both of them when their two bodies were linked. Alexander worked some magic to sedate the pain and forced his body to aid with the worse of the butler's wounds. He only healed the man enough so the butler would survive until the Medical-Magus arrived. Herman could have completely healed the man but Alexander could do no more for him, he was not well versed in medicine. That was not part of this role.

He stood and wiped the sweat of his face with his handkerchief. Looking around he noticed everyone watching him. He spoke calmly as he walked over to his table.

"It would not have sat well if he would have died. He is by far too good of a servant for us to find a replacement." He turned towards McGovern.

"That is right general. I am a Warrior-Wizard. Remember that next time you consider insulting me by prying into my games."

He took his chair and lit his pipe. General Geran was smiling and was almost on the verge of laughter. His tone was friendly.

"You are just full of surprises."

Alexander looked thoughtful for a moment before answering.

"I have found it much easier to discover who your real allies are when they consider you weak. Otherwise, it is too easy to mistake fear for loyalty." After a polite time had elapsed, Alexander excused himself and retired to his room. He needed the time alone to figure out just why he was playing the courtly game.

XVII

The private party was much smaller than Alexander had expected. Lady Eve and himself, General Albert and his wife and a couple, who he knew only in passing, were the only one's present. He entered without announcement which was common for such affairs. His walk and attitude were his usual one of command but it faltered when he saw Eveitio. He had resolved himself to the fact he was playing for the power but, upon seeing her, he was no longer sure. She rushed up and brought him to the seat next to hers.

Alexander was unusually awkward during the meal. Judging by the others reactions he did well in the conversation, but he felt exposed every time he looked at her. Even though the food was the finest available and masterfully seasoned, it tasted bland to him. He was trapped in something which seemed at the same time much worse and infinitely better than the chaos.

During the main course Lady Eve leaned over and whispered in his ear.

"Shelly told me what you did for her and the general. If it is not too forward, I shall ask why."

Herman smiled as he turned his head to speak in her ear. The closeness filled him with delight.

"Because love is such a rare thing between husband and wife for those of our rank, I felt it my duty to help them."

She retreated smiling. The pleasure of feeling her breath on his cheek lasted the rest of the meal. It was then he noticed how well the food was prepared. He grew uncomfortable again after dessert. They headed towards the den. Deciding that he needed to clear his thoughts Alexander walked to the balcony when they entered the small room.

He pulled out his pipe and a small gold cylinder. He had created a device for Tapps with which to start camp fires. It was easy to repeat the process to make a pocket fire, an item which impressed most of his friends. Lighting the pipe, he noticed the magical shield that kept the heat from escaping to the chilled air outside. Without thinking about it, he opened a small hole in the field to let the smoke out.

Alexander was not thinking well and he knew it. It felt like the time he had tried laugh weed. All except his mouth was not dry. Then even his mouth became very dry when Eveitio stepped next to him.

Her quarters on this side of the Shadow Castle had a nice view of the city. The lights in the dark, several hundred feet below, looked like stars. They talked of trifles for a short time but he soon felt awkward. He looked at her face. She was so beautiful and he knew instantly that he would give up everything for her.

"All the beauties in this world which I have seen during my travels, none have prepared me for you. My mind wars to hold back my heart from those things that it desires most . . ."

Lady Eve reached up and pressed her finger to his lips. She spoke as one reciting a favorite poem.

"If my will was strong, I would allow all the things I am most eager to say lapse with silence. Yet my heart takes captive my will and forces me to abandon all proper speech and drives me forward to show those things that I cannot find the words for. So, if my heart causes me to say anything that should embarrass you, I beg you to chastise me gently and hold no ill will." She smiled when her words became her own. "The Art of Love is one of my favorite books. I have read it many times. But please, let us speak honestly and without art."

Alexander looked down when Eve removed her finger. His voice was a whisper.

"I was being honest."

Her voice was sweet.

"I know."

They stood there in silence. He could not look at her. He felt like running away. It was not rational but he felt that he had betrayed her. Herman looked up as she moved closer. She leaned over and kissed him. Alexander blushed and he knew that the role he was playing was crumbling in her presence. His eyes and voice were shy.

"Why. . ."

He could get no more out but Eveitio knew what he asked.

"Because I knew that you would not kiss me." She noticed a strange look on his face for which she did not know the reason. "What's wrong?"

Alexander looked away.

"It's just that . . . I mean. . . I have never . . ."

He felt like such a fool. It was not like him to have a loss for words. What was happening to him? He looked up at her smiling face when she grabbed his hand and lead him to a dark corner of the balcony. The other guests sensing that it was time leave did so without disturbing them.

Angga looked up to the outcropping of rocks where Tapps would spend at least an hour each day in his prayers. High up the side of the canyon wall, he was nothing more than a dark figure. A stranger to the camp would most likely not even notice him. Even from the distance he was awe inspiring. A god looking down on his people making sure no harm comes to them.

Keith approached the clearing were Angga stood looking up. He stood back watching her. She was so beautiful. He knew that he had fallen in love and all the exercises that his mother had taught him did not help. He had stripped away all the fantasies but the love was still there. His father had always told him that love was real, but he had never truly believed until now.

He knew that she was looking up at Tapps. He had to fight hard against the tears that were forming. He started the mental exercise to purge the fears from his mind. Searching for each one, he brought them to the surface to examine them. It was not his age. Even though he was only twenty-three she had never treated him as only a youth.

Culture, race, social standing, none of these were the root of his pain. It turned out to be the most obvious one. Tapps. He was by far the better man, it was no wonder she looked at him the way she did even now. He knew what he needed to do. Keith walked up and stood next to Angga. He could not help but to smile when she smiled as she spoke.

"He is like a Marblen Gargoyle, keeping evil away from the valley." Keith looked up at Tapps for a moment before answering.

"Yes, it brought great comfort to many of us as youths when he sat up there." He chanced a look at her when she looked back up. "Are you in love with him?"

Keith's heart sank when her smile turned even sweeter.

"No, he is a remarkable man. What my father would call a hero to the heroes. I love him very much, but as for being in love with him, no, not yet, but I am sure it is heading that way."

Keith spoke without thinking.

"If anyone is worthy of you, it is him."

He suddenly felt exposed when Angga looked at him questionably. He had to turn his head away. It took a few moments for him to regain his composure and speak again.

"I am leaving this eve to start the final phase of my training and wanted to say goodbye. I will..." He paused. He could not voice that he would miss her in fear that she might learn the truth of his feelings. It was apparent that she knew what he was going to say.

"I will miss you too. I have never had someone I could really talk to before."

She reached out and gave him a hug. Keith smiled when she let go. He did not want to leave her. He forced his thoughts into order.

"Tapps wanted to see me before I left. I am heading up there now. Do you want to come?"

Angga shook her head.

"I do not have time. My next class starts soon."

They hugged again and parted ways. Keith felt like crying.

Tapps sat on top of a nearby mountain looking over the winter camp. It was his favorite place to pray and he would spend weeks up here at a time. Things were going on that were starting to become clear. Not only in his personal life, but in the Colonies as well.

He was going to have to turn over training to others. He reluctantly had to admit that he had enjoyed the task, but he was needed elsewhere. Officially, he had to deal with a Dragon that had been stepping across the line with some country folk. This would be the fifth one in as many years. There is more going on in the Dragon ranks than they are willing to admit. Of course, they are not infallible, so they may not even have seen it yet. He had laughed when the report was read to him. It was Turcan. A Dragon for whom he had been looking. It was KanaFinaTurcan and no doubt this had something to do with money. He was not sure whether dealing with the creature would be easy or hard.

There was too much going on in the Colonies. Tapps could not figure out what was causing his sense of coming doom. He wished Manker was around, he needed the prophet. It would be a while before he could get to visit his old friend. There were things that needed to be done. Dealing with the Dragon could wait as well. There was something more important to do. There was a wound in Angga with which they needed to deal. He had known of its presence for some time but only recently been granted the wisdom to know how to deal with it. She simply needed to go home.

She felt like she had betrayed her parents by leaving. She would have to face them. He did not know whether or not they actually held ill towards her, but after a decade it was time to deal with it. There was more to it than that. Her people needed her. He did not know why, but VivusDeus had made it clear that they would not survive without her, and he needed to go with her. Whatever she was to face, she was not strong enough to do it alone. He had heard the footsteps for some time and when he could make out the scent he knew who it was.

"I am glad that you decided not to avoid me."

Keith's tone was unemotional.

"As I am leaving tonight for the Purging, I could not put it off. What do you want?"

Tapps turned towards Keith as he spoke.

"I told you before that your mother's path is not yours. There is too much of your father in you. The choice is yours, of course. I am leaving right after Jennifer's and QuickPaw's wedding for Angga's home land. It would be for the best if you would come along."

The turmoil of Keith's heart was apparent on his face. It took Keith a moment to gain control. His words came out of clenched teeth.

"No, I am completing my training."

Tapps looked down. His voice contained a hint of sorrow.

"I will not make it an order, but it would be for the best. I can see your desire."

Keith's anger was thick in his voice as he cut Tapps off, a defense from the pain.

"Cannot you see that she does not want me?" Keith worked the mental exercise and it quickly calmed him. "You will not change my mind on this. If there is nothing else?"

Keith turned before Tapps could answer. Tapps let him leave. He had pressed too hard. There was something else in this of which he was not aware. The two of them had spent so much time together and there was so much energy between them that Tapps had assumed too much. He mentally shrugged. People always made things more difficult than they had to be. Tapps laughed out loud as he as he counted himself as one of those people.

Alexander woke abruptly and quickly rolled out of bed. He felt threatened so he let the chaos envelope him. Time slowed as he scanned the room with his magic. His reaction had been purely instinct. There was no one in the room. His mind coldly collected and analyzed the information as he sent his magic further out. Except for the presence of a few servants, the chambers were empty. Deciding it must have been a bad dream he stood and pushed away the feeling. He could not completely get rid of the darkness surrounding his mind. It was going to be a bad day, at least until he saw Eve again.

Walking over to his closet he chose his clothes carefully. Today would be special. He gave them a good brushing. He had refused Eveitio's offer for a valet. He was no dandy and was capable of dressing himself. He did not like the idea of someone else choosing his clothes. Well, that was not entirely true. Almost his entire wardroom now had been chosen by her. But he liked wearing the clothes in which she wanted to see him.

After dressing, Alexander stretched a bit and pulled the draw cord to signal that he was ready for breakfast. He would have loved to eat with Eve but she woke before dawn everyday no matter how late they had stayed up. No matter how hard he tried, he could not rouse himself that early. He smiled when he walked to the balcony.

His life over the past few months had been like a fairy tale. For the first time he felt truly happy. He had never liked those stories which were told to children. They seemed to give a false hope. Only in his dreams can the beast pretend that the beauty will love him. He always thought that in real life, the beauty always ran off with the hunter and the beast was left to retreat back to his castle, a little uglier and in a lot more pain. He could not help but laugh out loud. He was living the fairy tale. He was a beast who had found a beauty to love him.

He had had his doubts in the beginning. Even now it was hard to believe at times. After all, she had her pick of a great number of men and had very much enjoyed the attention. When he had asked, she quoted the eighteenth Rule of Love. Good character alone makes a man worthy of love. She always knew what to say. He had figured that they were to keep their relationship secret, as was proper in the court. She would not have it that way and had told her inner circle the next day. It did not take long for the word to spread because she was not shy about showing her affection in public. She let it known that she was off limits. It had not stopped the more aggressive men from trying but she no longer enjoyed it. Her change in behavior had allowed him to be open with her.

They had shared so much with each other. The wounds on their hearts were very similar but manifested in such different ways. It was the sharing of that pain which had created the bond between them. He could feel her even now.

He had moved into his own room in the palace. They had decided not to consummate their love. They had talked about it and decided to wait. They wanted everything to be perfect. He had his desire, but he enjoyed just being around her so much that it was easy to wait. He realized he was blushing when the servants brought in his breakfast.

He dismissed the servants after they set out the meal. He preferred to eat without them standing there. It was not that he minded their presence, but he was feeling giddy and even though they were too well trained to give a strange look, he still felt awkward laughing for no reason. Well, there was a reason. They had decided to get married. They would be hosting a party next week to give the announcement. They had not set a date yet. There was something bothering Eveitio about it. She was hiding something. He could easily forgive her for it because she was hiding it from herself as well. He knew it when he had asked her about it.

Alexander waited with anticipation which bordered on desperation for her to return. She had been gone for only a few hours but his anxiety increased with each minute. He knew that there was something wrong. He almost panicked when he spotted a gold rose on the table. He had made it out of a coin for her. It was not hard as he did have some minor artistic abilities but it seemed to please her immensely, so it made him happy as well. She would always wear it and rubbed it constantly. Why would she leave it today? Where would she be going that she could not wear it? He had just talked himself into believing that she must have been in a hurry and simply forgot it when the door opened.

His heart was elevated to heaven when Eveitio walked in. It was not long lived, for a white Kaltar and several guards followed shortly behind her. It was Snow. Herman almost panicked, but calmed himself. There was no way for Snow to recognize Herman as he now appeared. When Snow talked a pain rippled through Herman's body.

"Lady Eve told me of this foolish notion you have of marriage. You are a most unfortunate youth to fall in love with something that belongs to me. This is something that I will not be able to forgive."

The pain peaked in Herman and bent him over. He reached out for his magic but nothing happened. This had to be a nightmare. This could not be happening. Herman turned towards Eveitio with eyes which grasped for any hint of reality. Lady Eve's face and voice were cold but there were tears in her yes.

"The Shadow has deemed that I must give you up. I will obey."

She turned away. Herman eyes felt extremely tired and the room swirled to his senses. Another wave of attacks rippled through his heart, a pain greater than his loss of magic ran through his chest. He could not even find thoughts through the pain. Herman gave no protest, was not even really aware, when the guards grabbed him and he was manhandled to a prison cell.

Erinfist looked over the battlefield from a nearby hill. His solders, the Dragon's Breath, were waiting for his order to join the fight. The adults were standing at the ready. The children not large enough to carry a blade strung their bows and kept watch on those not yet old enough to fight. Nearly all of them had been raised in the Slave-Army of Mosk.

The tattoo on his left temple showed that he was born in the army, and those who knew how to read the markings knew his birth took place during battle. His name became the cry for that battle and many to follow. In the official Mosk dictionary it meant to deliver a fatal blow. A meaning to which he lived up to. His next mark showed more than him just being part of the army but that he was of the Dragon's Breath. Again, a meaning of certain death to those caught on the other side. A marking which all he commanded shared. Those outside the Slave-Army could not understand their bond. The culture of Mosk was one where everyone only cared about themselves, all except those with the Emperor's Mark. Each of them would give their life without a second thought for the Empire or their fellow slave-warrior. He had earned his freedom nearly two decades prior. Some would choose to be free instead of becoming a bond officer, but he could think of no other place he would want to be. This was his family and he had a duty to the Mosk Empire.

He spent the time waiting for the general to give the order for them to enter the battle in examining the enemy. The Eldon forces were in complete contrast to those of Mosk. The Musashi were the nobility of their kingdom. Erinfist often wondered what it would be like to have a ruling class which cared enough for their nation to fight for it. In his youth, just after the War Forward, there was talk of a revolt within the ranks of the Slave-Army. With the disappearance of Mosk the Betrayer, many thought that the slave-warrior should be the new ruling class. After all, they were the only ones who cared enough for the nation to give it their lives, and need be deaths, for its welfare. The new Emperor Mosk, gathered the generals and talked with them. They returned with news that there would be no rebellion. Mosk the Dark announced that the army was now completely in his charge. Many of the nobles balked at this but the slave army made it quickly known that they would have it no other way.

Since then, the Emperor had proved over and over again that he was loyal to the Empire and his army. They were a family and he was the eldest elder. He wondered if Queen Eldon was the same. He had fought on the KanaTo front many times and knew that it was not, but Eldon was different. Their warriors were much more than just highly skilled. They fought knowing that death was the price to pay for leadership. A messenger arriving at the general's tent drew Erinfist's attention back to his side. After a few minutes the flags raised and he prepared to give the order the charge. To his surprise, the order was for a retreat. His swallowed hard. He wanted to disobey. He raised his hand and hesitated. He wanted to order a charge. Those already on the field were no match for the Musashi. By ordering a retreat he felt like he was killing them himself. They were not part of the Dragon's Breath but they were still family. Still, if a retreat was called, they were needed elsewhere. Erinfist gave the order for retreat but felt like he was dying on the field with those slave-warriors.

XVIII

Herman sat on the floor of his cell plucking at a single thread on his garment. Hours passed and his fascination of the thread did not wane. Many have tried to muse on what he thought about; of his broken heart, his pain or plots of revenge. No such things were in his mind. He was trapped in the wordless thoughts of the chaos. When a rat came to the meal which had been placed on the floor for him, he merely raised his eye for a moment and went back to the thread. When the rat came near him to examine the human who shared his cell, Herman's pain turned to rage. His hand whipped out in a blur. Grabbing the rodent so strongly that it was dead before it left his hand, he threw it against the wall. The rat hit with such a force that it would take a close examination to tell what it originally had been.

The outburst had cost Herman dearly. He no longer had the strength even to play with the thread anymore. He simply curled up on the damp stone floor and stared. If anyone had been present, they may have assumed that he was watching the wall. He was not, that would have taken too much energy. Tired would be the best way to describe his disposition at the time. So tired, in fact, he did not even react when the cell door opened. Or even have the energy to be shocked when those who entered were not guards to bring him to his death but General Albert and his eldest son. He did not pay attention to what they were saying to him. He complied when they pulled him to his feet and walked with them as they hurried him along.

Even later he would have very little memory of the corridors that they went through or exactly how many guards were killed by the general and his son while they made their escape. It seemed to Herman to take forever and no time at all before they were standing in the forest outside the New Shadow City. He complied when they put a rucksack on him but paid little attention to their words. Something about how they could do no more. They told him something about a community to the west and sent him in that direction.

He walked. He continued in the direction of the west for nearly two days before his body would just not go without sleep any longer. He collapsed still trying to walk. When he awoke, he was in a cave with a Mountain Elf caring for his scratches and scraps. The creature smiled when she noticed Herman awake and watching her. She jumped back slightly when Herman sat up. He did not move after that. He just sat staring at her and trying desperately to regain his hold on reality. The presence of the Mountain Elf did not help. They shared their appearance with the Wild Elves, and like their forest-living cousins, they were legendary in their xenophobia. She was not more than a meter tall, and her skin seemed to be painted the gray and brown of rocks. Created by the Cult of Blood in the same project as the Goblins, they were unleashed on the Colonies to create havoc. Something had gone wrong for the cult, for even though the elves were as dangerous they were designed to be, they also were known to help those who they found in great need.

Herman looked around. The cave was not the creature's home. Not that he would have been able to tell what her home would look like, even if his faculties were fully working. They stared at each other for hours with the creature spending most of the time in tears. Eventually Herman realized that the Elf was crying because of his pain. A pain he was not letting himself feel. He looked away. By the time he had the strength to look back the Elf was gone. He had not heard her leave, but he did not care. He laid back down on the bed of grass and went back to sleep.

Mike Dirk Coursein looked over his shoulder as he walked out of the gates of the Dark Shadow City. He felt like crying. It was hard leaving Silver. The man had been his Night Father, and he had given an oath to serve him. He did not consider himself a moral person, but he was a professional. He had given orders to have dozens put to death. All them because their breaking of the Law of the Night warranted it, but this was just wrong. This place was evil. Not the kind of evil which lurked in the shadows of every city. The very city itself was dark. Not even Jappa had this feel to it. As if death had become a person and walked the streets of the New Shadow City.

Mike did not want to leave Silver. After all, the man had been more than just his Night Father, he had been in many ways a real father. Yet, sometimes bonds of kin or friendship were not enough. Mike hardened his heart as he headed to a place he did not know, to a fortune that he could not have foreseen.

"We have just received a large grant from the House Grut. They have not put any stipulations on how we spend it. So, our next agenda would be what would be the best way to use the resources."

The Chairman of the Board of the KanaTo Institute of Higher Learning sighed as the board members started their arguments. Each was the head of the seven departments at the Royal Institute. They always thought that their own department was the one most deserving of funds. Even the High Warrior thought he should have more money. There was no rational to it.

The War department had the lowest cost to train their cadets and, with them coming from the nobility, their admission was almost as high as the magi training department. He waited for them to become silent from talking angrily with each other before he spoke again.

"One of the first things is that the east wing of the library has fallen into disrepair and..."

The chairman stopped mid-sentence as a figure appeared on the middle of the table. He stood with a stern look. It was most likely a prank. It was common for the post grads to make minor alterations to each other spells. This student would need to learn not to be using such spells until he was ready. The prankster would be dealt with later. He opened his mouth to lecture the youth when fire erupted from the newcomer's hands. It cut through his protective wards like they were not there and fried him to a crisp in seconds. The rest of the council did not last much longer.

Shadow Fire was not having fun. This fight had been much too easy. Like most of those who called themselves True Magi, they served Elohim but they lacked even the basic understanding of the Great Game. In the centuries which have passed since the destruction of the Cult of Blood his enemy had become weak. It was because few of them had made a real commitment to their faith. They believed, but had not given everything to their God. If they had they would be far more of a threat to him. Over all, this would be for the best, but he was hoping for a much better game. Only two real threats were left. He was hoping to find their weaknesses in order to twist them his side. The first was his next target. The other was this cat man who people called Tapps. There were at least a hundred wizards out there who had the rank of Silver or were on the verge, but they would be easy to destroy. It would be this young wizard who would be the most problem. No, that was not true. There would be others. He would not know them until they appeared. He cursed Elohim for elevating the weak.

The Kaltar was not strong like White Bear, but Shadow Fire was no fool. He had not gained back all of his strength either. He had been neglecting his sacrifices. He would have to kill the other Silver wizards quickly and return to his alter so he could make a proper dedication to the Destroyer.

He would need the Serpent of Old's help in fighting this servant of Elohim. He disappeared after taking the moment to enjoy the smell of the burnt flesh

The mountain forest was alive with spring. Tapps could sense it everywhere. There was something else underling the feeling. Trouble was in the air. He turned and looked at Angga. She did not feel it. Tapps lifted his chin and took in a deep breath through his nostrils. Yes, trouble. The wind had a scent of blood in it. Something had died up ahead. No not one thing, but many things had been killed and killed brutally.

He turned towards Angga Sella again. She was standing with her hand on the hilt of her blade looking at him. She had sensed it as well. No, she had only sensed his reaction to it. Ignoring her questions, he kneeled and examined the magic flowing around him. There was a taint in its flow. Someone was using the Forbidden Rituals. Every magus knew of the rituals. It was undeniable that incredible energy was released when a creature died. It had been the basis of the Cult of Blood which had ruled during the Rule of the Giants. The life of every creature is found in the blood. It was directly from the Holy Writings. It was used for the basis of nearly every dark ritual to gain power but those who use it, as people often do, willingly forget the rest of the writings. No, they remember the rest, which is why the rituals have so much power. It is their covenant with all that is unrighteous.

It was the very reason that the Society of Sword and Spell was formed from the Academy. Before the Time of the Pain, it had been a school for the most gifted children in the Colonies. They lost their strongest members during the failed counterattack against BackBitter's rebellion. With the Shadow dead, and the empire lost, the school had changed its name and went into hiding. From the writings of the time, it had been a long wait for the Society. During the Rule of the Giant it was all they could do to keep the safe-house safe.

With the destruction of the Cult of Blood, and the overthrow of the Giant's rule over the Colonies, the priests of the Dark Church were scattered and many cults were formed. These cults have been a major problem in the Colonies and the Society has always been kept busy dealing with them. Every time they destroyed one two more popped up. Of course, neither one as strong as the one before. The Society called these scattered barnyard cults the Minor Cults. They very rarely caused any serious problems and were most often fueled by the leader's delusions and petty desire for power. There was always at least one Major Cult with which to deal.

Most recently the Major Cult has been the Vampires of Mosk. Formed by Mosk the Betrayer himself, they had managed to keep themselves hidden from the Society for nearly two centuries. In that time, they had managed to grow impressive in strength. The war between the two has been going on for nearly a hundred years and the fight had weakened the Society greatly.

The Vampires of Mosk were different from the other Vampire cults which dotted the Colonies. Besides being unofficially recognized by the Mosk Empire, they mimicked the records of the old Cult of Blood right down to their titles of rank. They have also revived most of the ancient rituals. The ones that were used by the high priests of the Dark Church. This worried the Society. Very few had access to the records of the Keep and no one else except the Dragons had the records on the ancient Cult of Blood. It was the fight which was the reason that the Society had asked Tapps to join. They normally would not put out the invitation to one who had not begun their training at a young age.

He was what the Encyclopedia of Shouker called a Udjuge. They described it as a holy warrior whose calling gave them charge over the physical realm. He was not fond of the title for it conjured images of someone like himself. Many often taught that they were the masters of spiritual fighting. It was sometimes hard to remember that the real fighting takes place in the Second Heaven. He could pick out a person serving the unclean and deal with them, but dealing with the unclean themselves was better left up to the ElMika. He had once envied those like Manker who could sense the patterns in the Second Heaven like Tapps could in the first. It was not until he had helped the holy man bring a revival to a church in KanaTo that he realized how much they had need of each other. He had some of the Gifts but nowhere near the level of Manker. His old friend had laughed when Tapps had voiced his envy and pointed out that all he had received from VivusDeus, that each was given Gifts and Grace according to their calling. He had learned much since then. Of most importance, was not to rely completely on what his senses told him but to let the Tongue of Fire show him what he needed to see. What he saw now made little sense. Yet, there could be no doubt that someone was sacrificing others in order to gain power from the unclean.

Could a Vampire cult be operating up here? No, there were too many dead for that, they preferred to work in secret. Besides, this area was too far away from the masses of people they needed to work their dark rituals. This was something entirely different and much, much worse. He caught the scent of a new message on the wind of magic. It was still going on.

Tapps looked at Angga. She was crouched with her blade drawn. She was also staring in the direction of the slaughter. He had taken here on as a pupil shortly after they started working together training the youths of the Clan. She had only recently become willing to commit herself to Elohim and still had a far way to go. Tapps did not smile and kept his voice low.

"What is up over that ledge over there?"

Angga looked questionably at him before answering.

"It is the town of Eagle Head, it is our most outward settlement. Or at least it was when I was still. . . "

Tapps took off in a run towards it. His words were as much a blur as his movement.

"They're under attack!"

A pale, thin man sat in the middle of the town enjoying the sounds of screams coming from the wounded. It was a fitting gift to himself for his two hundredth birthday. General Darrik Spith had never thought that one could channel so much power at once. Those fools in Mosk did not suspect even half the truth. He had been expelled from the Vampires of Mosk because he had been too ambitious. No, he had to admit to himself that it was because he was too quick in acting on his ambitions. He had made a bid for the High Priest position in the usual fashion. After much bloodshed, and his assassination attempt failing, he had found himself without any supporters. Even now he did not understand how they figured out the plot.

They had tried to kill him there but he was almost as powerful as Elson so the house guard could not touch him. They did manage to kill all the lesser and outside Vampires who he had hired. He knew that the Canables would be unchained and come for him next, so he decided it would be better to flee

Finding his way to the Dark Shadow had come very naturally. It was a strange encounter. The Kaltar who claimed to be the Shadow was filled with the unholy magic of the rituals. Yet there was no smell of the blood on him. It was more than that. The Shadow's name was always spoken with a whisper for it is said that he was one of the great enemies of the masters. At least a dozen will-o-wisps circled the Dark Shadow and the Kaltar had welcomed him and made him a general.

More importantly, the Dark Shadow had shown him how to take power from the dying without being limited by how much blood you could drink. The power did not come directly from the blood, but from the defiance of the Holy Law. With this new ability and the Shadow starting the war which would rebuild the Dark Empire, he no longer had to sneak around at night taking his victims one by one. He could take them in mass.

These winged people were pitiful fighters. When he had reached the border of their town right before sunset there was not even a single guard on watch. His men had moved in and within less than six hours had slaughtered nearly all of the hundred females of the town. It did take the rest of the night to flush out the few dozen warriors who were using guerrilla tactics in the town and trees.

A society of only female warriors probably would have caused problems for a leader from KanaTo. He was born and raised in the army of Mosk and a slave-warrior was a slave-warrior no matter their gender. He remembered, nearly a hundred and fifty years prior, when the Mosk Empire started to employ females in their ranks. It was a most brilliant move on the part of the Emperor, Mosk the Betrayer. The strategy was implemented to cause a major upset with the Musashi of Eldon. Their culture was not as rigid as originally thought and they had no problem cutting down the females who stood opposite them as warriors. In fact, the major advantage was seen to be against KanaTo. They were so reluctant to lock blades with the females that Mosk was able to take nearly half the fertile fields before KanaTo sued for peace.

Two hours after they secured the town the real fun had started. After he had prepared the proper procedure his men started their killing of the rest of the populace. It was not as fun as it would have been at night, so he gave the order to do it slowly so he could enjoy the inflow of power. One by one the noncombatants were killed in front of him.

Gesturing to start bringing the children, he sensed a presence which frightened him. One filled with the Light, a Spirit Warrior, was coming near. Fighting back the strong urge to flee, he called for one of his Lieutenants.

"There is a person coming from that direction. Take ten of the Shadow Warriors and capture him. You will know which one it is. The others with him may be disposed in any manner you wish. Just make sure to bring the holy person to me alive so I can perform the ritual."

The man smiled. This was going to be a great birthday. The life of a Spirit Warrior would be a great dessert. He waved off his men who brought the first child. He had lost his appetite for mortals when a Servant of Elohim was heading his way. The Spirit Warrior would be easily taken. They were unmatched in the Great Game, but their reliance on Elohim left them pitiful physical fighters. Pushing his fear deep down inside, he waited for the arrival of his prize. He did not have to wait long. Fear struck him as the man entered camp. He had been wrong. This was not a Prophet but a Judge and his fate was sealed.

Angga Sella was the first to see the enemy. Their armor covered with blood, and if Tapps was right, the blood of her people. With a shout, she let loose with one of her largest bolts of energy. It did not do as much as it should have, but the warrior dropped. The Lieutenant's face took on the appearance of shock. The man who had just died was a Shadow Warrior. They had been protected from harm by the Shadow himself. It was true that he did not want to go through the ritual which gave them their power, for it left them so horribly disfigured that you could barely look at them when their helms were off. Still, it gave them great power. None of the other winged people's magic could touch them. This one's had just killed one of his solders in a single blow.

Tapps was emotionless as he read the face of the leader of the force. He would have not been expecting any real threat here and it took him by surprise. Tapps charged without making a noise. He had reached the group of warriors by the time Angga had released her second bolt. With a short prayer he jumped into the group. A pain shot through Tapps claws as they bit into the man's flesh. They had been protected by magic and by the smell of it, powerful and forbidden. As the man dropped from the wound, Tapps turned towards the next warrior. The sorcery was not powerful enough to prevent their deaths.

The fight was short. In less than a minute the whole group was dead. Before the last one hit the ground the two were again racing towards the town.

The dead bodies lying everywhere sickened Angga. She had been a warrior her entire adventuring career, but had never seen the mass deaths associated with war. Focusing her grief into anger she sped up to reach the town at the same time as Tapps.

Tapps knew his target the moment he saw him, a detestable looking man sitting on the ground in the middle of a pentagram. He had the smell of a Vampire. As he raced towards the man, killing any soldier who got in his way, he could see fear growing on the man's face. The fear in the man increased tenfold when before he attacked Tapps slowed to speak, not to the man, but to the unclean near him.

"This is not your dominion and you have no more power here. It is Deos Venta that you now leave here."

Tapps said much more, but not with his mouth. The power which caused the unclean to leave was not found in Tapps' words, but in his prayers to Elohim. As the willow wisps fled the Light which radiated from Tapps, he prepared for a fight. But stopped as the sounds of the man's screams echoed through the town. The vampire tried to flee as well, but his body and soul had been too long corrupted by the darkness to withstand the Light of Elohim. He simply fell over dead without the willow wisps sustaining his unnatural life.

The warriors who made up the attacking forces started to flee. Tapps let them go but the anger that was in Angga Sella was not so forgiving. She let loose with bolt after bolt and cut down another twelve with her sword and magic before she could find no more of them. With her anger finally subsiding, she landed in the town's center. To her surprise some of those present recognized her and started to kneel. She spent the remainder of the day, and much of the night getting the story of what happened, burying the dead and hearing the praise of her rescuing them. Tapps spent the time in prayer. There was far more going on here than he could tell. He spent the entire night in prayer and did not stop when they started their movement towards next town.

Snow slammed his fist down on the hard stone which surrounded the spying pool. He had sent one of his generals out against the winged people who shared the mountains as a test. The man had appeared and knew many secrets of the Blood Rituals. He was able to release power which was found in blood that he could not. Grabbing the chance to learn, Snow had made the man a general. Knowing there were things that he could teach the man, it would be a relationship of equals, at least the teaching aspect of the relationship. Light so bright that it blinded him had radiated from the pool and caused him a pain deep in his soul. By the time he recovered, and the magic pool was working again, his general was just a heap of flesh. What magic was this?

What was Tapps doing up here? Had the blind man followed him, or was it only coincidence? What magic had he used against his general? There was no indication that any was used. For some reason this filled him with both anger and fear. He made a careful examination of the area surrounding Tapps. Not even a stir in the fog. It did not matter what power Tapps had used, Snow would have his victory. He would escalate the war against the winged people just to kill Tapps.

Snow had had several conversations with Divinus about it. His adviser always repeated the same thing, always the same. It was useless to pursue such a petty thing as revenge against one man. Once all of the Colonies were under Snow's foot then he could crush anyone he liked however he liked. He also had said something about moving with more caution against one with a complete set of armor, whatever that had meant. Except for some magical bracers, Tapps never wore any armor. Divinus always spoke of things which made no sense, insane things. Snow stopped listening shortly after that. Besides, Divinus was gone again and Snow was beginning to hope the man would not return.

He would have his revenge against the blind brother. From what he had learned from Silver he knew that Tapps would take the cause of the winged people as his own. Snow knew that Tapps would feel the pain of the destruction of the winged people. Snow laughed out loud. The death of those people would be only the beginning of the pain that Tapps would feel. By the time that he was finished with the man, Tapps would wish that he had never been born.

Snow had already been in a sour mood when this all started. The man that Lady Eve was in love with had escaped. His willow wisps would not tell him either where he went or how he managed to get out of the prison. They said it was the cost of him having them attack the man. Snow was baffled. The attacks by the willow wisps had left the man nothing more than mindless husk. He knew it had to have been an inside job. He would not have put it past Divinus to do it just to upset him. He would get to the root of the conspiracy even if he had to scourge half the palace staff.

There were others who knew the secrets he wanted. He did not know where they were but he knew how to find out. He called for a slave to be brought to him. He would need a fresh kill in order to summon the ones he wanted.

XIX

Angga Sella and the group of her people had almost arrived at the next town when Tapps motioned for her to come down to him. She landed not knowing what to think. His voice was full of understanding.

"We need to talk when we get to the town. You do not seem to be taking those deaths well. I will meet you in the town." Tapps raised his hand to ward off her forming protest. "I have something to check out first but I should not be more than an hour or two behind you."

After hugging for a long moment, Angga took to the air and Tapps ran in another direction. He had passed a familiar scent a little way back and he needed to check out if it was who he thought it was. Following the scent, he was led to a cave entrance so small that Tapps had to crawl in order to enter. Going in without hesitation he was taken back by what he saw.

Herman looked up when Tapps stood upon entering the cave. Herman's cheeks were pulled tight like he had gone without food for too many weeks. His eyes were sunken and blood shot like one who had cried too many nights. Herman raised a hand as if to cast a spell. Nothing happened. His arm lowered with a small thump. Water formed in Herman's eyes. He turned his face away from Tapps. His voice was as broken as his body.

"Kill me now, my old friend. I would have already done it a hundred times if I could have found the will."

With the words barely out of his mouth his body collapsed. Tapps moved across the cave so quickly it looked as if he took only a single step. He scooped Herman in his arms. Tapps gently laid him on the spread of leaves which was youth's bed.

Tapps examined the magic around Herman. There was neither ward nor spell, the youth was keeping it from himself. His mind was preventing it from even touching him. This was deadly for most who lived in the Colonies, but for a Natural the effects were exaggerated. Their bodies were part magic, they needed it just to be normal. Why would Herman do this? To block the chaos he was always talking about? Tapps looked deeper into Herman and tears came to his eyes. There was a wound on Herman's spirit which was the cause.

Tapps had to stop looking, the pain was too much for him. More than he had ever known as his own. If he felt it as such how much more pain it was for the youth.

He gently picked up Herman and carried him outside. Herman needed help beyond what he could give. Tapps sniffed the air but found no scent of his sister. He opened a teleporting portal. Speaking the password to the Keep of Secrets he entered the shining disk.

Tapps stayed in the Keep only long enough to make sure Herman was secure and to write several letters to those he thought might be able to help the youth. The guilt started for him the moment he stepped through the gate and was back in the forest. He should have put Herman in the Keep long ago. The only thing that had stopped him was guilt. He felt guilty of taking so long finding the boy. Herman had both a wild streak and one of pride which balked every time someone offered him help. He did a wonderful job of taking care of himself, and Tapps probably would not have given the child a second thought when they first met if he had not promised Herman's father that he would take care of him. Not that Herman needed much looking after.

There were only a handful of Trualja in the Colonies, and only one of them even came close to Herman's power. James Braker and he had the advantage of being raised in the Society.

Letting the magic of the portal slip he made a mental note that he needed to learn the pattern so he could transport a group. He had made that same observation at least a dozen times but had never gotten around to spending the time in study. He headed towards the town to meet with Angga.

"When we speak of the elements, of course, we are not talking of the weather but of the very items which make up all things physical. Unlike the common belief, there are not five elements but over a hundred. This semester in your chemical physics class you will learn their names and how they interact with each other.

"Now that you have learned the basics of magic, safety procedures and what is expected of you, let us now take a look at what it is and how we control it. The elements are made up of three parts, when separated from each other they give us the three forms of the particles of magic. You will learn all about the forces that keep them together in your albia physics class.

"This class is called practical physics because here you will learn to apply what you have learned as first years and in your present classes as second years. In the other classes your grades depend on how much you learn. In my class, your grade will depend on how well you can apply that knowledge. Be warned, I do not tolerate deviance from the patterns assigned you. It will not be until you are third years will you have enough experience with magic to improvise."

Greg paused. He felt as old as he looked. He had just gained the balance which the ancients used to mark with silver. He felt a bit betrayed by the Institute. According to the academic standards he had gained his silver over two decades ago. He had been misled into thinking that knowledge was all important. Gaining the silver used to mean so much more, and if he would have known before that so much more existed he would have searched for it.

Nearly everything he had been taught at the Institute about the concepts behind magic was wrong. He did not blame the Academics for this. They were teaching what had been taught since the Giant's ruled. He did blame them for not listening to him. He decided that he would start his own school. Unable to get funds he moved to Gormec and took on apprentices.

When he first arrived, he had thought he would have a hard time of it. He had to admit that it was due to his preconceptions. He had been taught that the Humanike races were limited to only combat style magic. They were just as capable of learning real magic and his only Human pupil was at the bottom of the class.

That had been just after the War Forward. He had seen his school grow as the nation grew. He now had a staff of nearly a hundred with five hundred pupils. He gained his silver too late in his life and would no longer be able to keep up with running the school and teaching as well. He was still undecided on which responsibility he would turn over to another.

"From what you learned as first years, magic is not an energy, but matter. That is the particles we control are a physical thing. However, we control them by manipulating energies. Everyone open up your manuals and turn to the section labeled spells. You will notice that there are only four, it may not seem like many but it will take your entire second year to be able to cast them as habit. They are the Basic Four and the principles taught by them will be used in all your castings.

"Your first assignment will be to learn how to use magic to see magic. As you see from the text Magic Sight is not seeing the particles of magic themselves, for they are too small and move too fast, but to see the effects of magic's presence. You will be broken up into groups in which to share ideas and insights. I will be here to give you guidance and to answer any questions that might arise..."

Greg was interrupted by a stranger teleporting into the room. He was about to ask the purpose of such a rude interruption when fire shot from the man. Greg had just enough time to yell for his pupils to flee before his protective wards collapsed. Because they tainted research, he had kept only the most basic ones active. Within seconds there were nothing left of him but ash. Shadow Fire ignored the screaming and fleeing youths and simply disappeared. He was late for a meeting.

Tapps stood and went to the window. His anger burned deep within. He had been asked to sit in on the Council because of his position in the Vagofrons. None of them wanted him there except for the Queen. Even the Queen's husband was against it and said something about how it was improper for a man to sit at the table. The rest of the Council took the same position.

The Shadow Army had been attacking their land nonstop. Six villages in as many weeks were destroyed and half as many towns. The enemy gave no sign of stopping and at the rate they were destroying, they would reach the castle within a month. Destroying was the right word. They were not conquering, for when one conquered one took what was there and made it one's own. These forces were killing and burning everything they could. Tapps could come to only one conclusion. The enemy was not an army, not warriors but Children of the Destroyer, bent on destruction.

He looked down at the streets of the small mountain city. It already was over crowded by those seeking refuge from the war. Food was not an immediate threat. They had sent out several groups of hunters to take whatever mountain goat and deer that had not fled from the destruction. Added to the stores they already had, it had given enough supplies to last for at least to midsummer. Still no planting was being done, and they were running out of time in the planting season. Even if they could start now, the mountains made for a poor harvest to begin with and they did not have enough land to maintain the population. His thoughts became a bit more critical. At the rate of death from the war, their supplies would last several years.

The Sella Queendom was losing this war and even the children below could feel it. They had an almost guarded movement about them. Tapps knew what needed to be done. He had suggested it but they had laughed at him. They would not give up the idea that taking the fight to their enemy was wrong. The laughter really howled when he had said that they should let the men fight as well.

He had broken protocol by standing and walking away from the conference table. He did not care. His anger was too hot right now. These women were worse than the human nobles. Even KanaTo allowed women to fight, even though it made them an outcast. Many often thought that Eldon was the worse in the matter. In truth, the only distinction that Eldon made was between the warriors and those the warriors protected. Once he had assumed that their Right of Protection only covered females, but to his surprise everyone who was not a warrior had that right, just as every warrior had to responsibility to protect the noncombatants.

It was fitting that Angga Sella had chosen that moment to come up. She had some sort of incident on one of her visits to Eldon. The two-weapon style of the Salk caused her to be challenged. Her skill in it was impressive enough to earn her the sponsorship of Prince Eldon. He had given her the privilege of not only the title of MusashiJut but of wearing his symbol as well. Even now she wore the armband of her rank. In fact, she had donned all of the honors she had earned as an adventurer. He figured it was to prove that she had done well outside the Queendom. She whispered in his ear for him to return, he thanked her and moved back to the table.

". . . trying to say is that we must do what we have always done. We should flee to another land and build anew." Tapps placed his figurine in the center of the table, marking him next to speak. "It is the way of our people. It is the only way to ensure that we survive."

When she finished, The Duchess looked at Tapps as if he really could have nothing important to say. Her face took on the look of surprise, then of regret for taking that position when he spoke.

"I agree with the Duchess. I see only three options that you possibly have. We can win this war, with your advantage of flight we can get behind them and cut off their supplies. By striking hard against their magi we can eliminate any threat they have and pick off the rest at ease. As I said before, it would require that you allow the men to fight as well." Tapps put his hand up to ward off the protest that was already forming in the elderly lady's thoughts. "As Queen Insa Sella has stated, and the rest of you made it very clear, this would not be acceptable.

"So, as for the only two other options, surrender or flee. I have studied your laws regarding my rights at this table to call for a vote and I am invoking it now. These are your options. Fight, surrender, or flee."

Tapps pulled his falcon off the table. A signal that he was finished with the meeting. With shocked looks on their faces, the ladies did the same. The only one that did not look surprised was the Queen. She liked Tapps. She knew that her mate did not approved of his brash actions and sharp words to the nobles, but he would get over it. After all, NetThin had nothing but praise to sing about the Hero of the War Forward.

"As is the right of anyone sitting at the table a vote has been forced. However, this is a serious matter so I will give a two-hour rest before the counting. Think hard on this for it will affect the very future of our people." She pulled her figurine of a Messenger off the table and spoke again when everyone had stood. "Angga, I would like to see you and Tapps in my waiting room."

Tapps almost laughed. He was so used to being the one giving the orders. It was strange being somewhere his voice carried no more authority than a friend. He had to admit that a part of him did not like it.

When the rest of the Council had left the servants moved the backless chairs into the Queen's office. Tapps found it interesting that the furniture of these people was very much like that of the Kaltars. His people had to deal with tails, these people had to deal with the wings. The only real difference was the ceilings. Nearly all the buildings had tall ceilings. Something about not feeling confined. The castle actually had ceilings tall enough and passageways wide enough for them to fly through. He sat down and waited patiently for the Queen to talk.

"Tapps De Toya, you are what the wingless ones call a True Magi? Do you have the ability of, what I believe you call, Pure Logic?" She continued when Tapps nodded. "Then use the logic paths for which they are famous and tell me what is the outcome of us surrendering."

Tapps blinked for a moment. Very few outside those who have gained their silver knew of the abilities of Pure Logic or the dozen other abilities that were at the disposal of the True Magi. In truth it was the hardest of the Balance for him to master. The talents and skills, had nothing to do with magic. The association was that few lived long enough, or trained hard enough to achieve the greatest potential in them. His senses faded out as he ran the different scenarios in his head. After a short time, he spoke.

"Given what we know of this person claiming to be the Shadow it is very likely that the surrender will be unconditional. Most likely he will kill those of the rebellious age. Between sixteen and thirty-five and the entire royalty. He will take many of the youths and train them for combat. There is a high probability that the elderly will be executed as well on the grounds they are unproductive."

"And if we fight?"

Tapps knew the question before she asked it and knew that fleeing would be next.

"Without enlisting the males, we can still win. However, the loss to your female population would be too great. You would be left with only a few handfuls of females of mating age and you would take a dozen generations to heal. There is a one in four chance your race would eventually die off. There is a four in five chance that your culture will collapse to be replaced by another.

"Enlisting the men to fight would have a short-term panic effect. Many of your people will feel that the war is useless and flee on their own. Once we start pushing back the Shadow Forces, the morale will turn back to normal. However, I do not have enough information to tell what the long-term effects will be to your society. By enlisting males, who out number your female population two to one now, would even out the number while preserving your base population. An all-out fight would, at best estimate, involve almost a fifty percent death rate.

"Fleeing will be difficult. You have a large ratio of youths to adults and many of them not yet at the flying age. Added to this, is the vulnerability to attack when moving large numbers of noncombatants. I cannot determine the loss of life but there is only a one in fifteen chance that your culture will remain unchanged even if a suitable place for settlement is found."

The Queen thought for a moment. Her face took on the look which showed she expected an argument from Tapps.

"I will be voting for fleeing, we just need to find a place to go. I am sure the rest will be voting the same. What I am about to do is something that is not allowed. If half the stories the Princess has told of you are true, then I am willing to take on the ones who will balk at what I am going to ask you to do. I want to know is what you need from me to cut the number of losses to the minimum until we get to safety."

To everyone's surprise Tapps did not argue, in fact he had bowed slightly before speaking.

"I will need at least fifty of your Eagle Warriors, and a hundred men. All of them volunteers who know beforehand that they will most likely be sacrificing their lives so the rest of you can get away. I want every single name to be taken down and put in your official history letting future generations of their deeds."

The Queen had a meaningful look.

"Why my Eagle Warriors?"

"Because they already have the arrogant attitude that all elite warriors share, they will not balk at the idea of the men fighting. They are secure in their own abilities and will not be threatened whatever heroics the men might be. I will need a group of warriors who are loyal enough to fight on even if their death is certain, so we will be able to hold off the enemy long enough for you to get to safety.

"We!?"

Angga Sella voice came out as an accusation. She had not right to use such a tone in front of her mother. Worse yet, she betrayed too much of the emotion she was trying to keep hidden. Ignoring Angga, Tapps' face did not change as he continued.

"I also know where your people can seek refuge, and if you stay there it is a place where your people will never have to flee. I will have to speak with who is responsible for the land, but she likes humans and should be able to be talked into it. With your permission, I will contact her and arrange communications between you to form your arrangements."

The Queen's husband was smiling. The Queen tapped him on the arm and he stopped. She turned towards Tapps.

"You have my permission to speak with this person, and if there is nothing else, you may leave. Angga you may leave as well, but we want to talk with you after the meeting."

The Queen almost laughed when Tapps left. The Kaltar looked so out of place dealing with royalty. The way he talked was as if they were just regular people. It was apparent that his education had come later in life, for the elegance in speech did not come naturally to him. Still, he had the command of nobility. She was about to turn to her husband when she was interrupted.

"You know she desires him." NetThin walked out of a portal into the room. "and she will demand to go with him."

Kelthin looked at his brother forgetting momentarily his irritation at his eavesdropping.

"What are you talking about?

The Queen laughed.

"He has pointed out the obvious, our daughter has developed an infatuation with Tapps. I cannot say I blame her."

"Your highness, I would like to go with as well."

"This is about Fenasy."

NetThin nodded. The Queen thought hard for some time. Finally, she shook her head.

"I am sorry but I cannot allow it. I need you and the Circles of Magi more now than ever."

NetThin clinched his jaw for a moment. Calming his spirit, he spoke humbly.

"Yes, your highness."

"See, I told you that he would stay to protect these people."

Snow was too busy laughing with glee to pay attention to Silver's words. The man was right, of course. Tapps had revealed his weakness today. These winged people were fleeing before his army and Tapps had stayed with a small force of them to give them time. If the Kaltar could risk his life to protect people he did not know, his wound would be severe from what Snow had planned.

Nothing could take away Snow's happiness. His Shadow Warriors had proven their worthiness in battle and the new ones would be ready soon. All indications were that they would be all but untouchable in battle. He had found a weakness in his enemy he could exploit and, to make matters better, Divinus had not been around for some time. The advisor was really getting on his nerve. More and more this mere advisor was not giving him the respect he deserved. He would have killed the man, but he had not yet gained enough control of his magic to do so. Divinus still had his uses, but the time was coming quickly when that would not be the case. He bellowed in laughter once again as he called for all his generals. It was time to declare the return of the Shadow to the Colonies. A declaration that would be written in blood and fire.

NetThin rounded a corner and came face to face with Tapps. He had need to speak with the Kaltar but had been putting it off. He had been torn between his concern for Fenasy and aversion to the meeting. Tapps looked down at him and examined him for a moment. The cat man spoke with recognition in his voice.

"Net, is that you?"

Nethin forced a smile before answering.

"Yes, it is me. It has been a long time."

Tapps laughed.

"A very long time, old man." Tapps paused for a moment and continued his examination of NetThin for a short time. The laughter returned with his words. "Do not worry about our past. Of all the things I have gone through in my life, the few lessons you taught me are not worth popping claws over. In fact, for what I learned from them was well worth the pain."

NetThin laughed as well. He had not been particularly nice to Tapps when they had been in prison together. He was sure that their encounter may have ended in violence. He had heard rumors about Tapps, but such things had a way of exaggerating the nobility of heroes.

"Well, I am glad to hear that. Since there is no bad air between us, let me ask you. What is your intention towards my niece?"

Tapps almost choked on his laughter.

"It is not like that. She is my pupil and nothing more."

NetThin eyed Tapps for awhile. Finally satisfied that Tapps had truly changed, he smiled.

"Then let me ask you a favor. The head of the Eagle Warriors is a lady named Fenasy Selka. She is very capable in both magic and Salk, but could you look after her? Make sure she comes back safe?"

Tapps felt the vulnerability of the winged man. Placing his hand on Nethin's shoulder, Tapps spoke with warmth.

"She has your heart?"

NetThin smile widened.

"After so many years of avoiding the issue, we have just admitted our love to each other."

Tapps' smile returned.

"This I promise you NetThin. The only thing that will prevent me from protecting her would be my own death."

Nethin thanked Tapps, then cocked his head to the side and asked with a tone which showed his curiosity.

"Tapps, you became a hero because of the War Forward. You had a great army at your command. Even now, and this far south, I have heard it said that all you would have to do is raise your banner and most of the nation of Gormec would stand and follow you. Why is it that you did not rule? Why do you not grasp and use the power in which you have?"

Tapps smiled, he had heard the question before.

"Yes, I could have been a king, can still be a king, but I did not then nor will I ever raise the Panther banner for such a purpose. I want power, yes, I am tempted such, but at what cost. I want the power, and that reason alone disqualifies me from gaining it. Power is like a drug, if sought for its own sake it becomes the master. Power must always play a secondary role to purpose. I am not a king because there is no need for me to be a king, the Panther Banner does not fly because there is no need great enough for me to risk the temptation." Tapps paused, and gave Netthin a wink. "Did I pass the test."

"Admirably, young man, admirably."

The two of them laughed then walked side by side for hours talking of the Queendom, of the land they would be moving to, and most of all, Angga and Keith.

XX

KanaFinaUn stretched his huge reptilian body as he woke. He had been asleep for a long time. The last battle against the Tecmen had been fierce for the Dragons. Over a dozen of his kindred had fallen that day. Only once before had more Dragons died at one time. He was not alive during the Giant/Dragon war, but he had read all the Dragon's records. The Battle of Freedom was most likely the most devastating in the history of the world. With almost two hundred Dragons and over a thousand Giants, the physical fighting alone flattened the countryside. The wizards on both sides had released so much magic that even the genetic alterations which allowed the populations to thrive in the radiation was not enough. Wide spread magic sickness was common over the Colonies and only the Dragons could survive in the area of the battle for over two hundred years. Even now life was difficult in the region. The Great Desert was home only to the outcast Dragons and little else lived there.

With the death of his people, and the wounds he had received, he had returned to his cave a broken being. He had longed for the OblivPercy, the Great Commune, but the needs of his people were too great then. It had taken him a full year to heal the wounds of those who he had led into the battle. It was the law and his duty. The wisdom of it could not be denied. It prevented the Keeper of the Scepter from calling the Dragons to battle too hastily. Just because it was good did not mean it was without cost. With each passing sun span his own pain increased. By the end of the year his pain was so great that he was sure if he did not enter the OblivPercy soon he would develop the Softening. The slow progression into madness that would rob the Dragon of his most precious gift. His link with VivusDeus. Without the guidance of LingueArdeo a Dragon would become the evil creature of the ancient legends.

It is said that the skin of a Dragon always represented the condition of their hearts. KanaFinaUn had started his life as a Dragon with skin as silver as a highly polished mirror. Even before becoming the Keeper of the Scepter his hide had darkened and now had near black streaks. It represented him taking his responsibilities seriously. The Softening would start with the Dragon's skin getting a tint of red to it. It was said that eventually the whole of the Dragon would become fully red. Long before then, the actions of the Dragon would become severe enough to require action. Because Dragons could not see the color red there was often problems in identifying which actions were truly evil and those which only seemed evil.

Out of the fifty cases where a Dragon had been judged red, twelve of them were later declared righteous. In one case, the dragon had managed to survive until the verdict was overturned by seeking refuge with the Outcasts. KanaFinaPrin had been emotionally devastated by the event that even after leaving the Outcasts he still refused to call himself KanaFin. He had eventually returned to the ranks of the Dragons. Prin even held the Scepter of the Dragon before KanaFinaUn. The inability of the Dragons to see the red hide was why the Ancient entrusted the Enforcers to police the KanaFin. The turmoil of a Softening would not last long for either for the Dragon or those around them, for the Enforcers would come and that would be the end of the Dragon's life. The Dragons always tried to intervene and help their soft kindred but in only two cases had the Dragon been saved.

Humans called it falling asleep or growing cold and there was little difference for a Dragon. The only real difference is the amount of power at the disposable of the Dragon. It would be easy for him to become a tyrant. It would take him simply to forget that the Fire which flows from VivusDeus. When he had entered the OblivPercy he had not realized how much damage needed to be repaired to his body and mind. It took almost twenty of the Human's years for the Great Commune to heal him. He had not expected it. The longest time he had spent in the Holy Time before was a little over six moons.

His eyes scanned over his cave. Nothing had changed except for the thick layers of dust over everything. He went to his treasure room. The room was huge with rubies lining the walls. The largest and best cut of the red gems had their own display cases. KanaFinaUn laughed to himself. He had been over that line which separates Humans from Dragons for over two hundred years and the rubies no longer were precious to him, except maybe a few for sentimental reasons. In his younger days he would have been almost willing to destroy a city for a claw full of rubies. Now, he had no desire to collect more.

In the center of the room was a huge marble pedestal. On the pedestal was a large scepter. It was a ten-foot golden rod that formed a Dragon's claw holding a huge crystal ball. At the center of the rod were three symbols and a ruby. The symbols were the Keepers before him and the ruby stood for him. He had been so proud when he had received it. The scepter itself was only a symbol of his office. KanaFinaIkKanaFina directly translated it was the Dragon of Dragons, usually when placed into the speeches of the mortals he was called the Keeper of the Scepter. He was the military leader of the Dragons. More than a general, but less than a king, he had the power to call the Dragons to war. A short piece of logic ran through his head. It was odd to him that the scepter no longer mattered to him. It as if some force which was in the air had ruined the meaning of it, or was about to.

KanaFinaUn needed to see what was going on with his people so he headed towards the exit of his lair. He paused shortly at the magical trap which guarded his home. It was designed by the best wizards that the Dragons have. Checking the records, the alarm had sounded. It showed how tired he had been that such a noise had not roused him. A skeleton of a human lay on the floor. He must have come to loot his lair and was stuck by the magic of the trap. Without KanaFinaUn to release the human, he probably died of thirst. He poked through the decaying gear with the tip of his talon for a few moments. Books, writing equipment, a scroll case. KanaFinaUn became mournful. Not a thief, a scholar had come to ask the Dragon of Dragons a question. A shame really, he always did like to hear what the mortals were thinking. KanaFinaUn turned off the trap, there was nothing in his cave worth another life. Anyone who was willing to travel this far into the Draco Mountains deserved his rubies. The thoughts left his mind as he started out of the cave.

KanaFinaUn stopped in his tracks before he even realized why. He sensed power, immense power. A level that he had only felt in the presence of the Ancient but this had a sinister feel to it. His eyes scanned the surrounding area. It took his several sweeps before he finally spotted the source of the power. He was not expecting it to be a mortal. No mortal, not even the Dragoon, emanated the kind of power that flowed freely from this man. Their bodies just could not handle it, and few ever overcame this limitation.

KanaFinaUn approached cautiously. He still remembered the lesson he had learned when he had attacked Death's Fang only in jest. He had caught that mortal by surprise and the leader of the Draco Army had grabbed him with his magic and thrown him into the mountain. It had taken him nearly an hour to dig himself out of the rubble. It was true that some magi used spells which only gave the illusion that they had incredible power and, like the Dragoon, some used spells to mask their real power. He would not take that risk until he knew for sure.

As KanaFinaUn approached, the man jumped off the rock on which he was sitting. He was shrouded in shadows which even the Dragon's senses could not penetrate. Only a slight glimmer of a smile under the hood. KanaFinaUn spoke with all the arrogance in his voice that was expected of a Dragon.

"I am called KanaFin. . ."

The man interrupted him. KanaFinaUn had to fight hard against the urge to bellow out in anger to the man.

"I am aware that you are the leader of the Dragons. I have been calling for you since I have been released. Yet, you have not answered me. I am the Shadow and you served me once. You must serve me again in my quest to bring order back to this land."

Could it be true? The Shadow released? KanaFinaUn's mind raced in the loops of logic. It could be, but only the Ancient would know for sure. The records told of how the Shadow created the Dragons, and how they served the man then. Was it not in the law, handed down since they became the Guardians, that they would serve no one except Elohim? But the law was written after the Shadow had been imprisoned. Could they bow their heads to a mortal again even if it was the Shadow? To bring the peace known during the Shadow Confederacy would be a grand goal indeed. Yet there was something wrong with what was going on. The man radiated power but there was a smell that was unclean about him. It was prophesied by the Law Speaker that the Shadow would return and bring a war of blood and fire with him. That there would be a split in the Dragons with many not serving the true authority of the One through which all authority flows.

KanaFinaUn knew that he had been raised to lead the Dragons against those outcasts. He had prepared his entire Dragon life to lead those who were still faithful against those who turned their back on what the Dragons stood for. It could not be doubted that this was now the time and he was strong enough. If this was the Shadow, he would follow the man but still he needed Ancient's advice. He spoke to the man almost as an equal.

"There are many things in the air in which I must seek guidance from the First Dragon."

The man's voice was full of fire.

"You do not understand. This was not a request. I created the Dragons to enforce peace on the land. The Dragons are too powerful not to be controlled. You will either be an instrument of my peace or you will be its enemy. Either lead your Dragons in the New Shadow Empire or I will find someone else."

KanaFinaUn's anger erupted. How dare this mortal issue such a threat. He had no right even if he was the Shadow. He was the Keeper of the Scepter, first among the Guardians. The anger of the Dragon's words erupted as hot as the fire that followed.

"HussKa."

KanaFinaUn was always impulsive, always prone to brash attacks. The many years of his life had barely tempered that trait. His breath melted the rock on which the man calling himself the Shadow had been sitting, but the man seemed unaffected. The illusion of his smile within the shadows of his hood seemed to broaden. He raised one hand and a dark energy came from his fingertips. It shot forward with the speed of lighting and nearly ripped off KanaFinaUn's right arm. He bellowed from the pain. He had not felt such pain since before crossing the line. No magic could penetrate a Dragon's hide like that. Not even the powerful magic of the Dragons could affect another in such a way of being anything but a nuisance. KanaFinaUn did not like this, but he was not without his own magic.

The Keeper of the Scepter reached out his own hand and let loose with a Dragon sized Palm Lighting Spell and took to the air. As he turned in the air to see what had become of his foe, he was shocked with what he saw. The man had taken control of the lighting and was circling it around himself. As it grew larger, it went from the normal blue-white color to that of the night sky. KanaFinaUn was sure what was to come next so he worked his magic frantically into an Insulating Shield spell. He had just finished the spell as the man released the shadowy magic towards him.

The dark lighting crashed into his protective shield and worked its way through. The agony rippling through his underside was beyond anything he had ever felt even before he crossed the line, if that was possible. He was sure if it had not been for his shield the lightning would have killed him. When he could see clearly again he spotted the man readying another attack. With his shield gone and no time to work another one he knew he would not survive. He had only one more chance and that was to flee. Working his aching wings he pushed with all his might. As he raced away form his foe he could feel the magic building behind him. He was working his own magic.

A simple spell, but one that was his only chance. Just as he felt the release of magic behind him he finished his own. The sudden burst of speed that magic had given him put him just out of range of the attack. He could feel the magic explode behind him and the currents of power made him lose his balance for a moment.

It was odd that the Shadow had not thrown another lighting attack. It was one of the few spells that could actually harm a Dragon. KanaFinaUn should have pondered on that thought, should have figured out what it meant, but there was something which occupied his mind. Something which was far more important to him, far more devastating than the question of why he was still alive. He had fled. The first time in his entire life he had done such. Was he turning into a coward in his old age? No, he needed to talk with the Ancient before he could decide whether or not he should fight and die.

Segax unhooked the gold starburst from his robe and took a silver ring off his finger. No need for them to be ruined by what was to happen. The starburst was his badge of belonging to the Temple of the Vassals of Xrist and the ring was from his membership in the Order of Truth. Stripping to his underclothes he folded his robe and placed it on his bed. No point in wasting it. Segax paused for a moment then took off his undergarment. Naked, he sat in the middle of the room hoping that he would not have to wait long in the cold.

He spent his time reflecting over his life. Segax, known as Segeada then, had come to the Temple of the VoX almost fifty years ago to study in their library. He never left. Being a True Magus was rare inside the house. At present he was the only one. It was not that they did not gain the balance which the academics marked with silver in their heir. It was just that most considered the dedication to magic a waste of time compared to the person as a whole. There had been a great number of wizards who had joined the VoX Templers over the years, but there was something about him which made him one of a kind.

He was not a Colonialist but African. After getting a doctorate in Biophysics and Genetics from the Cairo University of Egypt, he had a brilliant career in genome manipulation. His trip to the Colonies started when he was on the Holy Island because of his duty to the Order of Truth and met a Dragon. The Colonies ability with genetic engineering and especially post-birth manipulation was beyond amazing, it was impossible.

He decided right then and there that he would learn what the Colonies knew about genetics. That was over fifty years ago. He had spent the first two decades learning everything he could and sending his findings back to an old professor of his. From his understanding, with the knowledge from the Colonies combined with the research and application possible in the United Republics of Africa, great things were being accomplished. He had planned to return to the University but by the time arrived he had started thinking of the Temple of the VoX as his home. Most of them knew the truth of his origin and that he could not survive in the Colonies without the magic of his silver ring protecting him. In a way, he had advanced their knowledge of magic by learning to use it himself. It was supposed to be impossible for him to learn magic because he could have no physical contact with it. There was much he could not do and he was not very powerful. Another lesson for the wizards of the House. Being a True Magus had nothing to do with power but obtaining an understanding of one's self.

Being asked to head the Order of the Philosopher came as a shock. He had not thought himself worthy to sit on a Seat of Elders and only agreed because it was his duty. In all that time, he had spent many hours learning from White Bear. Segax remembered their first meeting well. White Bear had, out of nowhere, leaned over and asked if he had mourned his own death. At the time Segax did not understand. He had always had a great respect for the leader of the Order of Truth, but Segax thought that maybe the old man had mistaken him for someone else. As he became less himself, and more filled with Ferrun, it became clear. He had not asked for the title of Prophet and resisted it. He had not wanted to pay the price. Elohim had left him little choice. When he finally stopped running and made his choice, he had learned of his death and wept in a style uncommon for him. He knew that the man appearing in his room now was here to kill him.

The man shrouded in shadows was taken back by the sight of Segax sitting nude in the middle of his room and that the unclean spirits had not followed him. His words showed the arrogance which can only come from ignorance.

"I am the Shadow and there is no room in my new empire for. . ."

Shadow Fire's words were cut off by a warm laughter. Segax could feel the anger flaring in the man's spirit. Segax spoke with a gentle smile on his face, but his tone was serious.

"It does not matter what you call yourself. I know what you have come to do, but before you do there are things you must know. First the land you are now on is the Temple of the VoX and is set aside for Elohim, and is under the protection of White Bear since before your kind ruled the Colonies."

Segax was interrupted by several VoX Templers rushing in. They were the warriors of the House and would have felt the man's arrival. As they prepared for a fight, Segax's hand came up to stop them. His tone was level.

"Depart, you can do nothing here. Tell the Table that the time I told them of has come." He turned back to Shadow Fire as the VoX Templers started to leave. "There is more at risk here than my meager life. Let us talk of what is best for you and how you can bring yourself out of the grave you have dug for yourself."

Shadow Fire was worried about the unclean not following him here and the loss of power. It was true that this was holy ground. He had no more power than his natural ability in magic. If the VoX Templers had attacked he would not have been able to fend them off. Then how could they attack with their vow of nonviolence? There was too much that he did not know about this new Colonies. As the naked magus spoke, Shadow Fire was filled with indecisiveness. When the priest started speaking of wounds which needed to be healed, his mind cleared. His spirit flared with rage. The man sitting on the floor had more than enough power to defend himself. In fact, he would most likely win. Like all of his kind, he would not use it. Shadow Fire's words were forced as he pulled the magic to him.

"Enough of your words, Xrist teaches nothing but weakness and your faith is for those who have not the will for greatness. It is the strong who owns the earth. Even now I see the tears forming in your eyes."

Shadow Fire sent out his magical fire, a spell he created himself in all those years in prison. It was as deadly as it needed to be, but it caused a slow and painful death. As the fire engulfed the body of the naked priest, he spoke unhurriedly and with a gentleness that unnerved his attacker.

"It is not for myself that I weep, but for you."

The man did not cry out but simply prayed. As the man died, Shadow Fire almost regretted not letting the man finish talking. He felt as if he was lacking something and the man could have given it to him. He would have to think about what the True Magus meant but first he had to leave. Someone was showing up who he knew he could not face, even if he had the power the unclean gave him.

Just as Shadow Fire vanished, the room filled with VoX Templers, followed shortly behind by the two elders. The Keeper of Records fell to his knees and started weeping. Anger filled the eyes of the Marshall of the Temple. She turned towards her commander. Her voice was full of anger.

"Put together a team. We will hunt down who did this and. . ."

"You will do nothing but return to your prayers."

The voice came out softly but with enough authority that all stopped and looked at the speaker. The Marshall of the Temple turned to vent her rage on whoever would dare override her orders. Both her anger and her voice left her. White Bear entered the room and walked over to the bed. He picked up the golden starburst and silver ring. He pocketed the silver ring and handed the starburst to the Keeper of the Records. His voice held the familiar sureness and gentleness.

"Segax knew this was to come. It was his choice to continue his service to Elohim rather than come to me for protection. The Templers cannot be of help in this matter and will have other things to worry about. This fight is mine. The cost would be too high to allow others to pay it."

White Bear walked out of the room and went to the meditation garden. After taking a moment to let the pleasant memories of when the garden was built slip over him, he pulled out the silver ring and looked at it. After he allowed himself a few minutes to mourn the loss of another pupil, he closed his hand. When he opened it the ring had turned to dust. Letting the dust fall to the ground he vanished from the garden with the first line of the oath of the Holy Order of Truth in his mind. I will seek no glory except for that which glorifies the Lord.

"Attention!"

Brian Braker smiled as he entered the room and everyone stood. The Black Lighting had earned a name for itself in the Colonies. They had been credited with saving several dukedoms from falling to the Mosk Empire. Most of the members of the unit were natives, trained using the Tecmen's understanding of warfare. That was the secret of the Black Lightning, the original members had all been citizens of the Asionic Empire, Tecmen. Some of them had been children of people from the Colonies, the others had to wear magical rings which protected them from the radiation. All of them had planned to be stranded in the Colonies when Tecmen's fleet had been defeated. And none had ever regretted that decision, at least not openly.

They still considered him their Admiral even though he had given up that position long ago. This meeting was not what he had planned either. He had hoped to meet with just their leaders. He had come as a beggar, and did not want what he was about to ask them to seem like an order. After putting the team at ease, he nodded at Paul in the back of the room. Paul nodded back. It had been his decision to have most of the team here. It was a breach of their protocol because no one was supposed to know where people lived, but with the death of his wife and his children being members of the unit he had nothing to lose in having the meeting in his house.

"I cannot tell you much here about what this new assignment is, but I can tell you that it will mean a major relocation for you. Those of you who accept will have to move to the capital city of KanaTo for that is where the wards are found. This is of high sensitivity and only those who are assigned will know more. However, know that this is of utmost importance to the entire Colonies."

After spending a few moments answering questions he went into the bedroom to talk with Paul. Opening his briefcase, he pulled out the papers which contained the contacts and a letter of credit from KanaTo's Royal Bank. It should be more than enough funds for what they were to do. Opening up an envelope, he pulled out its contents.

It was a typed report of what had been happening in the Colonies and the individuals who they would need to protect. The Us and Bs were offset but it could be forgiven. The magical typewriter had seen better days. Out of twelve of the devices, it was the only one that still worked. The Keep had many books on the magical devices from the Time of the Shadow but none of the typewriters. None of the magi in the Keep specialized in tecmagic so they had to salvage the other devices to keep this one working. In a few years they would have to go back to handwriting their reports. That was something with which Daryl had to deal. As the High Magi it was his responsibility to keep everything running smoothly.

Flipping through the report, a small piece of paper fell out. Slowly he leaned over and picked it up. It was a hand written note from his son. James had inherited the best of both him and his mother. Just pushing seventeen, he had already mastered the sword and was a Natural with magic. He looked at the note with a curious eye. Just one word, Danger. It was unlike James

Braker. If he thought that there was danger here, he would have said something. This was something else. Probably just a feeling, but like his father, James had learned to trust his instincts.

Brian sat in a chair in the corner of the room. His eyes glanced over as he let his mind wander through his memory. Pieces of the puzzle pulled together and rearranged themselves a thousand times. Still nothing stood out, no pattern emerged that would require such a warning. The talents which James had inherited from his mother gave him pieces that he did not have, and being raised in this land he could read the flow of magic with a skill not seen in ages. The youth's specialty was application. Indeed, he was already able to out cast every wizard at the Society. He did not cast magic, he decided what needed to be accomplished and just did it. Knowing it was futile to look inside any longer, Brian opened his eyes.

Paul was standing there looking at him. He probably been doing so for a while. To the True Magus who entered the mental exercise, called Three as One, time had no meaning and what seemed like only a few minutes could very well have been an hour. There was a danger in this and the teaching of the method was highly restricted. Until one had mastered their own will they could easily slip into a cycle of deepening thought. By harmonizing all of your internal forces the mind, spirit and soul worked together in the way they were designed. The full name from the ancients was The Three Working in One Harmony. There were no words to describe it unless one already knew the feeling of it.

He stood and pocketed the note. He would have time to ask James what he meant when he returned. He smiled at Paul as he handed him the report. Paul glanced at it and tossed it on his bed. He had something else to talk about.

"Admiral, what are you not telling us? This is just not another assignment."

Braker laughed. He often forgot how long that Paul and he had worked together. Paul had gained his rank as much because he could tell what Braker was thinking as he did from his leadership skills.

"Someone is assassinating powerful wizards throughout the Colonies. It is the fear of the Society that these children will be targeted.

"Naturals?"

Braker smiled.

"No, it does boast itself as a school for Trualja but the children there are gifted in one way or another. Remember that you must make sure that no harm comes to them. It is equally important that you do not interfere with their lives. They must make their own choices for their lives. It is hoped that this threat will pass without any of them even knowing you were ever there.

"You are, of course, correct that there is more. A war is in the air. Many at the Keep do not want to believe it, but I have felt this before. Remember when we came to the Colonies. Remember the devastation that we brought with us. This war is going to be twice as devastating to this land. The force which is mounting is something right out of a vertgame. You remember the ones that had the great evil enemy at the end. The threat is large enough that even those who do not normally involve themselves with the common happenings of the Colonies are planning on a fight."

Paul smiled. Barker's ability to revert his speech to Asionic Royal amazed him. They had been in this land for over two decades and he had all but forgotten his old life, as a Tecman. After the two of them had talked of what was needed from the Black Lighting, and on other things for several hours Braker finally took his leave of the man.

As Braker finished the pattern for the Traveling Gate, he smiled. Many at the Keep laminate about how much knowledge was lost since the Time of the Shadow or even since the Time of the Dragon. They had no idea how advanced they really were. Their knowledge in subatomic physics well surpassed any other on the New Earth and they surpassed even EuroAfrica in their abilities in genetics. Traveling gates were beyond anything which the Asionic Empire would even dream. Gating and teleporting worked in two very different ways. Teleportation actually moved a person where a gate relied on splicing space. Pulling two points in space together and causing a hole between the two. Teleporting was harder and used more energy, but there would be no warning of the person's arrival. Even though it was quicker and safer than the gates he did not like it as much. Braker felt like he had no control of it. After all, it happened the moment the spell was cast, where the gate you had to walk through. It was a small thing, but one which kept him using the gates when he could.

With a wave of goodbye, he walked thought the gate. The sensation was the same as always. As if he was walking through a thin layer of plastic, or maybe, dry water. As soon as he had gone through, he turned to tell the warrior on guard to tell his son he wanted to see him. To his surprise, he was not in the Keep of Secrets, but in a forested area. A man sat on a fallen log with a sinister look on his face. Braker's anger flared and his magical shields instantly went up. The man spoke in a level tone.

"Do not be angered with me for deviating your spell to bring you to me. No, you should not be angered at that. You have a better reason to be angry with me for I mean to kill you."

Braker only thought was that the man's words and delivery was melodramatic as he allowed his instincts to start working the magic around him. It was not his nature for his mind to hinder his body in doing what it must in combat. Magic around him started to swirl quickly and flow into a pattern rapidly. His magical shield grew in strength to the point where even magic could not pass through it. He worked his magic into a pattern for an attack that he created himself. The air just on the other side of his shield condensed and even though it was not visible to normal sight, it would be as hard as any metal. He paused just before finishing the final piece of the pattern that would send it racing forward with the speed of a bullet. The man was not attacking but examining the pattern of Braker's magic. He had no concern in his voice.

"Can this be? You work magic like the people of my time. Without word or hand and more than that, your pattern shows very much more." The stranger looked up at Braker and the old Tecman could see the evil in the man's eyes as he continued. "Yes, you are not born to this land, for your pattern of thinking is that of those who understand the world of technology. It is a shame really. I was just a youth when the old earth was destroyed and I would be interested in learning what has become of the world outside the realm of the Colonies. But, alas, I must kill you, for no wizard who has obtained the Balance can be allowed to live outside of the Cult."

Braker knew that the man would not leave without an attack so he let the pattern complete itself and a loud crack resounded as the bullet of air went faster than sound. The man was quicker and, with what appeared only a slight movement, dodged the magical attack. Braker had already started his next. The man was too agile for such a consecrated force so he put the pieces together for an area attack. It would devastate most of the surrounding area and would probably destroy most of his shield as well but the man would not escape.

Braker looked up at the man as the pattern started to complete itself. The man had just completed his own attack and a small stream of magic flowed from him and hit the shield. It was not strong enough to even damage the shield. Braker grimaced. Was this just a young magus hoping to make a name for himself by killing a member of the Society of Sword and Spell. He could not have been more wrong. As the magic gathered that would clear a quarter acre of the forest with its force, Brian saw what his enemy's spell had been. Like a termite in a fallen tree, it had started to eat the pattern his shield. By the time the explosion from the Ingunus Pnue spell occurred the shield would not have prevented even a fly from passing through. Braker did not have time to even scream before the fire of his own spell enveloped him.

Shadow Fire stepped forward to examine the body of the magi he had just killed. As he wiped the blood from his nose, he pondered why he had not known that this wizard was so strong. The blast had hurt him and he would probably feel its effects for days. Very little remained of the wizard to tell anything. There was blood everywhere but no body. Just bits of flesh and part of a leg was all that was left of the wizard. No, he was not strong compared to the old days, he was just smart. He had been accustomed to using his magic as many did during the Time of the Shadow. Without thinking, it was just a part of them, very much like any other skill which had become habit after long hours of practice.

Shadow Fire had not expected that. Every other Silver Wizard he hunted down had not known the truth behind magic, so looked at is as more of an archaic art form rather than a soft science. Very much like he did before he met Death Bringer. He would not be so careless in the future. There would be others like this man. Shadow Fire put out a finger and gathered some of the wizard's blood. He no longer needed the Forbidden Ritual to gain power, but he still liked the taste of the red elixir.

He licked his finger as he teleported to take care of his next target. He had been pressing the Dragon hard. He was now tired of playing around. It was now time to set the trap. He expected an easy victory. This Dragon had the same weakness as that of many of his enemies. Nobility.

XXI

James Braker walked through the main hall of the Keep of Secrets. He was worried about Hermes. The Society's doctors could do nothing for him and all he could do was pray. Suddenly the world phased from his sight and his vision was of millions of strands. They came together and he understood what he had to do. It was the same way he understood magic. He simply knew which way the strands were supposed to go. He always knew which cord to pull to get what he wanted out of his magic. Life was never as easy.

He knew it was his father. It has been building for some time even though he had not known what the danger was. He still did not know, but he knew he needed to get his father back, and get him back now. Time slowed but he did not stop to ponder what it all meant. He stuck his arm out and moved it through space. As his had closed on what he knew would be his father's collar, he pulled with everything he had. A searing pain spread over his arm. As he pulled his father to the space he was in, fire spewed through the rift he had made. James had to let the gate collapse as the brunt of his father's attack hit it. His father was not all the way through and his lower legs were severed when the two spaces separated.

James did not have time to worry about the flesh peeling from his own arm. With his first thought, he sounded the alarm that would bring the guards and the medical personal. With his second thought, he had his magic constrict around the stumps of his father's legs. His third was to cool off the burns which covered most of his father's body.

By the time that the medical magi arrived, James had already started regrowing the skin on his own arm. He let them do their work. Even being a Natural he would not dare to try healing such severe wounds as his father. Healing one's self was easy for a Natural, but healing others was often dangerous. Magical healing required a fine balance between dealing with the wounds and not overtaxing the body's reserves. Healing could easily kill the patient, which is why James did not try to help the medical magi. That did not mean he was unconcerned. He did not leave his father's side for several days.

KanaFinaUn looked over the mountain top as the sun came up. He was almost there. If he could get to the Ancient before he was discovered by the

Shadow there may be hope yet. He looked down at the scepter in his claws. This was the first time that he had regretted becoming the Keeper of the Scepter. It had always been a joy. From proceeding over the different ceremonies to solving disputes between Dragons. Trying to call all the Dragons, he put some magic into the pearl. No response, he was sure that the Shadow had somehow blocked the ability. He had only called for the aid of the Dragons twice before. Once against the kingdom of Mosk when it was still young, and he had been lectured for what seemed like a decade by the Ancient about the abuse of power. The second time was during the War Forward. During the War Forward he was going to give the call to war the moment he heard of the Tecmen, but the Ancient said that he should wait a while, that he would know the time. He was glad that the Ancient had come to him then. He could not understand why the First Dragon did not come to him now. He had called to her over and over again with everything he had. She must have heard. Why was she ignoring him?

For five sun spans now, he had been on the run. Five days and three fights later, KanaFinaUn had so many wounds that he could barely fly. He had spent the whole night resting on this mountain top. It was called the Holy Mountain and it reached above the clouds. It was said that it was made by the White Bear himself and dedicated to Elohim. Even the Unholy Council during the Rule of the Giant would not come to the mountain. No mining and no settlements were allowed on the mountain. It was a place of refuge for no fighting was allowed here by the Dragons. The mountain was dedicated after the Shadow was imprisoned, so he may attack anyway.

After all, the Shadow had created the Dragons. So long ago it was ancient history to everyone except the Ancient. When he had crossed the line, he, like all the ones before him, had to spend time learning the history and secrets of the Dragons. For a mortal it would have taken a life time, for the mind of the Dragon with their ability for perfect memory it only took a year, as the mortals measured time. He let his mind pull out the information about the first Dragons. They were created by the Shadow from a group of volunteers. Part of his honor guard. With their new forms came the ability to defend the land against wizards who grew too powerful. They were the protectors of the people. In the Time of the Shadow only a handful of wizards had the power to take on a Dragon with any hope of success. The kind of power his adversary was using is unheard of in this time.

Looking around, he sighed. Like all the Keepers of the Scepters, he had spent time in fasting and prayer on this very spot. He had been resting long enough. The strength he had gained would allow him to use his magic to increase his speed enough so it would only take him a day to reach the Ancient. He had to get to her.

KanaFinaUn had just taken to the air again when he sensed the Shadow had appeared. The great Dragon had no more strength for fleeing. He brought his massive body to a hover and looked at his adversary. The small man brimmed with magical power. KanaFinaUn did not understand why this man who called himself the Shadow would not show his face. The Shadow's voice was level when he spoke to the huge Dragon.

"I am finished toying with you Guardian. You must make a choice. Either serve me in my quest to bring peace to this land as my god desires or you will no longer be KanaFin. It is time for the Dragons to take their rightful place as the true guardians again. Too long have you left the fate of the Colonies in the hands of the mortals as they war among themselves. They mock everything that you stand for and still you do nothing.

"You have shown me that the Dragons no longer care for the Colonies. Do you not see the importance of what I am trying to do here? To bring the glory back to these people. You must swear to serve me in this quest. I cannot allow creatures as powerful as yourself to live unless they serve the true way. If you cannot see that I speak the truth then I have no choice but to raise up a new Keeper of the Scepter, and elevate true Dragons to serve the Shadow.

"What is your answer? Must I kill you and all of your kind, or will you not follow me and bring peace to this land that so desperately needs it."

KanaFinaUn faltered in his flight. When he had received the scepter, he gave his word that he would serve the needs of the Dragon above his own at all times. He examined the man who hovered in the air by him. He had to be the Shadow. No mortal, not even the Dragoon possessed the kind of power that he did. All that he said was true as well. Since his youth he longed to bring peace and glory back to the Colonies. He knew without a doubt that this was the time of which the prophecy had spoken. The time when one Dragon will rise to reclaim the way of the Dragon and another will raise and forsake it. If serving the Shadow was the price, he paid to be able to crush the rebel when he came and to return the unity to the Dragons as the prophecy promised, he would be glad to do it.

Assenting to the Shadow, he started heading towards the ground to officially bow. The Shadow motioned for him to stay. The man still in shadows floated over to KanaFinaUn. Bowing his massive head, he felt the mortal's touch burn into the flesh behind his horns. The words of the man seemed to burn into the Dragon's brain.

"I have marked you as one of mine today. Know that many of your kind have grown weak and will not except the responsibility which is their duty. They will rise up against you. One who I see will be elevated and do war against you and all the Dragons who keep the true way. You and the true Dragons must bring them down at any cost."

KanaFinaUn eyes got as big as they could. His voice quavered.

"I know of the prophecy, but I cannot kill this Dragon of whom you speak. It is forbidden to kill another Dragon. It is the first of our commandments."

The Shadow thought for a moment and then smiled under his cloak.

"Yes, that is true, but you must remember that we have drawn a line today. Those who forsake the Colonies by not serving can no longer be called Dragons. They are only pretenders and have no fire in their voice. If the true Dragons are to survive there must be a unity among you. If that unity comes at the price of blood, then it has to be."

KanaFinaUn knew the truth of the words. It was the line from the prophecy. If the Guardians of the Truth are to survive, they must unite and stand as one. He had felt for a long time that the bond of many must be made whole again. He had never thought that it would be him who would be recorded as the one who brought it about. He had always hoped, but had never dared dream.

The man removed his hood and smiled warmly at the Dragon. KanaFinaUn could see the power in the man's eyes and his strong determination. He knew that this man would forge the peace and KanaFinaUn was glad he had made the right choice. He received his instructions from the man and flew off with a vision for his life.

Shadow Fire smiled truthfully after KanaFinaUn left. He had accomplished what so many had tried and failed in the past. He corrupted a Dragon. The others had been fools. They had tried to turn them to the dark. The huge creatures were too strong of character for that. It was always the easiest way to corrupt the virtuous. To have them to follow the Dark One by getting them to focus on the noble goal instead of their God. It was almost easier than he had expected. Only once did he think that all was lost. It was when the Dragon was heading towards that cursed mountain. It had been sanctified and he would have had no power there. Luckily the flying beast noticed his command and stopped heading there. Shadow Fire felt lucky, but he did not have time to revel in his victory. He was already late for an appointment.

Emperor Mosk the Dark examined the man in front of him. Elson had arranged the meeting. His younger brother had never before cared about politics of the nation. A fact that had kept him alive. It had come as a shock when Elson spoke of the man named Shadow Fire, the one before him now. The man radiated the power of one of the Dark Masters. Mosk did not know what to think about that. He remembered too well what Back Biter had done to his father. Yet, he was not his father.

"Elson tells me you are the power behind this new Shadow Empire." Shadow Fire bowed regally before speaking.

"That is true in a matter of speaking, your majesty. I am only a Wyle, here to offer...."

Mosk stood, anger thick in his voice.

"Do not play me like you would a noble dandy. I watched and learned for a hundred years as Back Biter sucked the life out of my father. I know what you are. Do not think you can manipulate me. I stood my ground with Back Biter. I am the one who forced him through the gate and closed it. So, keep it straight with me or you will regret it. I do not share my brother's appetites and neither do I share my father's foolishness."

Shadow fire smiled. He had been misinformed. Mosk understood the Dark Powers. He did more than understand. He was the first in the Colonies who matched him firmly as an equal. The willow wisps circled around the man and flared with his anger. Shadow Fire knew that Emperor Mosk was the one he was looking for. He spoke not honestly, he was no longer capable of honesty, but Shadow Fire spoke openly.

"I am glad that I have been led here. You are correct when you say that you understand, for I can now see that the Dark Power strong with you. You were also correct that I came here to manipulate you like I have done so many of the other nobles. However, I now have different plans for you.

"I have longed look for someone who was worthy to rule by my side. I did not lie to the fool that is running the empire now that I have no desire to rule the nations. He thinks that it will be him, and I am sure that he is planning on trying to kill me. That I find amusing enough to let him try and taste his fears when he learns the truth.

"As you pointed out and I believe, you have the power to kill me. Let me say though that I too have the power to destroy you. What I offer now is a partnership. You as the emperor over all the nations you want, but you must leave the church for me. You may have the people's bodies but I want their souls."

Mosk examined Shadow Fire for a very long time. The man was a liar and followed the Dark Path. Still, it was true that he cared nothing of ruling nations. Mosk found it interesting that it was the same arrangement that he had with his brother. It was also true that they had the power to kill each other. Then neither one would reach their goals and that would mean the other would win. He spoke with a commanding voice that he must have received from his mother.

"Very well, when the time is right, I will take control of the Dark Shadow Empire from your too, leaving the working of religion to you. But before we discuss terms and conditions, you should know that I will require a Blood Oath on our agreement."

Shadow Fire blinked, then smiled. The grandeur of the undertaking would call for such a permanent oath. He agreed and within the hour the two had performed the dark ritual that would prevent them from directly harming each other. And after the week it took to write the concrete, they had indeed become partners in their plot against the Colonies. Shadow Fire had second thoughts when he left. Emperor Mosk was most likely much better at attacking people through agents then he was, but as he said, he had no desire to rule the nations and if Mosk ever interfered with the Dark Church the Oath would be void. He went home pleased with everything he had accomplished.

Beyond the Barrier Mountains, a lone Human stood before the Council of Giants. He was alone with over sixty of the huge people who only the strongest of Dragons would face without help. It was the Giants who were afraid. He could sense it very strongly from many of the younger Giants. His reputation far exceeded his abilities, but he did have power. He was not only and Enforcer, but the Enforcer. The result of the centuries of research conducted by the Unholy Council. Genetic manipulation, magical augmentation, a lifetime of training of such intensity that he had been the only one to survive out of the two thousand who had started the program. After that they had made him into a living magical item. They had made him into the ultimate killing machine who was once known only as the Giant Slayer.

Very few of them ever overcame their fear enough to talk with him. One of those was Prince Incuertus. They had become friends and were working hard together to get permission from the Dragons to allow limited trade between his province and the Colonies. He caught Incuertus's eye and raised his right hand. The Giant raised his own hand and laughed.

Enforcer looked down at the floor at his feet to see at what his Giant friend was laughing. It was tiled with marble in the pattern of the symbol of pain. He looked at his palms. His right had the same symbol tattooed on it. The left, the symbol of power. Of course, the symbols themselves did not hold power but what they represented. To the ancients they were known as the heart and broken heart. Love and lost love. Amic the Great was wise when he declared the heart to be the most powerful of symbols. Enforcer sighed, it had been over five hundred years and he still missed the man. He knew how to wield power like none other. A benevolent tyrant was as rare as true love. He was reminded how much he wanted to go home. He put his palms together and smiled. Love could take away any pain.

The Council was making him wait. They were trying to intimidate him, but they were not doing a good job at it. He was becoming bored. To pass the time he closed his eyes and activated the tattoo behind his ears. Scanning the room's conversations, he found nothing of interest. The typical complaints and assassinations which were common among the royalty. He laughed out loud when he heard the three kings talking about him. They were uncomfortable about his presence. They had recently started trading with the Tecmen and were afraid that he was there to stop them. They did not know that Incuertus had been trading with the Philippine Empire since almost the end of the War Forward.

He had enough of their game. He longed to get home. He had been away from his beloved too long. It had been almost a year since he had seen her smile. This was the last thing he had to do and he could be home for a long time. He activated all of his tattoos. The sudden explosion of power and the shimmering ball of energy around him drew the attention of all the Giants. He spoke with a tint of irritation in his voice.

"I am finished being patient. We will now discuss the terms for the renewal of our truce."

The kings hardened their faces. They knew that they had made the Enforcer wait too long. The three stood, the one in the middle spoke.

"We stand face to face once again in order to come to terms for our two great peoples to live in peace. You have always showed your honor to our forefathers and to the present council. You have showed us the respect by understanding that our society does not hold the same views as the kingdoms of the little people. We ask that you continue such respect, as we have decided that the old laws against technology are not appropriate."

Enforcer felt like smiling, but did not. They had no idea how the introduction of technology was going to destroy the foundations on which the Giants' tyranny was built. Now that there would be enough food to feed them and the slaves as well, many of their subjects will start thinking that it might be worth fighting against the Giants. The weapons that will be smuggled into the Blood Lands would soon be strong enough to bring down a Giant. As soon as one Giant builds an army of humans and equips them with technological weapons, the rest will do the same and soon those armies will turn on their masters. Most likely setting up some form of democracy, or possibly themselves becoming the tyrants, but either way, the rule of the Giant was coming to an end as it did in the Colonies so many centuries ago. The Enforcer scanned the room before answering

"What do I care who you trade with. Our treaty has nothing to do with such trivial matters. There is only one thing that concerns me and that is where you stand in the coming war."

The Giants murmured among themselves.

"We have no idea what you are talking about."

The Enforcer smiled because it was true. He knew it was a tactical error, but there was no other way to find out where they would stand."

"One that was chosen by the Destroyer has been released and is working hard to rebuild the Dark Church in the Colonies. Even now his forces are gathering to forge his empire. An added condition of renewal is that you do not give united support to this effort."

The elder king spoke without even conferring with the other two.

"That is and easy promise to make. We have all been raised with stories of what life was like for our people under the rule of the Unholy Council. We had greater power then but we did not rule ourselves. We were forced to fight each other, not for pleasure or our own benefit, but at their whims. Even though such an alliance would give us access to the fertile lands past the Barrier Mountains, the price would be too high for us to pay. None of us here wants to be under the yoke of such creatures again. So, we accept your terms for a continued truce."

The Enforcer smiled as he spoke, for he would now be able to go home.

"Very well, the following conditions are added to the treaty between the Giants of the Land of Blood and the Agent of the Dragons. First, we will not interfere with your sovereignty including with whom you are willing to do business. The second is that now, nor in the future, will you give any unified support to any who are bent on resurrecting the Blood Empire."

They had never needed a written contract before, even though he knew the Giants kept a record, so he simply walked out of the meeting hall and went home.

At the edge of the southern forest nation of Lifkin, Elcin crouched on a high branch of a tree, thinking about life in general. She had not left her perch for three days. It had been over twenty years since she had been in the trees. She had been trying to work up the nerve to jump. It was not fear of falling that was causing her the problem. She was afraid that she may want to fall. She had been so miserable that she was not sure she wanted to live anymore. That was why she entered the trees again. By jumping she would know whether she wanted to live or die.

With the setting sun the three days of cleansing was completed. In almost ritual fashion she stripped off her clothes and donned the traditional armor of a Tree Jumper. Pulling her vine cutter out of its holster, she raised it to the back of her head. She paused only a moment and then cut off her ponytail. A Nite could not afford their hair getting caught in the branches of a high tree. She let the hair fall to the forest floor as she returned the vine cutter to its place. After double checking the buckles on her armor, she donned her mask. It smelled like her mother.

Memories of her mother flooded Elcin's mind. The Culrete, wearing her armor and mask, following the forms and duty of the forest people. Elcin had been raised by her mother deep in the Forest. For the first time Elcin felt like she understood both her mother and father, and their love. The two of them had met in this very valley. They lived together here until business had called her mother back into the forest. Elcin had hated her mother for such a long time because of that. For placing duty above her father.

Elcin fastened on the branch catchers onto her hands and ankles, making sure they were angled correctly, and then she leapt. Using the tips of the branches to guide her direction she landed safely on a tree limb. She held on until the branch started its upward movement, and used its upward movement to aid her in her next jump to a higher branch. Pulling herself up she jumped again without thinking. Tree jumping required entering into what the Culrete called the Falling Leaf, the state in which one moved in perfect harmony with one's surroundings. To the Nite it was not only needed for their rapid movements in the tree tops, but was considered a form of meditation. It let their mind go where it needed to be rather than be forced to go where they wanted it. She circled the valley over and over again.

Her mother had forced her to live as a Culrete. It was not that she had anything against her mother's people, it was that many of them had problems with her. With a Human father, Elcin was an outcast. When she was young, she had worked hard at being as Culrete as possible. Everything her mother's people were supposed to be good at, she excelled. Everything the Culrete believed in, she championed. It was never enough. She was never widely accepted because her ears were human and she was never happy.

She lost her footing and started falling. Out of an old practice she threw out a dart. It struck hard into a high branch and the spider cord attached to it swung her to a tree trunk. Without reflecting on her near death, Elcin started her movement through the trees again.

When her mother died, she had left the forest because she had not been happy there. She had found acceptance in the land of the Humans but never found happiness. That was not entirely true. She had been happy once in her life. Ankka. When she had met him, she had no idea what was going to happen. He was young and naive. How did he end up winning her heart?

It had to be his noble innocence. The way he always knew the right thing to do, even he did not completely grasp what was really going on. He had died in the same way. She had been on the ground watching him fly after the battle. The way he maneuvered in the air, without fear, without thought, as if he was part of the wind. She loved watching him fly. It filled her with pride.

She knew something was wrong when he stopped and hovered for a moment. She could feel him think in that way he did when he was trying to make a decision. By the time she spotted at what he was looking at, he was already in his dive. She screamed for him to stop, for others to help, she just screamed. It was too late by the time she could move, Ankka was already dragging the cursed hawk back into the air.

The Dragons were already mounting their attack on the Tecmen's ships by the time she reached his body. The poison of the shadow hawk's claws had already turned most of his body that dark color and made it soft. She wept. She had actually wept. She did not cry at her mother's death, or the dozens of adventurers who died next to her throughot the years. Yet, she felt herself die that day with Ankka.

She had no stomach for the festivals of the victory. She took his body and buried it in this very valley. Her father's valley. She had tried to return to the life of an adventurer. She could not. Somehow, she had changed. Every comrade who died would send her into the nightmares of that day she lost Ankka. The day her love, her first and only love, died. She returned to her home. Her father was happy but she was not. She continued her studies in human magic, she built additions to the house, anything to keep her mind off things. It helped at times with the loss, but most of the time she was just numb. She knew that she has never come to terms with Ankka's death. She knew that she never would. The very thing she held most dear about him, was the same thing which had killed him.

She had just buried her father. What kept her here? With her father's death the valley was hers. It was her home, but something called her away. It was her Culrete blood. Something was wrong that threatened the balance of the world. She was neither religious nor philosophical, but there are times when too much thought keeps us from doing what Elohim needs of us.

She leapt from a high branch into the valley, using a summersault and magic she landed safely on the ground. She did not retrieve anything from the house, nor bothered to secure it from thieves. The massive library and lab had belonged to her father. If they were gone when she returned, if she returned, they would not be missed. Without much thought she moved back into the trees and headed deep into the forest, to the home of her mother. Into the land of LifKin, the Forest Nation of the First Family of the First Circle.

XXII

Tapps threw himself to the ground, rolled and put his back to a boulder. The fight was not going well. It was the sixth real fight, but the first in which they had not done well. This Shadow Force was different. He had just come up with a new plan and was in the role of the bait. He hoped it would work. He looked over at his warriors and laughed as an enemy's spell tore a chunk of rock from the boulder. The soldiers were not his, they answered only to Angga. He looked over at her. She was hovering in front of the group issuing orders. Angga always knew what needed to be done but she was still lacking in the confidence she needed. But only when she had time to think about it. In the thick of the fight, she did not hesitate. Whenever the Princess did not have time to doubt herself, she would excel. Tapps looked over the boulder and scanned the canyon in which they were fighting.

The Shadow Warriors outnumbered them by least three to one but that was not what concerned him. This new force was far tougher than the others had been. They had some sort of shielding against magic, not even his own and Angga's could harm them. They had known that it was just a matter of time. With each wave of attacks, they had grown stronger. This morning their leaders had started to use magic. The Shadow Forces' unit commanders looked as if they had been twisted in a knot and then not completely straightened out again. They walked with a gait which made Angga comment that it reminded her of a story about a golem by a lady named Shelly. He had never read the novel. Very few books had been translated into brail. Of course, he knew that he only used that as an excuse. He was not much of a reader anyway.

He was brought back to the battle by a hawk-like screech coming from Fenasy. He looked up. The men in the force had started to channel their magic into the Eagle Warriors. That was his cue and he cast a Magi's Grenade. He stood and threw the ball of fire into the midst of Shadow Warriors. As he did, one of their leader's Fire Arrows hit him in the chest. It burnt through his cloths and fur but did little else. Tapps took off in a run as the Magi's Grenade exploded. He had not expected it to do any real damage. It was meant to be a diversion and nothing more. As he leapt, he heard another screech come from the captain of the Eagle Warriors.

The elite warriors of the Sella Queendom let loose with a massive attack in unison. It would have been enough to kill several of the Shadow Warriors outright but they were not the target. The energy from the Eagle Warriors crashed into the canyon wall. Tapps did not have time to watch but he knew that the cliff wall would be exploding into a hail of rocks. The Shadow Force would be trapped under tons of rock. Considering the power of these warriors they were not hoping to kill them with the attack but simply immobilize them. They were simply playing the waiting game.

When Angga gave the order to fall back to the next point, Tapps looked up at the sun. They had only a couple of hours of daylight left. This was the last day and would only have to hold out until then. The last of Angga's people would have already left the mountains and by sunset they would be out of the reach of the Dark Shadow Empire. But for how long? Tapps had a feeling that this new kingdom was not going to stop with just the Southern Mountains.

As always Angga looked relieved when he finally showed up. Tapps smiled and waved. He had tried to explain that there were only few things in the Colonies that could be a threat to him. Physically anyway. But he knew that she only worried because of her feelings for him. He had not realized it until NetThin brought it up. It explained a lot, and he felt foolish for not having seen it before. Keith had all but told him. That was something to worry about later.

Tapps scanned over the warriors who were getting as much rest as they could. Only a little over two score remained. They had started with fifty of the Eagle Warriors and a hundred men. All of the men who had volunteered had the same kind of wings as Angga. Many of them were able to concentrate their magic into an attack. He had to admit that there was a lot he did not know about Angga's culture. The force they brought should have been enough but the Shadow Forces did not act the way he had expected. They had not given chase to the winged people at all and concentrated on his force. Was it him or the Princess who was the target of this? The forces themselves did not seem to have a specific target.

It had been just a matter of hours since they had lost much of their force. It had started like all the others. They had struck from hiding. Their attacks did not have the affect they normally had. Not one of the Shadow Warriors had been dropped. They had little choice but to fight hand to hand while making the retreat. With all their agility in flight the Arvions were vulnerable to arrows. They had managed to get far enough away to take to the air. It had cost too many lives and when they thought they had reached safety the Shadow Forces had somehow managed to track them down. It was even the same group. Tapps knew that they would not be able to defeat this enemy. Nearly seventy had dropped in the first battle. Most of them were the males.

This new breed of Shadow Warriors was practically immune to magic but they could be brought down. Even so, they were not natural. He had disemboweled one and it still kept fighting. They did not slow when a limb was severed. They eventually would drop but it was only after taking an incredible about of damage. One was even bought down by the short bows of the Arvions. The thing looked like a porcupine with the dozens of arrows sticking out of it when it finally fell. Being the last day they needed to stay, the plan came easy. Incapacitate long enough to start their trek out of the mountains.

He was glad that it was over in a few hours. He had not gotten along with the force. Not that he had problems, but he was only a man. It did not matter he was from outside the Queendom. Even considering his reputation, he was just a man and they balked at the idea that they would be taking orders from him. The only ones who would listen to him were Angga and Fenasy. Luckily, they were in charge. It was inefficient at times in battle but it was something with which he had to learn to deal.

Once alone he stood watch at the edge of camp. It was high on the peak. On one side the only way up would to be climb a steep cliff that would take an expert. Any force that wanted to get to them would have to go back around the peak and come from the other side. It was at least six hours of travel and they would be vulnerable for attack most of the time. Of course, they had no plan on being there when they arrived. Angga's people should be well out of the mountains and out of the reach of the Shadow Forces. All they had to do now was wait until they could make their own escape.

Snow grew agitated as he watched the battles in the magical pool. He had set the perfect trap. Nearly a thousand Shadow Warriors had been sent to the area. Most of them of the new generation. The area which held his enemy was blanketed completely with them. They were completely surrounded. Slowly they pressed in but the Kaltar still evaded them. Every time he was located, Tapps was able to escape.

Tapps and the eagle people with him would then appear somewhere else. They would attack swiftly, and by the time Snow could get reinforcements to the area the group was nowhere to be found. As night started to fall, Snow was almost in a state of panic. He had let the rest of the eagle people get away so he could concentrate on Tapps. With the winged people safely out of his reach his real target would have no reason to stay.

The last hour of sunlight seemed to last forever. When darkness finally overcame the landscape, Snow collapsed into a chair. Tapps had escaped him. Silver turned towards him with a smile.

"Sir, do no despair yet, for I have an idea that will give us a much greater revenge than merely killing him."

Snow listened to the plan of the rogue turned general and was pleased with it.

Thorin stood on shore looking across the water at his city. He could not help but to think back on the first time he stood on that shore. Much had changed in those few years. He had become king of a nation which did not exist. He had become the Dragon King. He was still not sure he wanted the throne, but his only other option was to flee in the night like a coward.

He had not intended to take control of the city. Thorin simply had no patience for the bureaucracy which was hindering anything, everything from getting accomplished. This was especially true when it came to military matters. He had taken control of their guards, kept up their training and put them to work. DragoRue Henra started calling him DragoKeen, and asking him about other things about the city. Thorin had thought the DragoKeen was the title of the head of their military, a position he considered himself qualified for. A position he would not have hesitated to accept. By the time Thorin had learned that they had given him the Dragon Throne, made him the Dragon King, it was too late to abdicate. His sense of duty trapped him.

It had been an incident with KuAra which let Thorin know that he had become king. KuAra had been upset because he had been removed from the board of the school of magic. He was upset, even now, because Thorin had refused to veto the decision of the board. Thorin had been upset himself because KuAra had made the request formally instead of coming to see him first. Thorin, Cesdakar and Henra had to spend weeks developing the policies which would govern education. Thorin learned that he was in fact, king only when Henra presented the final copy for him to sign.

One good thing did come from the event. They now had an official educational system. One with its own board which could over see such request and complaints in the future. One which could, and has been making the decisions needed to get the schools operational. Only their Chairperson reported to him. It had set precedence, created a model for the other aspects of the society. The city now had its own board, Henra as its Chairperson, that took care of its infrastructure. Now he could spend his time focusing on growing the nation. The reason he was on the shore now.

The city was producing more than enough food now for its own need. They had salvaged enough iron to last a while, but they were in need of lumber. They could harvest some from the island the city sat on, but with the concern about erosion and the lack of running water for power, it would be far more efficient to set up a mill on the mainland. There was only one problem, the Goblins which lived in the area.

He had sent Cesdakar to see if they could not come up with some arrangement. The holy man had volunteered, saying in his cryptic way about how it was what was meant to be. It had been a year, with only a few commutations of Cesdakar informing that he was alive. Then a message came telling Thorin to meet him on the shore today. So Thorin and his guard came to the shore and waited. They had been there for hours already.

More hours passed before Cesdakar showed up with eleven Goblins. In some ways he appeared just the same, but in others he looked as a whole different person. Still wearing the dark glasses over his eyes, much of his skin was exposed, which had a reddish-brown color. More red than brown, and leathery in texture. He also had a scar across his face. By the look it was only a month or so old and must have been a serious wound. He left the Goblins at the tree line without saying a word to them and approached.

Thorin spoke as soon as he could be heard without shouting.

"Well, it has been a while."

Cesdakar cocked his head to the side. He knew that was all he was going to get as a hello so he spoke with a smile.

"Yes, three days short of a year. There is much more to the Goblins then we anticipated. A complex kin and clan system, which meant I had to convince not only the ones of this area but the entire Free Goblin nation."

"Just to get them to agree to let us harvest timber?"

Cesdakar laughed.

"Xenanor? Sorry, a common expression from an old Anear story. The point of which is that life is not without struggle. The Anear as they call themselves, in this area could not give permission because the land is held in common by the whole clan so I had to go up and wait why they gathered all the leaders together. They decided they could not agree because it might cause strife with the other clans. Apparently, their clans have not fought against each other for several generations, and they want to keep it that way.

"They were correct that allowing us to harvest lumber would upset the other clans. I had to travel to each one of them, wait until their leaders gathered, and gain permission from each of them. That took about six months, but then I had to convince them to call a Hurngha in order for them to negotiate with each other. A kind of great-meeting, where leaders from all the clans get together to deal with something which affects the entire Free Goblin nation. That took some time, and then even longer for them to come to an agreement everyone could be happy with. I sent the note as soon as it was considered official."

Cesdakar stopped because something on the ground grabbed his attention. He leaned over and picked up a small pebble from the ground. Placing it in a pouch he turned his attention to the water, giving no indication of continuing. Thorin prodded him.

"So, they have agreed to let us harvest?"

Cesdakar continued to examine the beach for a few moments and then returned his attention to Thorin. He spoke in a distracted tone.

"No, they have decided that they will not let us harvest. They do not believe that Humans are capable of doing it properly. They have given permission for us to build the mill we want, but they will harvest the trees."

Thorin was a bit surprised, and it showed in their voice.

"That sounds too good to be true, what are they expecting in return?"

Cesdakar laughed before speaking.

"To be citizens in the Nation of Many Faces again."

Thorin blinked hard.

"What?!"

"Apparently in the civilized lands Goblins have no rights, and are automatically considered a slave. These Goblins live in the wild because they will not be slaves. Anear in their language means freedom, and it is something which they hold dear. Though they have a longing to be part of the so-called civilized nations, they are not willing to give up that freedom. According to their oral history, they once had that during the Nation of Many Faces. I believe that is what they call the United Colonial Empire.

"They understand that you are the one that revived the old capital of that empire, and so they see the possibility of its rebirth. It has been the reason they have been defending this land as fiercely as they have. I cannot be sure whether it was a prophecy or simply something they desire. It was repeated often that they have been protecting this land because it would be what they pay for their civilized freedom. They have been waiting for a sign to give their allegiance to a human nation, and they believe the rebirth of the city is that sign."

Thorin was not sure he completely understood what was saying.

"Bottom line it for me, what exactly do they want?

Cesdakar looked back at the Goblins for a moment before speaking.

"In monetary terms, they want nothing except to be paid for the lumber they bring in. But more important to them is respect. They want to stand as equals with everyone else in the nation. To have their freedom and lives protected by the same laws that apply to Humans."

Thorin looked over at the group of Goblins. They had a look of anticipation, but Thorin did not notice any apprehension. He looked back at Cesdakar who had gone back to examining the area and was picking up another pebble off the ground.

"So, we can build our mill. They will harvest the lumber, deliver it, and all I have to do is create a law which gives them the protection of a citizen in NoraTo."

Cesdakar shook his head as he spoke.

"No, it is not that simple. They want to build towns, not only up the river but all over their lands. They want Humans to come and live near them and with them. That is, they do not simply want to trade with your nation, they want to become a part of it."

Thorin find that hard to believe. What he knew of the Wild Goblins, both from the stories he had heard, and his experience these Goblins had no love for Humans. He spoke such.

"That is hard to understand, Ces. If that has been the case, why have they been so vicious with those who travel in their land?"

"Think on its Thor. Respect is important to them, and the Humans do not come into their lands as if it belongs to them, but as if it belongs to no one. I am the first ambassador to ever go to them, and you are the first King not to simply send people to take what they want. That has gone a long way in convincing them that you are the one they have been waiting for.

"I have explained to them many of the details. They do not expect NoraTo to cover all of their lands overnight. It was hard to convince them as such, but they will keep possession of the land until it is needed for settlement."

Thorin nodded.

"How many Goblins are we talking about? And how large of an area?"

Cesdakar covered his eyes with a hand, a habit he obviously picked up while with the Goblins. He spoke as he brought his hand down.

"To their numbers I am not really sure. It appears that their numbering system is base ten instead of base eight, so it is a bit hard for me to understand. The best I have been able to gather, there may be a hundred thousand or so, but that may just be their warriors. I am unsure of their land as well. They control north to the City of Graves, which I am assuming is where the Human lands start. To the south, all the way to this very spot, and to the west as far to the land they say is controlled by the People of Stone. I am not sure where that is, but it is at least many days travel beyond the great river."

Thorin could not control his head jerking to stare at the Goblins. They were willing, asking to hand over a nation to him. Land enough for NoraTo to grow for centuries without the need for war. A prize worth more than all the gold in the Colonies, and all they were asking was something, at least to Thorin's thinking, they should have had anyway. It was hard for him not to feel the outrage growing in him. He grew to age in a democracy, where individual rights were paramount. He served in a military whose sole purpose, whose Honor was found in protecting those rights. He spoke from the heart.

"Tell them that they have what they ask for. Also tell them that while it will take some time to draw up the papers, they have my word that from this day forth, their rights are guaranteed more then by law, but by me. On my Honor I will make sure they will always be a free people."

Cesdakar smiled and did something which he had never done before. He bowed to Thorin. He turned back and started towards the Goblin. He paused to hear what Thorin said next.

"Ces, also I will need them to choose one of their numbers to come to live at court to represent Goblin interest."

Cesdakar went up and spoke with the Goblins. Thorin could tell they were pleased only because they were nodding their heads in agreement. Near the end, Cesdakar pulled one of the pebbles out of his pouch and handed it to one of the Goblins. As soon as that Goblin had placed the stone into his pouch, the group headed back into the forest. Cesdakar started that way as well, but stopped. Turning back around, he came back to Thorin. There was humor in his voice.

"I am in a habit of always moving with the Anicta, that is, the Family-Pack, that I started leaving without thinking about it."

Thorin smiled as he spoke.

"You did well Ces, very well. And it is good to have you back."

Cesdakar nodded his thanks, and spoke in that manner of wisdom which Thorin was used to from him.

"Speaking truth from the heart is powerful enough to move nations. It was easy for me, once you stopped thinking about what you wanted and showed your heart. That is why they were here. It was not my words, or yours that they wanted. They wanted to see the truth of your Honor. All my work would have been nothing if it was not for that."

Thorin laughed. Yes, it was good to have Cesdakar back. It was good to have someone around that spoke to him as a person, instead of as the Dragon King. Thorin motioned for the leader of his guard to have the ship come in to take them back to the city. They had much work to do, and there was no point in putting it off. As they were boarding the ship, Thorin turned towards Cesdakar.

"What is up with the rock?"

Cesdakar smiled, pulling the second pebble out of his pouch. He handed it to Thorin and spoke as soon as he had taken it.

"The Anear believe as I do that the Source leads a person to a place for a purpose and being in the right place is just as important as who you meet and what you discuss. It is not uncommon for them to pick up something from an area as a symbol of the meeting, especially when the meeting is of importance. That pebble which looks like many others, now has an importance because it is a reminder of a moment in time, a moment when the fate of many was decided." Cesdakar paused, looking over the water, then continued in that quite tone one gets when they fear of being overheard. "It is a custom of the Anear which I have learned from. A way for us to remember that just as with the pebble, a person may seem common and worthless, yet if they are in that place they should be, then they are important. Like that pebble, all it takes is for a single person to believe in us, that can see our worth, to make our lives better. Something you should know as king, that to see the purpose for a person, you can give meaning to their lives."

Thorin laughed as he put the pebble in his own pouch. Yes, it was good to have Cesdakar back.

KanaFinaGol looked around. She had been hoping the KanaFinaTurcan would be there. He was the newest Dragon but she had already found a great fondness for him. Of course, because of his age he would not share the feelings. Like most of those raised Dragon he did not find the body of the Dragon attractive. She was a born Dragon and so she could not grasp the beauty in the mortal body. Still, she found herself thinking of him often and loved spending time with him. The way he talked about economics was so much like she did of knowledge.

He was not at the calling and he was not the only one. The Ancient was not there and most of the elders had failed to show. They rarely showed up to callings which were not scheduled. Every fifty years the call was put out and new Dragons were welcomed, and the elders announced their plans to pass through the Gate. The next call was not to be for another decade or so. It was odd for it to be put out so early.

Many of the Dragons mumbled among themselves. The Keeper of the Scepter had put out the call and that was odd in itself, but the meeting place was what made most of them nervous. The crater at the northern base of the Holy Mountain was only used for the most formal rituals. The last time a meeting was held here was when her father was made the Keeper. She had been too young to attend but she had read the report.

A hush went over the Dragons as KanaFinaUn landed on the speaking rock. She shrunk back from him and she was not alone. She instantly knew something was wrong with her father. Something that went far beyond just the war that was starting. No, something had changed him completely. As if he had broken his bond with LingueArdeo, but that just could not be. No Dragon would give up his bond. It was what made them what they were. Without the bond they would become the terrible forces of evil that the legends of the old earth said they were. She worried for her father when he spoke.

"Gentle Dragons, listen to me, for I hold the scepter and I have come with a proclamation from the Shadow himself."

A roar went up from the Dragons as they all mumbled among themselves.

"SkaHu, Skahu, it is true. The Shadow has been released as the Ancient always said he would. He is the one who has built the castle in the Southern Mountains and has started his reclaiming of the Colonies. He will forge a new empire like the one before. There will be a peace which we have not seen since we ruled the Colonies. I have long said that we should take a more active role in the leadership of the Colonies. Now is the time. We will be once again in the service of the Shadow and take our rightful place in this land."

A real roar went up from the Dragons. Some were giving their support, others opposing it. KanaFinaGol just blinked. Did she hear right? Had her father just said that they would actually be taking sides in a war? She sniffed the air to see what the magic told her. She could tell nothing. Too many of the Dragons were near and they warped any knowledge that the magic would give her. KanaFinaFittus roar brought the gathering to silence.

"No! We do not fight in the wars of the mortal. Do you not remember what happened when you called us to war against Mosk?"

KanaFinaFittus was much older than KanaFinaUn and was a true born. He was known for being quiet but when he was angered everyone gave him a wide berth. He also had almost as much power as her father. He was after all the Silver of Silvers, he led the Silver Clan, the priests of the Dragons. The one who all went to with questions in their faith, a high priest or an elder is what the mortals would call him. Even those of the Gold Clan listened to his advice. She looked around. Many of the older Dragons shook their heads remembering that event. She was just an infant then but she knew that it had caused a crack in the unity of the Dragons. A wound that never healed. Father always believed that the Dragons should take a more active role in the Colonies and KanaFinaFittus advocated that they should maintain their distance from the mortals and do as the law dictates. This was not the first time these two had butted heads in over the centuries. The way they talked now it was hard to tell that the two had been close friends most of her father's Dragon life. KanaFinaUn's voice was full of fire.

"The Shadow created the Colonies and he created us. It is our place to do whatever he asks of us. We must give him all the respect which he deserves. It is time for us to claim our rightful place in the Colonies."
KanaFinaFittus own voice was full of fire. The kind of passion which can only come from true faith.

"As the father of the Ancient I give respect to the Shadow, but the Colonies is not his. He is not the one who created me. He is not my father.

nor is he VivusDeus. He is a man of power. No more."

"HussKa, we must rise up and rule like we did in the time of our parent's parents. It is my right to call us to war and I claim that right now."

"TicKa," KanaFinaFittus paused to calm himself, eyes closed in prayer. After a few moments he opened his eyes full of tears and continued. "This is not right. Your silver has turned red. You are not listening to LingueArdeo. It is true that we must take our service more seriously, but this is not the way. We must think what is best for those in our care rather than some mythical peace. I will not stand by and let you do this. We have worked hard to maintain our respect. If you join this fight, we will no longer be able to claim to serve the Colonies itself."

The other Dragons just stared as the two circled each other. KanaFinaGol could not believe her eyes. They were going to fight. Their behavior was definitely the ritual challenge. KanaFinaFittus did not stand a chance against her father. He was a mere scholar and the Keeper of the Scepter was a warrior to the bone. It would be a fast fight.

The two leaders of the Dragons locked in combat and the thrashing was enough to rock the ground. Within minutes KanaFinaUn had the neck of the Silver of Silvers between his teeth. Gasps went up among the Dragons when they heard the snap of the bones of the neck. A tear came to KanaFinaGol's eye. It was true. Her father's skin was red. There would be no other answer for him killing another Dragon, killing one of his people. Her whole life he had always taught her that the sole responsibility of a leader was the welfare of their people. That justice could not exist without mercy. The book of law allowed for the victor to kill his enemy but it calls for mercy as well. Every Dragon who had killed another in the formal fight had asked to be punished. She looked up at her father ignoring that her sunglasses had fallen to the ground. This was not her father. This was not the noble creature who had raised her from a hatchling. She barely heard his roar or his words that followed.

"HussKa, I have put out the TivKur, the Call to War and I expect it to be obeyed. We will meet in eight sun spans at the center of the Southern Mountains. Any Dragon who is not there at that time will be put on the List of Outcasts."

KanaFinaUn flew off without waiting for a response. The rest of the Dragons left soon after, not being able to look at the dead body of one of their own. KanaFinaGol watched them go and the Keeper of the Dead moving towards the body. Her scales were all one color which was rare enough but the color marked her unique. She was pure white like freshly fallen snow and the writings about her said that her heart was just as cold. She was an outsider among the Dragons for reasons KanaFinaGol did not understand. Only the Ancient and some of the elders knew anything about her. Very few, even among the Dragons, knew her name. She kept to herself and the only time anyone ever saw her was when she came to claim the body of a dead Dragon. KanaFinaGol went to comfort her when the Keeper of the Dead fell to her belly in sobs. Sometimes books can be wrong, even those written by Dragons. The white kin started when she felt a claw on her back.

She turned towards KanaFinaGol and could barely speak.

"He was my only child."

KanaFinaGol could not stop her own tears from falling. She did not cry for the slain Silver of Silvers. No, she cried because she knew that she would not be able to obey her father. She would have to become an Outcast. Lost in her grief, she forgot that she needed to meet her new PolisKanaFinis.

XXIII

Angga flew high in the air overlooking the throngs of people as they settled into their new home in the Draco Mountains. Life would be hard in the coming years as they had to leave most of their possessions behind. Thanks to the Circle of Magi it was not as hard as it could have been. With their gates they were able to bring many supplies to the new location. The mountain pastures were already full of livestock. The fields, the livestock and most of the mountain were theirs to settle. There was plenty of food and the shelter was sufficient for the winter. KanaFinaGol had taken care of both as she promised. Even though she had supposed to have been there when they had arrived.

Angga had made the mistake of calling the Dragon a he. She could not tell the difference and it appeared male to her. At the first meeting the Dragon had not corrected her, but Tapps eventually did. Still the Dragon did not look like a female at all. Tapps had said that if you looked at her with the eye of a Dragon not only did she appear feminine, but very beautiful as well. Tapps' comment had made Angga feel silly, but only because it made her feel jealous.

Angga, like her mother, balked at the idea of settling here. They would not own the mountain. They were mere custodians. It, and everything on it, including now her people, belonged to the Dragons who called it home. The Queen almost refused, but her husband had changed her mind behind closed doors.

She had never realized how much her mother listened to her father. As a child she never knew how much they loved each other. She had been watching them since her return. Her mother never treated her father like he was just a man. Even though her father would not stand for such talk, they stood together as equals.

Angga smiled. She had just fallen in love with their new mountain home. A new home for a new Queendom. Male and female, Mankarian and feathered, would have to work side by side with the Humans already making the mountains their home to build a new Queendom. They would be the PolisKanaFinis, People of the Dragon. It would be a new nation and she would be their Queen. But who would be their king? It would not be Tapps. She would have to face the fact that it had only been a fantasy. She had felt her loneliness sharply since realizing that. The two of them would not be good for each other. She needed someone who would always be there for her and he needed to free to travel on his missions. Tapps would make a great king, but not her king.

She looked down to where Tapps was talking with her father. Tears swelled in her eyes. She pushed the feelings away. The two of them had become friends since their return from their mission. At first, she had thought that it was only his service to the Queendom. But apparently it had something to do with Tapps revealing a mystery about her uncle. NetThin and Fenasy had barely been seen since their return. Her father was often commenting about reasonability and how there was not enough time for them always running off together. The Queen was heard replying that she wished that she and he would run off more often together. Kelthin stopped talking about it in the Queen's presence.

One thing that was baffling her was the humans who were already in the mountains. There was only a few thousand, but she could not understand why they were not upset with her people showing up. They had welcomed them. She had a chance to meet with some of them. Many of them bowed and all of them had called her Princess. Apparently, the humans were in the mountains to learn from the Dragons and in return they tended the herds and gardens that were the Dragons' primary food source. Many of them had been there since their youths. They seemed pleased with her people's arrival. One of them had commented about how it would be nice to live in civilization again. That would make sense. They had a pleasant life in the shadow of the Dragons but it would be easy to miss all the luxuries of city life.

That was what they had to rebuild, their entire civilization. Roads, wells, towns, a city, and they were starting with nothing. It was a hard path in front of them but one that she was determined to take. She had a duty to her people. Her father was right. The burden of leadership was a heavy one. Queens who did not feel the responsibility were not worthy of the title. He had always taught her that there was always the cost. She had no other choice but to pay it.

She headed towards where Tapps and her father were. It was obvious that the two had been talking about her. They both turned towards her and smiled. Tapps started to talk, but closed his mouth in order to let her father speak.

"So, what have you decided?"

She guarded herself.

"I will stay, but I need to go to the winter camp to get my stuff and say my good byes in person."

Her father nodded with approval. His words were warmer than she ever remembered.

"My heart will survive a bit longer. Return as soon as you can, there is much with which the Queen will need your help. Of course, you are not sneaking away this time, so I expect you to take your guard with you."

Angga went to protest, then thought better of it. He was right. She was now traveling as a Princess and it was proper for her to have her guard. Tapps bowed and spoke with a touch of humor in his voice.

"I will also be heading home, and can leave at your earliest convenience."

James Braker looked in at his friend. High Magus Daryl smiled grimly and shut the door. They had told him that he was too young. That his lack of experience would be more of a hindrance than help. He had argued with them to no avail. They did not understand the nature of Herman's wounds. They were not Naturals. Only the two of them who shared that trait would know what loneliness it brought. James had started worrying for his friend once he knew his father would survive. The elder Braker would be crippled and the medical magus' magic would only return part of his sight, but he would live. James almost smiled. Such setbacks would only strengthen the old admiral. A trait that he was glad he shared with his father. Herman was another matter.

Herman was like an older brother to him. James' power was beyond any other at the Keep and Herman had always made him look like a novice. He looked at the door. If this could happen to Herman, what about himself? He instantly stopped that train of thought. Herman was stronger and smarter than him but his wounds also went much deeper. James was just being born about the time Herman was turning his sister into a skunk. What a blow that must have been. To lose control was the greatest fear of every Natural. To lose control was to destroy everything one was.

James only had to deal with the wound that only the greatest of the Trualja shared, to be the murderer of their own mother. The Natural would react to the pain of childbirth the only way they knew how. They would lash out in violence, causing the magic to bend to their will. Only another Natural could survive such a birth. James' own mother had been a True Magi and had almost survived. Almost.

James wiped the tears from his eyes. It was not proper for him to be indulging his own pain when Herman had real problems. He jumped when someone placed a hand on his shoulder. An unfamiliar voice accompanied the motion.

"One must remove the board from their own eyes before they can help remove the splinter from another's eye. So, it is always proper to deal with our own wounds. But it is not yet time to worry about Hermes. He is in Elohim's hand still."

James Braker turned towards the man. He was a stranger to the Keep. The man was large, wearing the leather robe common with priests, just without a color. A sword was strapped to his side but there was something in his eyes which let James know that he belonged all the same. Braker thought he recognized him.

"White Bear?"

The man smiled as he nodded. His voice calmed James instantly.

"Yes, your father has called me. We will go to him first and then we will rescue Herman."

James forced back the tears.

"Teacher, my father has been injured. He no longer…"

James Braker could not say any more. White Bear hesitated, choosing his words carefully.

"I know…that is why I have come."

The two of them walked down halls in silence, and reached the room Brian Braker was in quickly. James could see the magical weave of the patterns which was keeping his father alive. If White Bear noticed them, he gave no indication. Brian's body had been repaired as best as it could. Besides the missing legs and a handful of scars he looked in perfect health.

White Bear bent over and placed his hand on Brian Braker's forehead. After what seemed like a long time to James he finally spoke.

"He fights to live, for you."

James looked down as he spoke.

"Because I am not yet strong enough to go on without him."

White Bear smiled sweetly and there was a warm humor in his voice.

"To the contrary, very much to the contrary. He fights because he fears he has really let you know how proud he is of you."

James looked at his father. On impulse he knelled down at the bed. His voice sounded almost prayerful.

"Father, I have never doubted your love or…"

White Bear ushered himself and the nurse out of the room and shut the door. After waiting a short time, he pulled an apple out of his pocket which he ate all but the seeds. Those went back into his pocket. Eventually James opened the door, his eyes red from the tears already dried on his cheeks. He looked at White Bear with an expression of thankfulness.

White Bear nodded in return, and then without delay unfastened the sword at his belt. He handed it, still in its sheath, to James. The young Braker took it, half pulled it and examined it for a moment. Putting it back in, he went to hand it back to White Bear, but the holy man waved him off. James' expression mirrored the questioning tone of his voice.

"I do not understand."

White Bear shrugged as is the topic was uninteresting. His voice, however still carried a touch of affection in it.

"I tried to give it to your father years ago, but he would not have it. He did not think he would be the one to bring Honor back to the Society. He planted the seeds, and you will be the one to harvest them."

James shook his head when he spoke.

" What does this sword have to do with it?"

A spark appeared in White Bear's eyes, as the awareness that he left a vital piece of information out.

"That is the Spell Sword.

James gaped and almost dropped the sword. The Spell Sword was the sword of the Society of Spell and Sword. It was a magical sword of legend, an artifact from which the Society had gained its name. It was the symbol of the Order, and according to their law, it belonged to the one who commands the fighting force of the Society. James shook his head, and tried to hand the sword back again.

"I am too young."

White Bear started walking as he spoke.

"Yes, you are too young to command but there is no one for you to command. The Society no longer has an army. You are the only one, so you command no one except yourself. But someday…you will be in command. You must ask yourself to what purpose. What would be worth asking those who will follow you to risk death for? You are young now, but you will not always be so. Someday you will be old enough that your voice will be heard, and you should start even now understanding what you will say with that voice."

White Bear chuckled as he continued.

"Besides, for the aged and wise to know what changes need to happen it is better to look to the young. We wise and old have many solutions, but we are typically hardened by life, and do not always know what problems there are in need of solving. It is all part of the Design of Life. The young need to aged for our wisdom, the aged needs the young for the sensitivity, and we need those in between to bridge the gap between us."

White Bear stopped in front of the door which led to Herman's room. He closed his eyes for a moment, but appeared to be looking around all the same. His eyes popped up with a start, and he turned towards James. His voice, while still gentle had an intensity which seemed to force James to pay attention.

"Not all which seems to be good is good, and not all hardships are evil. It is often the hardest lesson in life to understand the difference. To know when we must accept a pain, even though it is in our power to change it. To know when we must fight with every ounce of our strength in a cause that there is no hope. Thus, are the nature of Honor, thus is the nature you must seek to allow Elohim to guide you in. Come now, you need to be a part of this, for both his sake and yours."

Twelve of the most powerful True Magi in the Colonies were in the room, including the High Magus Daryl, examined Herman. Rakauther, the Society's High Medical Magus spoke.

"Except for some malnutrition and magic starvation there is nothing physically wrong with him."

Daryl nodded. The other ten were trying to overcome Herman's power and force feed him magic. One of them pushed too hard and Herman grimaced. The magic reacted to his pain. The True Magi look at each other. Herman had pushed all the magic out of the area. They were about to discuss what to do next when the door open. Daryl turned.

"How often are we going to have to tell you that you can do nothing," the High Magus paused, "Sire?."

When White Bear entered some of the Society's Council kneeled, others bowed. The holy man looked around then walked up to the bed on which Herman was sitting. He turned to those in the room.

"Out." When they did not move to go, he gave them a stare. "This is family business."

When the last of them left, without a saying anything, White bear turned to James.

"Shut the door, lad. And pay close attention because there will come a time when you will be called to do this very thing."

White Bear kneeled in front of Herman. His voice was gentle.

"Hermes, look at me." After a short pause, his voice became stern. "Look at me!"

Herman looked up with anger in his eyes. The passion quickly faded and White Bear continued.

"Yes, you know me."

Herman's voice was shaky.

"The others?"

"We are always with you."

"Upior."

White Bear cringed. There was only one place that word was found, in the Secret Text of Tymalt. The Umpiors and the Upiors, the names given to those like himself and Herman. Those with understanding and power beyond mortals, the descendants of old gods, at least according to the text. When the Tymalt was written, before time was recorded, they ruled without competition. White Bear was glad that Herman used Upior, the benefactors of humankind.

"You are well read. Yes, we are Upior, but not in the way of that book. The writer was wise but did not yet understand many things. He thought that secrets and powers were all there was to life. When he wrote that tome, he mistakenly thought that everything could be bent to the will including the Most High. Always remember Hermes, it is not our place to bend anything except ourselves. It is us who must bend to the Will to the Xrist and serve others."

Herman looked down and spoke softly.

"What is the point. To serve, to give everything but nothing ever changes. Many despise Tapps…" Herman looked up. "to give them what they need just mean they hate you because you do not give them what they want. Why walk such a lonely path?" Herman looked down again. "Why give anything at all when it does not change anything?"

White Bear smiled sweetly. How many times did he deal with that same feeling? He knew it well. He spoke out of this understanding.

"There is always a price, no matter what path you choose. And yes, the price of serving is often loneliness. But Hermes, you are not alone. You have those you call the others and we are always with you. Be comforted by that and your connection with Elohim. Be open and honest and you will find that it is not as hard as you feel it is."

Herman looked back up as he spoke.

"I was. More open than I have ever been, but then…"

Herman chocked on his tears. White Bear reached out placed his hand on the youth's shoulder. His words carried a healing with them.

"I know, and Herman, it was real. Not everything that you saw was as it seemed. There are forces at work beyond the people who are played by them. Time is short. You must go to her and find out how much truth there is. Before you do you must find what was true and what was fantasy in your own heart. You must face your pain and doubt before you will have the strength to return to her. If you do not…it is very important that you do this."

Hours more of conversation passed which were too personal to repeat here. The only thing that can be said is, by the time White Bear left the next morning both James and Herman were ready to face what was ahead of them.

NetThin, Fenasy, and Kelthin stood together as the Queen entered. Nethin and Fenasy had been asked to meet her here and the Queen's husband had stayed because he was curious as to why his wife would call a secret meeting. She stalled for a moment as she noticed her husband. It was apparent that she was trying to decide something, then moved further into the small barn when she finished. She looked at Nethin and then her husband for a moment and when she spoke, she kept her voice low.

"I was going to hide this from you until I had no choice but it is fitting that you are here, my love. I have been thinking a lot since we landed here. Not only about how to rebuild our lives, but about the very fabric of it. I have a chance that none of the other Mothers had. It is my intention to create a society where every one of my citizens can prosper. I need all of your support in doing this."

Nethin was smiling. Fenasy was listening in the way she always did, obediently. It was Kelthin who was suspicious. He knew what kind of changes the Queen had in mind. He spoke gently.

"I agree in the nobility of the matter, my queen, but your people have already had a major shock. If we try to make more major changes, you may lose them all together. Too many of your sisters would be willing to betray you to gain power. If you start talking about giving equality to Mankarians, or worse to males and the wingless ones, you may find a revolution on your hands."

There was silence for a moment which was broken by Fenasy.

"My lady, I do agree about the chance of revolution. There have been many times that the Duchesses have taken over the Queendom. Yet, they have never been able to rid themselves of the Queen Mother completely. So, each time there has been a strong Queen, like your own mother, they have been able to regain control. It is my opinion that the Duchess Mothers would seize upon your radical ideas to win many of the people to their side."

The Queen's husband spoke as soon as the captain of her guard stopped.

"You would risk too much. Would it not be better to rebuild your nation and worry about all of this later? I mean, why risk this now? After all, will all of this not be resolved when Angga takes the throne?"

The Queen turned to Nethin. He was listening intently to the conversation. She smiled while she spoke.

"Well Nethin, do you not have anything to add?"

Nethin looked at Fenasy then took her hand before speaking.

"Since my youth I have longed to hear those words, first from your mother then from you. They sound sweet to my ears. I must disagree about the chance of revolution. What you risk is far more. We are talking of a civil war. It is true that the Duchesses will win many to their side but many more will stay loyal to you. Word of the deeds of the male Mankarians, their sacrificing themselves for the Queendom, is already spreading. I have already felt the attitude towards me change.

"Still, it is time for this to come about. But, my Queen, it will not be for you to finish it. It is my advice that you only set the stage for your daughter. Do not make any new decrees on this but act as if you have. Show your nation the same heart that you have shown me."

Nethin let go of Fenasy's hand and took a step forward. To everyone's surprise he dropped to one knee and spread his wings out. His voice held a reverence which only Fenasy had heard from him.

"It is not my intention to sway you from the course that is set in your eyes but only have you to temper your strength with patience. I have sworn loyalty to the Queendom just as all of the Circle has, but I have never sworn loyalty to you. It has been salt in my wounds that Fenasy must always be more loyal to you than me. I now give you the same oath that she has given you. My Soul belongs to Elohim, my spirit is for my sisters and My Salk is yours."

Kelthin watched his brother in awe. Before Nethin had left the Queendom to further his magic he would not have knelt to anyone. He had proven this to be more than words when he had accepted a beating instead of kneeling to a Duchess. Upon his return he had made it clear that he would not kneel to anyone except for Elohim. Yet here he was on his knee before the Queen. Fenasy was radiating with pride when the Queen reached out her hand and placed it on Nethin's head.

"Since the Circle was formed your advice has always served me well. I understand the truth of it now. So, I will show the new path and I will start now. From this day forward you will be known as Nethin De Selka, Eagle Warrior, protector of the Eagle Throne. Raise Sel NetThin and greet your Queen as a sister."

Nethin stood and put his arms around the queen. She kissed him on the forehead as Nethin stepped back. The Queen looked first at Fenasy.

"He is now yours in more than just love. Instruct him in the ways of the Eagle Warriors. No longer will any be disqualified from serving their Queen because of wing or gender." She addressed the entire group. "I agree that it will be Angga who will build the new Queendom. The Princess is the future and must be protected at all cost. That is why I am sending both of you with her. Fenasy, take an entire flock of the Eagle Warriors and go with Angga. She is your Queen, for I plan of passing the throne to her as soon as she returns."

The Queen was expecting protests from the three, especially from her husband. No protests came, in fact Kelthin actually seemed pleased with the decision. She could tell something was bothering him behind his smile. She knew what it was. She had not consulted him, not only about the decisions she made but more importantly, what had been troubling her. The Queen had underestimated him. Even after all these decades she still sometimes forgot that his only desire was to be a source of strength for her. Even when he argued with her it was to persuade her from a path that he thought would be too much for her. The Queen knew well that he did not agree with the new direction in which she was taking the Queendom, but she should have more faith in his love. She had betrayed that love and she knew that she would have to ask for his forgiveness. She also knew that she would obtain it easily, like so many times in the past.

XXIV

Tapps and Angga entered the large cave. It was supposably home to a Dragon. Tapps walked in as if he owned the place. Angga tailed behind unsure what to make of him. KanaFinaGol was nice and from what Tapps said most Dragons were just as polite. At the moment the only one she could remember was the Legend of Neric Hofalf and that encounter with a Dragon did not end well.

She looked up at Tapps. It was true that he was powerful but she doubted that he had the strength to withstand a Dragon's fury. She hastily shifted all of her Kirtel into a protective shield. She was not sure how much it would take to get through her force fields and protective wards but she was sure that the Dragons could muster more power than her. Twice she had suggested that the Eagle Warriors, at least some of them, should accompany them. Tapps had rejected the advice, saying something about proper respect that even this Dragon deserves. Neither Fenasy nor Nethin wanted to let her go alone, but Tapps had made it clear that it was alone or not at all.

She did not want to miss the chance to meet another Dragon. If she would be dealing with them in her Queendom she had to become comfortable with them, still she would have preferred to have her warriors with her. When they had left the others, Tapps took her aside and told her that the Dragon would take too many as a threat and probably attack on sight. Angga figured it might make the Dragon think twice about eating them if they had a dozen or so solders with them. He just muttered something about KanaFinaUn and the Mosk's Elite.

They came to the main cavern of the Dragon's home. The Dragon was a huge specimen with a gold tint to his hide. His right arm was covered in some strange thin silver armor. He was sprawled out on huge oak bed, its wing tips barely touching the ground over the edge of the bed. Dragons always slept on their treasure to keep it safe. The room was full of huge furniture from desk to marble fireplace. Angga was amazed, this was not the way Dragon's lived in the stories. She looked at Tapps as he gently closed her gapping mouth. He did not look shocked at all, his lips curled into a smile. She was the first to speak.

"What do we do now?"

"We wait." Tapps sat down. "He knows we are here and we will have to wait until he decides to rise."

As they waited Angga started to get more and more worried. Between Tapps getting impatient and what appeared to be a smile slowly growing on the Dragon, she almost got up and screamed. Tapps broke the silence by leaning over to her and whispering.

"No matter what, just stay out of the way." Then he stood and walked towards the Dragon's head. "Turcan, you rude dirt chaser. You know how I hate waiting and do not ever think that you will best me face to face."

While still talking, Tapps reached out with his hand and poked the Dragons nose with his finger. Angga gasped, put her back up against the wall and readied herself to run. She nearly fainted when the Dragon lifted its head slowly. He rubbed the sleep from his eyes before speaking.

"Tapps, it is you. It has been a long time my old friend. You still carousing in bars and picking fights with beings who are much too powerful to be handle? You know, you really should call me by my formal. . . Hello, what do we have here?"

Within a breath, KanaFinaTurcan was next to Angga and assuming a human form. Angga was taken back. She had only seen Tapps' transformation spell, but it took Tapps almost half a minute to change. The Dragon turned man bowed to Angga Sella and kissed her hand, completely ignoring the protective shield that should have burned his hand to ash. His voice was sweet and soft like his grip on her hand. She barely heard Tapps' words break through the haze which was forming in her head.

"Stop it Turcan. She is one of my clan and is not only under my protection but that of KanaFinaGol as well. I will not let you use your magic on her. Should I tell her about that night in Tehawa?"

KanaFinaTurcan seemed to falter at the name of the other Dragon. The haze broke violently from Angga Sella as Turcan turned from her and spoke sweetly.

"KanaFinaGol? It has been too long since my eyes have…" The Dragon paused considering what Tapps had said. His voice took on a hint of anger. "You promised not to tell anyone about that!"

"No, my old friend, you begged me not to tell anyone but, all I promised was I would give it serious thought. About calling you KanaFin, you know me too well to think that I would be formal. Besides, I would only have to claim the right because of the length of our friendship."

Angga could not believe how easily she fell under the Lust Binding spell.

She always figured she would be stronger than the ladies in the tales who were seduced by evil wizards casting wicked spells. She would not fall for it again. She shifted her Kirtel into a Magic Sight spell to examine the flow of magic around her. She had been told that a Human magus would start to see the magic weaves as a side effect of working with it for so long. She wished it was the same with her but she always had to work magic to allow the magic to be seen by her eyes.

She looked at Tapps and the Dragon-man. It was hard to read the flow because so much magic was coming out of the Dragon. As if somehow the Dragon was a source of magic. Both KanaFinaTurcan and Tapps were covered with protective wards of such power and complication that it made her eyes water just trying to follow their patterns. She had never thought Tapps knew much magic, but they must not just give away the badges which represented the Warrior-Magi from the Society. She had a suspicion that his magic was limited to the combat sorts. Angga had never seen him use any other kind and did not think Tapps the type to learn useful spell.

She examined the room. Everything in the large cave was magical. From the bed to the writing quill glowed within her magic sight. Her amazement was cut short when the sounds of combat came to her ears. She turned quickly to see Tapps and the Dragon-man wrestling on the ground. After a moment of confusion, she grabbed a small staff that was laying against the wall. She ran up to the entangled two. After a moment of hesitation to make sure she did not hit Tapps, she brought the cudgel down. The stout staff found its mark. The hit was hard enough that the noise of it echoed throughout the cave.

The wrestling stopped. Turcan shook his head, then they both slowly turned their heads and stared hard at her. Angga did not know whether or not to run, so she blushed. Her embarrassment of realizing that they only played made her drop the cudgel. An unsteady apology was cut short by the Dragon-man's words.

"Tapps, it has always amazed me that you manage to get the most beautiful females for yourself, but do they always have to be so badly behaved?"

After they helped each other up, Tapps replied.

"Our relationship is not like that. Besides, I do remember a certain redhead. You remember. That one you tried your evil spell on, who left you with a split lip and a broken rib, if I recall right."

Angga's heart sank. As much as she told herself that there was nothing between them. As much as she tried to give up the fantasy, it still hurt to have him say the words. She felt like crying. Felt like running into the darkness of the cave's entrance to do such. He was a True Magi, and with the long life which went with that rank, they often did not look at other people in the same way. She felt so alive with him. She was instantly thrown out of her self-pity by the man turning back into the Dragon. He was still smiling when he sat on the huge couch that was made from some sort of leather. Tapps looked around as if seeing the furniture for the first time. He looked puzzled and he spoke his mind.

"Turcan, if you had not kept yourself hidden, I would have visited sooner. It has been twenty years since you became Unker. What has it been, fifteen since you became KanaFin? Do not look surprised Turcan, I may not have seen you since the war but I have heard many things about you. Answer me this, why do you still hold on the trappings of a human nature? Why not cross the line all the way?"

Angga was puzzled and became more so by the Dragon's answer.

"Remember how old I was when we met. I had reached old age during the time we adventured together. Not the old age of a Human but that of True Magi. I am KanaFinaTurcan but my habits and taste are still very much that of Zackery Morris. Even though I never truly understood the workings of the human heart, I would guess that it is the same reason that your tastes run towards that of Humans instead of Kaltars."

Tapps seemed satisfied with the answer. KanaFinaTurcan continued with a smile which seemed unnatural to the Dragon.

"Why have you come to see me? Are you finally willing to admit I was the brains of the partnership?"

The Dragon threw his head back and laughed. Tapps' face took on a grim look. The Dragon caught on to Tapps mood quickly and worry showed in the great creature's eyes. Tapps looked up to the Dragon when the laughter echoes started fading.

"I am here on Clan business. You are overstepping the boundaries that your rank grants. You have no agreement with the town of Spritewell, so should not be raiding their livestock. I have come to . . ."

Turcan's smile turned into a sneer. His bellow was loud enough to hurt Angga Sella's ears.

"You have always bullied me into doing the things that you wanted. This time I say no. Got that? No! I have only taken a few cows and sheep. I haven't burned any of their homes. Now I see that I should have. . . There is no way that I am going to leave. What I should do is…is…is eat you. That's what I should do."

Angga Sella saw the anger growing on Tapps' face. That was no surprise to her. She was surprised about Tapps' eyes. They were glowing a deep red. The Dragon, for all its size and power, seemed to shrink back from him. Angga Sella was even more surprised when Tapps' words were gentle.

"I have bullied you, that is true. If, for once in your life, you would listen to reason instead of seeing everything through the lens of profit I would not have to bully you. You would understand what going on around you instead of driving me to the point of frustration. Do not, for one moment, think just because you are KanaFin that you can start threatening me. Know that I speak with full authority on this, from both Fron and Dragon. Even though I am not a Dragon, my name has been put on the list with the rest by the Ancient. I am not a Rolfin. I am Unker, and not just any Unker, but Unker to all the Dragons. You would risk your standing, even with the gold clan, by attacking me. Now, for once, listen to me. I have not come to kick you out of your home. I have come to arrange a deal between you and the town."

The Dragon's head lifted when Tapps mentioned a deal. A twinkle of greed appeared in the Dragon's eyes. His words further baffled Angga.

"ShurSkaHu, but I understand."

Angga Sella could hear the tension leave Tapps' voice as his eyes stopped glowing.

"The town is not the wealthiest of places, but they do have good trade for their wine. They offer a cow, five gold and ten silver a season. In return they want to become your PolisKanaFinis and permission to name their wine after you. They want to call it Turcan's Breath Wine."

The Dragon hastily agreed. He would have bargained for another cow and more coin but he would end up with less after negotiating with Tapps. Besides, he would probably lose the wine being named after him and he wanted that more than all the rest. They talked of friendlier things. Suddenly KanaFinaTurcan's eyes widened in surprise.

"Wait, what about… you do not know then?"

Tapps smiled. This had to be something about money.

"What are you talking about?

"The Shadow has been released and he has started a campaign to reclaim the Colonies. KanaFinaUn has decided to support the Shadow Forces with the Dragons."

Tapps jumped up at the words. His disbelief was apparent on his face and in his voice.

"You must be mistaken!"

KanaFinaTurcan bellowed in laughter.

"Why do you never trust me? It is true. Bleeding Heart received the notice from KanaFinaGol. He brought it to me directly."

Tapps looked genuinely concerned and Angga realized that she had never seen him worried before. Not even in the thick of battle. His voice showed his mood.

"What about the Ancient? She must know that the Shadow Forces are in league with the Destroyer. Even many of the lower ranks know the taint of darkness. Has the First Dragon not corrected the Keeper?"

The gold-tinted Dragon shook his head as he spoke.

"She has been silent on the matter. From what I have been told none of the ones who tried to see her could. She is not even granting audiences with the elders. The only word that has come out of the Cave Palace has been it is now time for each Dragon to make up their own minds on who they will serve. I have not yet decided, but many of the others are planning to put their name on the List of Outcasts."

They conversed on the meaning of it all until the sun returned to the sky. Angga missed most of the conversation. She was rousted from her sleep on the huge couch by Tapps telling her it was for them to leave.

As they reached the mouth of the cave Angga Sella stopped Tapps. She had a thousand of questions about the night. She wasted no time in asking them.

"I figured out that KanaFin means Dragon but what are Rolfin, Unker and Sherhako?"

Tapps smiled down at her but simply turned and started walking towards the camp where the Eagle Warriors were waiting for them. For the first time Angga realized how small she was compared to him. She was sure that he would not speak, but he eventually he sighed and spoke quietly.

"There are things that should not be taught and many more that are better not spoken of, but as my pupil, I owe it to you not to keep anything from you. Besides as a PolisKanaFinis, you will be learning all of this at some point. KanaFin does mean Dragon, though literally it means the power of truth. It denotes a parental protection and guidance. As for ShurSkaHu, the best it can be pronounced by those with our tongue is Sh-r-S-ka-Hoo." He waited for her to say it a few times before he continued. "ShurSkaHu would translate into southern common as words or talk that enrages the spirit. When used as a lone phrase it would be the same as you saying I hurt your feelings, or when a slight trill is put on the R it denotes anger. This would mean that what you are saying is bringing me to the point of losing control of my anger.

"Rolfin is the Dragon word for ignorance of the truth. It typically is used for the unfaithful or for those who would dare to temp a Dragon to anger. Of late, it has been used too often instead of RoFin which means non-Dragon. I believe that it shows an uncontrolled pride growing in the Dragons. That is not for me to deal with yet, so I keep my mouth shut about it."

Tapps paused. Angga could tell that he was trying to figure out how to continue. Before speaking he stopped and looked at her.

"Unker has a deep meaning in which in which even a pupil or PolisKanaFinis should not know. But you will be a queen, and will need to learn the secrets of the Dragons if you are to rule their lands. So, you have to understand that this is not for commoners to know." He continued after Angga nodded consent. "For you to fully understand what Unker means I will tell you a story.

"Back in the days when I was living with the Shawlls I lived as one of them. I hunted with them. I slept in their pits and they thanked me for the warmth. It came to pass that the Shawlls had a problem with the Minotaurs to the east of them. I joined them in their battles with the Minotaurs. I fought like I was taught in the gladiator pits. That coupled with the ShorTunKana, a control of my blood lust that the Shawlls had taught me. I earned myself a name among the Shawlls.

"The Shawlls do not respect honor above all else like Humans do, so they have no way to reward those who show remarkable feats. All Shawlls are equal and if one was better than another at something, they are honored by being allowed to do it. The only way that they can honor a non-Shawlls is by making them one of their own. Now the ceremony is fantastic when the Shawlls do it, but I had a special guest at mine. A KanaFin was there to perform the ceremony. My idea was that it was just a way of honoring me, but as it progressed, I realized that there was powerful magic being worked. Powerful Dragon magic was being wielded. It was more than magic. There was the presence of LingueArdeo. It changed me forever.

"That day I became Unker, the word itself means servant but it is a title of honor. For in both the Shawll and Dragon culture it is the highest position one can have. To serve another is to be granted the highest honor. This is usually done when one serves another individual or village. It is not uncommon for a Dragon to take an Unker or two. as for me, the Ancient had made me Unker to the Dragons and, in a way, the entire Colonies. It is why I can accomplish what I can with them. The Dragons know that when I come, I come not only as an emissary from the Vagofrons, but as a servant to both sides. It is this which gives me the power to resolve disputes and declare judgments.

"So, everyone would understand, during my ceremony I was bound to a Dragon's egg. The egg was actually a child of the Ancient and our fates are linked together. It is this bond that gives me the insight to the Dragons that I have. That was over twenty years ago and not too far from now I will have to return and to finish the process. Me and that child Dragon will have to choose on how the bond will proceed, or even to keep it. I would have done it sooner but I met you and cannot leave until our time together is complete."

"What will happen if you do go meet this Dragon?"

Tapps took on a sorrowful expression.

"The bond will complete itself without us. If I do not have guidance for the completion I will die at best. At worst, I will lose my mind and kill many around me before I am finally taken down."

With that, Tapps smiled and winked and started to head to camp. Angga stayed where she stood. The seriousness of it hit her hard. Tapps was risking much to be her mentor. She felt again like crying, but this time at her own selfishness. She had been so overwhelmed by her desire that she had never understood love. She should have been meditating on what he was telling her instead of fantasizing about his arms around her. As Tapps entered the camp she vowed that she would dedicate the time they had left together to learning everything he had to teach.

XXV

Ukkert stood on a balcony in the center of the huge cavern. Lighting sped from her hand towards the advancing Denocte as she finished the casting of the Palm Lighting spell. Their wizards counter attacked. One of her Lifeguards threw himself in front of the attack. She pushed away the pain coming from the Unity and ignored his death. There was no time for grief, no time for pain. This was the Meritem Cavern, the very hub of travel in the deep ground. The Shawllin had held the cavern since their arrival and had turned it into a city. Creating a place in the Deep Ground where all those who were willing could come and trade in safety and, the Source be willing, come into the Unity. For the first time in the history of the city, it was in danger.

The last several years had been harsh for her people. The attacks had been nonstop and this was their last chance to hold the city. Lighting sprung from other balconies as well. It would not be long before the limited amount of magic available in the Deep Ground would be gone and the fighting would concentrate into melee. Ukkert decided it would be wise to save the rest of her stored magic. By the way she felt, she had enough for two or maybe three more bolts and she might need them later.

The Denocte hit the first barricade and within minutes had broken through it. There was just too many of them and they were just too used to killing. Her people knew war, there were none in the Deep Ground who did not, but they were a people of peace. One fought for defense and for food, but to kill for gain or pleasure was not the way of the Unity.

There were Denocte fighting along side her people. In fact there were people from every race of the Deep Ground. All of them had come to the Meritem Cavern for help. Only those who did not know the Love of the Source would fail to give aid to another, even if the other was an enemy. It was through her people's showing of the Love which allowed those of the other races to know the Unity with the Source. The Unity which they now defended with their lives.

The Denocte who battled on both sides were impressive in the way they fought with their blades. Their culture was one of conflict and death. They could not keep anything that they could not protect and they could not gain anything that they could not take by force. It was the great contrast that so many fought with the Shawllin. Being raised in an atmosphere of hate and without trust they were quick to see the Source through the Love of the Unity. Even though many of them had not picked up a blade in years they still fought with the skill of their people. The Denocte did not fight with finesse or any fancy moves. They fight only to kill and everything about them showed that they would do anything to win. It did not take long for every last defender of the first barricade to die.

Ukkert watched as the Denocte did not stop but charged towards the second barricade. The way that they were concentrated, a Magi's Artillery or even a Fire Ball would have brought most of them down. Any of the fire spells would not be used. The fire would suck the air out of the cavern and be just as deadly for her people. In fact, so dangerous was even a fire spell as small as Fire Seed, that she did not even know if anyone knew how to cast them.

As the Denocte poured over the second barricade and started slaughtering the defenders Ukkert knew that the other two barricades would not hold either. There was nothing she or the other brood elders could do to stop their advance. She stiffened her tail in determination. She knew what she had to do. If she was going to die, she would go out praying.

Ukkert dropped to all four, lifting her spirit to the Source. One by one others joined her in prayer. First those on the balconies, then on the floors. There was no reason for orders to be issued. The Source had told them it was time to pray. The Denocte were enemies of the Unity and most of them had faith that the Source would help. If the Source did nothing then it would be for the best for the Unity that they died here. By the time the Denocte broke through the second barricade, they found all the defenders in prayer. None of them hesitated to bring their blades down on their motionless enemy. If any of the Shawllin had not been in prayer they would have seen that the Denocte were enjoying the fight even more now that their enemy was not fighting back.

A few of the defenders broke with the Unity and fled. Many of the rest died with reassurance of their reward in the Source. Still, for the rest of them, death was not the will of the Source. The Light of the Source filled all those in the Unity. Their skin started to glow. All at once the light and heat of a thousand fires radiated from their bodies. Many of the Denocte died outright, many more of fell to the ground, writhing in pain. Most of them fled. Those of the Unity rose to slay their foe. Their arms were stayed by the very Light that was so visible from them at the moment. The Denocte left would be shown the Mercy of the Unity that they may come to know the Love of the Source.

Somewhere off in the distance lightning and thunder ripped through a cloudless sky.

Morgan sat at the table of the Unholy Council waiting for Shadow Fire to speak. There was a new member, Emperor Mosk the Dark. The man was harder to read than the others, but not by much. Mosk, like the others, had forged some dark pact in order to gain power. He was unlike the others in the fact that he had not been blinded by the power. All of them were hiding themselves better this time. He was here primarily to learn about them. They were too comfortable in their defenses for him to get what he needed today. The High Tymalt Boreta wanted to know if the order should give these people its full support. Before Morgan could answer that question, he needed to know how they handled the unexpected. Normally he would have just reached over and slapped one of them. That would have worked just as well here, but the cost would be too high. It would most likely end in the death of the person he slapped.

The Praus was watching him, trying to read him. That was what gave him the idea of what to do. Without hesitation he opened himself up completely. Even those with only a little ability with probing would be able to read his deepest thoughts. He would have no defense to anyone who chose to attack. Not that anyone present, other than himself, knew such methods of combat.

He was in the vulnerable state for only a couple of seconds but it told him everything he needed to know. The Praus backed off all the way. He took it as a challenge and was afraid. The Vampire Elson and the Annis Death Gate did not even know anything had happened. Shadow Fire knew something was going on, but did not know what. Only Mosk understood and used that opportunity to gather information from the Tymalt. When Morgan looked at him the Emperor smiled. Mosk faltered slightly when Morgan smiled back and bowed slightly. Mosk had thought it was a mistake on Morgan's part, but too late did the Emperor realize it was a test. He did not like giving himself away.

Morgan had his answer. He would return to the High Tymalt and tell him that the Unholy Council was only worthy of partial support. That the Tymalt should investigate Mosk further. Shadow Fire knew power but did not know control. The man may claim to understand Tym, the spiritual undercurrent of life, but he knew no more about it than his unclean would tell him. The very reason that the Order of Tymalt forbids such ways. As it is written in the Tymalt: do not deal with any spirit for to take even a drop of water from a spirit is to be owned by that spirit.

His experiment had changed the mood around the table. Later Morgan would look back at that moment and realize how his actions changed the course of events in the Colonies. They had been discussing the sphere of power that each would hold. After hours of arguments and veiled threats they had a break through. Their discussions had become friendlier and as close to honest as these men could manage. There had been a growing unity between them and Morgan's actions had ruined that. The Praus was first to return to his defensive ways. The rest picked up on the mood and started thinking about their small parts instead of the Shadow Empire as a whole. This may not have made a difference except it was at the end of the meeting and there was no time for them to regain the near unity which had been forming. Shadow Fire stood and spoke, not knowing anything had changed.

"Now that we are all in agreement let us get to work. It is time to announce the return of the Dark Church. Make all of your attacks swift and brutal. Remember this above all, those who are weak have no place in the Dark Shadow Empire. Use the Shadow Forces and the Dragons to spread death and destruction. Only those who are willing to bow to our strength will be shown mercy. Now go and conquer in the name of the Destroyer."

With that, Shadow Fire teleported himself away. One by one they all left until only Mosk and Morgan remained. Morgan stood to leave but the Emperor's words kept him from walking out.

"Why does the Order of the Tymalt give their support to this mad man?"

Morgan started to ask about Mosk's loyalty but the answer was written on the Emperor's face.

"For the same reason you do, Emperor Mosk. As it is written: when two paths take you to the same place, take the one which will give you more by following it."

Mosk laughed. He genuinely liked this Tymalt. He placed a ward against clairvoyance spells and spoke openly.

"What were you testing?"

It was Morgan's time to laugh. Mosk must have earned his power to speak so openly. Morgan had only taken him as a spirit chaser, but the Emperor was much more than that. It was written in the Tymalt: only those who hide the truth are unworthy to be given the truth. Morgan spoke honestly.

"I was seeing how people handled the unexpected and how much mastery they have over their own spirits."

Mosk smiled slyly.

"What did you learn?"

Morgan returned the smile. Mosk thought he was playing him. Morgan spoke unconcerned what the Emperor thought.

"That everyone here is too preoccupied with external power, including yourself. You will be the only one besides Shadow Fire who will be mentioned by name in my report. That even though, like I said, you are too concerned with external power, it has not stopped you from looking at what is inside of yourself. Now it is my turn. Why the interest, in other words, what do you want?"

Mosk actually bellowed in laughter.

"No wonder my father banned your Order from my empire. He never did appreciate the subtle things in life, nor had the wiliness to suffer bluntness. You have been honest with me and I will do the same. Even though I am supporting Shadow Fire, he does not have my full support. I am assuming that it is the same way with the Tymalt." Mosk continued with a smile when Morgan nodded his agreement. "Good. I would like to meet the head of your Order. The purpose is that my father was much mistaken when he threw you out of the nation. I am going to lift the ban and more than that. If both sides can be satisfied, then I will declare it an official sect of Mosk. To entice your boss to come and see me, I will confiscate several of the White Church estates and turn them over to the Order. This is only dependent on him coming to see me."

Morgan told the Emperor Mosk that he would relay the message and left. It was not hard to tell what the man wanted. If the Order would make their home in Mosk it would give the Emperor access to another resource. He was sure that the High Tymalt would take Mosk up on the offer. The Order had lost much of its wealth in the War Forward. The land would be a starting point to rebuild it. Too many of the Order were having to spend their time in unnecessary labor just to feed themselves. He spent his own time between these meetings building houses. It had been his work before the Order and he did enjoy it. Still, it took too much time away from his meditation. He mounted his horse and started the long trek home.

"Sister, there is trouble in the air, and I do not mean this impostor."

"I have sensed it as well. You need to talk to White Bear about it."

The Dragoon was deep in thought and was not really paying attention to the conversation. He looked up at the First Dragon when he realized what she had said.

"I went to his island but he had just left. Tell me why you did not help your General. Even the Illilita heard his cries for help."

The First Dragon shook her head in a completely human fashion. She too was in deep thought so it took her a moment to answer.

"I went to several times, but each time I was gripped so strongly by LingueArdeo that I had no choice but to ignore his cries. It is because…." The huge dragon paused. It took her a few minutes to speak again. "I am dying brother. I have tried to teach them all to rely on VivusDeus instead of me. Now is a time that they must learn it or die themselves."

The Dragoon just stared.

"You're dying? But White Bear never said anything about it."

His words failed him.

"White Bear does not know. He does not know everything, you know? And yes Marius, I am dying. Remember I was the first dragon, the experiment that calibrated the magic. My body keeps growing and even with White Bear's help it still grows too fast. Soon my body will be too compacted for blood to flow through it."

"I do not know what to say."

The great dragon, known as the Ancient, smiled in a very human manner as she spoke.

"Say what you must to comfort yourself. I have come to terms with it. I see nothing but happiness in the future. I do not see a rift forming but the closing of one. The Outcasts have showed themselves above the sand for the first time since that day I fought Novus. I am sure that we will be whole again. Will your Angels be getting involved?"

"Please sis, you know how I hate that slang term. But no, there was a great debate in the Council, but we finally decided to watch a bit longer to see what happens. There is more going on here than what is apparent on the surface. We are keeping our eye on the two. They have just been located. Most of us believe that the war starting is merely a herald of what is to come."

There was silence between the only two children of the Shadow who still worked for his dream. The Dragoon decided to stay with his sister until her breath left her.

King Thorin looked over the volunteers. His approval was almost completely ceremonial. They had been hand chosen by the leaders who would be taking them. All of them had been involved in setting up the town of Sorive and had worked close with the Goblins. And all of them had caught up in the Goblins' dream of building an empire of their land. The town of Sorive was a small thing compared to what the goblins, and the NoraTo would need, but it was a start.

The building of the town of Sorive on the Sarriu River, and the lumber mill it supported was accomplished much easier than expected. The Goblins had supplied much more then the wood. Many of them had arrived eager to learn how to build. And they labored without complaint. Far more surprising, was that all of them had showed up with an abundance of tools. Some of them had been taken from people who had come into the Anear's lands, but most of them the Goblins had traded for. There was a trader in the Draco Mountains that would give a good price to the Wild Goblins for the furs they brought in. Apparently, the Goblins had been collecting tools since the storm which had surrounded the city had stopped. No one knew, most likely not even the Goblins, how many tools they had acquired. No matter, there was enough that tools to build the towns were no longer a concern.

Nena entered the room. He had been chosen by the Goblin to represent them with Thorin. He had already been a Slachka of the RulHaKar clan, which Thorin had thought meant a leader. It had surprised him to learn that the Goblins where a theocracy. That the Slachka was both a religious and political title. He had doubted that Cesdakar had understood it as the Goblins seemed to live up to their name of Wild well enough that any form of official leadership seemed beyond them. It made sense once Cesdakar had explained that it could not be taken either as a priesthood or a nobility. That the word itself means on who serves.

Nena approached Thorin and spoke without bow or formality.

"Panea Brazie.'

Henra did not like Goblin's way of salutation towards King Thorin as soon as he found out that it meant 'Sir Sibling'. He thought that it did not show enough respect. Thorin liked it, felt more respect from a Wild Goblin calling him an equal than from being called Dragokeen. This was especially true because Nena came from the RulHaKar clan. Nena had been chosen in part because he was from the RulHaKar clan. From what Thorin understood the RulHaKar clan was the freest of the Anear Goblin. They were the clan in which Anear took on the double meaning of Wild. That of all Goblins, the Slachka of the RulHaKar clan were the only ones which had reservation about the alliance with NoraTo. If Nena was any indication, that clan had a wait and see approach. So Thorin knew that the greeting was Nena's way of saying that he saw the Dragon King as Slachka, one who served the Goblin people. It was a vote of confidence in which Thorin would do his best to live up with.

Without asking permission, or any indication of deference Nena turned his attention to the group of volunteers. His approval of them was not simply ceremony. He could reject any one of them, or all of them for any reason. Thorin knew that Nena would not be random with his decision. He was going to use one simple thing to determine whether or not he approved a person. Their reaction to him.

Nena was an extremely handsome man, according to Goblin standards. Which means that he was horrible, almost frightening to look upon for those not used to Goblin appearance. Goblin's lack of a nose gave them two slits. And Nena had huge craters in which one could see the mucus build up. All Goblins have uneven eyes, his were also noticeably of two different sizes. One little more than a dot, the other large enough to be a dominate feature. All Goblins had as much hair coming from their ears then on their head, Nena had both his ear hair and nose hairs made up in small braids. But all of the group had already months of experience dealing with Goblins. More than a few had learned the basics of the Goblin language, a fact which seemed to impress Nena.

Slachka Nena stopped in front of Tally Westerd. She was the choice as leader for the nearest of the two new towns. DragoRue Lisa Estests had recommended her for the furthest one because of her military experience, but Thorin thought it better that that town should belong to Lan Hembder as he showed a natural inclination towards trade. It was the only decision of the entire project so far which he had not gone with the recommendation of others. Dragorue Estests was watching intently now, apparently concerned that Nena would reject Westerd. The two exchanged words in the Goblin tongue for a moment, and then Nena went on with his inspection.

Thorin understood. He had to deal directly with the incidents in which had Estests worried. Tally Westard had been in charge of security during the building of the town of Sorive. This meant that she had to deal with many events in which Goblins were causing a problem. The individual Goblins complained considerably from the fines, and in some case a ban on them trading with the town. It had created a considerable amount of tension at first. Though while the Goblins seemed childish in many ways, they were not stupid. They watched, and Thorin knew, as Nena made it clear, that Westwerd was highly respected among the Goblins. A respect she earned by being neither more or less strict with the humans which were violating the same or similar laws.

Nena turned abruptly and returned to Thorin. His words were as pleasing as a Goblin could manage with their raspy voices.

"They are welcomed."

The Goblin then sat himself down on the Dragon Throne, and started picking through the fruit on the royal tray. DragonRue Henra went to say something but was stopped by Thorin speaking with apparent humor in his voice.

"Let us get this over with." He turned towards the group and raised his voice. He had memorized the speech for the occasion. "Lan Hembder and Tally Westard, you are invested today with the title of DragoRue. You are now the Dragon's Teeth. You are charged to take possession, and to improve the land which is has been laid out for you. I do not need to tell you to work closely with the Anear clan of your land. It has been by their gift which you have your position, and it will only be through their help that we will succeed in building the NoraTo nation. Go now, and live up to the duties and Honor which is yours."

The group left the throne room, as such groups leave a place, they are not completely comfortable in. DragoRue Henra bowed and left shortly after the last of the group. He would be representing Thorin at the celebration which the Dragon King was giving as a sendoff. Thorin's presence would have made too many people uncomfortable, and the point was to give them an official time to say goodbye to the family they would be leaving behind. Parents and siblings which in all likelihood they would not be seeing in many years to come. The group had been chosen because they were young, single or couples without children. Only their leadership had any years on them. Thorin did not envy the work cut out for his new DragoRues.

DragoRue? Throrin amazed how the United Colonial Empire had been so much like the political structure of his own time, and so much unlike it. It was structured in the same pattern, except that it was an empire instead of a confederacy. In his time the member nations, or their head of state had most of the power, with the Shadow only in charge of international affairs. In NoraTo most of the power was his, with the DragoRue having the power only to determine the policy within their own province. There was no clear line where his authority ended. All of the policies of the United Colonial Empire had been lost.

Thorin sighed. That was just one of the many things which had to be decided as time went on. One of those things that would be determined more as the culture developed then could be directed by policy. For now, he had to figure out what the next step should be for the expanse of NoraTo. And he knew, both by instinct and by his military experience, that it could be any moment when the nations to the east would notice what he was doing. And he could expect at least one of them to try to take advantage of their small numbers. That they would have to defend themselves, or become a part of another nation.

"Peace is always a better path then war. But as night follows day, only those who are capable of waging war will know peace. But then…once one is capable of war there is always the temptation to use that power to force others into how we should think they should be."

Thorin turned towards Cesdakar. His voice was full of humor.

"Reading my mind again? When did you get back?"

Cesdakar motioned towards the rough map which was on the wall.

"Love gives us an understanding of others which can easily be mistaken for telepathy. But it does not take love but only to pay a bit attention to your habits to know when you stand unmoving in front of that map you are worrying about that day that one of the other kings decides that they want what you have. If for no other reason than it is easy to take. And that is why I have returned, as I just have.

"I went and visited that trader in the mountains. An interesting fellow, ironically by the name of Rich, as he cares nothing for wealth. As the Goblins reported he deals fairly with them, more than fair. He makes fare less profit than he could. Even though he would not say as much, he pays the Goblins what their furs are worth, which is considerable. But that is not why I returned early. The Goblins are also correct that the reason that Rich is paying more for the fur this season is because there has been a large increase in population in the mountains. A whole nation worth of people has suddenly moved into the area with the need of the furs.

"I thought it important that you should now. According to Rich, they are also in need of building material. Considering our access to lumber, with the building of our towns we will have an excess of lumber that we can sell them. But the reason I returned in person rather than just sending a message is because, well, I think we should supply it to them at discount and as much credit as we can give. Apparently, they are refugees from some disaster. The whole nation had been forced out of their homes by some aggressive force.

"As they are planning on making the mountains their permanent homes, and we too are a new nation, that it might be well if we start off on a helpful tone rather than one of exploitation. That is, it is my opinion that we deal with this as a diplomatic issue rather than one of trade. But then, you know I have no love for the ideology that profit is the guide in all things."

Thorin was just starting to think about it when another voice sounded.

"Fifty percent."

Both Thorin and Cesdakar turned towards Lan Hembder, now DragoRue Hembder as he entered.

"My apologies, but I saw Cesdakar and knew that he was coming from the mountains by where my town will be so figured in needed to hear what he had to say. As the province which will be trading directly with them, I am thinking of fifty percent of current market rate."

Thorin looked at Cesdakar who only shrugged. So Thorin turned back towards his DragoRue.

"That is a rather deep discount. Can we afford it?"

Lan smiled, apparently it was something he had given thought to, and economics was one of his favorite topics.

"It is the number in which I am running my own calculations on. I know we are thinking of the harvesting trees only in terms of building the towns, but I think we are overlooking their importance. Just the clearing of the land needed for Sorive to produce enough food for itself will in the end create enough lumber to rebuild this city. We have not yet even started with the idea of breeding horses, or have dealt with population growth. That is, just accounting for the necessary clearing of the forest for living we are going to cause a ten to twenty-five decrease in the price of lumber, at least, in the short run.

"And I have already spoken to the Slachka of my clan and they are open to the idea of a managed harvesting of the forest in my province. In fact, the idea of actually producing lumber as a tradable good seems to excite them. That if the numbers I got from the Goblins can be trusted, the lumber production from my province alone will cut the lumber prices by at least another ten percent. Considering the time table for our towns, and including a sketch for transport costs, within five years we could be producing enough lumber to cut the market price in half in both southern Mosk and western KanaTo.

"And those will be our market. I was going to start trade at the current price and let the market adjust on its own. But I figured if we want to be diplomatic, we could offer them half the going rate now."

Thorin spoke in a friendly tone.

"You still have not answered the question as to whether or not we can afford it now."

Lan laughed. He had obviously forgotten that others did not pay attention to economics as he did. His voice carried humor in it.

"Yes sir, I can. like I said, I have figured my budget on that price already. Like I said we, that is, the Goblins and myself, was planning on using the excess to build the infrastructure of the province. Expanding the operations so the entire clan can be involved, the building of the roads it will take, the mills etc. The entire lumber operation will be owned and ran, at least for the most part, by the Goblins. As for myself, I chose most of my people because they want to be traders and not lumberjacks. The Goblins will produce the lumber and we will sell it. Even if we sold all the lumber fifty percent, there is still enough profits for everyone. While cost will go up when distance of transportation becomes an issue, we can produce the lumber as a small fraction of what it sells for. A lower price will simply slow down the expansion. And as Cesdakar believes, so do I. That even though I am sure I am more profit minded then he would like, I do think that relationships are more important than wealth. Besides, my provinces is, at least for now, going to be the only trade entry point. There is going to be more than enough wealth in the coming years to build with."

Thorin turned and looked back at his map. A whole nation which had to rebuild. It is doubtful that they would have the resources to purchase the amount of lumber which they would require. They would need so much. He spoke without turning.

"Lan, did your calculations take into account the affect the increase of demand that this nation would cause on lumber prices?"

"No." He paused for a moment. "I will have to recalculate, but most likely it will increase the market price initially, until our production will match what they need."

Thorin turned back towards the two.

"Ces, you have authority to negotiated a trade agreement with this nation in the mountains. You can promise then not less than half the excess lumber we produce at no more than twenty five percent below market price for the next five years. Explain to them how their demand and our supply will affect the price, and leave up to whether they want to set the prices now or pay according to the changes up to them. Also, you have my authorization to promise to their ruler that any amount of this lumber can be in the form of a loan to their nation.

"Lan, I will speak to Lisa, Nena and Tally, to see if the other clans would not be open to the same thing. Trade just enough lumber with the eastern nation to trade for the supplies we need and to cover the cost of any lumber traded to this nation in the mountains on credit."

Lan bowed and left quickly, obviously eager to get started working the plans for his province. Cesdakar stayed a bit longer, obviously spending some time visiting before he was off again. Thorin sometimes regretted using his friend as he did. But the holy man was by far the best diplomat he had. More importantly, Thorin could trust him to be honest, not only with him but with those he was negotiating with. This nation in the mountains would judge NoraTo on Cesdakar, and that would be a judgment in their favor.

Thorin turned back to the map once Cesdakar had left. Ces had said that the people in the mountains were refugees, fleeing some invader. He wished he knew more of those nations on the other side of the mountains. He had a little over eighteen thousand human adults, more than that number in young children. In twenty years, they would be able to field a real fighting force, but as for now, they only had a handful of combatants. Not enough to defend against even a small force one of those nations could send. That is why his advisors had recommended that Lan not be given the boarder province. That when they decided to attack, they would need a military leader there.

They did not understand that Thorin was planning on keeping the military separate from the political system. The military would be his, and when they had a force, he would appoint a leader there to take charge of the defenses. Thorin pulled a pebble out of his pocket, the one Cesdakar had given him from that first meeting with the Goblins and smiled. The Anear were the only ones which kept him from losing sleep over their vulnerability. The Wild Goblins had kept the Human nations from expanding into these forests for hundreds of years. Thorin was sure that they would be able to do it for a few more decades.

XXVI

Sir Bealson, High Marshal of Marduke, looked over the castle. He was nervous. He had always liked the duke, but Mark was becoming weak. Kerko had showed him that. The dukedom was the richest in the confederacy and only Duran's dukedom was stronger in military might. They should not be bowing down to the other dukes. The territory was the best and it should become the new capital. Sir Bealson did not understand why Mark did not see it.

Bealson had told him such during an evening meal. The duke had rebuked him in front of everyone. Mark had no right to humiliate his High Marshal like that. This pack with the other dukes would weaken the territory. If Duran decided to attack there would be no stopping him.

Sir Bealson looked over the castle guard. He had spent the last month rearranging the duty roaster. The bulk of the regulars were moved out to the edges of the territory and patrolling the countryside for bandits. Now the majority of guards in the city were mercenaries with loyalties only to him, or at least the money he paid them. The regulars who remained in the city were greens. Only the few veterans who were left to train the recruits would be any threat. Most of them were too old to be effective warriors but all had commanded most of their life and could bark an order that would make him jump. Bealson was no novice, he knew well enough that experience could overcome the lacking of a failing body.

The bell struck once for the midnight wake up and he noticed his mercenaries coming out of the barracks. They moved slowly and exited the building in small groups. Luckily for the rebels, the few regulars on duty did not have enough experience to realize that this was suspicious. They would not notice that more people were leaving the barracks then would be needed for a shift change. After looking around with the feeling that someone was watching, Bealson walked briskly to the signal tower.

As Bealson entered the bell room, the young regular stood and after only a few seconds he saluted. Bealson returned the salute and walked over to one of the windows. Looking out, the cold air stung his face. This was going to be much harder than he had figured.

The young man was Jason and was from an outlying farm. Sir Bealson had been out in the area a few years ago hunting some bandits. The group had been operating for some time and had drawn enough attention to warrant his personal involvement. They had captured or killed most of the gang, but two had escaped. They had been tracked to a farm house. Apparently, they had barged in on the family thinking that an elderly woman and children would be no threat. By the time that the guards had arrived Jason, at no more the fourteen, had beat the two bandits down with his shovel. Most of the guard had put off the boy killing the bandits as them being caught unaware of one so young. Bealson knew different. The boy was a natural warrior in both ability and temperament. He issued orders to the boy on the spot that he was to report for military training as soon as his siblings were old enough to take his place helping his grandmother. The boy complied and had finished the training in half the normal time.

Sir Bealson braced himself for what he had to do. He unhitched his blade from its hook. He was glad that he was never the type to wear a scabbard. He preferred to be able to take his blade out either by sliding or with a twist. As Jason turned to face his replacement the High Marshal grimaced and stuck his blade in the youth's back. He did not hear the young man gurgling as he flung the body aside. He nodded at the mercenary and the man rung the bell for relieving the watch.

Just moments later his men would be in charge of the castle. Then it would be an easy job collecting up all of the loyalists and having them imprisoned. First, he had to make sure that Duke Mark had been dealt with.

Duke Mark was awakened suddenly. He heard the single bell that marked the wakeup call. Someone was moving outside his door. Whoever it was opened the door just enough to enter silently. Mark put his hand on the dagger he kept in his bed. Lying silently, he waited for the assassin to come closer. The dark figure stopped at the edge of the bed and Mark tensed. He relaxed considerably when the figure spoke.

"Sir…sir, it is important… wake up, sir."

It was Ferra, a Lieutenant in the Panthers who was visiting her mother in the castle. Mark had been a Panther during the War Forward, and they were officially disbanded after the war. She was of the growing number of youths in Gormec which joined the unofficial militia, waiting for Tapps to raise the Panther Banner again.

Ferra was beautiful, which she must have inherited from her father. A kind of beauty which made you forget that she, like her mother, could match anyone in the use of the twin blades. Mark never forgot that, he had fought alongside her mother during the War Forward. He was not easily impressed, but Ferra's mother was impressive. The woman had birthed five children before the war, took a break to pick up the fight, and then went right back to her farm and husband and birthed three more. She had only answered his request to come live in the castle a short time ago after she had finished grieving for her husband. Mark sat up as he spoke.

"What is it, Lieutenant?"

She paused for a moment. It was apparent that she was nervous talking to the Duke. No, it was something else. Mark figured it was another tendency she must have gotten from her father. Rachel was never nervous. Ferra's voice was shaky.

"Mother . . . Lady Rachel sent me to wake you. She said that there is a rebellion in the castle and I am to bring you to her."

Duke Mark jumped out of bed. He did not notice Ferra turning her back on him. If this was true there was no time for modesty. He threw on his favorite cloak and a pair of britches. Grabbing his sword belt, he turned towards Ferra. His voice had recovered to one who ruled.

"Lead me to your mother."

Silently, and with only the moon light coming through the windows, the two made it to the kitchen just as the bell to relive the watch was sounded. The night cooks and aids looked nervous. Ferra gestured the Duke into the pantry. As he approached, he could hear the hushed voice inside. He opened the door and entered.

The room was lit by a single candle. Ferra's mother, Rachel, was talking to a band of youths. She held a short blade in her hand. It was apparent that her sixty odd years of life had not dulled her skill with the blade. When the Duke entered, she turned towards him, it showed in the tone of her voice that she gave no pretense to rank.

"Short Britches, the castle has been taken by insurrection. I should have seen it earlier. With the rotation of the guard, it was clear that this was going to happen, but I could not bring myself to believe that Sir Bealson would be capable."

Mark realized that Rachel must have been very agitated for her to use her nickname for him. She had given it to him all those years ago during the war when he started ordering her around. She had simply called him Short Britches and would not explain why. Even so, she had never called him that in public. She may have been a strong woman who would not take any disrespect from any person no matter their rank. Yet, she was also the first to box an ear when someone did not show the proper respect for rank. He thought for a moment but still could not make any understanding of it. It showed in his voice.

"What are you talking about?"

"Sir, we do not have time for me to explain, on the bond that comes from bleeding the field of battle together and on our Death Oath, you must trust me."

Duke Mark blinked, then blinked again. Rachel had sworn on their bond several times, but by the Death Oath was a different matter. Neither one of them had spoken of it since they survived that last battle. He had no doubt now that this was real.

"My life is yours."

Rachel turned in a blur and started issuing orders. Ferra stared at amazement, first at her mother and then the Duke. She knew that the two were close from fighting side by side during the War Forward, but the Death Oath was a different matter. Why had her mother not told her? It explained just about everything in her life since mother came back from the war. She was too young to remember anything about the war except that her mother was gone. When her mother had come back, she had instantly started teaching the blade to her. It had never made sense before. It was the Death Oath. She was the second child in the family and the oath would fall to her.

A Death Oath was not a private matter. She would have to talk to her mother about it. What could have been so important? The Death Oath was a powerful oath and was not given easily. Were the Duke and her mother lovers during the war? No, her mother had been only in her forties at the time but the way the two acted when together, there was no hint of romance. Why the Death Oath? Her mother had bound the families together for what reason? Had father known? He must have, he had always been against teaching the children to fight. Then after the war he let mother teach her and her youngest brother. She jumped when her mother sharply called her name.

"You will be in the middle with me and the Duke. Our honor is at stake here, Ferra protect him like you would me."

The team that moved out of the pantry was as rag tag as you could imagine. The bulk of them were young warriors who have never seen a battle. The only real veterans in the group were the Duke, Rachel and the Minotaur tailor named Karlon.

The Minotaur was large but had seen better days. He was reaching near the end of his life. He moved unhurriedly from the arthritis racking his body but the look in his eyes made the youths skittish. It was apparent in the Minotaur's face that he was ready to use his huge hammer on anyone who got in the way of him saving his Duke. The Minotaur had appeared after that last battle of the War Forward swearing loyalty to him. According to Karlon, the Duke had saved his life during the battle. Mark had no memory of it, but the horned man was persistent.

The Duke sighed. He did not know why this was happening or why Rachel would implicate Bealson. Still, she was not one to jump to conclusions and if things were as half as bad as she said his life was literally in her hands.

The group had just entered the secret passage which would take them out of the castle when the alarm bell sounded. They were in a part of the sewage system which smelled grotesque but it was the safest way out of the castle. The sounds of the bell were dulled by the layers of rock but the implication was the same. The team hastened their steps but could not run because of the slime that covered the ground.

They nearly made it out without incident. At the exit into the city, guards had been posted. As soon as they came into view they moved to attack and Karlon rushed. The three bolts that slammed into his chest did nothing to slow him. His roar deafened the youths who just then started their charge. By the time they reached the fray Karlon had already crushed three of the guards a fourth was running.

The counter attack by the mercenaries was devastating. Three of the eight youths had already dropped and the Minotaur was beginning to slow. Mark could stand it no longer. He was a warrior born and bred. Being protected like a child while others died was beyond him. He pulled his blade and charged. Rachel and Ferra had no choice but to follow. Within seconds the battle was over and the Duke was left with mostly dead soldiers.

Karlon fell to the ground. His wounds were too great for his age and the Duke rushed to his side. The Minotaur looked up at his Duke.

"One of the mercenaries fled. No doubt they will have reinforcements here any moment. You must flee, go to the armor-smith Nealkor and tell her what happen. Let her know that I died with honor." The duke tried to speak but Karlon grunted loudly. "No, I am dead already but at least I have repaid my debt to you."

Mark felt like roaring in the tradition of the horned people. As they headed across the street carrying the wounded youths into a dark alley, Duke Mark spotted Karlon getting to his feet. As they reached the other end of the alley, he heard his tailor's roar but it was cut short.

Laughter flowed freely from a man looking through a spy glass sitting on his horse. He was a black-haired youth, a few years past his second decade but in both appearance and attitude he was just old enough to be called man. He had inherited his mother's stern looks and his father's skill in reaching for goals. He was General Dackery McGovern, second born of the Lord McGovern. At the first news of the mounting of the Shadow Forces his father had sent him with an offer of an alliance. The Shadow accepted, and as a measure of good faith on both sides he was made a general in the Shadow Army. He was too young to have fought in the War Forward but his own uncle was the hero. A brave man, even if he was killed in the last by a turncoat in his own ranks. He had enjoyed reading the exploits his relatives in the family library. After all he was named after one of his heroic ancestors. It never really bothered his logic that Dackery McGovern the Noble never had any children. Nor the fact that Dackery McGovern the Noble was disowned by the family. A part which is left out of the McGovern's library.

Now it was Dackery's time to lead a great conquest. Of course, this time it was against the Dragon Banner. He loved the way his father played both sides. If the Shadow was as powerful as the rumors insisted, he would soon rule all of the Colonies. For his father's help the Shadow had promised the crown of KanaTo. The McGoverns would once again rule from the Dragon Throne of KanaTo as was their right. Of course, they would first have to overthrow the false Royal Family. From what he saw in his spy glass, it would be very easy.

He had been given three legions of the Shadow Army. Like all the nobles of KanaTo, he had always been partial to the cavalry but he had to grudgingly admit that these horrible looking Shadow Warriors were the best in his force. They were worth at least five warriors on horseback. He would have put them on horse but the equine would not go near them. He could not blame the horses, for he did not like being near them either.

He watched with glee as they attacked the town of Freeport. It was the most southern town in the KanaTo nation. It was the guard and trade town of the mountain pass which connected KanaTo with Shouker. He did not fool himself into thinking this was a real test. Shouker was a peaceful nation and the guard posted here would be more used to searching wagons for contraband than fighting. It was a good place for him to get a feel for what his warriors could do. He only wished that his spyglass had been magical so he could have seen the looks on the townsfolk's faces when five thousand warriors came rushing into the town. By the time they recovered from their shock, they had only managed to get two runners away. Of course, he had the cavalry on the other side of the town by then and the messengers did not get through.

Dackery McGovern put away his spyglass as the signal that the town was taken was given. He was very happy indeed. He knew that this was the beginning of a new era for the McGoverns. He had taken his first victory in the many he was sure would follow.

XXVII

QuickPaw examined the silver-skinned Shawll who was standing before him. The Shawlls had changed since his youth. The Shawlls from then did not grasp even the rudimentary aspect of other cultures. Now they seem to have become not only familiar with other cultures, but had become the perfect negotiator between cultures. It appeared to QuickPaw that the Shawlls had taped into some long-forgotten talent. He started to pay attention to the Shawll's words once he had gotten past the formalities of these meetings.

"I conversed with all holy people of clans and we agree. We are in danger. A hand of darkness stretches across the land, ready to crush us."

QuickPaw stood. He had heard it all before, but never before from the elder healer. If it concerned the old Shawll then it needed to be dealt with haste.

"Then let's convene the Council of Elders and bring all of the clans into the winter camp."

"Camp not be safe. Barrier not strong enough for this threat."

QuickPaw's eyes widen and his voice rose.

"But the Dragons created the barrier to. . ."

QuickPaw was interrupted by the sound of an explosion outside his tent. He ran outside to see what the cause was. In the center of camp, a small comet had struck and set fire to a tent. QuickPaw examined the small crater after calling for the scholars. There was a blood-red liquid oozing from the surface of the rock. As the first scholar arrived someone spotted more comets far off in the sky racing towards them. There were so many coming toward the camp that it looked like a swarm of locus. At first, he thought it was a Fiery Hail spell, but by the size and number it would have to be more than a hundred True Magi using all the magic they had. There was something else behind this.

There was a saying in the Vagofron which stated; every person has two things. Something to teach and something to learn. QuickPaw's talent was the way he thought. He was a natural leader who excelled in strategy and tactics. This was why QuickPaw had become the Speaker of the Clans at such a young age. Without thinking, he pulled a short-spear from its quiver and threw it into the ground as he started barking orders. In less than a minute, over fifty of the clans' magi had surrounded him. He was nervous. He had only practiced the linking before. There had never been a real reason to risk the danger involved in such a large one before. Links were common enough, but there were limits

The linking started. He felt the magic of those surrounding him increasing to the point where it felt hot in his mind. As the magic started to flow into him, he started to work true Dragon magic. The secret of the link was one of the gifts from the Dragons when the Clans were formed. Dragon magic was more than just larger patterns, it was also more power. So powerful, in fact, that it would burn even a True Magus to a cinder who tried to use it. By linking the power of at least twenty magi they were able to focus enough magic to cast some of the least powerful spells of the Dragons. QuickPaw using his own limited power was the focus of the magi's power.

Completing the spell, QuickPaw let loose with a bolt of magical energy. It sped from his finger tips and destroyed dozens of the incoming comets. He instantly knew that there was not enough time to destroy all of them and shifted from offense to defense. Pulling together all the magic he dared, he hastily worked it into a shield. They had reached their limit. He could see out of the corner of his eyes the magi dropping one by one to be replaced by the ones waiting behind them. As the first wave crashed into the barrier and exploded, he felt the pain from the backlash. It dropped him to his knees, he ordered for Winter's Bite to be brought to him through clenched teeth. He was able to stand once more, and started issuing orders by the time the elderly Winter's Bite arrived.

"Expand the Circle! At least two more rows and another Furciena!" QuickPaw lowered his voice so that only Winter's Bite could hear. "Open up all the gates and start moving everyone out of here."

With a glance he let the old Lost One that the order was based that survival of the Clans which goes beyond politics and honor. QuickPaw returned his attention to the incoming projectiles, but spoke his last recorded words.

"and tell Jenifer…and her father, I died by my spear."

Shortly after the leader of the Insanus Unum left, the second wave hit. The shield wavered and cracked but held. Seconds later it was pounded by the third, and then fourth wave of comets. Tears formed in QuickPaw's eyes. Wave after wave, for time uncounted they came, and he knew they were failing. He only hoped that they had gained enough time for the others to leave. Another wave of the meteors of blood and fire smashed into their defenses. The power of the explosion was too much and shattered the shield. The backlash killed several of the magi outright and knocked most of the rest unconscious. With his dying breath he gave thanks that Jenifer was away visiting her siblings and for Elohim to keep her safe.

The rest of the comets pounded unhindered into the Vagofrons' winter camp. It continued for nearly an hour, destroying any remnant that the area once held the hopes and dreams of countless years. When it was over, there was nothing left of what the Dragons once called the Free City in the Mountains.

The Dark Shadow, as the name Snow was almost forgotten to him, watched with glee the destruction of the Vagofrons in the magical fountain. He had enacted his revenge on Tapps. A wicked smile spread across his face as he imagined the reaction of his foe when he found his home destroyed. He giggled with the pain it would cause. He had not yet recovered from giddiness when Divinus entered the room. His advisor's angry words made Snow jump back.

"You fool. You little fool. You have not even the slightest idea what you have done, do you?"

Snow's anger quickly replaced his confusion. He dismissed Silver and vented his rage on Divinus.

"How dare you talk to me like that especially in front of one of the help? I am the Shadow and you need to learn your place."

It was time to get rid of his advisor. He had learned all he could from the man. After all, Snow was more powerful than ten, fifty, no, a hundred True Magi. What was Divinus compared to that. The magic he had seen from the man was but parlor tricks compared to what Snow had. Snow concentrated to gather the dark magic to destroy his advisor. Nothing happened. Shock and fear played across his face when he realized that Divinus was preventing him from working the magic. The will-o-wisps were laughing in his ears. He opened his mouth to tell them to be silent but his words were drowned out by Divinus.

"Do not presume to talk to me like I am a servant. You do not have a tenth of the power the Destroyer has given me and you rule only because I allow it. The will-o-wisps who give you your power answer to me. I gave you the name of the Shadow, but I see now that you were unworthy of such a honor. This Kaltar you have tormented into acting against us is more powerful than any other I have seen on this piece of rock. He rivals White Bear's Faithful. The only reason I will let you live is that it is not worth the trouble of finding a replacement. Do not fail me again. You may find that I am not so lazy after all.

"With any luck his desire for revenge will prevent him from listening to his cursed God. I may be able to use this to pervert him to our cause. From now on when I tell you something, whether in the form of advice or not, you will do it. Understand."

Snow could not get a word out, he could only nod and watch in amazement as Divinus left the room. How could the man have blocked his power like that? How did he prevent the will-o-wisps from aiding him? The power of the Shadow was his. None could stand against him, but then, how could Divinus do what he did? His advisor was more a threat than ever. He had to find a way to rid himself of Divinus. But how? That was the question which would plague his days and his dreams for months to come.

Far off the eastern seaboard of the Colonies on a huge island no longer found on any map, White Bear looked up from the letter he was writing. White Bear took his hands off the keyboard of his computer. He closed the books which covered his desk and then his eyes. After hours had passed, he opened his eyes and pushed a button on his desk. Just a few minutes later, Chang Tzu appeared. White Bear spoke unhurriedly.

"Chang, I will be returning to the Colonies. Prepare my bags for an extended stay. There is much to be done. Not the least of these is to look in on the two children of the First and to find my old friend."

Chang spoke in a tone which showed his new rank of Elder Pupil.

"So, you are sure that Marius has been released?"

White Bear laughed soberly.

"I have always been sure that he had been released. It just has not been the time to search. The Serpent of Old is now concentrating on this silly conquest and I will now have greater freedom to move about. I should be able to get to him without much trouble. Once I have brought him to safety I can deal with the Sons of Disobedience. However, you will not be going with me. You have something else you need to do, and I am sure you know what it is. I do need to leave now."

Chang nodded his head in serious agreement. He did know what he needed to do but he had been hoping he that he had not been hearing correctly. Chang would have brought it up to his master before but he feared that White Bear would have done what he just did. He was also sure that it was the same reason that White Bear had not pressed him on it before. Chang had put it off too long and now he had no more time of waiting. Like White Bear he needed to leave now. So, Chang Tzu packed the gear quickly and, within the hour, White Bear was in the Colonies and Chang was on his way back to the Asionic Empire.

XXVIII

Tapps knew something was wrong when he was not greeted upon coming over the hill which marked the beginning of the Vagofron territory. It was possible that the guards in the heavily camouflaged post were asleep. It was not unheard of. Any small groups would not be harassed, and an army which would require the main camp to be notified would make enough noise to wake them. Still Tapps knew something was wrong. He could not figure out what was bothering him but the feeling became worse when he entered the guard post. It was empty and had been such for at least a week.

Tapps returned to Angga and her Eagle Warriors just as a group of Insanus Unam appeared. Keith was with them and he was wearing almost the entire traditional garb. He had finished the purging and would now only have to last a year in the field. That is when most dropped out of the group. Tapps greeted all of them and asked if they knew why the post was abandoned. None of them knew.

They moved on together and the feeling in Tapps' heart grew and grew, and grew. Finally, he could stand it no longer and without a word took off in a full run. Everyone tried to keep up but even the Arvions in their flight could not keep up with Tapps. He was fueled by an almost panic. He traversed almost a half day's travel in a little more than an hour. He did not slow until he stumbled at the sight of the destruction which had been caused to the winter camp.

Tapps picked himself up to his knees and threw his head back. His roar filled evening air. Rage boiled up from his soul and he was gripped in the Shortun. Anger, pain and confusion filled his mind. Bending over, putting his face into the ash which had once been a building, he did the only thing he could. He cried and he prayed.

Hours passed before the rest of the group caught up to Tapps. Everyone was stopped cold from what they saw. The Eagle Warriors did not know what they were looking at and the Insanus Unam could not understand it. Angga went to go comfort Tapps, but Nethin placed his hand on her shoulder to stop her. His words were almost a whisper.

"There are times in which we are tested by a flame so hot that we must turn only to Elohim or be destroyed."

Angga looked into her uncle's eyes and realized that he spoke from an understanding which could only come from knowing that fire. She knew that he was right. As her eyes left her uncle her attention was drawn to the Insanus Unam. They stood with unemotional faces as they waited with patience for Tapps to finish. This was not what drew her attention. It was Keith. The youth had fallen to his knees and was ripping off his armor. Tears were running down his eyes. She did not hesitate to go comfort him.

Angga dropped to her knees and put her arms around him. He accepted her embrace and started to truly sob. She looked on as the Insanus Unam closest to them turned their backs to them. She became angry over this. Where was their hearts? There were tears in some of their eyes. Why was Keith's grief so different? Angga felt like screaming at them all, but it would not be right. She bit back her anger and allowed herself to cry. Queen or not, the grief became too much for her.

As the sun set, the Insanus Unam took up defensive positions around Tapps. The great Kaltar had not moved from his spot and did not stop his prayers until the sun came up again. He rose and turned slowly towards those who were waiting. The fur of his cheeks matted from the tears of the night. His eyes glowed red as if his anger had sparked some light in them as he looked at the ruins around him. Tapps Toya barely spoke above a whisper, but it was said that his proclamation carried in it the power of lightning and thunder.

"Send out the runners. The Panther Banner flies again."

XXIX

The Dark-Skinned Bard let the images fade. He looked around the common room of the inn, at the wide eyes of everyone who had been watching. His own eyes were red from the tears his own stories always produced in him. He spoke with no little strain in his voice.

"Thus, the War of Blood and Fire officially started. As with all events which change the course of civilization, there were many things which came before. The events that come before, giving the form of what comes after. One into the next, as with society, as with our own lives. Now you know many of those events, both good and bad, which happened before the story which history tells. But we all are all in need of rest, so the rest will have to wait. Goodnight."

Without another word, DSB quickly drank the cider which remained in his mug, and headed to his room before the questions could start.

KanaTukFin

Translating NokoShor Shivna

The events which lead up to the War for Blood and Fire have, for the most part, have been largely ignored within academic circles. This is due mainly because most of the traditional indications of a pending war are missing, and there is little information regarding the figures which lead the Dark Shadow Empire. Because of this, there is no shortage of theories, both reasonable and exaggerated, on where the forces came from, especially in the southern aspect of the war. This also means, with few exceptions, the majority of the writings about the War for Blood and Fire is on the war itself.

The international language of the Colonies, or Imperial Trade, has two distinct root words for dark, 'Nok' and 'Uet'. Nok is the darkness which comes from the lack of light, such as in a dark night or dark cave. While uet is reference to shading, such as dark rock. Example of this is found in two characters, *Sophen Euta*, which literally means bard with dark-skin, and *KanaMoskNok*, whose name literally meant 'powerful Mosk with no light'. The addition of the 'o' on Nok, pertains to vision, or sight. Shor, while meaning blood in the language of the Dragons, means soul or life-spirit, in Imperial Trade. NokoShor is generally used in the Colonies for the evil of one's own soul, or a person's 'inner shadow' they cannot see, and in Colonial Philosophy is the source of a person's emotional pain.

Both of these made KanaTukFin's written account of the Dark-Skinned Bard's telling of the War controversial from the start. Tuk had to bypass the Bards' Guild Association in its publication because they considered it inaccurate, or at least not provable. Most of the controversy came from Tuk's using NokoShor to describe the Shadow Empire. More so, by giving it the title of NokoShor Shivna, which gave a clear indication that the evil of the Dark Shadow Empire was simply a reflection of the evil already found in the Colonies.

www.ingramcontent.com/pod-product-compliance
Lightning Source LLC
LaVergne TN
LVHW010601100826
845148LV00014B/2796

* 9 7 8 1 6 3 8 6 3 0 0 3 6 *